Lions Vineyard

Loyola van Rooyen Buck

Published by LIONS VINEYARD, 2024.

It was 2015 when my husband and I decided to undertake a major island hop from Vancouver Island, Canada to the North Island, New Zealand with our dog in tow. I soon discovered a history so intriguing that the telling of it, along with some interesting character development, became paramount. However the writing of this story would not have come to pass without the inspiration of my family and friends, and those in history who have bravely gone before me. I was never alone. Lyndsay Wells, Gail Spence and Barry Ogle get all the credit for boosting my efforts right when I needed their wisdom, talent and gifts most. And now I have the great privilege of thanking you, my reader. In gratitude I dedicate this book to all of you who have the courage to live, laugh and love.

In memory of our beloved Leo van Rooyen Buck

FIRST EDITION EBOOK May 5th 2024
　　First Edition Print July 1st 2024
　　ISBN 978-1-0670154-0-4
　　Published by: LIONS VINEYARD

Chapter ONE

1994 *Aotearoa New Zealand*

When Tony and Hannah King unearthed the scarred wooden box full of Malefyt family history at the onset of the foundation work of their new home at Lions Vineyard, neither was expecting the swelling of curiosity that would bring them to this moment. Yet, here they were, sitting hand in hand, as their Air New Zealand flight taxied down the runway to commence the start of not one but two long flights that would end in a windmill and tulip landscape.

Tony adored Hannah. He appreciated her dedication to his rugby way of life. Without fail, she was there for his local games and many regional test matches. She had been witness on numerous occasions to the silent struggle he was having with an inner anger issue when on the field. The last thing Tony wanted was to let his teammates, family, and himself down, but his problem was real. He had no idea how to control the rage that swelled within at times, without warning. He knew that his chance to be selected for the nation's top team would end if he did not find the answer. This team valued integrity on a par with all the other skills a player needed to be counted one among this elite team of Aotearoa New Zealand national ambassadors. Inner peace prevailed when they were busy working on the farm, but the recent death of Uncle Jonty made for fresh troubled times. This adventure seemed like the perfect way to clear his head and give back a little something to Hannah, too.

Hannah would fight a legion of warriors with Tony, even though she had to admit some wars needed to be fought led by his own determination. Her inner strength, fuelled by the unending power within, was legendary. She often possessed enough for them both. She had to develop an inner resilience at the tender age of eight, or let her own lively and decisive character be suffocated by the new reality she woke up to after the accident that left her in a wheelchair. Things changed drastically after the car accident that killed both her parents in 1981. Friends continued in their usual way as outdoor explorers, but this no longer had the same appeal for her. Living with Uncle Jonty also took some getting used to. He was no great cook, and having to master the skills her Mum had taught her far sooner than expected took up most of Hannah's free time. Her endeavours added a sense of purpose and direction to her days.

With a little help from WWOOF, an organisation that paired volunteers to the local farms, Hannah settled into her new way of life. Millicent van Dam, better known as Millzy, and Hannah made a quick order of claiming dominion over the kitchen in her Uncle's villa at Lions Vineyard. This course of action proved fruitful. Hannah developed her craft to become an expert in the kitchen, channelling creativity through her love of developing new recipes and testing the results out on the men in her life. She was relentless in her determination to have independence.

With the help of friends in the publishing industry, Hannah's first cookbook *Full Steam Ahead* was a success. The ingredients used were from the land she cherished. The pages reflected her passion for taking what one has on hand and making the most of it. Her most recent cookbook, *King's Table*, was ready for the printer now. She wanted to foster a desire for the young and young at heart to enjoy bringing affordable, nutritious meals to their own tables. It would make a nice companion to the series she had published over the years: *Cups & Cakes, Athlete's Oven, Harvest Bowls, Chilly Bin Treats*, and finally *Kiamoana*. Food that had been gathered from the sea.

A local television network had approached her early this year with a very generous offer to establish her own primetime show. This she was now giving considerable thought to. It would be a progressive and practical way to start 1995. Of course, this would take up huge amounts of her time. She would no longer be free to see as many rugby games as she liked. *Maybe it was time to let Tony make it on his own,* Hannah thought. By the time they returned from the Netherlands in two weeks she had promised the network an answer.

It was a good thing Tony worked out so often and had such a huge physique or he may have lost some of that lean and muscular build. He and a few of his teammates were Hannah's test market and her hardest critics. They held nothing back when it came to their opinions. She expected nothing less, welcoming their honesty. These players knew good food fuelled the body. They were like warriors that engaged in battle in seasonal frequency and were given leave on occasion when they would retreat. She was used to having them around. Because they appreciated, supported, and encouraged all her efforts, she was always eager to welcome them with a home-cooked meal. Uncle Jonty found plenty of work for all the boys. He was of the mind that if they could test the results that came from her kitchen, he was going to get some work out of them.

What would I do without him? Hannah never was one for many tears, yet, each time memories skipped through her mind, the parade of happy times filled her heart and her eyes threatened to spill over. *He was such a good man.* God-fearing, hard-working, unselfish. Yet, when he set a line, it was tougher than number 8 wire and no one dared to cross it, even her, ever. Some found great comfort there. *Why was there never an Aunty Jonty,* she thought.

Looking over at her travel companion, Hannah could see Tony was settling in without letting his fear of flying prevent him from engaging in full as he does in all their adventures, selecting the film *Iron Will* to lose himself in. She could see the humour of the predicament he found himself in. He would not let her go it alone, knowing she was going to follow the leads in the old family journals that they had recently found. Gently peeling her fingers from his relaxed grip, she reached into her carry-on to also begin her settling-in ritual, determined to read as many of the journals they had found as time would allow on each long flight.

Hannah's palm rested momentarily on the soft worn leather cover of her mother's small Bible that she had also decided to pack. The pages had been turned often as she had searched many times through the years for answers to life's questions, and above all, some grounding truth. The words had first sprung to life as she listened to Uncle Jonty read to her when she started her recovery after the accident.

Hannah's Mum, Johanna Heath, was not one to leave anything to chance. This was the reason Hannah believed her Dad fell hard for her. He was first a great husband and Dad and a close second, as he would say, "a fabulous insurance salesman." The best in his field, even in the early stages of his career, he often claimed the top insurance sales award for all of Oceania. Alvan King, Hannah's dad, lived for his family and thrived on order. Hannah could distinctly recall his pleasure in her mother's endless joy in a simple, uncomplicated life.

Though one page was missing from the well-worn Bible, to Hannah this book was a perfect library of resources. She had read it through several times, and absorbed for herself the stories of inspirational, strong and determined pilgrims who lived as though the lives of those they loved were of a value greater than any gold or precious stone. To her each book revealed depth and meaning, telling of love through creation that would bring those willing to a place and time of perfect existence with God as one universal family. A whanau and unified gathering composed of all His children. Coming to know the character of God through the network of threads written and spoken on the pages was life-giving.

Safely packed away in her pack, along with a few other personal items, were the documents they had discovered in the wooden sea chest, along with the old journals, and other carefully preserved items indicating a far different family history than she had ever known existed. It would appear Anna Malefyt had sailed to Lions Vineyard on the North Island from the Netherlands in 1814 at the age of twenty-one with the mission group of Samuel Marsden, motivated by the hope of finding her twin brother Ashton, who was thought to be dead.

The descendants of Ashton Malefyt, who had changed his name to Tony Heath, were in some way heirs of an estate that was still in existence today in the Netherlands. The Heath descendants had lived at Lions Vineyard for over a hundred and eighty years. Hannah was now determined to follow the clues, and, if need be, drag Tony along also. All the while letting him believe it was his idea.

Chapter TWO

S *ame day, different land.*

"I am all for getting to the Bed & Breakfast and a good meal before we talk about any more plans." Tony's mind was not often far from food. Today was no different and he was glad to have his feet firmly on solid ground. With little appetite over the past 28 hours of travel, he was now solely zeroing in on his next meal. He also was finding it a challenge to not focus on the fact that cutting this adventure short was out of the question. *Who was he kidding?* He would never deny Hannah anything, but even he had to admit this was going above and beyond.

Loving her as he did, though, had made his life richer and full of laughs. Hannah could find humour in the least obvious places. When he needed it most, she often aided in defusing his temper long before any explosion could occur. Though he told Hannah he would do this for her, what he really wanted was to be working on the foundation of the new house that had come to an abrupt halt only a few days ago.

"I have warned them well in advance that you would be needing topping up as soon as we arrived. Our hosts, the van Dams, have made reservations at what I have been assured is the best steak house in the province, only minutes from their front door." Hannah was used to thinking and planning ahead. Not only because of her needs. Because she also knew by experience that travelling with Tony meant there needed to be plenty of opportunities for outdoor exercise and an abundance of good food options rotating at regular intervals throughout each day.

The taxi driver was soon pointing out that they were travelling on the narrow streets that bordered the property of the estate they would be lodging at, to Hannah's pleasure the one mentioned in the documents.

She had found a brochure of these accommodations in Uncle Jonty's things and soon discovered it was once the gatehouse to Bergen Op Meer. She was pleased that at such short notice they had been able to accommodate two Kiwi guests for the next thirteen nights. *A coincidence?* The price per night had to have been one of the main reasons they had rooms available on such short notice. Slowing to a stop in front of an imposing brick home, with whiter than white lace curtains in every window and cheerful flowers spilling out of numerous flower boxes in a festival of colour, Hannah was thankful once again to Uncle Jonty for providing the means for this adventure. His legacy enabled them to travel in comfort and Hannah held no reservations about spending the money in these terms. As Uncle Jonty always said, "Faith is the priceless currency and material abundance adds responsibility."

Hannah had felt an immediate connection to the woman in the journal, Johanna Malefyt, the mother of Anna and Ashton. She had desperately longed to have children, an experience Hannah could never hope to have, and the journals told of a betrayal that would rock anyone's world. Johanna wrote of a need to forgive the man she adored for something Hannah was not sure she could ever forgive a man for. On the tear-stained pages of the journal, Johanna poured out her silent, hurt feelings leaving Hannah with the impression no one was ever meant to read the words written out of her private pain. And here Hannah was, entering into a world that Anna, Johanna's daughter, had left behind and may have never returned to. The thought of unravelling the mystery gave Hannah a chill. She would follow the leads left behind with her usual determination, until the truth was revealed. Hannah never started anything she did not take to its full finish, ever. Tony had better buckle in. She was sure that, as their lives had taken more than one turn through the years, this one would be a big one.

Tony had helped the driver with their things and returned to collect her. *I don't mind.* There he was, arms strong and sure, to lift her from the taxi to the chair, always with love and patience.

The impressive two-storey, red brick, entryway, with towering columns and huge shuttered windows, left Hannah wondering. *If this was the Gate House, just how spectacular the estate house must be.* Even Tony seemed dwarf-like standing next to the two massive green doors.

Neither size nor the obvious weight of the door had any effect on the diminutive, blonde haired, blue-eyed hostess who cheerfully stepped through the door with her hand outstretched to Hannah in preparation for a friendly handshake, with warm, perfectly spoken English introductions and a welcoming smile.

She was to call her "Anita". From the outset it was crystal clear she meant hospitality.

Hannah was willing to give Anita her full attention and admiration not only for her obvious passion for her home, but also for her confident carriage and style. Nothing about her tiny size said small. She was precision, class, and a sparkle of fun. I liked her on the spot.

As she turned to give the same attention to Tony, Hannah expected to see no less of a greeting.

Now Tony was used to being stared at when in public, because his fans recognized him, and the woman could not help but admire his looks. He was handsome, strikingly so, much to the chagrin of his best mates.

Cropped blond, to the point of white at times, curly locks, blue eyes that you could lose yourself in their cool depth, and body of a tall, sculpted mountain. His mates loved him like a brother though did tire of being eclipsed at times. Tony had no regard for the attention, brushing off the female intentions as though they were not even there. This all too often sent his friends into further depths of despair over the situation they found themselves in. What happened next was a look Tony had never received before.

Anita van Dam from birth had seldom experienced a loss for words. She came into the world at 2 pounds 6 ounces and never reached 5 feet. She made up for it in many other ways though. Very little in her life had the opportunity to surprise her, because she planned for everything, taking that ability into the running of her establishment. She had been born in this house.

With the confidence of a brigadier general she prepared for each guest's arrival and stay as though to win a war without a single messy shot being fired. All facets of her life reflected her determination and iron will to see everyone who entered through her doors warmly welcomed and enjoying their time at *The Gate House,* no matter who they were. She had been host to leaders from many faiths and nations, royalty from dozens of countries, not a few wayward backpackers that wanted a day or two of luxury, and every type of traveller in between. But nothing, not even after what their daughter had revealed last night, could have prepared her for the waterfall of shock and disbelief that threatened to overtake her when she turned to welcome the guest at her right.

In his preparation for a similar greeting that Hannah was currently the recipient of, Tony stepped forward with his hand outstretched and readied himself with his most charming smile.

When he wanted to turn it on, he knew exactly how.

This small cup of a woman was his gateway to the kitchen and its contents. He wanted to make friends fast.

Hannah could feel his charm meter start-up.

As Anita van Dam turned to greet Tony, Hannah also turned to watch the show.

"Good day, Tony King." Tony stepped into the space between them.

Anita's hand never reached Tony's. It flew up to cover the gasp that escaped from her glossed lips.

As his face came into the full-frame of her gaze, her world tipped with the effect of an iceberg hitting an unsinkable ship. The colour drained from her face. *She was not sure if she was going to stay on her feet.* "Onse leife heir!" There are times when only *Our loving Father* can get us through. This was one of those for her.

"Miss, are you alright? Let me help you, here, sit here." Tony guided the pale and shaken tiny woman to the stone bench near the door.

"I truly am fine, yet find myself needing a moment. My sincere apologies. I feel peculiar but I am sure it will quickly pass." Anita took the needed helping hand and without her usual grace sat down.

"Can we get someone for you?" Hannah, always the practical one, asked, as she made her way over to the bench and took the stone-cold hand of their hostess.

As their eyes met Hannah saw the spark of understanding of the situation Anita was finding herself in. Exploding within their depths was what seemed to Hannah, an energetic calculation of just how their hostess was going to restore her dignity and move forward. The embarrassment was now firing up her cheeks to a lovely pink shade that was in a close match to her lip gloss.

Hannah was certain blushing was not a common occurrence for the refined and well put together woman that sat before her now. Everything about her, and her surroundings and appearance shouted precision and competence. Anita's discomfort was obvious.

Tony and Hannah held a silent communication over her head.

Before they could plan the next move Anita was back on her feet.

Once again she held out her hand and gave Tony his formal yet somewhat less warm greeting than the one Hannah had received only moments before.

Without further ado she ushered them in.

Chapter THREE

*G*etting a meal is complicated.

Everything about our hostess was once again all business. Business in a manner that was textbook though.

Something had thrown her rhythm and it had to do with Tony. Hannah could tell by the questioning look on his face he was not quite sure how to proceed, but in true Tony form, he found the opening that often pleases.

He offered to help.

"The bags are no problem and I am happy to take them to our rooms." Tony offered to our hostess as we both followed her into the very impressive reception hall where the love of fresh flowers was evident. All the beauty of nature's intoxicating scent was equally present indoors, as we had witnessed on our arrival.

The reception area held an air of precise invitation.

Sunlight filtered in through the tall windows with perfectly white lace curtains bordering the walls of the obvious library on our left, and the breakfast room on our right that held tomorrow's cups and saucers in a formation like soldiers at attention facing North waiting for the call to battle.

"A continental style breakfast is available on the sideboard in the morning room to your right between 6.00 and 10.00 am and your menu card for a full breakfast is in your reception package in your rooms. Orders are needed by 7.00 pm the night before. Oh, yes please, Mr. King, that would be of the utmost help. Here are your room keys. I have given you the ground floor adjoining rooms as requested down the hall to your left, rooms 4 and 6."

"All good, call us Tony and Hannah," Tony said.

"Pardon," Anita turned to take one more glimpse "of course, Tony, and Hannah." Placing the keys with purpose in Hannah's hand, Anita continued with her textbook format of the order of business.

"Please excuse me as I have to attend to the request of the guest in room 12 as they seem anxious about the fresh flowers I placed there earlier today. I can be reached until 9.00 pm and as early as 6.00 am. After these hours, our daughter is available when you require any assistance. She is a competent young woman, and I trust her implicitly with all my guests. Now, if there are no further questions," as Anita turned to remove herself from the reception hall she recalled one final thought, after which she was going to get herself to the kitchen and sit down in private with a strong cup of tea and go over exactly what had just happened. "The directions to T. Price Bistro are also in your welcome packages in your rooms and your reservation is in," Anita consulted her ever present Rolex "45 minutes."

Never before had she been so shaken. She was even unsure if she could continue to keep herself together standing in the presence of this young man.

Tony and Hannah watched in curious fascination as their hostess exited with the speed of a petite model on a catwalk wearing designer roller blades. "I think we just witnessed an award-winning performance." Hannah thought she was stating the obvious.

"Turning on the charm has never had that effect before. I will dial it down a notch next time." Tony supplied his own opinion of the matter and seemed pleased with himself.

"Tons, that performance had zero to do with anything you turned on, or up. Her reaction was more of a surprise face to face with an apparition. Let's get settled in. I can freshen up before you fall over from hunger. We have less than forty minutes and I am going to need every one of them." Even though Hannah knew the exact outfit she was going to wear, she still wanted to brush out her long midnight black hair until it shone with its glossy glow.

In every way, Hannah was the opposite of Tony.

Her skin tone was coffee and cream, heavy on the cream, eyes of the darkest soft brown, full burgundy lips, elegantly sculpted neck, arms like those of an athlete, and curves in all the right places.

Her appearance, like most young women her age, mattered to her. Twenty-three was only the beginning of her life.

14

As soon as Hannah's income from the sale of her cookbooks would allow, she hired a strength and conditioning coach. Someone she hand-picked who would understand she always wanted to look and be at her physical best, no matter what. After only a few months of training with Dr. Nic Gill, the same strength and conditioning coach as the All Blacks, her efforts paid off. Now, five years on, she was happy with the results.

The dress she had chosen for tonight was from the latest line of her favourite North Island designer, black raw silk, form-fitting, and sleeveless. Even Tony's head turned the first time he saw her in it. Her hand-made midnight black merino wool and silk wrap from BaaBaa Black Sheep & Co. was the perfect accessory.

The trembling of Anita's hand prevented her from safely lifting the delicate teacup from its saucer.

What appeared as an almost transparent white cup and saucer at first glance revealed the images of the Magi following the star that leads to the first Christmas imprinted in its delicate, slightly blue tinged, glazing. When the user held the cup to the light, at its base was a star. *They are enchanting.*

She gently slid the cup and saucer a safe distance from her, deciding a stronger libation was called for.

She went to the sideboard and splashed herself a generous portion of the amber liquid on hand into one of the crystal glasses standing in neat rows on the armoire.

"Ahhh, now that's better." As soon as the heat hit her belly she felt a calming warmth flood through her.

"What's better?" Wim van Dam had caught his wife in the act of drinking the good stuff. As he knew her dislike for strong drinks, this came as no small surprise.

Though they kept it on hand for a select few who she knew would enjoy a nightcap, and of course she wanted to offer only the best, Anita never touched it.

The kitchen was the inner sanctuary of the house and had remained a cosy, private environment for them to retreat to through the years. Wim secretly loved this part of the house most. He thought his beloved wife felt the same, even though she had worked so hard to maintain the grandeur and elegance of the entire establishment that she enjoyed running. It is true, the rest of the house was a picture on the level of a van Gogh. Many came from afar for the pleasure of knowing everything would be perfect. *It always was.* He was proud of her and told her so every chance he found appropriate.

"Mein lieveling." *He truly was her loved one.* "The most extraordinary thing has occurred. I don't think you will believe until you see for yourself." Anita and Wim had known each other all their lives. They had been married for over thirty-five years. In all that time he had never once seen her as undone like this.

"Tell me Moopje, I am sure to believe you." With his usual teasing in twinkly style that he saved for only his dear wife, patiently, he waited. He wondered if this had anything to do with the news their daughter had shared with them last night.

Hannah could not reach the little silver bell left on the reception desk. As she heard voices coming from the back of the house, she made her way to what she thought would be the kitchen. The smells wafting from that direction spoke of fresh baking.

Anita and Wim turned in unison to see the elegant young woman who had recently arrived glide into the kitchen. "Excuse me, I hope I am not interrupting." Hannah reached out her hand to Anita's male companion in greeting and without hesitation introduced herself. "Hannah King, and who is this charming gentleman?" Hannah could tell she had interrupted an intimate conversation and had entered a private sanctuary but the clock was ticking. Losing their reservation was not going to make for a pleasant evening with Tony. She jumped right in with the hope her confident manner would be enough to keep the moment brief and all relationships on pleasant terms.

"This is my husband my dear," was Anita's diverting reply as she discreetly placed the half-empty glass down.

"Simply put, I am Wim, very pleased to meet you." Taking her delicate hand in his well worn calloused one, he thought she looked familiar somehow. She had a good grip and a smile that lit the room. *What a striking, confident woman he thought. How do I know her?*

"My apologies for interrupting. I could not reach the bell." Hannah gently extracted her hand and turned to Anita.

Anita made a mental note of this fact and was inwardly annoyed she had allowed this to happen.

"Would you have an extra umbrella? The night is fair but I would not want to be caught out." Hannah pulled the soft wrap resting over her shoulders a little closer.

Tony was beyond hungry by this point and thought Hannah was taking far too long getting what she needed. Going in search of her was his only option. Making sure he had their keys and his jacket, he expected to find her at the reception desk.

Tony felt his temperature rise when she was nowhere in sight. With his acute sense of smell for fine baking, Tony followed his nose.

Wim could hear the footsteps echo down the hall and wondered what delight would enter into his wife's private sanctuary, as he was enjoying seeing his unravelable wife experience a new dilemma. Nothing prepared him for the sight that eclipsed the doorway.

Tony took in the scene and rested his eyes on Hannah in a way that said *"What's keeping you, I'm hungry."* He failed to see the look of shock on Wim's face.

Hannah, used to not being intimidated by Tony, took in every detail of the entire scene. Something about Tony was unsettling these two dear people, and Hannah was going to have fun unearthing the treasure of that discovery. *Tony could wait.* She was sure this efficient and well-prepared couple would have something in the cupboard that would satisfy even him.

The silence that followed Tony into the room was filled with the ticking of the wall clock. It sounded out the awkward moments that painfully filled the void marking off the passing of their chance of getting a steak.

To Wim's relief, he felt his own heart start once again. He had just had the shock he now knew his wife had experienced earlier this evening. Standing in his kitchen now stood the past. "What brings you to Bergen Op Meer?" asked Wim, as he moved into Tony's space and gazed up.

"At the moment, food." Tony offered as an obvious reply.

Hannah and Anita's intuition locked. They both knew these two men needed to sit down. One to eat and one to get the answers he was obviously soon going to be demanding.

How curious, thought Hannah. Once again, in less than an hour, something about Tony had turned moments in time into pieces of an evolving puzzle. She was enjoying the anticipation of their appearance immensely.

Wim finished what was left in Anita's glass and gestured for Tony to take a seat.

Tony saw Anita and Hannah opening well-stocked cupboards and felt assured they were going to produce what was looking like a feast. He gestured to his fellow mate if filling another glass was an option. Upon a positive nod, Tony poured himself a glass and topped up the glass of the man he was assuming was the caretaker.

"Let's start this again, I am Wim van Dam, Anita's husband. And you are?" Extending his hand, Wim waited.

Husband, Tony did not see that coming. The man holding out his hand to him seemed gentle, more of a simple life kind of guy, with a passion for the garden. *Ahhhh, that explained the flowers.* He was a perfectionist and his demeanour said he was firm, fair and friendly.

Tony took his hand and gave as good as he got. He did think his host was squeezing a little too hard. "Hello Mr van Dam, Tony King. We have come at the whim of Hannah, no pun intended of course. She thought it was the right time to unravel the mysteries of Johanna Malefyt's journals. It appears there is a family connection and this seemed like the logical place to start." Shrugging off the information as though it had no consequence, and stuffing the first bite in his mouth, Tony did not see the exchange between his hosts. Hannah did not miss a thing.

"Have you lived in the area long, Mr van Dam?" Hannah took the full weight of their attention.

Tony was glad he could just sit back and enjoy the incredible bread and cheese he was now having his second helping of.

"Long! Yes, you could say that." Wim's English was excellent and his impish grin revealed a pure heart.

Anita gave the glance of a wife to a husband that spoke of a warning, but Hannah was not concerned. She was enjoying herself and the excitement of discovery was building.

"Do you have the journals with you?" Wim asked.

"Yes, I do, Mr van Dam," Hannah replied. "Why do you ask?" Of all the questions that could be thought of, this one seemed odd.

A collective exhale from the others around the table did not go unnoticed by Hannah. Anita showed a sign of deep thought at this news, Tony was just plain thrilled to be finally fed something and relaxed back in his chair with glass in hand. Wim also displayed an expression of what Hannah thought was immense relief.

"My dear, please call me Wim." With a renewed sparkle that Hannah was sure did not only come from the fine amber liquid he was filling his and Tony's glasses with at regular intervals, she basked in the warmth of his glow.

Giving Hannah her full attention Anita placed her warm hand over Hannah's "And lieveling, your arrival is a welcome one. You are our honoured guests." Hannah had rarely felt love that she thought a Mother's love would feel like, but every fibre of her told her now that it would feel something like this. Anita looked at her with a warm kindness that drew Hannah to her and reminded her of kind Millzy who had been there for her all those years ago.

Hannah took this as a sign to let all the pieces of their evolving puzzle remain airborne for now. She filled her own plate and took in the atmosphere, while Tony and Wim talked rugby and Anita busied herself.

It was as though information had been received that brought about a paradigm shift which Hannah could only describe as *lightening the air*. The food was of the best quality and began to fill that empty place that she enjoyed filling as much as Tony did.

Looking about the room, a strange sense of *having been here before*, a sort of familiarity, began to take over Hannah's thoughts. There were aspects of the kitchen that she was sure she had seen before. "I have not had time to read all twelve journals." Hannah soon explained.

"Twelve" was the shocked reply of their hosts.

Hannah felt a small sense of guilt for constantly upsetting these two sweet people. "Why, yes, there are twelve of them. Plus documents and certificates that we were hoping to get some answers to over the next two weeks of our stay here."

Anita had taken all that she could for one day. She was sure this second piece of news had had an effect on her husband's heart also. She decided enough was enough for one day. Back to her business-like self, Anita packed up the feast and made a tray of fresh fruits and what looked like a stack of waffle biscuits that they could take to their rooms.

Tony and Hannah allowed themselves to be ushered out of the kitchen with the promise of seeing them both tomorrow.

"Wow, that was some kind of crazy." *Tony sure had a way with words,* Hannah thought.

"One thing we know is that you have a way of rocking the world of others around here," Hannah shot over her shoulder as they made their way down the hall. "I don't know about you, Tons, but I am going to get a good night's sleep. Tomorrow will be fun and I want to be ready for anything." Reaching up Hannah snatched the stack of waffle-like biscuits from the tray and kindly left Tony all the fruit. "Good night, sleep tight."

"Hey, I want one of those too," Tony said to the retreating form now entering her adjoining room.

"I'll let you know how they are tomorrow." And with a wave over her shoulder, she disappeared behind the door.

Chapter FOUR

In walks the matriarch.

The next morning Tony found Hannah in the breakfast room working on what was most likely her second cup of coffee. So deep was she into the journal that she did not see him coming. On his second "Good Morning" greeting she peeked at him over the rim of her specs with a look of *really, can't you see I am occupied*. "Hello to you, too. Sleep well?"

The grin displayed to Tony told him just how this day was going to go. She was going to be in charge and he was not at all sure he liked it. "My head hit that firm pillow and I was out like a light. Before things got too busy along the canal this morning, I got a run in and am now ready for more of what was on the plate last night. Excuse me, Hannah Banana." He hoped using her pet name would soften her a little.

Tony made his way over to the trays of food and heaped enough on the plate to show appreciation but not embarrass himself. *Besides, he could go back again.*

"I want to go over to the main house first thing today. This is a popular tour I am told because of the artefacts and the gardens. Eat up, big fella, we have a schedule to keep." She knew he was trying to get on her soft side. This was not going to work today. Time was short.

Tony rolled his eyes at Hannah, but they both knew he would deny her nothing.

Like the athlete he is, he tackled his first plate like a pro just in time for the additional menu items he pre-ordered to arrive right on time and be consumed also.

"Hey! Look at this, these fried potatoes are cut into stars just like Millzy used to do." Tony smiled down at his plate and wondered what had ever become of her. *I guess star potatoes is a Dutch thing.*

As they made their way through the tulip-lined pathway later that morning, Hannah warned Tony to be ready for anything. It was his presence that threw the van Dams off last night. After reading all of the journals of Anna Malefyt, and her mother's too, she was convinced today was going to be a whole new adventure.

Bergen Op Meer was run by Katerina Wolf, most likely one of the descendants of the caretaker Hannah had read about in the journals. In residence was her brother Thomas and their grandmother Batina Wolf Blass, *"though either not often seen during tour hours"* she was told by a helpful fellow guest over eggs this morning.

The brochure she had read gave her some good information on the family and Hannah was now keen to make the acquaintance of Katerina Wolf. She would be a great source of information. Hannah hoped she would have time to spend with her going over the documents and journals. There were years of information that told of family ties to this place and they had only twelve days left.

They entered the courtyard an hour before the scheduled opening time. Already there was a young woman setting up the queues of orange velvet ropes to mark the area to wait in for the next tour.

Kat had heard the voices in the garden much earlier than was standard and decided she would set up early but start the tour as scheduled. *They could wait.* She was still in her riding clothes and needed the time to freshen up fully before a day of greeting and tours.

Each day hundreds of admirers came to enjoy the many priceless artefacts only found in their home. She considered each one of them a welcome guest and wanted to present to them only her best self.

When Hannah informed Tony they were in fact an hour early and would be waiting in the secure border of velvet orange for a while, Tony took matters into his own hands and approached the *busy Miss* setting up. She had to have known he was standing right behind her, the gravel in the yard and his steps through it would have told her so loud and clear.

Kat knew someone was standing right behind her. She also knew that if she turned and engaged in conversation, in no time she would lose her chance to get ready for her day the way she planned and be giving a private tour before schedule. Tony looked back at Hannah and conveyed with a shrug that he was not sure how to proceed. Hannah's silent gesture of *tap her shoulder* seemed logical. So he proceeded to do just that.

Kat was not used to being touched by those on the tour. The shoulder tap she just received left her shocked and a little annoyed. The one perpetrating the interruption of her morning was going to get a dressing down. So with hands on hips she turned to face the culprit and give him or her a piece of her mind.

Tony had played the game of rugby all his life and there was never a time he was not ready to catch a ball. It could come from any angle. Catching was second nature and he rarely missed. It was in this instance that he had never been so glad that he could. The young woman fell in a dead faint and with well practised reflexes, Tony swept her up into his solid arms.

Anita and Wim thought it would be wise to make their way over to Bergen Op Meer as soon as possible today. Massy and Kat were going to have their lives irreversibly altered, not to mention the effect the news of their guests from New Zealand would have on Oma. They wondered if her heart could take it. However, they had missed their chance to warn the family. How could they have known the young couple would be so eager to get answers that they would slip out the front doors hours before others had even finished their first cup of morning coffee.

It was at this moment they entered the courtyard to see Hannah giggling at Tony's predicament of the still form of Katerina Wolf in his arms. Tony looked sheepishly at the three others in the courtyard and then down to the most beautiful face he had ever seen. His world tipped.

As though all by one thread the three spectators moved forward, all giving direction. Tony silently pleaded to Wim for help with a look of, *what do I do now.*

The woman in his arms was beginning to come to life and he wanted to put her down as soon as possible.

Wim gestured for Tony to follow him and led them all into the entryway and straight through to what appeared to be a library.

Hannah and Anita were presently sending out commands that Tony ignored. *Wim was his man.* He instinctively trusted him with his life.

As he placed the young woman he held gently on the leather couch, Anita stepped forward to take Katerina's hand and lovingly comfort her as she came back to life.

"What in God's green earth is going on here?" Massy pushed his way past the tower of a man standing by his sister who was looking half dead in their library.

Taking her other hand, he checked her pulse and smoothed a wayward hair from her cheek. This tender act sent jolts of jealousy through Tony, the like of which he had never felt before. He could feel Hannah's eyes on him. The blush that spread across his cheeks could not be hidden from her eagle stare.

It was obvious to Hannah that the young woman was going to be fine after fainting dead away at the sight of Tony. The young man now attending her had to be her brother or close relation, as the family resemblance was striking.

"What happened?" Kat looked up at her brother for reassurance, but found herself needing to reassure him at that moment as his concern was etched into his face. "Oh, this is a mess I have made, all in front of an audience. Have you met our guests yet Massy?"

Tony was beginning to wonder if everyone in this country spoke English.

Massy had in fact not given the others in the room a moment's notice. Helping his sister to sit up, he plopped down next to her and faced the small group that had gathered so impromptu in their library at this early hour.

"Good morning Tante Anita, and Oom Wim, who have you brought with you today?" Massy had full confidence and trust in the couple that he adored.

"May I introduce Hannah King, mein lieveling" Anita said. He gave Hannah his full attention and scrutinised her as though she was an exotic species one looks for for years but rarely ever finds.

"You must be Thomas Wolf, it is my pleasure to meet you." Hannah held out her hand in anticipation of the standard greeting being reciprocated. But he sat speechless next to his sister. It was only the elbow to his side by Kat that he jumped into action and returned the greeting in fluent, flawless English. "Greetings to you, Hannah King, please call me Massy." A bell rang in Hannah's head. *Massy?*

Massy did not want to let the silky hand he held now go. He was looking at a woman that held him enchanted. He hoped the huge presence of a man taking up so much space in their home was not her husband. "And may I introduce Tony King," said Wim. Massy's heart fell as he realised his hopes were dashed in that simple introduction. All eyes watched his reaction to meeting Tony.

Kat found it impossible to believe what she was seeing and wanted to pull her brother into a private conversation as soon as possible. *Tante Anita and Oom Wim must have known meeting Tony would come as a shock and came early to ease them into this vision.*

Reluctantly letting the hand go that he held, Massy turned and extended his hand to what could only be described as a mountain of a man. "Hi Tony, this is my sister Kat and I am Massy Wolf, pleasure to meet you." Standing he gave Tony his full measure and wondered briefly why this guy looked familiar.

Tony for his part was relieved, though he could not explain why, it mattered that this guy was the brother of the woman he had just been holding in his arms.

Kat could not believe how blind her brother was and decided to take this moment to interrupt. "I would like to begin again and welcome you both to Bergen Op Meer." Tony liked her voice.

"Thank you, Kat. Is ending up in the arms of a stranger in a dead faint a common greeting?" Never one to let anyone build a guard, Hannah got right to business with a calculated grin.

"It is first important to note," Anita said, "that the King's found the missing journals of Johanna Malefyt." The bomb dropped. Now time for triage.

The leather couch caught Massy as he ungracefully once again sat down next to his sister and stared at Tony. It was just now beginning to dawn on him why he looked so familiar. "Oh my, now I know why you look so familiar."

"Oh, can you tell us why?" asked Hannah

"I can." An ancient voice heavily accented came from the double doorway into the library and all faces in unison turned to her like six needles of a compass finding true North.

Chapter FIVE

The Matriarch takes charge.

"Oh, Oma, we are having a morning like no other today. Did we disturb you?" Kat doted on her beloved grandma and admired her above all women in this world.

Massy jumped up to escort who had to have been Batina Wolf Blass into the room. With a firm gesture of non-acceptance that her two grandchildren had never witnessed before, she turned from them to Hannah. "Finally, you are as beautiful as your mother." To say Hannah was speechless would be a massive understatement.

Anita tried to follow every train of thought that was whirling through her mind. *The queue is growing outside. Kat and Massy have to face the hard facts of what Tony's arrival may mean. Batina thinks she knows this girl's mother.*

"Oma" spoke Kat gently. "I think it's best if you sit down."

Man, these people have class, thought Tony, *they speak English better than I do.*

"I have longed for this day. The relief of it is a gift. You must be Hannah." Batina opened her arms and, as though she belonged in this nurturing space, Hannah moulded in.

In time Hannah found her voice in the form of a giggle and shared her glee with the ancient all-seeing eyes of the woman that now held both her hands. *This was going to be such fun.* Massy's and Kat's world tipped on its axis as they thought they were watching their beloved Oma lose her mind.

"Can someone tell me what is going on please?" Tony had had enough. "Hannah?"

"You may also call me Oma. I think you, Katerina, need to deal with the first tour of the day." With the wave of her hand towards the outer courtyard Oma took full command of the moment.

"Oh, my glory." Kat sprung into action and uncharacteristically charged out the door and started the first tour of the day right on schedule. Tony felt the light go from the room as she left, but was soon somewhat restored when Anita suggested they retreat to the kitchen as it was part of the private domain of the family. There they would not be disturbed.

Massy was finding this situation most unsettling. *Did this young couple have any idea what might potentially be unfolding?* He followed the small party at a discreet distance as they made their way to the heart of Bergen Op Meer, his family home. *He intended to keep it that way.*

Anita knew her way around the kitchen and Hannah could immediately see why. Hers was a perfect miniature to this one. In this kitchen, also, the space welcomed anyone who entered.

Hannah once again had that feeling of having been in this place before. *Keep your head in the game girl.* She was now in the presence of not one but two of the key people who could crack some of the mystery in the journals wide open. Batina Wolf Blass, or to us all Oma, opened her hands in a gesture for them to be held by those on either side of her during the thanks-giving prayer, and blessed the food they were about to eat. Tony was glad Uncle Jonty had taught him to be patient at everyone's table. *"The food will still be there, Lad, after giving thanks,"* he would say.

Though her prayer was in a language they did not understand, both Tony and Hannah knew briefly a moment of remembrance of Uncle Jonty, for he, too, had said his thanks-giving prayer in the same language. They both considered it ancient and had never bothered to learn it, even though their mother had also spoken many languages. Uncle Jonty never missed an opportunity to give thanks and Tony was now sorry he had not been more diligent in learning the prayer. He had a strong desire to gain the approval of Batina Wolf Blass. *Why he had no idea, but wanted it he did.*

The conversation moved on to light and casual matters. Things got lively as Anita and Wim spoke of a guest they had recently entertained that always travelled with their beloved Rhodesian Ridgeback Leo van Rooyen Buck. "A descendant of the mighty Kia we were enthusiastically told." He, the dog that is, was no trouble at all, and was soon granted his own place in front of the cosy kitchen fire each night of his stay when Anita and Wim closed off their days with a night-time snack.

"Oh, how we miss him. There were times I was certain Leo was speaking to us and we understood him perfectly," said Anita with a dreamy-eyed look. Wim took her hand in his and in a loving gesture gave her palm a kiss.

The clock was ticking. Hannah thought it was time to get on with her search for the facts. Dozens of questions were lining up in neat rows in her mind. As the morning progressed their number only grew. Batina Wolf Blass beat her to it. "Do you have Johanna's journals with you?"

"Yes, Oma, I have just this morning finished reading Anna's journals, also. Would you like to read them?" Hannah liked calling her Oma. A sense of belonging was growing within her heart.

Massy gave his grandmother a look that spoke volumes. He was hiding something and instinct told Hannah she could not trust him. "Yes, how thoughtful. You are here now, what else have you discovered?" Oma felt relief and was enjoying the gathering and meal. Hannah liked this woman, she got right to the point. Wim and Anita both felt an inner sense of calm that the morning was going so well.

"I have learnt recently that Johanna's daughter, Anna, went looking for her brother, who was believed to be dead, in the early eighteen hundreds and in fact did find him very much alive in New Zealand and..." Hannah's words were cut off as Kat marched through the door.

"I have 20 minutes before the next tour and would like to show you two something." Massy shook his head side to side. Kat ignored him and gestured for Tony and Hannah to come with her.

Standing too quickly, Tony's chair was in threat of toppling over, as if answering Kat's request was urgent, "Our thanks for this lovely meal, Oma." Tony's charm met its mark as he caught the chair mid-fall.

Hannah could see the making of a grin starting on Oma's face. She was smitten with the little Taniwha and he knew it, too. *Tony often reminded her of a shape-shifting mythical creature.* "It is best we answer Hannah's questions first, Katerina." Oma said and was obviously firm on this point. Hannah thought Massy was going to explode at Oma's mention of her digging any deeper. *Yes, she needed to watch out for that one,* thought Hannah.

Tony quickly pulled out a chair gallantly for Kat and Anita made good use of the awkward moment by setting a fresh cup of tea in front of her.

Was it just my imagination or was Tony acting very odd each time Kat appeared, Hannah silently wondered. "Thank you, Oma. We will be staying for a fortnight and would like to use our time wisely." Hannah placed the journal she had on hand on the table between them and decided it best to use the same tactic. Getting right to the point Hannah asked, "How do you know my mother?"

Chapter SIX

1970 *Lions Vineyard Aotearoa New Zealand*
Their parents had had children late in life. The two of them, Jonty and Johanna Heath, had the best that life could offer. All the joy a child could ask for.

When their parents both died in their seventies within a year of each other, the two siblings found themselves orphaned. Left to manage a large dry stock farm and vast orchard.

Johanna used her grief to move her through the many boxes, cases, and family stuff that had been collected and stored through the many generations of her family that had been living on the property since the early 1800s. There were sheds with old equipment and an attic stacked full of boxes packed to the rafters. *This was therapy to her.*

Jonty tackled the outdoors. He worked with the farm hands and orchard workers and dealt with the many day to day needs of the family business.

It was on the day that Johanna made the decision to start on the pile of boxes in the old family villa that she began to feel the hold of some grief ease. It could have been because of the photo albums that gave a perfect documentation of the life their parents had shared that Johanna had found on top of the old wooden sea chest marked with the initials AM.

Her parents had grown up on neighbouring farms, both only children, and the earliest photo of them together was at a very tender age that left no doubt that Adam Heath would protect Stephanie Cross with his entire heart, mind, body, and soul.

As the tears began to fall Johanna dusted off an old wonky stool made of a material she could not identify and settled in.

To reach her commitment of clearing out the dusty debris, she decided this wooden sea chest was as good a place as any to start. It was hard to not be distracted and wonder who AM was. As she dug deeper into the contents of the wooden box, she soon realised the history of AM was at her fingertips.

There were original birth certificates of Ashton and Anna Malefyt, land deeds, coins, journals, what looked like a flag, various other historical items, other family birth certificates, and foreign land titles to the estate Bergen Op Meer. Deeds to the land she and Jonty now owned, identifying clearly the descent of ownership from the humble beginnings of the past family members to the present ones. All neatly placed in their own leather-bound file.

Johanna was getting nowhere and everywhere at once. *Maybe taking one journal out of the case and placing the rest back in for safe keeping would be the best plan,* she thought. Disappearing later with what she hoped would be a further distraction from her constant heartache, and an interesting read at the end of this day, was what she would do.

But first, *back to dealing with some of these other boxes.*

The land held Jonty captive at times. *Today was one of those days.*

Surveying the paddocks and surrounding vineyard hills that were now his and Johanna's was a staggering thought. *How was he going to maintain all of this without his Puppa as a constant companion?* They had been a team spirited by a sense of belonging from the start.

Jonty's first childhood memory was of the two of them bringing home to Mumma a new horse from town. Her greeting was so joyful, He could remember each detail of the moment, including how she smelled of honey and cooked sugar. "Hello, my dearest son, I have been waiting for you." *She held me so close. I remember feeling safe. I was so relieved to be finally home again. I cried into her apron as she ran her hand over my head and gently patted my back.* The comfort and safety of her embrace in that moment he could still feel today.

One day, when Jonty and his Puppa, Adam Heath, had finished digging the many holes needed for the fencing poles on the north side of the property, they settled in to enjoy a basket full of their favourites. It was then Adam Heath told Jonty how their family first came to buy some of their land as whalers when trading with the local Iwi in the early 1800's. A section of their land had been a gift. The majority of the land had been purchased over the years to add to the vast dry stock and vineyard holdings it was today. When Steph and he married, adding the Cross holdings to the land, it had nearly doubled in size.

"Talbot Heath had been a whaler and traded for the first parcel of our land in the 1800s. His son, Tony Heath, or so the locals believed him to be, acquired the land just over the rise there to the west. My Puppa, his Puppa, and his Puppa before him, and so on, had bought more land. When your Mumma and I married, the vineyards and all the paddocks that you see came under our ownership. This will all be yours and your sister's responsibility one day. It has not always been easy. There have been wars, floods, droughts, and there is even a legend of a shipmate of Talbot Heath being killed, just over the rise there, by a widow-maker. We have always asked you kids to stay clear of the trees that have the plants that take root in the branches and become massive. The locals say he hid treasure on the land and for a time lived in the old stone sheep shed that is near the river; we use it for storage now at Lions Vineyard." All of this said with the deep knowing contentment of being firmly rooted on the land.

Jonty and his sister would now take care of their parents' legacy. He secretly hoped his sister would always live on the land. He could even find it in his heart to have Alvan also living on the land, if that meant Johanna would stay.

Alvan and Johanna were high school sweethearts.

Though Jonty could not choose a better guy for his sister, he hoped he and his sister would get a little more time together, before she devoted herself to a life with Alvan and the family she had always wanted.

Johanna let the warm water of the shower cascade over her, washing away the aches and dust of the day. She was happy with how much she had accomplished, but was now ready to settle into reading what was by date the first journal of Anna Malefyt, and enjoy a long drink of hot tea.

Wrapped in her favourite dressing gown, wet hair still held in the turban style towel on her head, tucking her feet under her, she settled down by the fire in her Puppa's well worn leather chair and opened to the first page. *There were days coming soon when she would wish that she had not done so.* For now the moment was idyllic.

Though the words were written in Dutch, Johanna would find no trouble in reading each page. Her parents had encouraged her love of language, having her tutored in Hebrew, French, German, Spanish and the local native language. She excelled in them all.

Written inside the front cover was the date Christmas 1809, and signed:

To Anna Banana, with unexpected loving devotion. Ash.

September 6th 1810

Louis (as I refuse to call him Lodewijk the first) has fled to Austria leaving us entirely free to live no longer in a state of defensive preparedness.

Friend that you are to me journal, I am in need of your pages. To rid myself of turmoil so that I may find some peace in this night. Therefore, I place inkened thought to the parchment. In the hopes of reprieve.

This fortnight is the longest in my life I have been apart from Ashton. My father is behaving peculiarly in a most disturbing fashion. Instincts tell me these two matters are related. As only a twin can know, Ash believes the fire was his fault. I do not. The manner in which the fire overtook the vineyard was unnatural and nothing of his making. I know in time this will be proven to be true.

My Father, however, has slipped away from me. He sits listless in his chair day after day. I am wholly uncertain if he will ever return to me.

If I could put all the facts together, these turns of events may come right again. I have faith this is so.

And this is where I leave you journal. I am beginning to feel the weight of the last few weeks lift just enough that I may say my prayers, without interruption, and proper dedication.

LIONS VINEYARD

September 16th

The most extraordinary events occurred today, even at this late hour, I am compelled to document their happening. In hopes of making sense of it all.

Of course my instincts were correct. Deposits of gunpowder were discovered in the lower hills of the vineyard that the fire did not reach. Ashton may have been the conduit by which the spark gained a soul, another had laid the plans to ignite the entire crop.

Jude's hands have healed nicely. Now, too will his heart begin the process.

The question remains, who would plan such a dastardly outcome. Could Louis have taken our unwillingness to relinquish Bergen Op Meer to him, and his entourage, as such an insult, that he wanted us ruined. Possibly?

Sadly, this new information did nothing to aid in my father's melancholy state. Upon my visit to him in the library this evening, I expected a more lively conversation. It was not to be. He was moved, however, to choose today, of all days, to pass on to me, my mother's journals.

I have longed to know the woman who died giving birth to us. I now have in my possession six journals composed by my own mother. And it seems at first glance that our Mother was meticulous in her attention to detail. Be still my frantic heart.

These events leave my mind reeling with thoughts, and thus my reason for turning to my parchment confidant, to clear my mind in readiness for my evening prayer. Tomorrow I shall find the time to extend my knowledge. In hopes I learn more about who she was. For now I begin, "Our Father who art in heaven....."

LOYOLA VAN ROOYEN BUCK

December 30th 1810

The funeral was peaceful. Yet, one could feel the drums of rebellion beating out a tune an octave below the hymns today. My mind is reeling from the day's events. I am now the sole owner of Bergen Op Meer, and I have no right to vote. The scales of democracy are as yet one sided on this matter.

Here in this private moment, I allow the pen to bring the question before me, did my Father love us? Today at his graveside I felt the weight of responsibility lift. The loneliness of loss taking its place. Resentment is looming like a shadow, waiting to overtake what little peace I can find, in this moment of much needed solitude. How this would be so much easier to bear if Ashton were here. We would mourn the losses as two pillars of strength in a fortress. I now see this is how we have managed to come to this point in our lives with our faith firmly intact.

That I can not tell him about Moses is a blessing, yet nothing will soften the blow when the day of telling comes. That horse was often the only comfort he had. Since the day Uncle Tally brought him from across the sea, the two of them were locked in the bond of friendship. Now, on the same day, both the Master of Bergen Op Meer and Moses enter into eternal rest. That old horse loved Ash when one had to question if our only parent ever did.

How will Ash take the death of our father I wonder? No, that thought is too dangerous. Why is it that these two men never bonded?

I had never seen my twin cross my father, not once. How I could use Ashton's strength today. Wherever you are brother, I send you my Love, and may the grace of our Lord Christ Jesus and the comfort of the Holy Spirit be with you, keeping you safe. Believing Ashton is lost at sea is simply absurd. I will find him one day.

LIONS VINEYARD

Here is my commitment, that reading our own mothers' journals will become high on my duties list, in hopes she has left some clue behind that gives answers to the many questions I find myself burdened with each day.

I will rise tomorrow to a new way of living. Tonight, as I seek solace, I ask the Lord my God to grant me a peaceful night's rest. To fortify me for what tomorrow will undoubtedly have in store.

The honest clock ticking away the minutes left Johanna no room for doubt, she needed to get to bed. *How poignant the words of the journal were.* She thought. It was not lost on Johanna that the women of this family love deeply, with the sobering thought that loss happens to us all, it seems.

As she unwound her almost dry hair from the terry cloth turban she thought, *tomorrow I will hopefully discover who these people are and how we may be related.*

Chapter SEVEN

I *am going on a trip.*

Johanna needed to get her thoughts sorted and soon. Her heart knew Alvan could not wait for her forever but she had to be sure she was making the right choices. So, in true Kiwi character, she started to plan her Overseas Experience. An OE, against the silent protest of her doting brother Jonty.

She had read the six journals. Now determined to finish what Anna Malefyt started over two hundred years ago, she was heading to the Netherlands, alone, tomorrow. And when she got an idea in her determined head, there was no stopping her.

The next day Alvan could not believe what he was hearing. For the first time he and Jonty agreed, Johanna was being completely irrational. That she promised to settle down and get married when she returned did very little to calm his nerves. He liked order. This was anything but orderly.

The two of them started off as friends five years ago, when they met at a test rugby match. By chance, they had each taken single seats at a sold out game. Those seats were next to each other. They sussed each other out through easy conversation and soon discovered they had plenty in common. He had just moved to the North with his parents that summer, and, as the two avid rugby fans discovered, they had a lot to talk about.

Alvan would be attending the same school as Johanna. He was glad to have ticked the box of meeting the first local his own age and promised to look for her when class started up in a fortnight. Life had plans he could not have improved on.

They ended up in some of the same classes and Johanna was happy to introduce him to her group of friends. He fitted right in.

Just like that, life began a fresh new chapter. He was determined to bring order to the mess his parents had made of his life by moving him from Auckland.

On the one hand he could understand why his Dad wanted to make the move. Even he had to admit the dairy co-operative he would be working for was a rock-solid choice for employment. The small accounting firm he was working for had no ambition to expand and grow with the times. They were a Mom-and-Pop operation. Even Alvan could see they would soon be swallowed up by one of the many firms in Auckland that could see the commerce potential at hand. *But the North, really.*

Alvan was determined to find an occupation that would respect both his need for absolute order and be a prosperous venture. His Uncle Max had an insurance company in Paihia and had offered him an apprenticeship when he finished school. He had already decided to give it a go, and worked with his Uncle every chance he got. Alvan quickly began mastering the ins and outs of serving the needs of the local families.

The insurance business had turned into the right choice for him. He had more than once achieved the highest sales in Oceania for the entire company. Providing his clients with fair, affordable choices was rewarding. He spent as much time as needed with each client, until they all knew what was going to protect them and their loved ones. Johanna had often waited patiently for him to finish his day. *God, I love this woman.*

He had long ago invested in a policy that would provide him with a comfortable retirement. Uncle Max was a great mentor. He explained all the benefits of starting early and letting the compound interest do the work. Uncle Max said "in life, it is our choice if we want interest to be a thief or a profit maker for us", *I choose that latter thank you.*

Johanna was everything to him.

That she did not mind his quirky sense of humour was a constant gift.

They spent more time laughing than anything else. She had many of the same likes as him. He thought God had got it right when he made a woman that enjoyed a simple life, where family was at its centre. He felt exactly the same way. For now he would see Johanna off and wait.

At the airport, Johanna took a moment to look into the faces of the two men she loved most in this world. Jonty held that place in her heart reserved only for him. He was older than her by nine years, though often seemed much much older than this. He was her constant. That friend you could depend on for anything.

Until recently, she had never noticed that they did not look alike at all.

Looking through the photos she had found while sorting through the old wooden case marked AM, she realised there were no photos of Jonty before the age of four, nor a birth certificate. *Why was that?* The thought prompted her to investigate further and this led to her reading all the journals. The shocker was discovering she herself may have a much different heritage than what her parents had led her to believe.

It was not like them to keep secrets from their children, at least she thought they wouldn't.

Johanna and her Mumma, her Puppa would always say, were like two peas in a pod. *My sweet peas* he called them. She had never thought to ask her parents why her name was Johanna, which, she now knew from the documents found, was the name of Anna Malefyt's own mother.

Johanna took one last look back as she passed through security, adjusted her pack and waved farewell to the two most important men in her life. *There was no turning back now.*

Johanna had pieced together this much: Anna Malefyt was told her brother had died in a shipwreck, however, she refused to believe it. He had in fact changed his name to Tony Heath, and Johanna was now confident she was his direct descendant and one of the possible heirs to a large holding in the Netherlands. Anna Malefyt had no descendants and had legally ensured her brother's children would remain in possession of the family estate, Bergen Op Meer.

Johanna had no intention of making any claim. All she wanted was a simple life with Alvan and Jonty, although she did want to know why her parents had kept this information from her.

It was this hope that led her to follow her intuition, before she settled down and laid this whole unsettling mess to rest. The most difficult news Johanna now had was the fact she had every reason to believe Jonty was adopted.

This would never matter to her, he would always be her constant. She would not want to lose him to another family or a totally different life altogether. To give her mind ease she found herself on this adventure, happy that she had enjoyed learning languages and would have no problems communicating in the country she now found herself travelling to.

As Batina waited for the young woman to arrive, she caressed the silver frame and wondered at how life could be both so cruel and such a blessing in the same instant. Joshua was saved from the full horror of the war. She did not regret her decision to accept the missionary's kindness to keep her son safe. Not a day went by that she did not wonder about the man he had become. Her return to her home from the concentration camps was a miracle, and for a time she had much joy in finding love once again with Jurgin Blass before he was killed in a skiing accident. Leaving her with a baby to raise on her own. Batina decided, at this point, she would live a life dedicated to running Bergen Op Meer and raising her daughter Ester Maria Wolf Blass.

Ester from a very young age gravitated towards nature. It seemed only fitting when she chose to study the birds of this earth at university. She often travelled in her studies and so met the love of her life on assignment. Markus Wolf was a marine biologist who took Ester by storm. They were a perfect match from the very beginning. You could say penguins brought them together and took them both from Batina.

Ester Wolf Blass and Markus Wolf never took the time to marry legally.

Though there was no family relationship they shared the surname Wolf.

It was on a beach somewhere in the South Pacific that the two of them said their vows before God and a handful of witnesses in a ceremony that included combining their collection of beach glass in a jar. For them it was enough. Batina often thought the angels were fortunate to have been in attendance. Time existed as an adventure for them. As it never stops, neither did they.

When using a new type of submarine equipment for their research into penguins off the coast of New Zealand, things would go horribly wrong in the future. The sea would claim both their lives. Batina would become more than just an Oma that day to her future grandchildren Katerina and Thomas.

But for now, she was blissfully unaware of this tragic future to come.

Johanna rested the outcome of today in greater hands than her own. Placed the documents she needed and the journals in her pack, and off she went. Pedalling her rented bike along the canal by the hostel, letting the wind push her towards Bergen Op Meer, she let her thoughts wander.

Immediately enchanted with the charming tiny streets that seemed to go in every direction. *What would she discover in her meeting with Batina Wolf Blass? She sounded very kind on the phone.* This comforted Johanna. They spoke briefly yesterday. When Johanna had explained she had the journals, and that she was shocked to recently discover she was possibly a descendant of the Malefyt family, the silence extended to the point she thought the call had dropped out.

At the end of the line Batina soon found her breath, though laboured, and invited Johanna to pay her a visit at 10.00 am the next day.

She knew this day would come. Batina had a duty to protect her home. She also had to accept the possible hard truths. If this young woman was who she said she is, Bergen Op Meer and all its priceless artefacts would become the possession of a complete stranger that same day. With a determination to face the facts without fear, and an acceptance, without reservations Batina answered the door at the appointed time.

Chapter EIGHT

A *ll she wanted was a simple life.*
  Johanna had never been in such an opulent home before.

A delicate tea service was set out. As Batina poured, Johanna took in the room. An obvious library, filled to the ornate ceilings on two walls with books. The massive windows overlooking the lake stood straight and tall like soldiers dressed in fine white uniforms. The view was breathtaking.

This must be the lake that had been mentioned in the journals Johanna thought. Imagining her potential ancestors would have stood right where she was now, this sent a shiver through her whole being.

"Are you chilled, my dear, here have a restorative cup of tea." Batina's English was impeccable.

The two women settled into small talk and soon found that they enjoyed each other's company. Batina proved to be witty and very open to hearing about life. Johanna, for her part, listened with interest, as stories of a past that seemed more fiction than what could possibly be real, were told over not one but two pots of aromatic tea.

Soon Batina asked "Would you like to see more of the estate, my dear?" And so it was that Johanna was given a private tour of the beautiful home and grounds.

Bergen Op Meer was enchanting. It was obvious Batina Wolf Blass loved each corner, cupboard, and carnation.

As a very pleasant day passed Batina felt no threat from this *kind-hearted, unselfish, humble, young foreigner* and was compelled to invite her to stay.

Without a moment's hesitation Johanna accepted.

She could sense the older woman's loneliness, as her daughter was away on assignment, and saw no reason to not enjoy the hospitality of such a gentle woman. This would give them both more time to work out exactly what they were dealing with.

Batina had alluded to the fact that she, too, could now conclude Johanna was most likely a descendant of the Malefyt family.

As matters had been so for this long, tomorrow would be soon enough to confirm the facts.

After enjoying a walk through the grounds in the early morning, the next day Batina led Johanna into a private suite that she had not shared the day before.

It seemed the house just went on and on, thought Johanna. It was here they would lay out all the evidence and together determine what would be the next course of action.

Johanna neatly laid out all the proof she had, along with the journals and the photo books of her own family.

As the two women settled in, Johanna soon discovered it was a good thing they were sitting down when she opened up the treasured photo book of her own parents.

Batina had requested they start there. She knew Johanna was struggling. *She was now going to have to accept the fate she uncovered in the attic of the old family villa.* Batina thought this may bring her some much needed comfort.

"My brother and I have never wanted for love or money. Our parents shared much joy and poured abundance into our lives. They were older when I was born and what I now suspect, my brother Jonty, nine years my senior, is adopted. You see, there is no family resemblance, and not a single photo of him before the age of four. I find this questionable. Why would our parents keep this from us?" Johanna asked.

Batina could hear the hurt in Johanna's voice over this choice her parents had made.

"My dear, there are times in all our lives that withholding a truth seems like the right choice. I understand this better than most." Wisdom was often a nurturing companion of Batina's.

Johanna helpfully flipped to the page of the first picture in the book of Jonty. She pointed out the obvious.

Batinas' heart leapt with shock from her chest. Rising from the table, she reached for a silver-framed photo among the many in the private sanctuary and placed it next to the one in the book. It was the same face. It was the same boy.

Both women turned in unison to each other with looks of awe.

"That is my Joshua." Batina broke down and wept.

With a tenderness beyond her years Johanna gently wrapped the dear, sweet, sobbing woman in an embrace. She waited for the moment to pass. In truth things had now become even too big for her to direct into any kind of sense.

As time will do, the moment settled.

With once again a fresh pot of tea between them, Batina started at the beginning. After much discussion she confirmed. "You are the rightful heir to all that you see and your brother is my very own son." Batina was now certain of both.

"I don't want it, any of it. Jonty and I have a home we love. I have no intention of letting any of this change." Johanna had never been more serious in all her life.

"My child, it is not for you to want or not want, it is so." It was Batinas' turn now to console the distraught young woman whose world had been irreversibly changed forever. Johanna let her hand rest in the caring hold of a woman she now wanted to run as far away from as possible.

"How can my brother be your son, this is crazy. How can this all be my responsibility now?" Side to side Johannas' head moved in her effort to reinforce the facts not being what this woman at her side was now claiming.

"It is so. Moments ago, you admitted it yourself that he was adopted. Tell me all you know about the man you call Jonty." Batina had never given up the hope that she would one day be reunited with her son. She now hung on every word this wonderful young woman was speaking.

"Our Mumma had always said Puppa had brought him home on the day he went to town to buy a new horse. We always thought this was a tale of fantasy. Something to laugh at. Never to believe. He is happy on the land that our family has lived on for generations. I want none of this to change. Batina, I have no intention of claiming any part of Bergen Op Meer, nor will I make a change to any part of my life that will disrupt the plans I have to marry Alvan. They are everything to me, and all I have left as a family." Earlier in the day, Johanna had told Batina of the promise she had made to Alvan. She had every intention of keeping life as it was and following through.

And so it was, in the remaining time the two women had together, Johanna told Batina everything she could about Jonty.

Batina, as her contribution, shared every detail of the Malefyt family history starting with Jacobus and Damien Malefyt. When they parted, Batina promised to remain steward over the vast estate in the Netherlands until such a time that Johanna could begin to come to terms with full ownership. She was encouraged to listen to her heart for guidance and trust in the Lord's plan for them all.

Chapter NINE

1792 *Bergen Op Meer Netherlands*
"Hah, I have an even greater possession." replied Jacobus,
with the halting incredulous tone saved only for the mirror image of himself
sitting across the dining hall. Damien would find a way to make it impossible
for his twin to get away with having anything that took his fancy. He also
knew if Jacobus could find a way to have both, marriage and the tea set, he
would. Most of the family treasures would go to the first to marry. That was
agreeable to them both, however the artefact they now discussed was a
contender to their undoing.

The first one to marry would lose the right to any claim to it.

The legend of the Malefyt Tea Set remained a safely guarded family
secret. Damien had every intention of enjoying the fact that he would gain
full ownership of the said porcelain. Of such value was this seemingly
innocent looking set, it took precedence over the family's Vermeer and
Rembrandt collections.

Johanna Heath had recently accepted Jacobus' offer to wed. The problem
was Damien, too, was going to ask for her hand at a more romantic moment
than on a stroll in the vast estate. However, the colours of the changing of
the season in the vineyard turned into the perfect setting, and Jacobus had
won the day and her hand. A winter wedding was now the talk on everyone's
lips. As the year turned to 1793, Jacobus and Johanna would begin a life as
husband and wife.

Damien refused to become an outsider in his own home that was sure
to fill with children within the year. He truly had no feelings for children
and this was now his downfall. In truth, this was the reason he had waited so
long before asking for Johanna's hand. He had hoped that in time his paternal
desires would ignite and the problem would be a matter of the past.

Johanna had made it clear she *adored children* and wanted to start a family right away. Jacobus admittedly announced he was ready to be a father and Johanna became his willing bride-to-be without a moment's hesitation.

The only barrier he had to overcome was that of her overbearing brother, Talbot Heath. Jacobus thought, due to the fact Talbot was often away sailing on his whaling ship in the South Pacific, that he would want Johanna settled with a family of her own, but lo and behold, this proved to be false hopes.

Johanna used all her abilities of persuasion. She was determined to convince her brother that she knew what she wanted was the right choice for her.

Talbot thought she was far too young to start a family. His fear of losing her in childbirth, as they had their mother when Johanna was born, was a fear all too real to him.

Johanna was sixteen and was painfully realising the tick-tock of time passing with what she considered alarming gong-like intervals. If truth be told, she found both of the Malefyt men suitable. Through their life-long bond, marrying either one of them at this point in time would suit her without question.

To be honest, she found it almost impossible to tell the two brothers apart. If it weren't for the birthmark in the palm of Damien's hand she would be lost. Their mannerisms, and looks, were a perfect mirror image. In the past they had taken great pleasure in playing the game of switching places when out riding, as then they were wearing gloves.

When she was younger, this was fun. As she matured and set her heart on marriage, she refused to be in their presence when they were wearing gloves.

Johanna's father, Mac Heath, had been the financial overseer of the vast Malefyt holdings for decades and had always kept a dwelling of moderate yet elegant status near Bergen Op Meer. Shortly after his beloved wife Sophie had died giving birth to Johanna, the Gate House became their new home. *He thought it best to keep the newborn child close at all times.*

Mac knew Batina Wolf, the new governess, would give the child the love of a mother. Her natural maternal instinct was unquestionable, even though she herself was not that much older than his first born Talbot.

Mac and Talbot did not see eye to eye. They were both strong minded-men with such a gap in interests. Mac found it impossible to relate. He found it at times hard to believe Talbot was his son, yet the resemblance was too striking to deny. He had secretly hoped to have more children right away, but it was not to be.

Johanna was a gift that entered into his life as a huge shock seventeen years after his first child.

Sophie was overjoyed to be expecting, taking all the precautions she could to ensure all would be well with the baby. She ate well, rested often and enjoyed the fresh air regularly. Together, they took early meals and turned down their social calendar in the nine months leading up to the birth of their daughter. It was a time their love for one another shone like a new gold coin that had undergone an unnecessary polish.

Even the strain of Talbot being so much more his Mother's son than his, this had no adverse effect on Mac's loving bond with his beautiful wife. Sophie and Mac were to the very end dear friends and very much in love.

Talbot became bitter towards Mac at the death of his mother.

Though he loved his sister with a complete abandon from their very first meeting. Johanna was two when she met Talbot for the first time. He refused to return home when his mother died, choosing to measure out his bitterness towards his father sailing to various places across the South Pacific.

But a hard heart had no chance against the winning charm of the adorable two-year-old who greeted him when he finally returned home to convalesce and recover from his injuries sustained in battle.

This was a hold she had over him her entire life.

From the moment she wrapped her chubby arms around his weather-toughened neck, christened him Tally, and sealed it with a kiss to his tanned cheek upon his return, he was irrevocably all hers.

This even helped to smooth things with his father and the three of them enjoyed some treasured, happy times.

Mac had also realised that his son was now a grown man, had survived the battle of Dogger Bank and was one of the lucky ones off the *Holland* that sank.

With a sense of pride Mac, with his small daughter safely tucked in the protection of his arms, listened to the harrowing tales of his only son's sea journeys and the battle's lost and won. Even Mac had to marvel at the fact the boy was barely just a man and had seen far more adventure than he was ever likely to.

Johanna, along with her free spirited nature, grew up without the two men at her side.

Her father died when she was five in the bubonic plague that swept across Europe. Tally, though she knew he loved her, could never stay on land for more than his sea legs would allow.

Batina remained her mother figure and doted on her young ward as though she herself had knitted her out of rainbow threads.

The Gate House of Bergen Op Meer became the Heath permanent residence. *This arrangement suits me fine,* Tally thought. This suited them all. He could indulge the little minx and feel no obligation to do more for her than ensure she was well provided for and have the comfort of knowing she was loved. And this he did with great pleasure.

He grew very protective of her and had made the decision to find a suitable husband for her, though not before the age of twenty.

This decision, he knew, was going to give him a marvellous amount of grief at the hands of his sister. *I have her best interest at heart.* Captain Talbot Heath always listened to his instincts. Any good sea captain knew how to read conditions and he trusted implicitly that God-given instrument.

He had every intention of following through in this nature, but even the best intentions can be tossed about like a ship in a rolling sea.

Chapter TEN

The caretaker has something to say.

Talbot spent more time on land one particular trading season than was natural for him, but the pleasure of his time with his sister was worth every moment.

It was during one of these times that he wished he was in the middle of the South Pacific on his ship *Wind Whisperer*.

At the very tender age of sixteen, Johanna had decided she had had enough of being without a family. She was attempting to convince her brother that either of the two young masters she had grown up with would make suitable fathers to the many children Johanna was explaining she was ready to have.

"How could you possibly understand, Tally? What you know about women could not fit into this tea cup," indicating her point, lifting the delicate Malefyt family heirloom at her fingertips for emphasis.

"Besides, you are always away on some misadventure and I am here on the estate with Jacobus and Damien. Batina watches over me as though I were a babe and not a woman." With an adorable pout she stated her case as they talked companionably in the library of their home, after the weekly church service.

"You are all I have in this world, little one." Tally played the chords of her heart. He had every intention of ending this conversation with the tune he chose to play being the final note. "Why not pack your things and come with me on my next voyage? You could see some of the world outside this estate and forget this crazy notion of children when you are still very much one yourself," emphasising this by dotting the tip of her nose with his gloved finger.

There Tally had said it, the truth, he utterly failed to see her as a woman. "I have long ago left the nursery, Tally, as if you had not noticed, and have decided to remain right here where I have always belonged. I am the obvious choice for the next mistress of the Malefyt estate and the brothers know it." Johanna shared this fact with absolute certainty.

Tally had to inwardly admit he had noticed that she had grown into a delicate version of their mother. But she was so small and his fear of losing her, too, in childbirth was very real. *If only he could convince her that all she really needed was some adventure on the high seas?* He thought. Surely she had developed other interests than just having a family would allow. He would consult Batina this evening.

"Besides, you would then be totally free to sail away and never return." Johanna knew Tally would always return to her. The frustration that was building up inside was beginning to take hold and gain control of her better judgement.

"Now, now, little minx, let's not have wasted words that we will both regret. Did you learn nothing in today's reading? *Don't turn your back on wisdom, for she will protect you. Love her, and she will guard you.*

Johanna knew not to argue with Scripture. She decided she would continue this conversation with Batina this evening.

Convincing Batina that she was truly ready to start her own family took more than Johanna's usual efforts. Both Tally and Batina thought she was just too young.

It was fear that she saw in both their eyes. For this she felt some shame in placing two people who loved her deeply in a position that they believed only loss would be the outcome. When all she could see were happy moments ahead and all the children there would be to nurture and adore. *Who could help her convince them that all would be well, and their fears unfounded?* She wondered.

To Johanna's amazement, the rescuer was an unlikely source.

Jude Wolf had been caretaker of the Malefyt vineyard since he transplanted his family's noble grape vine twenty years before on the estate. He was thirteen at the time and had vast knowledge even then.

The Wolf family had been producing fine wines for hundreds of years and each son was taught from a young age the value of producing a vintage the markets would demand a high price for. As Jude was the youngest son of a large family, he was forced to find his own way in the world. So when the first vine had been delivered and placed lovingly in the ground at Bergen Op Meer from a new strain of grapes also propagated on the Wolf family estate, their youngest son convinced his family he needed to remain with the new crop, as he felt it was his duty. *Who could argue with such logic?* A wage was negotiated that included lodging and Jude permanently shifted.

The years quickly passed.

Jacobus, Damien and Johanna often found themselves after a ride on a crisp, cold winter day calling in at the caretaker's cottage.

Jude always had a fine fire going and could be entrusted with any confidence the three young wards could have, without any judgement at all. He grew to love them as his own. There was less work on the cold winter days, and he welcomed their lively company.

Jude knew very little about true love, the kind shared by a man and a woman, but even he could see that both boys could see no fault in their female companion. He was certain one of them was going to ensure she would become the next mistress of the estate. If there was one thing he had learnt, it was that nothing could stop passion when you loved.

This is how he felt about the vineyard.

So it was with trepidation that Jude went in search of the governess, Batina, to explain his findings.

"Love is its own seed and will grow when tended by a passionate master." Batina was still in awe of the fact this gentle, tender-hearted man came to the Gate House where she and Johanna lived to explain his findings.

Of course Batina knew her young ward was in love. Either of the young masters would have been a suitable match for her. *What this giant of a man could not know was the fear she felt at the thought of childbirth.*

She herself vowed to never have children.

Batina had seen far too much pain and loss and knew of no logical reason to inflict this on herself. But even she had to admit Johanna was not her. She was fearless. She would have a family.

It was more and more obvious that the young masters had taken her fancy. The inevitable could not be prevented. *What was she to do?* For now Batina listened to the observations of the caretaker with complete sincerity. She began to accept what seemed far from possible only days before, Johanna becoming the mistress of Bergen Op Meer would soon be a reality.

Jude knew he was looking at a bright and warm hearted-woman. Her compassion for her young ward's circumstances shone from her eyes like starlight. Batina had never visited Jude in his cottage, nor had he ever set foot in the Gate House to her knowledge.

So when Johanna breezed through the open door, her shock at seeing this sight left her momentarily speechless.

Jude found it best to leave the two women to their own matters. He nodded his head with a farewell to each of them. Placing his cap back where it rightfully belonged and out of his fidgety hands, he left them in momentary silence.

Not many days thereafter it was announced that Jacobus Malefyt and Johanna Heath were to be wed on New Year's Eve.

Chapter ELEVEN

Wine in a teacup has the same effect.

Damien now knew that Johanna had meant far more to him than he had known but a few, short months before. He had placed the full ownership of the priceless tea set before happiness and now was beginning to bitterly regret his choice.

Since the announcement, Johanna and Jacobus had been inseparable. Damien no longer felt welcome, though he knew neither of them intentionally caused this. They only had eyes for each other now. Damien felt a deep sense of loss, not only for what could have been, but what no longer was.

He now spent his lonely days holding back the growing envy and contemplating his next course of action. He had no intention of living in a home full of children that were not his own. The estate was quickly becoming worthless to him.

The issue was he could no longer see himself with anyone else. Only with his twin brother's future wife. The three of them had grown into who they all were today, as a set. How was he to find anyone that would match his personality as she had done. *What a fool you are Damien Wolfgang Malefyt.*

Turning to the cellar seemed like a logical answer.

With clear direction that he had not felt in days, Damien collected one of the priceless unassuming teacups from its resting place and headed to the bowels of the manor.

Though the Malefyt family had always grown a fine grape to be sold to select buyers in domestic markets, they had acquired an envious collection of the fermented variety.

This is where Jude found him two days later.

"Come on, Lad, let's put some tea in that cup and get it into you." Jude knew it was going to take a lot more than the cook's strong brew to get this one remotely close to sober. At least it was a start.

And so it was that Jude dusted off the delicate cup, tucked it in his pocket and endeavoured to use it for its rightful purpose. By the looks of it, the vintage that was set aside for the wedding was now seriously depleted.

The young Masters had always shared everything. Jude thought this was a sign of things to come if Damien did not come to terms with Johanna and Jacobus making a life together. *These are the times a true parent was needed.*

Jude had done his very best when the boys had lost both their parents within months of each other. Their Father had died when he fell through the ice on the lake on Christmas Eve and their mother had died within a year of the plague and a broken heart, leaving two distraught twelve-year-old boys. Forced to grow into men long before their time.

Mac Heath did all he could to keep the estate running, but he, too, succumbed within two years leaving two children behind.

Talbot had not been home at the time, and hired an overseer to manage the day to day operations. Naturally Batina continued to maintain constant supervision. The three orphans found solace in spending time together on the estate. The young mistress and the two youthful masters maintained a bond through loss and were seldom ever seen apart again.

Miss Johanna was to become Mistress of Bergen Op Meer, Jude's heart was glad. That way he would always have her and the two Masters close. They were the family of his heart. There was nothing he would not do for them. To see Damien struggling was now a concern he had no idea how to deal with. It was obvious he, too, had loved the girl deeply and was at a loss.

Damien needed someone to share his life with.

Jude committed to seeking an opportunity to encourage a new social schedule that would increase the numbers of young female adults at the estate. And he knew just how. The harvest each year was a joy for the entire estate and the villagers. This year Jude would include Johanna in the planning and encourage her to add a much larger number of young women her age.

For now, Jude lifted the limp body of the young master over his shoulder and made his way to the estate kitchens.

The wedding day dawned crisp and bright.

Everywhere one looked, the twinkling of the season and the joy of the wedding day lit each room. *Today is my day to outshine it all.* This was Johanna's wedding day.

Tally would be in all his captain's splendour.

The striking entrance they would make had Johannas' heart fluttering with excitement.

Batina had ensured that not a single detail had been overlooked and she fussed about the glowing bride like a mother hen. Johanna had recently moved into the refurbished suite furnished for the two young newlyweds to start out their life in private comfort.

They had decided to put off the honeymoon tour until the spring. It was then they could freely enjoy the full splendour of the world class vineyards they were planning to visit.

Jacobus wanted to show Johanna the world. He thought there could be no better way than to accept the invitations that had come in from several of the finest families who shared the passion of grape growing for generations, starting at the Blass Estate.

Today would be the beginning of a new and full life for Johanna with a wedding night to hopefully start her on the path to the family of her own that she had always dreamed of.

Tally had never seen a more beautiful vision than his beloved sister. His heart refused to succumb to the melancholy thought of how wonderful this day could have been if their parents had also been present to share in it. Today was going to be a celebration of the love he was assured Johanna had for her new husband. *Fear would have no place in what outcomes their union may bring.*

Damien had spent the months leading up to this day going over and over how he could have it all.

A life with Johanna now seemed out of reach. Yet he still could not let her go. He had truly believed becoming the sole owner of the tea set would be the only salve he needed to overcome the depressed state he had fallen into in the cellar that day, a state he never came out of, no matter how much effort Jude had put into it. Even now as he watched the newly wed pair dance flawlessly across the floor with eyes only for each other, he seethed inwardly with renewed envy. *How could it be that my brother has all I now want?*

LOYOLA VAN ROOYEN BUCK

In this moment, an evil thought that would change the course of the lives of their descendants for the next two hundred years, began to take form.

Chapter TWELVE

A *fter we say 'I Do'.*
Johanna was beginning to fret about the hours that were to come, the time when the music would stop and she would be preparing herself for the intimate time ahead with Jacobus. Batina had on numerous occasions attempted to impart knowledge of the duties of a loving wife to her, but it was painfully obvious that she herself had little or no idea. *Who could she take her burdens to at this late hour?*

Johanna went in search of Wilhelmina van den Bloom, who had married this spring and was already with child. She would know how to put this silliness to rest.

Jacobus knew he was the luckiest man on the face of the earth. Yet his deep desire to wipe the devilish grin off his brother's face took his mind time and time again away from the happy moments of the wedding day.

The moment Johanna left Jacobus's side, Damien stepped into his line of view. He offered an invitation to his newly wed brother for a private celebration of a special vintage he had saved, just for them.

When Jacobus entered the library, he expected to see two silver wine goblets and a bottle of fine red airing on the side board. *Why was the tea set sitting front and centre?* This left him feeling uneasy, unsure of what was now to transpire. Damien waved him over to the priceless set that had been in the family for over a thousand years, then said the unthinkable.

"Allow me to swap places with you tonight. One hour and the set is yours." Their eyes locked.

The blood drained from Jacobus's head. He had lusted over this artefact all his life. Now it could be his and Johanna, all in one night. He knew what Damien was thinking. They were identical. Even his new wife could not tell them apart, except for the birthmark in the centre of Damien's hand. Jacobus dared to think about the idea. She would never know. *Was her virginity worth his possession of this priceless set of six saucers and cups?*

There had been numerous offers made through the generations by the same descendant of buyers to take over possession of the set for a small fortune. The answer was always the same. The auction house used by the Malefyts would take authority over the sale, if ever the set was to be sold. What remained a mystery was, how did this other family know of its existence?

Damien then produced the fine wine he had promised. He poured it into the unlikely porcelain vessels and the unthinkable was discussed.

Later that evening, Johanna entered the room they were to now share as husband and wife. The soft candle light would make it impossible for Jacobus to see her embarrassment. She was thankful for this mercy. Batina had assisted her with dressing and Johanna felt exposed as she made her way to the large bed. Like a frightened child, she blew out some candles to dim the lighting and relaxed impatiently under the feather duvet.

Damien entered from the secret door that only he and Jacobus had known about. He was pleased to see how dim the lighting was. The soft gasp from deep within the large bed set his blood racing. For good measure he blew out a few more of the candles closest to the bed. He began to remove his dressing gown.

Johanna had been told by Wilhelmina "the joy of intimacy is so excellent, you will want to spend the next three weeks wrapped in the comfort of each other's arms, uninterrupted by trivial matters such as eating." She would quite happily have Batina bring her a customary hot chocolate and one of those delicious biscuits that melted in her mouth right now, as Jacobus had yet to join her under the soft inviting bedding.

His pause at the bedside left her feeling unsettled. He then abruptly turned and made his way back to the secret door. She assured herself she would investigate this door first thing tomorrow, and was left wondering if he also wanted hot chocolate.

Damien quickly passed the dressing gown to his twin waiting in the secret passage and hurried away. To look at his brother now was impossible. Coming face to face with his bargain, the cost was too high. Johanna meant far more to him than he had ever imagined. He could not go through with what he knew was so wrong. Her happiness shone even in the dim candlelight. He would do nothing to cause her any pain. *Jacobus could keep the blasted tea set, too.*

Jacobus hurried into the room, lit a few more candles, and proceeded to tenderly kiss his new wife. Johanna's thoughts of hot chocolate dissipated into mist, as her body began to catch flame. No one saw the newly married couple for three days, as they explored and enjoyed all that was theirs in each other.

Eventually Batina did slip into the room when she knew Jacobus was checking on estate matters. She brought that much needed hot chocolate and was pleased to see the new mistress of Bergen Op Meer content and well loved. If there was not the pitter-patter of little feet within the year, it would not be for the lack of trying.

Batina was right. The honeymoon tour had to be postponed. The morning sickness that overcame her mistress within the first month of marriage was too severe to allow her to travel. Tally met with Batina each time he was on shore to ensure all was well. While Jacobus met Johanna's every wish and whim, the estate prepared for a baby.

Damien took over the Gate House, as his twin made it painfully clear he was better off without him. Though they never spoke of it again, Damien was glad he had not gone through with deceiving Johanna. She did not even miss him, so wrapped up was she in the prospect of being a new wife and soon-to-be mother.

It was Jude that kept the lonely master occupied, with his company.

On a very hot August day, when Johanna was resting in the shade by the lake, her bliss would have an abrupt end. Jacobus and Damien had not been spending much time together and Johanna was pleased to hear them discussing what she thought were matters of estate in the library. It was when voices raised that she made her way towards the sound. In her hopes of being helpful, she overheard what could not be even possible. *Why was Jacobus screaming for Damien to take the tea set back?* Then words that could never be taken back were spoken by her beloved husband, *the truth*. Johanna's world tipped on its axis and she fainted.

"The twins are fine," the doctor said to the two men and one woman hovering at the bedside later that day.

"Twins." To their surprise, Johanna had finally surfaced. She took in the news with a weak yet joyful cheer. Gone for the moment was the memory of what she had overheard the two brothers fighting about.

Batina had thought there was a possibility of twins, of course, even more so, when Johanna began to show so quickly after the wedding. There was no chance Johanna had been with child before the wedding. Batina had ensured she would not be permitted the opportunity to enter into any vulnerable situation.

Jude had confirmed that he believed Jacobus was also innocent on the night of his wedding.

Long-forgotten fears began to make their way into the forefront of Batina's mind. Johanna was small, but very strong. Batina would consult with the doctor and Jacobus in private, just as soon as she had ensured Johanna had all she needed and had found out what she was doing out in the sun in her condition. Talbot also needed to be informed.

"Batina, I am feeling quite restored and would like to inform my brother right away about the news. He needs to come home, as I want him to share in the joy of our family growing, not by just one, but two little ones." Johanna was fully restored. She had also recalled everything she had heard. The only one she could trust with the information was her worldly and wise brother.

"Dearest wife, you must now rest for a while. I can stay with you, if you would prefer." Jacobus was most concerned, but his motive to find out if she had heard what the two brothers had been fighting over was now his main reason for being alone with his young wife.

"No, I would like to be with Batina for the remainder of the afternoon. Batina, please also have a maid fetch my journal. I do believe it has been left under the big shade tree by the lake." Johanna had every intention of clearing her thoughts on the pages. *She had to think clearly.* When Johanna had her mind set, there was no changing it.

With a look to his brother of, *what have we done?*, the two brothers followed the doctor out of the room. Batina would consult with the doctor at a later time. For today, Johanna would get her undivided attention for the remainder of this day.

With haste, a letter was dispatched to Tally at his city office. Due to the fact it was from his sister, he was somewhat relieved, because it meant that she and the baby were doing well. This calm did not last long, once he had opened the short but effective message. *Twins.* He would be leaving the office sooner than expected.

Johanna had indeed spent the afternoon documenting all she had heard onto the pages of her journal. She had ensured the letter to her brother would reach him within that day and finally rested. Batina, true to her word, remained at her mistress' side. As Johanna became agitated and restless later that evening, she had a bed made for herself in the room as well.

Batina was awoken in the early hours by a sound from within the folds of the large master bed, a soft whimper more suited to a small wounded forest creature than the lively mistress she doted on. Within seconds Batina was at her side.

"I am here, my dearest child." Johanna was soaked in sweat. Gently Batina lifted back the covers in hopes of not seeing her greatest fears. Blood soaked the bedding. The scared eyes staring at her for reassurance were not disappointed. With her usual steely will, Batina looked into her mistress's eyes with the reassuring look of *all will be well*, gently placing the blanket back. She quickly rang to see if the doctor had remained overnight, as was discussed earlier.

Within moments the house lit up and fires were rekindled. A dishevelled doctor was quickly ushered into the room, still in the process of putting his dressing gown on. "Have the maids prepare plenty of hot water and bring fresh bedding."

As if Batina had to be told this. With an unladylike, hands-on-hips stance, she eyed the doctor with fury. Which had no obvious effect on him.

The doctor knew within moments he would be saving lives today and was determined to not lose a single one. With a tenderness Batina had never seen in a man, he examined and reassured her frightened mistress, explaining to her what had happened. Her waters had broken. "The amount of blood was much less than was at first glance revealed, but still a concern my dear." With a strength Batina did not think he possessed, the doctor lifted his young patient in his arms and held her close as the bed was quickly stripped and re-made.

Maybe she had been too harsh on the doctor. Batina thought. She and the maid had the bed refreshed within seconds. Clean night clothes had materialised and Johanna was resting comfortably within the span of a butterfly's breath.

It would appear the Malefyt family would soon grow by two. The entire staff was on alert to ensure not a single detail for the new masters or mistresses of the estate were overlooked. Johanna had the undivided attention of a dedicated and capable team of five. Jacobus and Damien were all but forgotten.

This suited Damien just fine. Once he had been told Johanna's life was not threatened, he retired once again to the Gate House to wait out the inevitable. His twin had made it perfectly clear he wanted nothing to do with him. This cut deeply.

Jacobus focused his attention solely on being ready to welcome his children into the world. So there he sat in the downstairs library, alone, waiting, just waiting. The doctor had indicated these things can take time. "With twins one never knows...." he said. A girl arrived first.

Shouts of joy rang down the stairs in less than an hour, that he had a daughter.

In a flash Jacobus was at the door of the master suite. Out stepped a maid with a tiny bundle wrapped in the Malefyt crested cloth and tenderly placed the infant into his arms, before stepping back into the room. There he stood, alone and enchanted, with his daughter. Jacobus had never known such joy. The infant that peacefully rested in his arms was a perfect miniature of her mother. "We shall call you Anna", and he gently kissed her sweet-smelling forehead.

Batina was running the comings and goings of the master suite like a general in command of her army and momentarily entrusted the wrong soldier. "Where is the child?"

The room had settled to a new calm to face what would now be the birth of the second infant.

Batina scanned the battle ground, expecting to see the little one in the arms of the maid. The three maids looked at each other, then back at Batina as if to say, "Don't you know?"

"In the arms of her father," was the youngest maid's reply.

"Where is the father?" Batina's calm had evaporated in an instant.

Could these young women truly not know that Jacobus would have no idea how to deal with a newborn, let alone know how to even hold one?

Her exit out of the room seemed almost comical to the doctor. He dared not let the dedicated governess know, as she did not seem to have much of a sense of humour.

As she soon found out, there was no need for concern. There before her very eyes, seated on the landing just outside the master suite, was a besotted father confidently holding his newborn daughter in his arms. Tears spilled out as she took in the sheer beauty of the tender kiss she saw him place on the infant's forehead.

"Come, Jacobus, the infant will need her wetnurse soon. I must have the child." Batina gently kissed the new father's cheek. With a tenderness born of experience, she extracted the baby and turned to re-enter the master suite.

"Her name is Anna." Jacobus thought Batina would need to know this important information, before she and the child disappeared.

Batina's focus was so intent on getting back to her mistress, she did not acknowledge the quiet, spoken words of the Master of the house. She entered the room with the sole focus of ensuring the wet nurse was brought to the room immediately.

In all his years the doctor had not witnessed a first child entering into the world so quickly. His concern for the new mother showed in the creases of his face. *Yes, the first child is small, this is true.* Intuition told him to be cautiously optimistic.

Johanna was resting between contractions. As they had slowed and her pulse was only slightly elevated, he eased himself into a bedside chair and took the tea offered by the maid.

The hours ticked by slowly.

Jacobus had made his way back to the sanctuary he was most comfortable in. The wait had become unbearable and he thought he would go mad. This is how Damien found his dishevelled brother, lost in a daze, late in the day. *Maybe this was an appropriate time to simply sit with his twin and wait.*

Moments later, this is how Talbot found them.

He could never tell them apart, so spoke to the room at large. "How is she?"

Startled, Jacobus came to his senses. "Anna is thriving. She is with her wetnurse."

"Johanna, how is she?" *Could all have gone well? Would he soon be celebrating the birth of his sister's children?* Talbot wondered.

"The doctor has been with her the entire time. The second child is taking its time." Jacobus was beginning to grasp the magnitude of the moment. *Was his beloved Johanna truly in danger?*

"Is Batina upstairs?" Talbot knew where Johanna was, so too, Batina would be and every answer he would need.

"Yes." Two identical responses from two identical faces.

In his wake the twins followed the man who took charge. They made their way to the master suite.

Talbot gave a cursory knock on the door, but had no intention of waiting.

The smell of blood that hit him like a tidal wave would have overwhelmed a weaker man, but he was used to it after all these years of whaling. What he was not prepared for was the look on Batina's face as she held the naked, crying newborn. His little hands waved in the open air.

The two men at his back came to an abrupt halt. Neither missed the mark in the centre of the boy's hand, identical to the one on Damien's. Jacobus' heart fell to depths it would never recover from. His first thought was not for the woman he had loved. It was that the father of the twins was not him.

Chapter THIRTEEN

*O*ma tries to explain some of the history.

    Oma gave careful consideration of where to begin and how much to tell, leaving Joshua's identity out of the tale, for now. Much to everyone's silent amazement she had answered Hannah's question. She told an extraordinary tale of having spent time with Johanna Heath. The fact that all four of these young people had met before, *that story would be for another day also*. She thought.

She produced a delicate page torn from a bible, from the book of 1 Samuel, Chapter 2. Hannah saw the page and knew immediately what she was looking at. "You see, your mother asked me to keep the legacy of the estate a secret and I agreed. In turn, she also agreed to keep a secret for me. When you were born, she sent me this page. I knew she had named you Hannah and one day you would come."

Hannah produced the Bible from her bag and Oma placed the missing page back in its rightful place.

In unison Massy and Kat turned to each other, both thinking the exact same thing. *If Hannah is the direct descendant, then why does Tony King look like the mirror image of Ashton Malefyt?*

"My Loved Ones." Oma looked into the eyes of the four young adults around the table. "After today, all your lives will never be the same."

What an understatement this proved to be.

"We can do nothing about the outcome now. You see, your mother Johanna was taken from us before she had told the love of her life about the understanding we had formed. The estate is rightfully hers; this is very true. When she died, it became yours, Hannah. As she had kept my secret, I had no choice but to keep hers. *The tea set is a matter for another day.*

"This does not explain why Tony looks identical to Ashton, Oma. Or why their Uncle Jonty is not the one to inherit." Kat could no longer hold back her statement.

"How do you know I look like Ashton?" Tony was finding this all too much. The blaze inside him was beginning again.

"I don't understand how Hannah can be a descendant and also be married to Tony?" Massy was confused about his feelings and blurted this out.

Tony and Hannah, both in utter shock, looked in his direction and together burst into gales of laughter. This helped to take the full edge off Tony's rising anger. "It is because we are brother and sister, Massy. Tony is my younger brother. Our parents died in a car crash leaving me in this state." Hannah waved her hands over the wheels constantly at her sides. "Tony has been my champion ever since. My mother's older brother took us in and raised us."

"And how is your Uncle Jonty?" Oma asked, trying to cover up the embarrassment being felt by her family members. *Of course our mother would have told Oma about Uncle Jonty.* Hannah found the loss too fresh so the telling fell to Tony.

"Oma, the story is a sad one for us." Tony said. Batina Maria Wolf Blass prepared herself for the worst.

Jonty had no intention of keeping those blasted hearing aids in. They bothered his ears and the squawking of mating peacocks in the yard drove him mad.

Hannah was relentless though, and from time to time he made a show of it and had them in for her benefit. Today was not one of those days, but, even with the pesky aids sitting next to him on the table he could hear the distress call of one of the cattle.

Hannah loved all the creatures of their farm. She would not allow a single one to end up on their very own table. Jonty and Tony never argued. Hannah did all the cooking anyway and was gifted with the ability to boot.

Recently a calf was born. Hannah had assisted with the difficult birth as the first-calf heifer would not let anyone other than Hannah close to her. If Jonty was right, the distress call was from that ornery new mother. *He had better go check things out, before she kicked up too much of a fuss and unsettled the whole herd.*

Yup, Jonty had been right. There, in the new patch of the tilled garden, stood the baby calf. Its' mother stood with her fellow cows, curdling her milk on the opposite side of the fence.

Jonty slipped on his wellies, boots he had spent thousands of hours in, and gave a prayer of thanks that the calf was small. He would have no issue picking up the little thing and taking it right back to the irate heifer.

The ground was fresh and looked alive. For years Jonty, and generations before him, had rotated crops on the land, resting the ground every seven years and letting nature nourish, restore and then give back again. As he stood looking over the valley, absentmindedly scratching the soft downy head of the calf Hannah had named Skippy, Jonty, without his hearing aids, did not hear the oncoming thunder of a mother who had battered down the fence behind him to get to her offspring. He never knew what hit him.

Hannah drove up to the villa late in the afternoon. She was shocked to see a ring of cows standing in the garden. Her first thought was just how annoyed Uncle Jonty would be once he sees the mess they had made of the freshly ploughed land.

Tony was not far behind in his ute, the truck he had restored and had modified to his own specifications.

Hannah would let him take care of the mess and she would deal with Uncle Jonty. He may be a little harder to convince this time that butchering the cattle was not necessary.

Tony saw the ring right away and knew tragedy had struck. Springing from his ute, he ran to the circle that cattle make when they protect something. In this case, it was someone. "Call 111 now, Hannah, it is Uncle Jonty." The urgency to do so was obvious by his tone.

In silence, Tony and Hannah waited for news. *How much longer would they have to wait for the doctor? Had they not suffered enough,* Hannah thought bitterly as she sat next to her brother in the emergency waiting room. Tony had seen the damage done by the cows' hooves and held little hope. *Why, Lord, why?*

"We should call Charlotte." Hannah's mind was humming.

"Already tried. She is at the prison today. I had to leave a message for her to ring us." Tony leaned in and put his head on Hannah's shoulder as they waited.

Hospitals are at the same time places of hope and new life, as well as hopelessness and the end of life. The Doctor knew Tony and Hannah had suffered more than most. It was with a heavy heart he now stood before the two young people he had walked with through Hannah's recovery. He had to tell them the worst.

"Your Uncle took a blow that caused internal bleeding that was extensive. We could not save him, I'm sorry, kids." The pain was clear on his face.

Tony expected the news, turned to Hannah and took her hand. "Thank you, Hamish, can we see him?" he asked.

"I care too much for you both to let you see him in this state. Jonty would not want it either," spoken with a firm depth of compassion the doctor truly felt. Hannah dropped his hand and left the waiting room, knowing Tony would soon follow. *He was ever faithful.* She needed to get out of here. Hospitals are nothing but bad news. She had had enough to last her a lifetime.

"I'll take care of everything here, Tony." Hamish Macdonald quietly said.

Tony stood torn between arguing with the doctor and following the retreating form of his sister. Nodding to Hamish, he chose the latter, knowing Uncle Jonty would understand.

In continued silence they drove back to the villa, their home they had shared with their Uncle since the death of their parents. *So much loss in one lifetime,* thought Hannah. Tony soon pulled up to their home. The boys were lined up ready for their arrival. Hannah froze. "They know, I called them," Tony said.

"I don't want them to touch me. Come, get me and take me inside." Looking straight ahead, she looked like an exotic marble carving. With a wave to the lads that said give me a minute, Tony gently lifted his sister from the ute and carried her inside.

Hannah allowed herself a brief secure moment in the safety of Tony's arms. Feeling the beat of his strong heart against her ear, she took a breath and then another. "You can put me down now, Tons, I am going to be okay." Gently, Tony placed his sister in her chair that had magically appeared at his elbow. One of the lads had discreetly placed it in the room, then gave them some space.

Hannah looked around the kitchen. She saw it all as if for the very first time.

Uncle Jonty had made his home theirs. Two orphans lost and alone. He had never asked for a thing in return. A love for him swelled in her heart as a strength that can only come from on high. *She was going to be okay.*

Tony looked at the show of emotion on the face of the anchor of his existence and waited. All he wanted was to be carried by her for a brief, safe minute, too, and have her say it was all going to be okay again. He did not have long to wait.

Hannah, strong, constant and peaceful, patted her lap, cuing him in. Where she found safety in the security of his arms, she could return it in larger proportions when he rested his head on her lap. She gently ran her hands over his head. *They were going to be okay.* The lads filed in. All of them waiting for Hannah to give them orders as to what to do next. The house was going to fill up with neighbours soon, so everyone would now be designated a task.

"Bros, you okay?" Tony asked.

Hannah looked to see some of them openly wept, while others hid behind faces that said: *I am here for you because I am lost right now.* There was shock everywhere.

"What would Uncle Jonty have us do now?" Hannah took the lead. "Let's get some tables up and start cooking. I guess everyone knows?" There was a chorus of yesses. News had travelled. *At least that was taken care of.*

The funeral was nothing short of beautiful. Charlotte was given the lead and everything at the church ran smoothly. She shared her affection for Jonty Adam Heath in a eulogy that left no-one wondering just how well she had known him and his depth of feeling for life and those he loved.

Tony and Hannah were both glad with their choice in having Charlotte speak for the man she loved.

The congregation surrounded each other with open compassion and tenderness, just the way Uncle Jonty would have wanted it. Tony's teammates took care of all the heavy lifting. The families of the parish prepared the huge meal served on the grounds of Lions Vineyard.

What a joy the celebration was, to honour a man who, by his own words, *'loved the Lord and placed whānau above gain',* which he had done. His faith in Christ, each and every day of his life, would now be his lasting legacy.

Stories were shared of times gone by, some long before Hannah's and Tony's time in his life. Beau Retallick, whose family had a neighbouring farm, told of a story that 'one day old man Heath went into the village to buy a horse and came back with Jonty in the bargain.' We, too, had been told this story by Uncle Jonty and heard it as nothing more than a tale of fantasy.

The solicitor called the day after the funeral to ask when he could come by? This meeting was now set for today and we both wanted to get it over with. "Whatever happens, Tons, we are in this together, equals forever, agreed."

"Agreed, Hannah Banana," Tony replied without hesitation.

They all sat comfortably around the kitchen table. Now that the delicious scones, preserves and cream had been enjoyed by all, Job Palmer opened his briefcase and took out documents that he had waited a very long time to share with his clients.

"Well, you two, here it goes. Let's start at the beginning. As you both know, your Dad was a successful insurance salesman helping many families prepare, mine included. Well, he also made sure he had the best policy for himself and your Mum, just in case. As it turned out, Jonty was to oversee the claims until you reached maturity or anything happened to him. He never used a single penny of the payout and invested the funds wisely. Here are the proceeds." Sliding the two pages across the table and placing them in front of Tony and Hannah was the finest moment to date of his illustrious career. To give these two young people some good news was a relief.

Silence filled the room normally full of chatter and the clanging of pots and pans. Tony and Hannah had never wanted for a thing all their lives. Here, now in front of them, was not one but two statements, both showing figures of seven digits.

"Is this ours?" Tony could not believe it.

"Yes. You both receive equal shares of these funds. Plus, Tony, you are now the sole owner of the holdings of Heath Cross Enterprises Ltd., with the proviso that Hannah is also to receive a generous income from Lions Vineyard and a home to live in for her entire life." Job grinned from ear to ear. He knew these kids and was certain they would both be happy with this arrangement.

"I can't take more than Hannah. Change this so we are equal partners." Tony did not even have to think about it. Uncle Jonty had taught them about wealth and keeping a clear head.

"Ton's, it's this way because I can't have kids. You will have a family one day. All good Bro." The ever practical Hannah could see why it was so and this gave Job encouragement. She gently placed her hand on the arm so long ago healed and pleaded with him with her eyes.

"Yes, you are right, Hannah dear. You will also see here," Job slid another statement over to them and explained, "all that is in your Uncle's personal accounts today, now also belongs to both of you. Not a sizable figure in comparison, as he was unfailingly generous. He wanted you to have a detailed record of the contributions and gifts he had been making so you two could choose to continue, add some of your own, or cease giving altogether. As I said, Jonty Heath was unfailingly generous. I spoke to him about this through the years as there have been some hard years when crops have been destroyed by pests and dry stock wiped out by disease. He would not have a bar of it." The man who had raised them was far more complex than they realised.

"And so you see, I started construction on our second home and that is when we dug up the old wooden box of family records and the journals that led us here." Tony looked around the table and wondered what could possibly happen next.

Chapter FOURTEEN

What could happen indeed?

Oma looked as though she was going to pass out. This alarmed everyone and shifted the focus quickly once again to high gear. "Oma, are you alright, you look very pale?" Massy was at her side checking her vital signs.

"Lieveling, my son, my son." Oma looked into Massy's eyes, as though he could understand why she was calling out for her son.

"This day has been too much for you, Oma, let's get you upstairs." Massy and Kat stood each at a shoulder but she was not having it. Hannah was beginning to come to an impossible conclusion. One that was too fantastic to believe, but she could see it now. As plain as the nose on Oma's face. Hannah leaned forward and took Oma's stone cold hand.

"He was your son. Uncle Jonty is your son, isn't he, Oma? Was this the secret that you asked our Mother to keep for you?" Hannah looked deeply into her eyes.

"Yes." The natural colour was returning to Batina's cheeks. Time froze yet again. "We were taken to the camps and he was hidden here, at Bergen Op Meer. One day, the estate was searched. The missionaries who had been assisting Jews through the war time knew it was only a matter of time before he would be discovered. If these priceless artefacts had belonged to a Jew they would have all been taken, so they moved him to New Zealand. One day, news reached the missionaries that I was killed in a gas chamber. They needed a permanent home for him. He was adopted by your grandparents. Your mother and I stumbled over this truth, when she brought the same documents you have brought now and your family photo album. I knew it was my Joshua, as soon as I saw the photo of the brother she called Jonty. Why Johanna or Jonty would bury everything is a matter I do not understand."

Wim and Anita turned to each other in silent dialogue. *What was that all about?* wondered Hannah.

"I think we have all gone through enough today," Kat said. "I am so sorry for your loss Oma." Gently she leaned in and kissed both her cheeks.

As he held the other cold hand of his beloved Oma, Massy saw his moment. "Hannah, would you like to come stay with us? Tony, of course you are invited. Well on second thought, I guess, it is up to her."

"Since Anita and Wim have given us all we need at The Gate House, I think Tony and I will stay on there. We have a lot to think about." They could all see there would be no arguing with Hannah.

"Say the word you two, and I will bring your things from your rooms." Wim thought it would be wise to move them as soon as possible. He knew his daughter would need some time.

"Whatever you think is best will be just fine with us." Anita did not want to have Wims' offer look obvious.

Tony and Hannah each gave Batina a gentle kiss on the cheek and promised to have tea with her the next day. They wanted to ensure the shock was not too great for her.

"Tomorrow is a new day." That Oma's eyes held sparkle after all she had been told today gave Hannah hope that she, too, could shine through all that she and Tony had to face.

Later that evening Kat consoled her brother. "Have you considered what this means to us, Kat?" It was obvious to her by the distraught look on her brother's face that she needed to tread lightly.

"I do, lieveling." Kat tapped the desktop indicating she was putting this all together piece by piece, as Massy slouched in the old leather armchair facing the desk she was sitting behind, the desk she had used as her very own, as the commanding hub, to run the estate for years. *Did she have any idea that this could mean that that desk, along with their entire home, could be in the hands of another within days,* Massy wondered.

"Oma has never allowed us to believe the estate, the revenues and all this priceless art would pass on to us, brother. You know this. Today, we have seen why she never led us to this conclusion. Tony is obviously a descendant of the Malefyt family. I am confident, once I go through these documents that Hannah has left with me and Oma reads the journals, that we will discover this fact is the absolute truth. I don't think Tony and Hannah really understand the true nature of their findings yet. Massy, we need to help them. Hannah will need us to show her how to run the estate." Kat waved her hands in a gesture indicating the entire vast surroundings.

"How can you be so matter of fact?" Massy's tone held an edge of defence.

"I always knew this day would come. Certainly I harboured a small hope that somehow you and I would always remain stewards long after Oma had left us. I am only human." Kat felt a little defeated. Massy finally saw the sadness etched on the corners of his sister's eyes and decided to pull back just a little. He was relieved to see that she, too, wanted the same outcome as he did. Hope remained alive within him.

"Kat, what can we do? This is our home. We can't just move Oma into a senior's village. That would ruin her." It was obvious Massy's head was taking off in all directions. As usual Kat's clear-headed thinking would prevail.

"We will face the future head on, with our usual faith. This situation cannot be harder than the death of our parents. If Oma can make it through that loss, I am sure she will walk with her usual dignity and grace through any change we all have to face now. You have a thriving practice. Oma has a generous income from all her careful investments. Maybe it is time for me to continue my education. God knows I will soon have plenty of time on my hands." There, she said it. In truth, some relief flooded in. Both siblings sat for a moment in quiet contemplation.

Kat was right, thought Massy. I had followed my dreams when she had put hers on hold to run the estate. *To leave his home was asking more than he could digest in one day though.* He would also have clients to see in the morning. It was time to get some sleep, that is, if he could.

This could be an answer to a prayer. Starting in the fall at Bircham University would be a long-awaited dream come true, thought Kat. She never minded ensuring that the estate got her undivided attention. This was her way of assisting Oma with the legacy she had taken responsibility for all these years.

Not only was Oma the guardian of millions of dollars worth of priceless artefacts and a successful vineyard that she would see no benefit from other than the home she had to shelter in. She also became a mother again at an age when most women would be learning to lawn bowl and take cruises. Yes, Oma had a legacy fund that was hers to draw on, a fund that Kat knew Oma never abused the privilege of. *How would it truly feel to leave the only home they had all ever known?* This thought left Kat heavy-hearted.

Chapter FIFTEEN

The resemblance is uncanny.

"Let me show you something first, come with me." Kat said.

Hannah and Tony had arrived right on time for tea the next day. She had met them at the door. For now, all tours had been cancelled. Her time was free to help everyone with the changes to come. She led them through the halls of the exquisite estate.

This is like a palace. I am sure I just saw a Rembrandt, thought Hannah. It seemed to go on forever. It was beginning to sink in that this was all her responsibility now.

In a room free of much furnishing and just a few select artefacts Tony could finally see why Anita had responded to meeting him the way she had. On the wall before him was a painting of him. An exact likeness. The goosebumps rippled over his flesh as though a wind had gently disturbed the peaceful waters of his soul.

"This was painted by Anna Malefyt and is the painting that changed all our lives hundreds of years ago." Kat once again became lost in the gaze that had looked back at her all her life. Many times she had pulled up a chair and sat quietly in this room, wondering how fascinating it was that she had come to be one of the descendants that was to help the family that had originally owned this painting. Her parents had been of no help. They had often been on expeditions. Oma never wanted to say much about the circumstances, other than the fact her ancestor had inadvertently become responsible for the entire estate, and all of the priceless art, when he purchased this painting as a gift for his wife. Kat began to giggle. *I guess this means we will be taking one painting with us,* she thought. *Life is so strange at times.* As long as she had

Oma and Massy to love, she would be fine. She had stayed up last night after Massy had left her and thought about her future. *It was time to bring FRUIT of the VINE to life.* Going back to school in the pursuit of developing her own line of organic skin care was what she had decided to do.

Despite the effect seeing the painting had on Tony, it did not hold his attention long. For the sake of Kat, he made a show of deep interest. It was her he was having trouble keeping his eyes off. She was beautiful. He liked her. She had felt so right in his arms only three days ago. So much had happened since then.

Because Tony and Hannah saw a change in Wim and Anita, they decided to move their things today over to the big house, which is what he and Hannah had come to call it.

It had eventually struck Tony and Hannah like a lightning bolt that each of them now had properties that would need their attention. Tony would have to get back to Lions Vineyard, though he had promised Hannah he would stay on with her here an additional two more weeks. Hannah was going to ask them all today to remain for as long as they wanted. Secretly she had hoped this would be a permanent arrangement. Somehow she knew this may suit Oma, but she was not at all sure about Massy and Kat.

"Kat, unless I had seen this painting I would have never believed it. It's as though Tony had sat for the painting." Hannah liked Kat and hoped they could build a bond like sisters.

"It truly is remarkable." Kat turned from Tony to the painting and back again.

"Well, girls, I'm ready to enjoy more of the fine food I have been eating lately. I hope there are some of those waffle biscuits." With no more parting words, Tony headed for the kitchen. Massy had just finished with his last client of the morning and met Tony coming down the hall. "Hey, Bro. You comin' with me? I'm ravenous." Tony said.

It was hard not to like Tony, thought Massy. "Wait, Tony" Massy had to run to catch up to him. "Can you tell me a little bit about Hannah's injury. I did not want to offend her, but I was wondering if I could help a little."

"Mate, there have been all kinds of specialists that have had a go at Hannah. She is firm now that enough is enough." Tony had started to warm to Massy. That he was thinking of his sister's welfare gave Tony hope that he may even come to like him.

"I see." Massy liked this new Tony. He had relaxed and moved about the estate as though he had lived here all his life. It was becoming increasingly hard to not like both of them.

Everyone had eventually found their places around the huge dining table and had settled down. Though her eyes were puffy from tears, no one mentioned it. Oma blessed the meal and chatter broke out in all directions. Having regular meals together was one thing they had all had in common.

"I have been thinking." Hannah had everyone's attention. As Tony now had a full plate, she knew she would not be interrupted any time soon. "I have to admit this is all far more than I have been able to take in," gesturing with a wave of her hands to the opulent surroundings "I cannot fathom being here without all of you. And as Tony will be needing to return to New Zealand for the start of the rugby season and all the responsibilities of Lions Vineyard, would you please let me join you." *What does this pause mean? Maybe she was being unclear.* "I want us all to live together, here, at Bergen Op Meer." Silence, except for the scraping of Tony's knife on his plate as he sliced through a chunk of cheese.

Oma was the first to respond. "What a lovely thought. There is nothing I would like more. Kinderen, wat denk je? *What they were thinking was of the utmost importance to her.* "Thomas, Katerina, would you make this old woman very happy?" Oma glowed with hope.

After the shock Oma had received yesterday, Hannah sure hoped her happiness was at the forefront of everyone's minds. Hannah looked at them both with such hope and sincerity until their answer became obvious. "I have so much to learn. Though I will not expect you to give up your lives to help me, I would like to get to know you both a lot better and I can think of no better way. The place is certainly big enough. Kat, Massy, what do you say?" They soon both agreed and the rest of the meal was spent discussing which room would be best for Hannah. She, of course, had the pick of the house.

Massy sat back and watched the candid discussion between his sister and the new woman in his life. They talked excitedly about Kat's plans for school and her ideas for product development while Hannah divulged her love of cooking and wanted to know all she could about local produce. She had decided to turn down the offer from the network, telling Kat how this was not a difficult choice. Hannah liked not being tied to a schedule that restricted her from coming and going as she pleased. Massy had decided then and there that he was going to ease any burden Hannah may have. If she would let him assist her, he could use some of his expertise as a physiotherapist, too.

Tony was going to miss Hannah. Oma saw the look on his face and smiled in his direction. It made him feel like everything was going to be alright. *We are the protectors and nurturers of our next generation. This is whānau, life is rich.* As the words *It is the people, it is the people, it is the people* played across his mind, he returned the smile to the dear matriarch across the table, with one of his own. The kind that shone from his soul through his eyes. Oma melted.

Chapter SIXTEEN

Becoming orphans.

    Over the next few weeks Tony got to know the ins and outs of the property. He discovered the same grapes grew here as on their land in New Zealand. Tony and Hannah mutually agreed that each property would be home to them both. Oma had discovered in Anna's journal that she had taken a vine with her. It had obviously flourished. Lions Vineyard had its humble origins from here. That knowledge gave Tony a warm feeling in his heart.

Kat spent every waking moment at the side of Hannah or Tony. She was determined to pass on everything she knew before the first term started. Tony took to the land like a pro and he and Kat were often found on horseback, dining at one of the great local establishments, *T.Price Bistro was his favourite*, or enjoying a walk along the canal. Massy was a new joy in Hannah's life and she was surprised to find that she truly could come to trust him, possibly to the same level as she shared with Tony.

As they had experienced a mutual loss, Massy opened up the conversation first and told Hannah how his parents had been on an expedition off the coast of the North Island in New Zealand. "They had been given the opportunity to do a deep sea dive in a new state-of-the-art submersible owned by the research firm they both worked for. The sub never returned to the ship. The radar had malfunctioned due to interference from a rare type of crayfish. They were never found."

In the far reaches of Hannah's mind she thought she heard a bell but it was so faint she disregarded it. Massy had asked her gently over dinner one night when it was just the two of them, "what happened the day your parents died?" Oma had professed to being tired and took dinner in her own rooms. The story came easy to Hannah. She started at the beginning.

"Mom, Dad, we need to go. We have got to go. I want to go so bad. We have got to support our team." Tony turned up the charm and smiled with that impish grin of his when he was not going to let an idea go. Tossing the ever-present rugby ball up and catching it over and over, he pleaded with his parents to take the family to the Springbok Tour of 1981. Johanna and Alvan had been watching closely the unfolding controversy following the tour and were reluctant to tell both their children that they already had tickets. Hannah snatched the ball from the air and took off down the hall, with Tony in hot pursuit.

"What do we do, Aroha?" *Alvan was going to leave the final decision to the Love of his life.* Yes, he was concerned, but he did not think for a minute Kiwis would act up to the point of truly letting anything dangerous evolve and get in the way of the All Blacks playing a match.

"Let's be ready for anything. If we need to leave the stadium early, so be it." Johanna was glad they had a nice surprise for the kids. She was sure that all would stay peaceful. Jonty had turned them down when they had made plans to get tickets. He had told them he just felt "unright", did not want a bar of it and would "watch the game on the telly."

Tony could hardly sleep for days leading up to the game. The excitement in the stands he had to admit, when he got there, though, was a little overwhelming. Hannah did not seem worried, so he was not going to let it show. Hannah loved family time. Her Dad openly shared that joy and today was extra special. They were watching the All Blacks together.

Hannah had decided she was going to marry an All Black when she was old enough. Mum and Dad had always said they seemed like such nice men and she wanted to make them happy. Uncle Jonty said 'I need to be with a fine lad that knew something about grapes and dry stock, loved the Lord, and if he wanted to play rugby could find time for that, too.'

This felt different. thought Johanna. The crowd on the inside of the stadium was okay; it was the goings-on outside that troubled her.

Things had been peaceful when they arrived, though she had wondered if they should turn around when she saw the barricades.

Alvan assured her that Kiwis would be outspoken, but will always keep it peaceful, and there was Tony looking up at her with those eyes. Alvan was not going to take any unnecessary chances with his family. At the first sign of trouble he was taking them home. He had to admit he was beginning to feel a little uneasy. *How did the bros on the field take all the pressure?* He wondered. The players seemed focused, confident. It just became too much of a risk when Gary Knight was knocked out cold by a flour bomb dropped from a low flying plane that had taken a risk to interrupt the game in peaceful protest.

Alvan and Johanna had seen enough. *When political unrest reaches these heights they want their children safe and far away from it. They should not have come,* thought Johanna.

The two carefree Canadian prairie boys from Cadillac had not anticipated being in the middle of a mob scene. Vaun Rainbird and Matt Lacelle had saved up by working on the local farms for the past three summers. Now they had enough money, if they were frugal, to travel the North and then the South Island for a year. The first purchase was this caravan that they registered in Matt's name. Fully equipped to live in, no problem. Travelling from the cape on the North Island to the fjords on the South Island was a reality and this was week two. It was Vaun's turn to drive and all he wanted to do was get clear of all the protesters.

Alvan had safely navigated his family through the stands. Sweat was running down his back in rivulets. It was a warm day, granted, but he knew this was a bad situation and his nerves were running really high. What a relief it was when they cut through a residential property and made it safely to the car. Johanna turned to Alvan with that look of *You are my knight and your armour is shining.* Turning to his disappointed son he said "Sorry, little mate, we had to get out of there. Maybe we can check the highlights on the telly tonight?"

Tony was a little disappointed. "Right, Dad, let's get our women to safety and have some ice cream too." Tony's laughter helped take the edge off the moment.

"I don't feel scared, Mum, do you?" Hannah very seldom was ever worried about anything. She had her life pretty much planned and knew her parents would always take care of her and Tony.

"Not one bit. Your Dad will always take good care of us and everything else we leave to our loving Abba who made you," tapping the end of her daughter's nose for emphasis.

Vaun was glad to be free of the mobs and chaos and decided to gun it. Having started driving when he was twelve, he was the more confident driver of the two even though things in this country were crazy with both the driver and location of traffic being on opposite sides to home. His extended family had a large farm on the prairies and driving all kinds of vehicles came naturally to him, Matt's Dad ran the local bank. They would make good time now and be all set up in Northland at the beach in no time.

Alvan opened up the windows and let the cool air of the trip wash over them. They would be home in a few hours. The kids were safely clipped in and had both fallen asleep. It was just he and his girl, side-by-side enjoying the open road. "Best keep an extra eye out for anyone distracted, sweetheart. We are not the only ones travelling these roads today. Slow and steady will get us home, too." Johanna squeezed his thigh her hand was resting on.

They were entering a high crash area, so Alvan understood why Johanna was thinking this way. "All will be right, my Jojo." Johanna blushed. Oh how she loved this man.

Vaun had just pulled back onto the state highway after a quick pitstop. Neither he nor Matt realised until the last minute they had pulled out into the lane of oncoming highway traffic. Matt by reflex grabbed the wheel, but it was too late. Alvan had less than a split second to avoid the caravan in their lane. He did not stand a chance.

Jonty made it to the hospital in record time considering the main highway had been closed off for hours. That had no bearing on him getting to those kids. He knew every road from here to Auckland and had no need to use the main access. The shock of the loss of his sister and Alvan was going to have to be put off until later. When Tony woke he could not work out why Uncle Jonty was sitting next to his bed. "Lad, how is it?"

"Fine Uncle, what happened? Why are you here?" Tony tried to sit up and look around the room.

Jonty took the hand that was not in a cast. In relief the tears began to sneak out of the corner of his eyes. "You have been in an accident, Tony, your arm is broken." Jonty thought best to give him some of the facts.

"Where is Mum?" Fear began to show and the nurse stepped forward. Tony frantically looked around the room. "I want my Mum." Tony began to scream. The nurse, Clarisa Strongbow, was ready to give Tony a sedative through his intravenous and did not hesitate. Nothing was going to change the news. Her patient, this dear sweet boy the same age as her own son David, was going to eventually have to hear it. The least she could do was remove some of the shock factor. As this was the Doctor's orders, she was ready. Jonty knew he needed to get his bearings, but he was struggling too. He would have switched places with Johanna if he could. Soon Tony had started to settle down a little. The nurse gave Jonty an encouraging nod to start again.

"It is going to be you and me, little man. Mum and Dad aren't with us any more." Jonty needed the lad to take in the impossible and hear the news that he and his sister were now orphans. *How could this even be possible?* Clarisa was ready for anything. There was a reason she had been assigned to Tony's case. Known for her unwavering compassion and attention to detail, the Doctor had asked her to do a double shift and stay next to the boy like a plaster. She watched the play of emotion over Tony's face and could see he was taking in the news through the haze of the sedative.

"Hannah, Uncle, where is she?" Tony instinctively knew that the news was going to be bad, because no force on earth had ever kept his sister from his side when he needed her. He really needed her now. Jonty looked up at the nurse for guidance. She nodded to affirm it was best to tell him everything.

"She is still in surgery, my boy. God has her in his hands." A tear slipped from his eye.

"But does God have the doctors in his hands, too, Uncle?" Huge wet tears began to flow from the corners of his eyes as he lay there looking up at his Uncle for reassurance.

"They are all excellent doctors, Tony" Clarisa stepped into his view, "and as soon as I have news you will be the first to be told. How does that sound?" All Clarisa truly wanted to do was take the sweet child in her arms and hold him. For now, showing him understanding was enough. Maybe later, he will be ready for a hug. God knew he was going to need some serious help along the road to recovery. While he was in her care, she was going to ensure he was given everything within her power. "How about I leave you two for a minute and go check now?" Clarisa thought these two needed a little privacy. A moment to breathe and hope. "I won't be but a moment."

"Okay, but tell her I am okay too, because she will worry." Tony's eyes held her briefly with the calm look of sleepy peace.

"You bet, Tiger, she is going to be so happy to get that message." With that encouragement Clarisa left the room, walked down the hall, stepped into a private office, closed the door, sat down and wept. *Keep it together Strongbow.*

Jonty could see sleep overtake Tony. *The poor little lad must be exhausted.* He had to admit to some shred of relief that this part was over. When Clarisa came back into the room she found both of them asleep. As there was no news, she quietly checked her patient's vital signs and gently closed the door. She left them in peace.

Jonty woke from a gentle touch on his shoulder. At first he did not recognize Tony's nurse Clarisa. Then the recent events came flooding in and he knew why she had woken him. She indicated for him to step out with her and let Tony sleep a little longer. She whispered, "there was news." "Lyndsay, can you sit with my patient just in case he wakes up? Come get me immediately, please, if he does," Clarisa asked as she walked past the Nurses Station, expecting her request to be met without fuss. *This family had had enough.* Immediately the nurse stood up and headed for Tony's room. "She is in recovery. The Doctor would like to see you." Clarisa gently touched Jonty's shoulder and hoped the softness of her tone gave him comfort. There was more bad news to come.

Relief washed over Jonty. "Of course, lead the way."

"The spine has been badly damaged. You can see here on the x-ray the compound fractures. We have the best surgeons on staff and she is young. The soft tissue damage is extensive. This may complicate her ability to have children when the time comes. We will know more as she begins to heal." The Doctor looked into the eyes of a man that was doing his best to take it all in, in all confidence he knew he could not have done more. "She is in God's hands, my friend."

How true. Thought Jonty. "Thank you, Doctor, when can I see her?" Jonty felt numb. All he wanted was for this nightmare to end.

"She will be taken to the Intensive Care Unit soon. In the ICU you can have a moment with her then. Brace yourself. Seeing children in this condition is never easy, even for us. They are so delicate and small, but often tough and resilient. We never lose sight of this here." The Doctor wanted to have better news. How much suffering could one man take in a day.

"Let's check in on Tony, sir. The doctor will send for you." Clarisa gently led Jonty back through the maze of hallways and assisted him to have a seat next to the still sleeping child that he could be with. She went to get him a cup of tea. Later that evening, nothing could have prepared Jonty for the sight he took in. Hannah could hardly be found among the wires, tubes and devices. They had given him one minute. It struck him soundly in the gut that he was going to have to eventually tell Hannah about the loss of her Mum and Dad also. He got down on his knees and prayed.

The Doctor found Tony sitting up watching the comings and going of the Nurses Station with enrapt fascination. "Do you know who that is?" Gary Knight had been brought in for observation. He was standing at the Nurses Station still wearing a muddy All Blacks jersey with flour stains powdering his whole upper body.

"Yes, sir. Is he okay?" Big eyed, Tony watched the player that he knew had also had a very bad day.

"Yes, he is one tough player. He left this with me. Would you like it?" The doctor produced a game ball with a signature on it and handed it to Tony. Moving his head up and down, Tony took the ball into his good hand and brought it to his heart like a lifeline.

"You know who else I know who is tough?" The Doctor looked into Tony's eyes in hopes his patient would see strength reflected back. Tony moved his head from side to side. Jonty was hanging back in the room watching the interaction between Tony and the Doctor. *He sure hoped the doctor was not going to expect his broken-hearted nephew to be the tough one. He needed to just be a kid and all that came with it.*

"Your sister. She is going to need to be. You see, Hannah is going to need us to help her. She got badly broken up. If she is anything like you, and I think she is, I believe, with all my heart, you two are going to be okay."

"Does she know about...." Tony broke up here. He could not bring himself yet to talk about his parents. That would come in time, Jonty was certain.

"Not yet, Sport. She is getting some sleep right now because that will help her heal." Some days as a Doctor are unthinkably hard. This day would go down as one of his toughest. "When do you want us to tell her?" Jonty admired the Doctor. He was wise and an answer to a prayer.

Tony said "I will tell her."

The Doctor and Jonty's eyes met. "Okay, but first she needs to get some sleep, is that okay?" *Man, I admire this one's courage.* Thought the Doctor.

"Yup." Every adult in the room could see the conversation had taken its toll on Tony. He needed some sleep, too.

Clarisa stepped forward and placed a kiss on his forehead. He fell asleep still holding his new rugby ball.

Tony was discharged three days later. Jonty had decided to not let Tony see Hannah until she had come out of ICU. He assured him she was on the mend and they would come see her in a few days or so. Hannah would eventually be moved to a hospital closer to home and then they could see her everyday. When the visiting day finally came, Tony insisted they pick up flowers. "They have to be the live ones, those ones in the vase die" he informed his Uncle. Tony knew how much getting the rugby ball had helped him and he wanted Hannah to have pretty things in her room to enjoy.

She looked really small in her bed. The same nurse that he had met only a few weeks before was sitting at Hannah's bedside when they walked in. A lot had changed since then. Even Tony had to admit he had done a lot of growing up.

Clarisa smiled at Tony. "I see you are on the mend, how is the arm?" She walked over and tousled Tony's hair in a friendly gesture. He liked her and decided to give her a hug. *Maybe he needed to get some live flowers for her, too,* he thought.

"All good, I will be back on the field in no time, the Doctor said. But first, I need to take a season off, so my throwing arm has time to heal properly. That's okay. I am going to take care of Hannah," Tony informed her.

"She is getting better every day. I am sure she is going to like the roses; they are my favourite. Do you want me to stay?" Smiling down at him, she waited.

I really do need to stop at van der Bush Nursery again. "Nope, I got this." Tony acted far more brave than he felt. "Can we call you if we need anything?" *Best to keep help at hand,* he thought.

"You sure can, I will be just outside that door." Clarisa knew that Hannah and Tony needed to share their grief. What Tony did not know was that Hannah had worked out the worst and had begun the long road to recovery knowing she would be doing so with her brother as a champion. This would help him too. They now had Uncle Jonty as guardian. Hannah knew she was going to need to mend quickly, as Clarisa had been told in confidence he could not cook.

Jonty was in awe of the young man he was now responsible for. Overnight, he had accepted his new role in Hannah's life and had pitched in the best he could with one arm to prepare the house for her homecoming.

"Hi, Tons." A tiny weak voice came from the covers. Tony squared his shoulders and headed towards it.

"Hi, Banana. I brought you these." Bashfully Tony presented his very delicate sister with red roses still in the pot. *He would explain later.* "Are ya getting better?" Tony had decided he would be telling Hannah the news about their parents right away.

"Yup, I think so. Did they tell you how bad it is?" Hannah was still feeling like the inside of a soft cushion most days.

Tony affirmed her question with a silent nod. His sister may never walk again. "I got more bad news too."

"Shhhhhh" Hannah lifted her hand and Tony saw this as a good sign, *at least she was still going to be able to catch a rugby ball.* "I know, Bro. Mum and Dad are not going to be with us anymore."

Jonty stood as still as a marble statue, just far enough away from the exchange to give them space, but close enough to hear if he was needed, prayer humming within him.

Tony began to cry in relief. Hannah rubbed her hand over his bowed head that was resting on her bed. "We got this, Tons." Hannah turned to their Uncle and held out her other hand. The statue moved. When he took her hand, hers was warm in the ice coldness of his. Tears finally began to fall down Hannah's cheeks. Clarisa had discreetly been observing from a distance, just in case, and breathed a sigh of relief. These were her patient's first tears.

"I have never spoken to anyone about that day. We moved on. All three of us overcame the shock. Strong in our faith that all is as it should be, even when the hurt is so big. Not a day goes by that I don't think of them. Do you have photos of your parents?" Massy was speechless. The woman before him had a dignity and grace that left him longing to take her in his arms and never let go.

"Yes, yes we do. There is a great one of them on the beach holding a jar of beach glass. It's in the library. I will show you later if you would like?"

"Yes, please. Maybe I will put a photo of my parents there, too?"

"Of course." Out of impulse Massy reached out to hold Hannah's hand. She was taken completely by surprise.

Hannah was sure this was a gesture of comfort. She was not concerned. Things could never go further with any man. She could not have children. That was her pain and no one else's to bear. "Tell me what you know about Ashton and Anna Malefyt." *Let's take this conversation elsewhere.*

Chapter SEVENTEEN

Aboard Captain Tally's ship Wind Whisperer.

Ashton trailed his fingers over the surface of a calm, at first glance, silent ocean. His melancholy swing of boredom created twin waves to those formed from the gentle lapping of water off the side of the boat he had converted from an old oak barrel. The sun's light caressed the tar surface, releasing an intoxicating smell. Floating at his leisure over the Rangitāhua abyss, further and further from his uncle's whaling ship, *Wind Whisperer*, Ashton was granting himself a much-needed reprieve from their current state of doldrums and the ever-present vexing first mate, Paulo Santos.

Just shy of six months of sailing logged since leaving his home, Bergen Op Meer, Ashton was beginning to second-guess his hasty choice to finally accept his uncle's offer to board his ship. *Would it have been better to stay with his familiar troubles and constant heartaches or answer the call to go to sea?* The silent reply was a kiss of warmth bronzing his lithe athlete's body to an even darker tone of coffee - a beverage he had recently acquired a taste for.

The weight of so many thoughts caused his mind to stagger. To think, even for a moment, that maybe, just maybe, his newfound freedom could be a tougher fate than remaining on the same continent as his father. No, he would refuse to believe that any form of defeat would follow him. With a determination yet to take full hold, he trusted the mighty hand that guided him and remained focused on the tranquil moment.

Allowing his train of thought its own direction brought him within a heartbeat, once again, to the inner dwelling of heartache. A threshold he never stepped over, he had no intention of starting now.

His father had made it painfully clear he found his only son unworthy of love. No matter how much effort Ashton put into pleasing him, nothing would, and due to recent events, he was now certain nothing ever could. Ashton had claimed, with some of his father-pleasing efforts, the highest sports awards in the district three consecutive years running, and was now honourably positioned to select the university of his choice. Offers had come in from five of the top schools in Europe to join their rowing teams, starting in the autumn of 1810. This fact had given him a refined sense of purpose, knowing he was finally making his own way without any help from anyone, alive or dead. Only a few short months ago, with confident certainty, he believed this was his year, and a rewarding path would present itself.

Shaking off the risk of plummeting into the dark depths of his thoughts, Ashton turned his gaze to the watery womb at hand and silently wondered if he had anything left of any true value to lose. *Or was it wisdom guiding him to accept the current chain of events* - a nudge to push him along an unknown path to the land his uncle so lovingly described as, "a land to weave a full life on rich, fertile soil." Did he dare begin to believe he could be welcomed and granted the beginning of a new and worthwhile future? Taking stock he thought, *his older sister Anna was next in line to inherit the Malefyt family estate. There was no love lost between him and his only living parent,* and to complete the trio set of his thoughts, *he had not only literally burned the bridge to Jude's love, the only father figure he had ever known,* but his recent actions had also ensured that love, too, *must have been annihilated.*

When Ashton was the tender age of five, Jude began to teach the young master all he knew about the grapes lovingly tended and prized on the Malefyt estate. Ashton's palms cupped together were too small to hold one clump of the huge clusters. That did not hinder his determination to pick his share.

Jude Wolf had been the one to bestow upon Ashton the parental love he secretly longed for from his own parents. Now the shame of knowing that he was the sole destroyer of that love, which the caretaker unconditionally bestowed in abundance from the onset of Ashton's life, was proving to be too great a task to overcome. Branded into his mind forever would be the image of Jude's face covered in ash and hands blistered to the point of bleeding from his attempt to save the vineyard from the complete ruin Ashton had only recently unleashed on it.

With all his thoughts leading to these tender points of pain, the pressure within finally became too great. Human nature opened the massive dam, and a great flood of long-held-in-check tears flowed, blending their salty numbers with that of the sea.

In time a deep need for relief flooded into his bruised but slightly refreshed soul. So, with a cleansed and renewed desire for answers, Ashton looked past his reflection into the eyes of the liquid looking-glass at his fingertips.

At first glance, he was unsure what he saw cradled in the water. There, right before his bluer than blue eyes identical to his uncle's onboard the ship, hung silver shadows reflecting the morning sun, three stories long and wider than some homes along the canals of Amsterdam. "Whales!" The whispered word slipped through his lips and rode away in all directions on the mirror's surface. As only time can bestow as a gift, the pulse of excitement took melancholy's place and Ashton began to fully realise the urgent need for discretion.

These majestic sea creatures of the deep lived peacefully in these waters and he saw no reason to disturb them. In the past few months, the bloody and devastating effects of whaling had been shown to him first hand. He had no intention of aiding in feeding the hunger for wealth that rode aboard the *Wind Whisperer*. Ashton could at this very moment feel the eyes of the ship piercing his back.

Said in the hush of a whisper to keep a secret safe, but heard it Paulo did. He was relieved to have Malefyt off the ship. If it were his choice to make, he would hoist sail and leave Ashton Malefyt on the vast sea, to make land with the current.

His beloved cerulean mistress would carry the captain's nephew on her salty tail, as she had done so many times before, for others who needed her guidance to safely reach the islands Paulo had called home for more years than he could be bothered to count. The Sea was kind and often misunderstood by those less knowing of these matters, but he knew her intimately and loved her with a reckless devotion above all else in his life. As a child-sailor, he had safely matured while cradled tenderly in her embrace. In later years, she gave up to him the creatures of the deep. Revenues filled the sea chest of gold he carried with him everywhere.

In his many years of sailing, he had never known a shipwreck. By only two laws, five generations of Santos sailors had managed to never cause their mistress a moment of jealousy and remained dry above the waves: no other women on board, and no one on board, ever, by the name of Malefyt.

Paulo currently watched Ashton's every move from his bird's-eye view and elephant-ear positioning. Though the boy's face was turned from him, the tell-tale shaking of his shoulders revealed the weakling was crying like a sailor who was out of funds for ale and had no prospects of a ship to sail on. An experience Paulo considered lower than low, one that he had never known.

Tapping the residue from his pipe on the ship's rail, he gave up his position above deck and went in search of Captain Tally. Paulo was sure the scallywag had spotted blubbery wealth and was keeping the prize selfishly to himself.

Talbot Heath, Ashton's uncle, had been devoted to his baby sister Johanna. Since the birth of her children, Ashton and Anna, he vowed to be guardian and guide as they faced life without a mother. *Life can play a cruel hand at will.* It turned out, one of them faced life without a father as well. Ashton Malefyt had never seen a single day of love bestowed on him by either of his parents. For the past eighteen years, far more than his share of unfairness had befallen his young nephew.

For more reasons than Tally could number, the captain found it a blessing to finally have the lad on board his ship. Voyages on the *Wind Whisperer* took him often far away and for long periods of time. Yet the bond of love the three of them shared stayed strong and grew steadily as Anna and Ashton became fine young adults, both willing and determined to leave each place, time and experience in their lives better than how it was originally found. Anna, through her dedication to missions and social justice, and Ashton, through his determination to overcome life's challenges with humility.

The captain's admiration for them knew no bounds, yet came second to his love for them.

The physical similarity between Ashton and the captain was so great, that he was certain his whānau, the people of his Island home, would not believe that the boy was not his own son. He was hoping a new start in life would help Ashton forget some, if not all, of his past heartaches. The great mystery of why Ashton's father had never taken to his only son was beyond the captain's understanding. *Oh, the many times I wanted to take the boy to sea and show him all the wonders of the islands I call home.* But there are few more stubborn than his nephew's father. Until the devastating recent events, Jacobus would never allow it.

Pondering the thought further, the captain had to conclude he had never met anyone who came close to the magnitude of stubbornness Jacobus Malefyt had displayed with steady dedication. It was as though his dominance over Ashton gained him a form of constant and oppressive control.

To date, Ashton had shown none of his father's arrogance, a blessing the captain gave thanks for in his daily prayer. And then there is Anna, who fearlessly faces her father's dominance over her brother, steering her only parent discreetly and with true grace into a position of redirection, as though by an unseen force. A marvel to behold, indeed.

Her mother had the same gift, but used it to get what she thought she wanted, often succeeding with others. The captain gave in to her only once, and it had cost her everything.

There was no doubt in his mind that Jacobus and Johanna had been deeply devoted to each other. As Johanna's guardian, Tally at first found great relief in her joy of being in love. He was often away sailing and only wanted what was best for her. For Johanna's children's sake, after her death, the relationship that Tally had with his brother-in-law was kept on civil terms. Long ago, any true feelings for the children's father had died a slow and painful death.

Talbot Heath had had high hopes for his sister's happiness. In the early stages of the newlyweds relationship, there were no signs of the odd behaviour Jacobus displayed after their children were born. Granted, the death of Johanna at their birth affected everyone in different ways. *Jacobus*

NEVER showed the boy a father's love. This left the captain feeling less than charitable towards his brother-in-law, and Tally felt shame over this at times. *Accepting our fellow man as they are, and meeting them where they are at in this life, takes an ongoing supply of patience and an endless need for reliance on Christ's guidance.* God alone knew how hard the captain had earnestly tried to offer true, mutual friendship to a hard-crusted Jacobus.

Anna, from birth, was a miniature replica of her mother. In time, Tally came to believe this was the reason a proud and arrogant father like Jacobus Malefyt openly accepted her, a female, as the rightful heir of Bergen Op Meer, the Malefyt family estate. The boy was born only hours after his sister and was instantly shunned by his father, as though it was the child's fault he had been born at all.

Batina, Johanna's governess, had attended Johanna at the birth of the twins. As she had been there for the birth of other children through the years, Tally had complete confidence that if he was at sea and the babe came early, his beloved sister could be in no better hands than in those of the woman who had watched over Johanna her entire life. *I could see instantly in Batina's eyes, as she stood before me with the newborn boy in her arms, that Johanna was gone. Sorrow struck like an arrow through the heart, as my nephew cried out for his mother.* What a loss it must have been for the child, to come from the safe home of his mother's womb which he had shared with a companion to this, a place of sorrow and rejection.

"Captain Tally, the sea informs me we have a catch waiting for us at the port side." Paulo broke into his thoughts, shattering them asunder. Turning his full attention to other matters immediately at hand was a relief the captain welcomed. Paulo could always be counted on to bring him a new challenge that they could undertake and execute with precision and their usual companionable finesse.

Gazing out at the scene unfolding above deck, Tally believed Paulo had misjudged the old girl's message. "I see the calm of a flat-chested beauty, Paulo, my mate. Within seconds, concerns flooded the empty space of Tally's mind, as he spotted Ashton in his makeshift vessel, bobbing like a discarded cork on a vast empty lake, drooped shoulders and all.

"That menace of a boy has intercepted the message; he is trying to keep them from us. You know he dislikes the sea for how she rewards us," Paulo informed the captain, with a tone reflecting his obvious dislike for Ashton.

Finding it difficult this time to believe his first mate, the captain was now sure he needed to get Ashton to dry land and settled. His presence was truly affecting Paulo in ways Tally had never seen before, none of them any good.

With perfect timing, winds made a grand entrance and filled the deflated sails, showing the two seasoned sailors and their crew an end had come to the doldrums. They could now head for their Island home.

Chapter EIGHTEEN

*G*uided by an unlikely sea creature.

"Ash, my boy, let's head for home." With his usual booming voice, the captain expressed the urgency for the youth to get back on board. The wind had entered into the day. It was pushing the two vessels in different directions. Ashton was going to need all his might to paddle to the safety of the ship.

Tally watched as the dance of the sea became turbulent. Without much effort at all, as though Ashton was born to it, he glided through the waves and was soon packing his things away and finding his place as one of the crew on board the *Wind Whisperer*. Tally had experienced this type of weather pattern only one other time at sea. It nearly cost him and the crew their lives, and he was not eager to face the same trials again.

Headfirst into what had quickly become a full-blown storm, the trusty ship glided at the master hands of Captain Tally. His crew expertly answered his bark over the crashing of the waves on deck. As one, they read all the signs and sailed over the waves like a sharp sword cutting through the soft white fluffy butter icing whipped up in high peaks on a party cake. Ashton swung in the riggings like a sailor born to the sea. The storm was nothing more than yet another challenge to face. He could see Paulo below, keeping his footing on the deck as though the rolling of the ship through the tempest was a stroll in wooden shoes through a shallow stream.

This is different, the mistress is in a mood new to me. It is that no-good passenger on board, thought Paulo, as he made his way to the captain at the helm. "Captain, what do you make of the signs?" Paulo was greeted with a look he had never seen before reflected back at him.

"Heading to the protection of the open sea is what is called for now, my old friend. Time is wasted on trying to outrun this temper tantrum", the Captain said.

Paulo had never questioned the captain's many choices through all the years they had sailed together, other than keeping the boy on board. With a quick nod, he agreed. Giving orders to the crew that for a split moment gave them all pause, except for Ashton, left the captain feeling uneasy. With trusted instinct, he shouted the order again over the sound of the crashing waves. There was no turning back.

As only water and wind can do, when their collective forces are combined, the ship was blown towards land. As soon as the ship entered the waters protecting them from the wind on the sheltered side of the uninhabited island, surrounded by shallows riddled with submerged reefs, the welcoming calm was a relief to the crew, although a greater concern to the captain. He now had to bring his ship through the maze of underwater jagged rocks. *God, you have been a kind master to me. Do not let this journey end in this way. Bring us all safely through this test; give me your divine sight to know the way through. I ask this all in your Son's name.* The quickest and the shortest prayer the captain had ever prayed, yet the most heartfelt he could recall. Ashton was experiencing the worst conditions at sea the Captain had ever had to face. It seemed as though one more unfairness was being added to the boy's life. Yet, as Ashton approached with shoulders held high, and a strength of confidence more often seen on a much older man, the captain's uncertainty disappeared in an instant.

Giving his uncle his due respect, Ashton waited to be acknowledged, "Captain, we are being guided to safety. I need your word; will you protect the creature who now leads us?" He pleaded with his uncle in a rush before Paulo could reach them.

"What are you saying Lad? Tell me more. You have my word." The captain thought Ashton's timing could not be worse. It was obvious his nephew was serious, so Tally thought it best to give him his full attention.

Much to Ashton's horror, Paulo reached them just as he began to explain. "There is a dolphin off the port bow, sir, that I am certain is leading us through the danger that lies beneath the ship."

Knowing the boy was never one for fantasies, and having no time to waste, Tally gave him the benefit of his many doubts. Responding over Paulo's gales of laughter, the captain's only response could be, "Show me." At first, Ashton was astonished that his uncle had not belittled him in front of the other sailors. After a moment's hesitation, he took to the rails. In tow was almost the entire crew that Paulo had called together so he could enjoy the show of madness with his mates. Sure enough, there, right before all their eyes, was a lone dolphin calling out a greeting at the bow of the ship.

"Watch." Ashton felt no shame in his instincts; they had brought him through life this far and had never failed him.

The captain soon beamed with pride and scooped Ashton into a bear hug that nearly crushed him. "Wahoo! Right you are, my boy; we have a guide. Prayers have been answered." Tally could have been knocked over by a pelican feather, and with jovial glee, he commanded his crew. "Man your stations. We are going to get through these waters in one piece after all."

Losing all patience, Paulo witnessed his last injustice from this young menace. Ignoring the captain's orders, he went below to get his musket. He would get the upper hand and soon put an end to this madness.

The journey had finally taken on a new meaning for Ashton. For the first time in what seemed forever, the magic of nature lifted his spirit in a way he had not felt since his uncle had bought him Moses, his horse, the devoted companion he had to recently leave behind.

Paulo soon returned and made his way to the rail, raising the gun without a moment of hesitation. He was sure the captain had gone mad. Giving full focus to his aim, he did not see Ashton throw his body through the air. He was too late. The gun discharged just as Ashton tackled Paulo.

Without much effort he pinned the shocked sailor to the deck. With a control he did not know he possessed, Ashton held back his desire to put a complete and absolute finish to the sailor he now held, face down, on the deck of the ship.

Hearing gunshots on board his ship was a rare occurrence. At first glance Tally did not know what to make of the scene on deck, nor why the trail of blood in the water troubled him. He was used to that, having been involved in whaling for so many years. When he did get to the two tangled on the deck, it took all the captain's might to lift Ashton off the screaming first mate held beneath him, and even more force to keep them apart.

"What were you thinking, Paulo? We had a guide. Now look, nothing, nothing but jagged rocks, and the wind picking up with the force of ten dragons in flight." To say Tally was furious would be an understatement. The wind broke into the moment with such force, it scattered the crew that had gathered to watch the show. This gave Paulo a chance to break free and distance himself from the scene he had created.

Nothing had ever prepared the captain for the forces of nature that bombarded them now. His main concern was for his nephew's safety and that of his crew. The cargo could always be replaced. Despite the fact they were all well-seasoned sailors, he was sure they had never before seen these forces coming together as though they were under attack by demons of nature.

"Get that menace of a boy off this ship!" screamed Paulo over the turmoil boiling up out of the water to anyone who would listen. He was convinced the sea had turned on them because of Malefyt.

"Ash, get your boat ready, now." With a shove from his uncle and without hesitation, Ashton headed in the direction he had just come from. Stopping only long enough to grab his wooden sea chest, as he dodged the clutches of the other crew. They were now also convinced. Paulo was right. The menace had to go.

Tally soon met Ashton midship. He could see the boy had listened and was as ready as he was ever going to be. He handed his beloved nephew a leather-bound pouch and instructed him to not let it out of his sight. Holding him briefly, with a kiss to his forehead, he reassured him that he would make it to his new home. "The tide will carry you." They waited for the next wave. Within seconds, Ashton, along with his few possessions safely stored in his boat, went overboard. Tally watched as long as he dared, the son he could never have drifted further and further from the ship.

Chapter NINETEEN

Home at last on the tide.

The crew had one brief moment to rejoice before a fierce captain, like none they had ever seen before, cried out like a wounded animal and turned to wipe the smile off Paulo's face with a left hook that sent the sailor through the air to land flat on his back, just as the next big wave overcame the ship.

Paulo was glad to have the threat off the ship. He was certain the sea would now calm and not let him down. This time he was wrong, and the captain knew it.

When the *Wind Whisperer* hit the reef the first time, there remained briefly some hope. As the ship's timbers took a beating, again and again, the fists of stone won the match.

The sea swallowed her prize with the captain and crew on board.

Talbot Ashton Heath's last thoughts were of his sister. His final prayer was for her two beautiful children whom he had loved as his own. His last request of hope was for Ashton, that the ever-constant currents would take him to his new home safely with the package that Tally had given him. The lad needed to start a new life. *Bless him Lord.*

Paulo wasted no time in thought. Sprang into action. Grabbed his possessions floating in the debris of his cabin and made way for the only lifeboat. If the others made it, so be it. Even though the pain in his face had yet to subside, he did not hold the captain's reaction against him. His hope was that the sinking of the ship would not take his friend with it. Yet, if his beloved mistress saw fit to take her share of lives in repayment for the offence they had obviously dealt her today, who was he to argue?

How many days passed, Ashton did not know. The dawn chorus of birdsong greeted him like an anthem to his new home. Upon fully awakening, the darkest set of eyes anchored to a face with the brightest smile he had ever seen greeted him. Newfound joy broke free from his chest like a spring of pure water. The two young men bonded in an instant through their mutual joy - Rawiri Kavinga, at the wonder of his discovery while fishing at dawn; Ashton, for the simple but beautiful fact that he lived, and that a welcoming smile greeted him upon arrival at what was to become his new home.

With a determination that can only come from perfect hope, he left the past behind in the ashes. That day he decided to become Tony Heath.

At Bergen Op Meer, Anna knew her brother needed her. She could feel his distress as though it were her own.

Jude, Batina and Anna had just finished a meal together. She was now taking a tray to her father in his study, a practice that had recently become a regular occurrence. But this night she would not inquire of his well-being. She needed time alone to work out her own thoughts and wondered if he would even notice.

She knew Ashton blamed himself for the fire. That she did not need to feel - she saw it on his face the last time she had seen him. *So much hurt, so many years of rejection,* and now any chance of forgiveness seemingly impossible. *How does one person carry so much pain and still manage to find joy in life?* It marvelled Anna that he always found a way and she loved him all the more for it.

Later that evening, to gain some peace, Anna finally took pen to page. Using the instrument as a voice for speaking words she dared not say. How was she to know these markings would one day be carried through time, into the hands of future generations. To guide them right back to these rooms, not only revealing the hidden history of her family, but also the legacy of love hidden by layers of deceit yet to be revealed.

Chapter TWENTY

1981 *Aotearoa New Zealand*
Vaun and Matt sat in stunned silence.
The kind that takes over when you are in shock.

It would be years before they would return home. Matt had no more tears left. He had cried them out long ago. The shame of what they had done was too much for him to bear. He had been on suicide watch from the moment they were taken into custody. Vaun let the feeling of being totally numb hold him for as long as it would stay. He wished that death had taken him instead in the accident.

They had been sentenced to four years in prison, and given no chance to say goodbye to their parents. *Four years seemed a lifetime,* he thought. His Mom did not cry when the sentence was read out. She simply looked into his eyes with the undying faith she has. From across the courtroom she comforted her only son without a word.

Della Rainbird was not worldly. This was her first time out of Cadillac Saskatchewan. She loved Vaun, *her boy,* and knew that he needed her here. Montey Lacelle could see that she was going to be with her son, no matter what. As he was leaving the bank in good hands, he offered to make sure she got where she was going in one piece and back again. They had no idea what to expect today, but neither was ready for the devastating news they had just received about the lives of their two sons.

Della looked into the scared face of her beloved son and willed all the strength she could muster to be given to her child. *He was a good boy.* That another's life had changed, tragically affected as the result of his actions, would devastate him. She now worried about him. God knows she had prayed for the two little ones that had been left without a parent. Della silently spoke to her *Father on high*, to walk through these four years protecting and loving her boy that he may come back to her whole.

Jonty watched from a safe distance all the proceedings that had taken days to come to this moment. Nothing would bring Johanna back yet he knew he needed to be here today. *My God, these boys are barely out of school uniform. None of this makes any sense.* Four years was an eternity when you are their age. In truth, Jonty had prayed for no jail time. These lads needed to pick up the pieces, too. He could see they were devastated.

Hannah greeted her Uncle Jonty as he came in that evening. As children do, she was making amazing progress. To see this lightened Jonty's burden. However, he could not hide his sorrow at the injustice of it all. Millzy had just made a fresh batch of Anzac biscuits. The three of them sat in communal silence as he enjoyed the simple pleasure of being with the girls.

Hannah knew that quiet times came over her Uncle, and if she was strong in the way that her Mum would want her to be, she could learn to *sit in the silence* with him. Eventually he said "These Anzac biscuits are just like those my Mother used to make. Well done, girls." Millzy was glad she could bring some happiness to this dear man's life. The children were resilient. Though they had their moments of missing their parents and their old way of life, they had both embraced all that was new as an adventure. Uncle Jonty, as she had come to call him, needed a little more gentle care. Today was one of those days.

"Where is Tony?" Jonty had not seen him at his usual place when he drove up the drive.

"Oh, he has a new place to spend his time when not eating." Millzy supplied this information with a gentle grin. "Since his arm is not fully recovered and in his full use to throw that ball that is always in his hand, he is at the pitch kicking it between those two white poles," pointing with an up and down motion using both hands.

Millzy's simple description of the uprights brought a little light into his heart. "Do you mean the sticks?"

Her command of the English language was excellent but even she did not know all of the terms for the sport that was a part of the family, indeed the whole country for that matter.

Snapping her fingers, "That's it, the sticks." She was always glad to extend her knowledge of English.

"Of course, I should have guessed. Shall I take a few extra of these and go pick him up before the sky opens?" Jonty reached for the full container of cookies Millzy had already prepared. Sometimes she knew him better than he knew himself. How could he have ever come through these first months without her? It was as though she had been sent.

"I am sure you will find he is not alone. The ever-present Brogang is with him, to be sure." Millzy had come to adore them all. Her mind wandered as she thought about the circumstances that had brought her into the lives of a family she now considered her own to love. *Whānau*. She watched the retreat of a very sad looking man and let her thoughts wander back to Bergen Op Meer. She missed her family there too.

That evening when Tony and Hannah had gone off to sleep, the two unlikely companions sat at the kitchen table.

Over a hot cup of tea and the remaining Anzac biscuits, Jonty and Millzy discussed what had happened at the courthouse that day. "Those boys had their whole life ahead of them. Now they will always carry a prison record. To see the look on their parent's faces today will always remain with me. The odd thing is, I wish I could do something for them. I just cannot accept that there is nothing that can be done to help them through this time and when life goes on in four years." Jonty tapped his finger on the rim of his warm empty cup and contemplated options. *Nothing was impossible for you, Lord.* He had complete faith in this fact.

"How do the men in prison spend their time? In the Netherlands there are options to be educated while in prison. This is seen as a form of rehabilitation. I do know of one woman who completely turned her life around in prison and worked towards a Masters Degree. She is now assisting others who are struggling with addiction and live on the streets of Amsterdam. Is it possible that these programs are available here too?"

Millzy also believed that there was always hope. Jonty knew she had a good heart. "My Dear, that is a brilliant idea. I know the Chaplain at the prison, whom you have also met, and will contact her tomorrow. I am sure she will be a great help." Feeling just a little lighter, Jonty made his way over to the doorways of his niece's and nephew's rooms and silently spoke a blessing over them. Leaving Millicent with her own thoughts of Bergen Op Meer and the task at hand.

Chapter TWENTY ONE

B*ergen Op Meer a few months before.*
"Here, Oma, let me help you with that." Millicent was entrusted with the care of Massy and Kat until Batina had fully recovered. They kept everyone on the go all day. These quieter times sitting and reading with Oma after those two had been all tucked in were a complete bliss. "There, is that better?" Millicent fluffed the immaculate white pillow at Oma's back and waited.

"Yes, lieveling. Please read from Hebrews, the page is marked." Letting out a sigh, Batina relaxed into the downy cloud. Millicent knew Oma would soon be fast asleep. *I love sharing these special moments.* She thought. Everyone was still reeling from the fact Oma had taken ill so quickly. Mumma had said it was heart sickness, that with all our love poured out to her she would recover. *I think Mumma was right, as always.*

"This is a very old Bible, Oma. It is falling apart. Would you like me to replace it for you?" Coming to know the Lord was new to Millicent. Her bible had seen much less use than Oma's well-used volume.

"No. When the word of God is spoken over and over into our lives, we are united with the Lord. As you can see, the Lord has had many occasions to speak to me through the years." *Did Oma just giggle.* Millicent thought. Her face always glowed when she spoke of Christ Jesus.

"Is your Bible showing use?" Looking directly into her eyes, Millicent felt on the spot.

"I do not know where to start. Each time I begin, this overwhelming feeling of how far I have to go takes over. I don't like it. It is as though a light begins to shine into places inside me where I am not sure I want it to." Plopping down onto the stool, Millicent looked defeated.

"Oh, how I know your pain." Batina patted the space on the bed and motioned for her to come sit a little closer. "When the journey began in earnest for me, I was pregnant and unmarried."

Millicent knew Oma was not perfect, but she did seem very saint-like to everyone in the family. "Oma!!!! What did you do?"

"Well, first I prayed. Then I told my mother. She was devastated. I had shamed my family. But I was not sorry. The baby's father was taken from me. I was glad to have a part of him close. It is hard to explain those times. People were disappearing; no one knew who would be next. The plans to wed had been organised for us and we could not wait. He never saw his son." In flooded the past and thoughts of love lost as Batina absentmindedly ran her hand over Millicent's open palm.

Oma looked so lost in her own thoughts. "What happened to the child?" From far away Oma looked into her eyes and just as quickly returned.

"To keep my little Joshua safe, the Missionaries took him into their care at the time I was believed dead. That I survived the camps, that anyone survived, is a miracle. But when it came to my son, his life was to take another path. He was adopted into a family that I am told could not have children. I do wonder if he knows about me."

I think I had better change the subject. Oma looked so sad. "I will try again, Oma. Even if the light shines so bright that I have to take it very slow, I will start reading my Bible." *If Oma could get through all that had happened in her life, I certainly could too.*

"The Good Lord will never allow any of the children God has given life to, to face more than what is possible for us to be saved through and to be strengthened from," patting the hand she was touching as she spoke. The fatigue of the day was taking hold. Her eyes closed and she soon surrendered to peaceful dreams of love.

Batina fell asleep holding Millicent's hand. *I wonder where 'becoming stronger' is meant to take us?* Millicent thought. She did know about the promise of an eternal life. She could even accept the fact that more than 2000 years ago a man lived right here on Earth who, by his death and even more remarkable, by his resurrection, altered the outcome of her life today. What she just could not work out is, what was today for? God did not need anyone. *Even she knew that. Maybe we had free will so that choosing to love, as I did Oma and a few select others, meant more than she realised.* She longed to stay within the comfort of the peaceful moment.

Slowly rising to not wake the sleeping beauty now resting after an arduous day, Millicent moved to place the well-worn volume reverently back on the shelf that had been its home for as long as she could remember. The shelves were filled with old favourites, some that had been in the family for numerous generations. There were so many. Some of the shelves were two books deep, like the shelf she was now placing the Bible on. It was at this moment curiosity took hold.

Millicent moved aside a few books in the front row and picked out a small book with no marking of any kind on the old leather cover. No title, no author inside. Just hand-written words. Millicent had always had a healthy curious appetite that had, on more than one occasion, plunged her deep into matters that she knew were none of her business. *Oma had probably not looked at the journal now in her hand for over a hundred years or more. What harm would it be to anyone if I just sat here in peace for a little while longer and read some of the hand-written notes on the pages from the past?*

In the quiet of the upstairs suite at Bergen Op Meer, with only the sound of gentle even breathing from the beloved woman sleeping in the bed, Millicent discovered the story of the descendants of the great family that had once graced these same rooms.

They became real to her.

Johanna Heath/Malefyt had meticulously made known the history of a family that had been more a fairy tale to Millicent than reality. Each night when Oma was sound asleep, she read more until she had read all six journals. By the time Oma was well, she had completed her research and had a plan.

Millicent secretly removed the six journals. She began to investigate what had happened to the children Johanna was carrying when the journals came to an abrupt end. The local mission group, supported by the family, that had been in existence for hundreds of years, had been very helpful. It was here in the archives that she had uncovered the letters that Anna Malefyt had penned, explaining how she and her twin brother, Ashton Malefyt also known as Tony Heath, continued their support of the mission from their location in what is now known as Aotearoa New Zealand.

New Zealand, hmmm...... does this mean there are descendants? There was no turning back.

Everyone at Bergen Op Meer and The Gate House knew that when, and if, a direct descendant of the Malefyt family was to claim their birthright, the Wolf Family would be quickly removed from the premises. A home that they had known for generations. However, the family at The Gate House was secure due to the legal documents the family possessed, tying them to rightful ownership.

This had always unsettled Millicent. *Did not Massy and Kat deserve the same security that she had? Not to mention Oma.* She thought. *Of course, they could all move in here at The Gate House, but would that be the best-case scenario?* It was time to tell her parents.

"What do you mean you are going to be a WWOOFer? What could have possibly come over you, my dear daughter?" She was joining the organisation of World Wide Opportunities on Organic Farms.

Anita was seldom ever surprised by anything. Her daughter managed it, this time.

Now that Oma was fully recovered and back on her feet, Anita had no reason to not give her blessing for her only child to experience life through travel. That she had chosen to volunteer for other families, on a farm, so far away, seemed an odd way to learn about life outside of Bergen Op Meer though.

Later that week, Anita and Wim watched as their only child weaved her way through the masses at Schipol Airport. Secretly they were very proud of her for choosing to step out into the world. Where would this year away lead her? *They hoped right back to them.* She was a beautiful girl. Anyone would be blessed to have her in their lives. They had never seen her show the least bit of interest in having a serious relationship to date. They sure hoped it would not start now.

LIONS VINEYARD

Beau Retallick was ready for the upcoming harvest. He had hand picked from the options who they thought would be most suited to fit into their family-run orchard in Northland. Everyone lived on site and the meals were all eaten together. Through the years the family had met and made friends with WWOOFers from around the world. This year would be no different. With excited anticipation on everyone's part, one by one, they began to arrive. Millicent seemed like a sweet girl. Beau liked her on the spot. She was hard-working, smart, great with kids and an extrovert to a level that he was sure no Kiwi had ever reached. When tragedy struck his neighbours, the Heaths, she was the obvious choice to approach.

Jonty was stubborn, but not stupid. Even he would have to admit that having help with Hannah was going to be needed for a time.

The Retallick family was sorry to lose her. Helping out was the right thing to do. The girl was more than willing. In the second week of her arrival she packed up and joined the Heath Family on the neighbouring farm.

Millicent could not believe her luck.

She had worked out the area that Anna and Tony had settled in and thought she would begin her research there by applying for a WWOOFing placement of which there were plenty. She had every reason to believe the family she had now agreed to assist, after a tragic accident, would know even more. They held the same surname of Heath.

The child in the chair was small, delicate, exotic. "Hi, I'm Millicent. Your Uncle has asked me to help around here. You're Hannah, right?" Millicent tossed her backpack onto the kitchen floor. She knelt down to Hannah's level so they could see each other eye to eye.

"Yes. Where are you from?" Hannah was not at all sure she wanted help, but even she knew that Uncle Jonty could not cook. She hoped the volunteer from the neighbours' orchard could do the trick. *This might help Tony feel better, too. He was sad a lot of the time and good food cheered him up.*

Oh, I see you are very astute. "I am a WWOOFer from next door." Millicent did not know how much this family knew about Bergen Op Meer, if anything at all. She wanted to keep her identity a closed book.

A sweet giggle bubbled up from Hannah's chest "No, I mean your home. I know Mr Retallick said to Uncle Jonty that you were perfect for us right now."

"Ohhh, got yah. I am from the Netherlands." Millicent was conscious of the eyes on her. Mr Heath had remained discreetly in the room. The eyes looking into her now had the ability to see into her soul. She could feel it, or *am I just being self-conscious?*

"Is that far from here?" This was the beginning of many happy conversations in the year to come. Hannah knew that Uncle Jonty loved her and would only do things that were best for her and Tony. Hannah hoped that she and her new friend would have lots of fun and be happy together. Later that day Tony took his wellies off, added them to the neat row, crashed through the door and headed for the smell of food. "Hi, Ton's, this is Millzy, she is from the Netherlands." Hannah helpfully indicated to the apparition in the apron at her side.

"Hi, what's cooking, it smells good." Tony got up on the stool, leaned over the pot on the stove top and sniffed in the heavenly smell. Millicent certainly knew how to cook.

"You must be Tony." Giving a final stir, she looked down into the most adorable little face.

"Yup." With a rugby ball held in its usual resting place, Tony looked up into the eyes of a stranger and smiled his most charming smile.

"Well, it's chicken soup today. How about a grilled, cheese sandwich to go along with it right after you wash up?" Millicent tapped the wooden spoon on the side of the soup pot for emphasis. "And if any of those friends of yours hanging back there want some, there is plenty, but they need to wash up, too."

Hannah could hear the scurry of activity just outside the kitchen door and smiled. *My goodness Millzy was sharp. We need her around here.* Silently Jonty faded away with the hope of some joy returning to his heart. The girl was a godsend.

Chapter TWENTY TWO

What do we do about these two in prison?

Charlotte had known Jonty through their mutual parish for what seemed a lifetime. She was not surprised by his request. Only he would have the heart big enough to even think about how he could assist the two young men who had recently joined one of her many Bible study groups within the prison. With a happy heart, she stopped by Lions Vineyard at the end of her day.

"I cannot tell you anything about the boys, of course, as this is all confidential. But I can tell you there has been in the past a financial sponsorship program to assist inmates with an education that I may be able to help establish. If the boys show the initiative, they can sign up for a University Degree. At least then, they will be leaving here in four year's time with a solid direction to help them when they enter into society again." Charlotte knew that the boys were kind-hearted. This was evident from her first meeting with them. After the shock wore off fully, they would need to be shown all the options open to them.

For now, they were both settling in, not sure how to be resilient enough to be with the other men their age without isolating or losing themselves. This was always complex in the early days of being in prison.

"Yes, that would be good. I am happy to act as a benefactor. Just pass on to me the figures. I will speak to the bank, but would prefer the lads never know." Jonty was still trying to work out why the future of these two young men mattered to him.

"Of course. Give me till the end of the week and I should have some information for you. It was really nice to see you. How are the kids doing?" Charlotte assisted at the funeral but had not seen Hannah yet.

"Oh, you know how children are, they are living each day as it comes. They amaze me and I am ashamed to say, they are my inspiration at times. I have help now. She is a delightful young woman who both the kids have taken to right away." Jonty held a gentle smile on his face as he thought of his loved ones.

"You feel ashamed?" Charlotte picked up on his feelings and leaned in. She also felt a little jealous, as she had harboured feelings for Jonty, though this had never led to anything.

"Yes. I should be the one who lifts them up, yet often I feel it is their strength that pushes me along. The loss of my sister has left a hole in my heart so deep, I hate to admit I fall in it sometimes." Jonty lowered his head and spoke the last words in a whisper. Placing her hand on his Charlotte waited for Jonty to take hold. When he did, he held it like a lifeline. Tears began to fall.

Millzy was a great friend and Hannah enjoyed all the time they had together. She was sad when she had to go back to school. *What would Millzy do all day?* She wondered.

As the school bus made its way down the drive, Millicent decided today was the day she would finally continue her quest for information. *Where was a good place to look?*

The Villa was not huge.

There would surely not be too many places to hide clues about this family, if they truly were direct descendants of the Malefyt Family.

Uncle Jonty had explained earlier that morning that he would be out for most of the day. He had banking business that was urgent, then he would be stopping in to see about some much needed fence posts that he could order from the timber mill in Kerikeri.

With the children both in school, there should be no interruptions. *But where to start? Where would this family keep historical documents?* She thought.

As she walked from room to room opening drawers and sifting through bits and pieces of paper, a sense of guilt began to form in the pit of her belly. *What am I doing? Doesn't this family deserve to know the truth? Why don't I just come right out and ask?*

She knew why. *Massy and Kat.* Two other children who she dearly loved and wanted to protect. The morning was quickly passing and a sense of hopelessness hung just far enough back that she remained determined. And glad she did. *The attic.*

The words shot across her mind as though truth had spoken them directly to her loud and clear. She beelined for it.

Oh, my goodness, look at this mess. Though it did look as though an attempt had been made at some point to bring order to the collection of long-forgotten things, Millicent looked at the amount of boxes, furniture and, to put it kindly, stuff, and felt defeated. *How will I ever find anything? That is, if anything is here at all.*

Some of the boxes placed neatly together seemed like a good place to start. They were also labelled. *Toys, Books, Dishes, Linens, Keepsakes, Photos.* Millicent moved each one to the side of the room that had more light with no fear of anyone noticing. As the dust would show, no one had been up here in decades.

This was how, once again, the sea chest marked AM was discovered, behind all the neatly stacked boxes, as though they had been placed there on purpose to cover up and hide it. Her heart began to race. She knew without a doubt secrets had been hidden and stored in the old sea chest. *This is it. Someone hid it to keep its secrets?*

It was heavy. It took all her strength to drag it over to the small window. To be on the safe side, she checked her watch, a copy of her own Mother's ever-present Rolex. *Yup, all good. I should still have time for this. And time to start a batch of cookies before the kids get off the bus. Uncle Jonty was not expected for hours yet.*

As soon as the lid was open and the musty smell of old books and papers hit her nose, her heart froze. Right at the very top, neatly stacked, were journals. She knew this, as they were crafted in the same style as the ones she had in her backpack, those written by Johanna Malefyt. "Phew. Here is the mother lode. I found it."

Relief flooded in and was soon followed by fear. *What would she discover?* Picking out the six journals that lay as if covering the documents that rested one layer down, Millicent placed them on the floor. Glancing at her watch again, there was just enough time remaining to replace everything, just in case anyone did check up here. *She could not believe her luck.*

As the first batch of biscuits baked, journal one, as they had been dated, became the centre of her attention. The others had been safely stored away under the mattress in her room. "Onse Leife Heir!" So engrossed was she in the writings on the pages of the journal, Millicent did not hear the early arrival of Uncle Jonty.

"What is it, my dear, anything that requires the urgent attention of Our Loving Father usually means bad news." It was not his intent but he had startled the girl to the point she lost hold of the book she was reading and it hit the floor. *How strange that I understood what she had said.* He thought. "Here, let me get that for you." Jonty, always the gentleman, bent down and picked up the book.

Millicent looked up from the jacket cover of the old journal that now rested once again in her hand. She hoped that the guilt she felt was not written across her face.

"Interesting reading?" Jonty thought she was acting a bit odd, but in truth he did not know her all that well and decided to make light of the matter.

She did seem uncomfortable though.

Maybe she felt guilty that he had caught her reading, so he thought he would put her mind at ease. "Care to share what you are reading there? I like reading, too. Then we can discuss it over some of those Anzac cookies that are going to be extra crisp if one of us does not pull them out of the oven now." With his bare hands Jonty lifted the hot tray from the oven.

"Oh, it is nothing you would find interesting." Thinking fast, she decided to stick to as much of the truth as possible. "These are the thoughts and writings of a young woman about my age."

"I see. You are probably right. Say, the children are due any minute. I am going to surprise Tony and get in some practice throwing with him before dinner. His arm is getting stronger by the day." The smile on his face lit up the room. Seeing his nephew recover gave him such joy.

"And I will finish baking these cookies with Hannah. She also wants to learn a new recipe that we are tweaking. Tea will be ready at 5:30pm." Millicent packed a few of the warm, and yes a little crispy, biscuits into a cloth napkin and handed them to him. "Here, best take these with you." As Uncle Jonty turned to leave she slipped the journal into her apron pocket.

"Right. There is the bus, off we go." Jonty took the offered package and headed for the door.

Later that same evening, when all was quiet, Millicent closed and locked her door. It was time to find out the truth.

And so she did.

The dawn light was creeping across the floor when she finished reading the last entry. *Best get breakfast on.* She thought. When the house was empty again, she had decided to place the journals in the old wooden sea chest and work out what she was going to do next.

"Uncle Jonty?" Filling his cup with steaming hot coffee, Millicent brought his second cup over to him that morning and waited.

"Yes, Dear." Jonty looked up from his morning paper and thought she looked a little tired this morning. *Maybe we should all go to the beach this weekend.*

"Once I have finished the regular chores today, I was wondering if I could clean up some of the dust that has collected around all the boxes upstairs? I was vacuuming up spider webs yesterday, when I noticed the opening to the attic and peaked in. I hope you do not mind. It could use a good dusting and I have the time." *That explains that.*

"Oh, my. No one has been up there for years. It must be a mess. I do not want you overdoing things, but if it makes you happy, sure, be my guest. And maybe this weekend, we should all take a break and spend the day at the beach." Jonty really admired this girl. She worked hard. The Villa had never been this clean and her cooking skills drew in the crowds daily. Hannah and Tony loved her too. *My word she is going to be missed.*

"That sounds great." Her smile shone through and lifted the tiredness from her features.

Later that day Millicent spread out the contents of the sea chest and found all the evidence she needed. With a sinking feeling she knew the truth. It would seem that Hannah would eventually be the owner of Bergen Op Meer. *And what of Massy and Kat? Not to mention Oma.* She knew she had no right to keep the truth from the sweet family she had come to know and care for. They obviously had no idea that a fortune in artefacts and a profitable vineyard were part of their legacy. *Would it hurt if they did not know? Look what they have now. Obviously not wanting for anything and very happy. Bergen Op Meer isn't going anywhere. The truth may come out later in life all on its own.*

Millicent placed everything back in the sea chest, added the six journals from Oma's bedroom and lugged the whole bundle out of the house. She placed it in a wheelbarrow, grabbed a shovel and walked as far as she could from the house into the field without being noticed. The lush soil was easy to dig, and, with a lot less effort than she thought it would take, the sea chest was three feet under in no time.

"There, now, that is that. Can I live with myself? Yes. What no one knows will not hurt any of them. That is what I can live with." The trees were there to hear her testimony. With only a slight nudge to her conscience, Millicent brushed the soil from her hands and she returned the shovel and wheelbarrow to the shed.

Chapter TWENTY THREE

1813 *Bergen Op Meer Netherlands.*
Anna refused to believe the false tidings that Ash had perished in a shipwreck on his way to her Uncle's home in the new land in the South Pacific.

Though there was enough evidence that everyone had died in the freak storm that had taken more than one ship to the depths of the sea that day, she was certain her twin was not among the dead. That she was now a woman of her own independent means meant there was no reason for her not to follow him. The missionaries that were often beneficiaries of her family had informed her recently of their plans to set up a mission on the island that Ashton was destined for. If she was willing to assist with the travel expenses, she would be welcome to journey with Rev. Samuel Marsden's group.

They would be first travelling to a large continent in the South Pacific, then on to islands where her Uncle Tally owned land. Though they warned her *'the journey may end in disappointment'*, her companionship would be considered a blessing.

A blessing for them also, Anna knew, because she would be generous with her contribution. *Kind of the men at any rate, to have made her so welcome.*

Jude and Batina could be completely entrusted with all the needs that would have to be dealt with at Bergen Op Meer for the year or so that she would be away; there was nothing to hold her back.

With her usual unwavering determination, Anna made her plans which included several healthy grafted vines that had not been damaged in the fire. This seemed like a sensible idea. In sure fashion she could show Ashton that not only would the crop fully thrive again, she was also determined to see to it that their legacy flourished in the new land.

With her painting paraphernalia stored safely in a travel case, and not just a few favourite books including her Bible and her mother's journals, she would now have plenty of time to read them at her leisure. With hours of help from Batina, her luggage was scrutinised and approved for boarding right on schedule. As Anna watched the shores of her home disappear in the sunset, her conviction also sailed to new heights.

Kenyon Lewis watched the vision at the rail and wondered at his good fortune. This beautiful woman would be in his presence for months to come and he had every intention of making her his wife before the end of this voyage. Miss Anna Maria Malefyt had always been just out of his reach. Kenyon often tried to join the landing crew at their home. Due to the other officers also wanting to make their best impression on the family, the junior mate was last on the list to receive an invite. It would seem good fortune had smiled on him and planted a congratulatory kiss on his cheek today.

He knew that she had spurned the other officers, professing to have no interest in involving herself in a long term liaison that would restrict her from pursuing her many humanitarian passions. Yet she had never met the charming Kenyon Oliver Lewis. He was confident she would soon see things his way and they would be settling down together at some point in the near future. Kenyon would agree that this new life together could be on her family estate if this made her happy. He was not a domineering man and intuition told him this would please her.

The days began to pass by in pleasant conversation and experiences that Anna fully enjoyed. To her absolute pleasure, she discovered that away from the daily trials of land and life the officers saw her more as a fellow member of the crew.

She enjoyed taking fresh air on the deck and painting portraits of those with delightful characters. There was one, however, that she knew would be best to avoid. *She had seen that look before.* The one that gave her the distinct feeling she was being made part of a plan that she had no intention of partaking in. *Anna had her own plans.* Those included her dear brother and nothing, and no one, was going to get in her way.

Once she had Ashton focused in the correct direction, her pursuits of equality for women would take the forefront once again.

Anna wondered what it would be like to meet women from other cultures so different from her own. *Did these women also struggle with societies that saw them as pretty things for show and self honour?* All of the presumed essential needs of the male gender pushed against her patience. Anna had always envisioned herself as part of a society that knew the value of each citizen, from the youngest to the ancient. From within her own family she had experienced just that. Anna had held a place of leadership; the men in her life worked with her and she with them. This allowed her to cultivate a sense of value for all humanity that she carried through to her desires for healthy communal living and human rights for all.

Kenyon could not believe his continuous misfortune. *Miss Malefyt was never alone.* Her hands found constant focus in those blasted paintings she was always engaged in and there was always a willing subject that dominated her attention in full. He had even tried to show his prowess in her sight by revealing just how strong he was when climbing the rigging with an impressive speed and agility, but she paid him no attention.

Anna found the evenings most pleasant. The meals were of the finest quality and the conversation stimulating. Reverend Samuel had brought onboard several varieties of grapes that he also planned to cultivate in the new land. Anna's vast knowledge was often in good service as they discussed the need for just the right soil, optimum temperature and, of course, the ever-present need for pest control.

"But what of the need for workers?" one of the officers had asked her one evening. "How will you train those you need to deal with the harvest each year?" In truth she had not thought that far, but reassured everyone at the table that her beloved brother would have this matter well in hand before she arrived.

Captain Jock Smit, the officers and fellow missionaries found her unfailing trust in the fact that her brother was still alive to be a disappointment in the making, but none of them shared this in her presence. Most of them had lost revenues in the storm that had taken many to the bottom of the sea that fateful day.

Jock could not, to this day, come to terms with the fact that this was a world without Captain Tally and, for that matter, his dear friend Jacobus.

Each night after the ladies had retired, the men would share their misgivings. They discussed how they could assist her after she discovered her journey would end in sorrow. Obviously she was a determined woman who had a great deal to offer. They admired her fortitude and knew she would take this to the very end without fail.

It was not by chance that Anna was included in this mission trip. She had a way about her that spoke competence, just what was needed in a woman to make her way in a new land. Anna would find ways to adapt. Her knowledge of Scripture was equal also to that of most of the missionaries, making her also a candidate for the school that was being planned to bring the Word Of God to tribes of the Islands in the South Pacific.

Captain Jock had known the Malefyt family for decades. The sad loss of the twin's Mother marshalled in the beginning of the demise also of the life of his dear friend Jacobus. He was never the same man again.

Jock had on numerous occasions attempted to entice Jacobus to move on with his life. He had still been so young and had so much living still ahead of him. But it was not to be. Jock had been with Jacobus as the life emptied out of him on that sad morning not long ago.

Tears fell as Jacobus removed the gun from the wall, primed it, and began to lead the old tired horse from the barn out to the pasture where they would soon cremate him. "This is my fault, all of this is my fault." Jacobus kept repeating. Absent-mindedly Jacobus stroked Moses' soft mane as he listened to Jock's offer. *Why was his own heart racing as though he had just run a race?* The horse was ancient and he was suffering from the infection that had spread throughout its body.

Jock came to warn Jacobus that the military would soon be upon Bergen Op Meer as they required the use of these noble beasts to carry the officers into battle. *Over my dead body,* thought Jacobus. Jock watched in sad fascination as the two, one being led and one gently leading, walked on, both seeming old and at the end of their lives.

"My friend, the creature has had a good life. Let me do the right thing before there is any chance of him being taken." Jock knew Jacobus did not have it in him to shoot his son's horse. For that matter, Jock was unsure at this point if he could pull the trigger.

Ashton had taken to Moses as though he had been thrown a lifeline.

The two had been constant companions from day one. What it must have done to the Lad that he left without his beloved horse, Jock could only imagine. It seemed as though it was only days ago that his first mate, Talbot Heath, had convinced Jock to pull the pony from the water and transport the feisty beast from across the South Pacific to his new home right here at Bergen Op Meer.

"Excuse me, Sir, are you Jacobus Malefyt?" So wrapped up were the two friends in the complete sadness of the moment, neither of them had seen the young officer enter the paddock. A man much older than the officer had expected to meet, turned to him and gave a single nod of affirmation as though the movement took a great effort.

"By order of his Majesty, I must take that horse you are leading there." This had been a long day of dealing with these stubborn families. Obviously they did not see service to the Crown as the noble call that it is. Young Simon van Dam held nothing back as he took on each task given to him with pride for his King and country.

"Lad, can't you see the animal is old and of no use." Jock could not let this blow to his friend happen. He did not think Jacobus had it in him today. To see the horse led away by a total stranger would be asking too much.

"It is Corporal van Dam, Sir, and yes, my eyesight is perfect." Simon firmly tugged the rein from the old man's feeble hand and turned at once to return to the waiting wagon.

Jacobus' heart shattered into so many pieces, he knew the damage was irreparable. The pain now running up his left arm was all he needed to confirm his life had finally come to an end. So without reservation, he raised the gun and fired. As though the bullet had gone through Jacobus' own heart, the pain shot through him, too, with lightning force. Jock reached his lifelong friend within seconds and gently rested Jacobus' head in his arms. "You have always been a better shot than me. Moses is resting now."

The two men cared nothing for the young soldier now pinned under the huge beast and calling out in aggravation.

They only had eyes for each other as the light faded from Jacobus.

Jock was the only one present to hear the final testimony of a dying man. "Ashton and Anna are my children." The words came in a whisper and seemed odd to Jock, but who was he to question.

Later, he would ponder these words.

For now he gave devotional love to the man in his arms, and with the peace born from above, he began to recite from heart the 139th psalm.

Chapter TWENTY FOUR

A *nna was right.*
Anna felt the trip took only what seemed moments, many pleasurable days linked together to make a fine golden chain of sunrises. Her journals were the place of testimony, recording each fantastic sight, sound, and experience. She was going to share it all with Ashton.

Her excitement of being with him again lifted her spirits even higher each day. Not a single drop of doubt filled her that she would not have more adventures with her brother, even though she could sense the doubt of those she now sailed with. Each day she lovingly tended the vines in her care and watched them thrive like a new life eager to burst from containment. *Much like how she felt at times.*

They spent time in the British Colony of New South Wales at the mission station for three months. The fellowship with others turned into a welcome diversion as the constant attention of Kenyan Lewis had truly got on Anna's nerves.

In spite of receiving no encouragement, he remained relentless in his attempt to have her undivided attention, achieving only the embarrassment of himself in the many weeks they had been at sea.

Though none of this would deter Anna from the excitement she now felt at the prospect of successfully fulfilling the mission group's aim of bringing the glorious message of Christ's birth to the tribes of this new land, and spending Christmas day of 1814 on the island that Ashton had been destined for. The disturbing reports of attacks at sea did give Anna a sleepless night or two, but she had come too far to turn back now.

With her usual determination, at dawn she stood at the rail and watched in fascination as a long white cloud in the distance blanketed the horizon which Captain Jock assured her would lift and reveal the land her brother was destined for four years before.

Kenyon had never felt such defeat.

Silently from the shadows he watched the apparition at the ship's rail. Dawn was gently unwrapping her features. With each revelation his longing to hold her grew stronger. He had completely misunderstood the true glory of her passion for life. Her depth of compassion had been revealed in its entirety when they had visits from the village children at the mission house recently. Her joy in sharing the songs of Christ's love for all his children filled the air and enveloped the joyful children tenderly. He had never seen them ever show such intense focus and fascination. She loved them all. *If she could only turn to him with even a small measure of her attention. Would he even be worthy of such a woman?* A thought that until recently had never entered his mind. He felt sheepish, thinking back on all those weeks of flaunting his masculinity before her.

As though an unseen force blew gently at the mist with the dawn, the Island came into clear view, just as Captain Jock had explained to Anna. Reverend Marsden in his finest ministers' robes joined Anna and blessed the new day. Today was Christmas Day and all glory to the Lord burst forth with the light.

Tony and Rawiri had spotted the ship and were now quickly becoming one of the many that would greet the landing party.

Ever since the two had met they never again spent a day apart. Hunting, fishing, horse riding and answering to the call and demands of their iwi.

Uncle Tally had been right. The local tribe had seen Tony for the rightful owner of the land Talbot Heath had traded for and his entry into life within the area was seamless. He shared with them his knowledge of growing new crops and left the life of whaling to others more suited. Tony was prospering and was very happy, though there were still days he longed to be with his sister. He regretted that she thought he was lost at sea, but he liked it that way. Never again did he want to have contact with his remaining parent. *Them thinking him dead assured this would not happen.*

Anna opened her hymnal at the instruction of Reverend Marsden as they stood on the shore amongst the tribe's people. She fearlessly followed the lead of the other missionaries and broke into another of the well-known hymns now being sung on the beach by the mission group at the Christmas service. This would be an event she would never forget, nor the rest of the country.

Rawiri had never seen such a strange sight before on the beach. The ariki, the first born of the families, showed reverence and honour to all. He had learnt long ago, the hard way, it is always best to follow his elders lead.

Tony joined in with his strong tenor voice in the familiar words that the missionaries now sang. His heart began to ache for the loss he now felt deep in his soul. All the tender memories of Christmas past came flooding in and his heart ached anew for his sister. So much so, that he could almost hear her clear soprano voice above the sound of the waves hitting the shore.

As Anna listened to the words now being spoken, her mind began to wander. *Where was Ashton now? Was he celebrating the birth of the Lord with loved ones today?*

Rawiri spotted her first and watched in fascination. He had never seen a female from Tony's people before. Questions came to his mind as he observed her. Once again he was pleased to have a friend like Tony who would spend hours telling him about his whānau, especially his sister. *I wonder if this woman looks like his sister?* He thought.

Tony knew it must be difficult for Rawiri to keep his focus on any given task for very long unless it was fishing or hunting, yet he seemed to take in the scene with full calm interest. Tony followed his line of vision and knew the answer, a female, and a European at that. This would be a new experience for his friend. Tony made a mental note to introduce himself and Rawiri to the female missionary as soon as the service was concluded.

Anna could feel the eyes on her. She was sure Mr Lewis was not far away; his concern for her was unfounded. She was a good judge of character. Nothing about the group that now stood in worship with her gave her any cause to fear. These welcoming, obviously fierce people seemed deeply spiritual, even to a level that she thought may surprise the missionaries she had travelled with.

More than once a shiver had gone down her spine as she stood with such powerful people in worship. Christmas is a day for celebration, yet she was fighting an inner battle of selfishness. Now that she was onshore her patience was being tested, as she longed to begin interviewing the locals. Thoughts of finding Ashton could no longer be held at bay. *I am sorry, Father, you as always have everything in hand. Give me the strength to be present with the Lord now, here on this glorious day.* Even as the unspoken prayer came to its end, Anna was restored to the full majesty of the moment.

Rawiri was not known for his obedience.

When Tony gestured they move in the direction he wanted to go most, with full surrender he uncharacteristically obeyed.

As they came closer, Rawiri saw she was lively and delicate. Like the fantail in flight.

Tony lead them right past a huge barrel of a man who stood at attention. Even Rawiri could see this delicate creature had a strength of her own. He thought the guardian was wasting his time. He had seen women in his tribe with the strength of ten warriors. She had the same power.

Tony eventually made his way directly towards the object of his best friend's attention.

Anna knew before she turned to those now approaching her that she was more of an object of curiosity than anything else. Little did these unassuming parishioners of today's service know she had an ulterior motive. *Let them come*, she thought.

Kenyon knew if he stood in the path for too long of the Islanders heading straight for Miss Malefyt that she would not be impressed with him. He had to settle with knowing these two now knew he was watching and they had better behave.

Tony entered into the young woman's view and immediately the day began to spiral. Rawiri watched as the woman's eyes came to rest on Tony. With a tribal yell of the like Rawiri had never heard before, she flew at Tony with a force no one on the beach was ready for, except Tony.

With the reflexes of a true champion, Tony responded by catching her in mid-flight with his strong arms, as though this event happened to him every day.

If this was the greeting Rawiri was to expect, he was now ready, though not sure if he wanted to be a part of this ritual, as he needed to determine if there was any threat intended.

Where only moments before a peaceful service had been underway, now pure chaos broke loose as Tony began to grasp the unlikely possibility that he was now holding his beloved sister in his embrace.

Kenyon and Rawiri stood over their self proclaimed charges with fierce protective determination. Each willing to give their lives.

As Tony began to spin the woman he held in his embrace, she held back her head and laughed with a beauty no one with eyes on the beach that day would ever forget. Kenyon and Rawiri soon saw the scene for what it was; it was one of joy.

Kenyon's heart fell as he watched the woman of his earnest pursuits place kiss after kiss on the face of the man who now held her close. Rawiri was not sure if he still wanted to meet the woman of Tony's tribe. Even for him this greeting seemed strange. He was not sure if he could respond to it with the same reply as Tony had given.

"Ashton, Ashton, Ashton. No greater gift has ever been given on Christmas day." Anna placed kiss after kiss on her brother's face. Tony could not get in a word edgewise. Anna claimed the moment. To be honest, he was in a state of shock and could not find his tongue. "I have so much to tell you. Mother had journals and I have gained knowledge as to why Father had suffered so." Anna's normally controlled mind was spinning.

"Had?" Tony heard the word for exactly what it was. The explanation as to why his beloved sister was standing before him started to take shape. If for a moment there were any thoughts of his return to Bergen Op Meer, she would be soon very disappointed. "Are we now truly orphans then?"

Where only moments before Anna had felt such joy, melancholy had swept in. "Ashton, I have so many things to tell you."

"Let this be known here and now, Anna Banana, I am home, and here is where I will stay." With absolute clarity Tony knew his heart. Anna knew by his tone nothing would change it, but that would not stop her from trying.

"Let us not let anything get in the way of this moment, Ash. There is time for all of that later. For now we rejoice." Anna held tight to his hand. She turned to the native at her brother's side and said "Aren't you going to introduce me to your friend?"

"Rawiri." Ashton had taught him enough of the language he spoke for Rawiri to know he was being added to the moment.

"Hello, Rawiri, I am Ashton's sister, Anna Malefyt, a pleasure to meet you." With her most radiant smile Anna warmly introduced herself.

"Who is Ashton, Miss?" Rawiri stood in absolute silence as he waited for the peals of laughter coming from the most perplexing creature he had ever seen to stop. Tony's silly grin told him that the laughter was because of what he had said. A feeling came from the depths of Rawiri's soul like none he had ever experienced before. The heat on his face could be seen by everyone continuing to watch the exchange on the beach.

Tony loved his friend, but was enjoying his embarrassment just a little too much, so it was time to put Rawiri at ease, he hoped. "This is MY sister. I am Ashton." Each of the three young lives now facing each other on the beach shifted like the sand at their feet in a receding wave. "Anna, this is my brother, Rawiri, and in turn now your brother too." Tony let the two people he loved most in this world come to terms with their new truths.

Rawiri knew only one way forward "The hāngī is prepared for all the people and comes from the ground now. Will you eat with us?" Food. Anna could smell the most delicious aroma now mixed with the salt of the sea air, as though one was created purposely to flavour the other.

"I would be delighted." Tony let a sigh of relief leave his lips at the kind reply from his sister. In no time he was certain that Anna would have charmed his best friend into her good graces.

Without reserve she took the hands of both men and headed for the smell that was now making her mouth water in a very unladylike fashion.

Kenyon had no choice but to follow at a discreet distance. He continued to harbour hope once again, discovering a joy for Miss Malefyt that she had in fact found the purpose of her journey right here on the beach today. She really mattered to him in disconcerting ways he had not felt before today. He respected her.

The other missionaries had already found their way to the enticing smells and were mingling among the tribe's people. The historic moment altered the lives of many people that day, but none more than those of the three who now stood in companionship enjoying the bounty of the earth.

Who was the man who to Tony's observation clearly had designs on his sister? He knew she had no significant bond with him, or she would have indicated this in some form in a timely manner. Keyon saw his chance. "Good day, Sir, Kenyon Lewis." extending his hand to Tony.

"A pleasure, Ashton Malefyt, better known as Tony Heath, at your service." Though the crushing pain that shot through his hand did not show on his face, Kenyon knew this man would protect his sister to the death without fear of losing his own life. By a warrior's instinct, Rawiri knew he was to stand next to Tony and be present. No more was needed. The three men shared in a voiceless dialogue which went undetected by Anna. She was far too busy enjoying her meal from the earth.

Chapter TWENTY FIVE

A *new friend with four legs.*
A new routine quickly became the norm for the trio. Anna continued to assist the missionaries and delighted in presenting Tony with the grapevines that had flourished under her tender care on the long voyage.

Reverend Marsden spent many hours discussing with Tony, *would Anna ever become accustomed to the name Ashton was known by in the new land?* which would be the best area in which to begin and cultivate his own vineyard. Tony imparted the need for discretion when seeking land, as it would need to be a gift, or in exchange for a fair trade, and offered to help in any way he could, imploring the Reverend to not have sheep in the same area as the vines. This will not turn out well, as Tony had already discovered.

That Tony now knew the destruction of the family land was not entirely his fault was a balm to his bruised soul. But the extraordinary turn of events with his father and the loss of Moses left him once again reeling within, giving him heightened feelings of gratitude to the Creator for his new four-legged companion. Diddy, short for Doubting Thomas, had entered into his life as an unforeseen joy. This is how they had met.

Tony had been sleeping off the hottest part of the day in the shade of a pūriri tree, when he had woken to the sense he was not alone.

He had not been in the new land long and was still unsure of his environment. This left him on alert at all times. *What is that familiar smell?* Tony lay as still as a statue and waited. Off to the left he could see a slight movement in the underbrush. He slowly moved his right hand to the hilt of his dagger in preparation. And then it struck him like lightning, a horse. He could smell the familiar scent of Moses. *Was he still dreaming?*

Tony moved with silent grace and climbed the tree in hopes of getting a glimpse of the elusive wild horses he had been told of. The beast was majestic. Dappled and sinewy. Tony remained hidden and downwind contemplating his next move. *How will the Lord weave our paths into one?* He knew with every fibre of his being, he and the beast would become one.

His heart called out to the creature and with senses born of survival, Tony could see the beast knew he was now being watched. Their eyes met and locked. Who would be the first to turn away. *Don't doubt me friend, I mean you no harm.* The words played across Tony's mind like a script. *Were these his doubts or the horse's?*

With confidence Tony descended the tree and humbly approached the wild animal. Head bowed and even steps, he presented himself into the space of the now dancing pony. Letting the creature of his attention come into his space took steely patience. Time ticked by, yet there they remained. One curious and one humbled, bowed down and ready to wait for eternity.

Tony knew he had gained a companion when he felt the breath from the horse's nostrils gently blow against the back of his ear. Gracefully, Tony lifted his open palm to gently stroke the cheek of the beast now hovering over him in a proprietary stand. In a moment only the Lord can identify, the two became one.

Diddy could not fill the empty space the loss of Moses had left in his heart, yet Tony now felt a new lifeblood spread within, that allowed room for a full love for the new beast in his life to expand. He understood why his father had shot Moses. Tony believed he would have done the same in those circumstances. This helped soften the pain.

With the flourishing of Lions Vineyard, a name that their Uncle had given to the land to honour the King of kings, and the need for spiritual guidance to spread across the Island, Anna stayed on and took over the running of Tony's home.

To her relief, and Kenyon Lewis' self-proclaimed sadness, he finally departed with the Marsden mission and left her in peace, though not before she had written to Jude and Batina.

Entrusting him to deliver the letter. Anna knew Mr Lewis felt a loss, as any chance of a bond between them was definitely out of his reach. She hoped in time they might become friends. Anna had given much thought as to how she could explain her unprecedented choice to Batina and Jude. In the end, she penned a simple missive explaining her joy in finding her twin and that she wanted to stay on with him for now. The estate would be dealt with through the solicitors. The needs of those Anna held dear would be met. Kenyon Lewis was also entrusted with the letter to the solicitors.

Anna's life blossomed with meaning. She was beginning to comprehend why Tony would not want to return home. She felt closer to the creator here, more than in any cathedral she had worshipped in. She had opened to new blessings and the Lord was pouring.

Over time the women of the tribe had warmed to her and she befriended them. Anna admired their love and feirce devotion. She often thought their knowledge of the spirit of creation was on a level that was even new to her. These women elevated each other and family at all times with an abiding equality and grace she admired. At least, this is what she thought, until the day she too became a mother in the most unexpected way.

Did she want a family? At times when Anna assisted the new mothers her heart felt a tug when she held their babies. Today she was called to assist Anahera with a difficult birth, a dear sweet captive who had accepted the Lord as her personal saviour. The women of the tribe had not accepted her. She had been captured, and it was soon discovered she was already with child. This rendered her to be an unsuitable bride, the reason for her being taken in the first place. To Anna, Anahera seemed more like a child than a woman knowledgeable of intimate matters.

The two women had bonded out of a need and want to belong. The Lord became their constant focus, manifesting a deep joy for all they delighted in. Each of them marvelled at life forming so perfectly within the safety of Anahera's body. They both had dedicated intentions that this new life would enter into a world full of love's abundant sense of belonging.

When the day came for the infant to join the outside world, Anna arrived thinking the women of the village would have been busy with the preparations. To her dismay, Anahera lay in a heap on a mat in obvious pain. This caused Anna a moment of hardened heart.

True to form, Anna comforted and protected the soon-to-be new mother with every fibre of her being and knowledge.

Though it would not be enough.

"Shhhhhh, child, we will face each moment together." Anna gently wiped the perspiration on Anahera's brow with a cool cloth in between contractions. Anahera's young body was not ready for the trials of difficult labour. The two women fought with all they had to bring forth a not so little baby boy eighteen hours later. He was strong and beautiful, a perfect miracle.

"Koraka, his name is Koraka." Anahera's breath was leaving her.

Anna projected calm, but inwardly screamed out *"Save her, Lord"*.

"What does it mean, lieveling?" Anna touched her forehead to Anahera's as the newborn lay nested, protected between the two women.

"His father is a chief. He is a child of the South." She softly spoke.

Anna had patiently waited for Anahera to share her origins in their many communal hours they had pleasantly shared and tell her story, but the young woman never could speak of her heartache. Anna's heart broke as she held the sleeping infant and the woman-child as her breath slowly stilled to a lifeless silence.

Practicality mixed with Anna's weeping, as the realisation formed that Koraka would need a mother. With a fierce intensity of that equal to a protective lion, with her lifeblood, she claimed the child as her own. She gently covered her beloved friend, washed and swaddled the child, and prayed. As she stepped from the hut, Anna saw a crescent moon and the last star of the soon-to-be morning sky. It appeared the entire village had been waiting also. *Had they known this child was a leader among them?*

Anna found it difficult to look at them. Anahera had not been treated kindly in the end and now their hearts seemed cold towards the infant.

There was no harmful force on this earth that she would allow to touch the child and this flowed from the power of her bearing. Silently they watched her as she walked through them towards Tony, a force that parted them like Moses through the Red Sea.

When she reached him, he knew the need for acceptance by a parent. With determination born of understanding, he, too, accepted the child into his heart without a moment's hesitation.

Determination and protection walked shoulder to shoulder through the village holding the child, and guidance followed right behind in the form of Rawiri. *His foreign brother and sister were going to need him even more now,* he thought.

So enveloped in the moment was the entire village that none of the seasoned warriors noticed the scout who, from the edge of the village, watched the unfolding of the first moments of the people of the South's future chief. He could see the child would have protection, until his people could claim what was rightfully theirs. Silently, he once again became one with the forest. With the speed of a time traveller he took his message back to his iwi.

"Anna, we have an obligation to this child. It will be seen as though he was taken from his people. If what you tell me is true, they will come." Tony decided to prepare for war and was digging into the ground at the centre of their home. His sea chest with all their documents and valuables would be safely stored in the belly of the earth. "Rawiri and I will travel to the tribes of the South and offer peace. This will not be the first time I have traded and had dealings with these men. There is some hope."

"How will you know if the tribe is Anahera's tribe? She gave us such little information." Anna gently traced her finger over the forehead of the sleeping child in her arms and with fascination watched the pout of his lips on his enchanting face.

"Oh, there is little doubt that word has not already passed from here to its destination. All we have to do is be alert, the information will come to us." Tony and Rawiri shared a glance of common knowledge. Each one not wanting to tell their sister what she would most likely be facing, sooner than later.

As it turned out Tony was right. Before the dawn of a new day the first cry of attack sent the sleeping village into immediate chaos. The smoke of burning timber quickly filled the skies.

Without fear, Anna swaddled the child and made for safety. If she could make it to one of the many boats near the shore, safety would be hers. She was confident the men would find her eventually. She slipped unseen into the shallows, released one of the boats from its mooring, placed the sleeping infant into the safe, dry hollow of the waka and guided them both away from the destruction unfolding on shore.

Tony, as always, had Rawiri at his back. The men had taken to the fight with warrior intensity. Equally matched, the tribe defending had more to lose and so fought with fierce determination. Tony had seen Anna slip away with the child and was forever grateful his sister could fearlessly face her own defence with such wisdom. Their home was now nothing but ashes, and Tony wondered more than once in the days to come if this was to be his fate again and again.

Anna eventually found a quiet cove to dry off in and feed Koraka as soon as she had felt safe to rest. The day dawned bright and remained so. *How long would it take to rebuild their home*, she thought, for she was certain Tony had made it through the day's battle and this would be his plan.

"Shhhhhhh, little one. You are safe. I will never let anyone harm you." Anna released the child from all his bindings and playfully tickled his tiny toes producing a surprised look from the child. So intent was she on her task that she did not hear the two men approaching.

Tony and Rawiri had guessed right that Anna would take the child to a familiar yet secret place. She was bedraggled and enchanting all in one vision. The two men stood in silence allowing themselves time to take in the serenity of the moment far removed from the battle they had so recently overcome. They were both battle-weary. The village had been burned to the ground. There had been no loss of life. The wounds would all heal.

The warriors of both tribes had, as if by a miracle, found peace. The story of the pain experienced by the southern tribe over the loss of their daughter and the newborn was spoken and understood. The child was to be seen and raised as a leader to all people and remain at his birth place for now, *phew*. This came as a huge relief to Tony, as he knew no force on earth would take the child from his sister. All efforts and resources would go to rebuilding now. Tony had already decided to build a villa suitable for a lady to raise a child and he knew the perfect spot. "Anna Banana," he whispered.

"Yes, brother of my heart." With a glow shining from misty eyes, Anna slowly turned her gaze away from the now sleeping babe to rest it on the outcome of her brother's news that would be sure to follow his entry into the secret grotto.

He was smeared in soot, glistened with sweat, had a few non-life-threatening cuts and looked like he was at peace. Rawiri stood next to him and shone with a warrior's power in a high vibration of victory's glory. She finally let out the breath she had been holding. She knew all would be well.

Chapter TWENTY SIX

A*t Bergen Op Meer Hannah is settling in.*
Vaun was enjoying the diversion the speaking engagements were allotting him. Lotti, too, was happy to be away from the many day-to-day pressures of their practice in Vancouver. *She really was amazing.* Thought Vaun.

That they had never married he knew was his fault, but that never seemed to bother her. They had met at medical school and had not been apart since. For years he had thought that he did not deserve the kind of happiness the love of a sweet and compassionate woman brought into his life. She never let go and he loved her all the more for it. That he had never told her about his past did at times bother him. *Would she leave me if she knew?*

The two women he loved most in this life had met at his graduation. He had written his thesis on stem cell rejuvenation, as this had become his passion. Della Rainbird made her second trip out of her comfy little life in Cadillac to attend. The two hit it off and he was relieved.

Though Della never brought up the accident, he knew she was disappointed in him for not telling Lotti. "This will help to bring you closure, and bring the both of you closer," she said when he had told her Lotti did not know. He knew that closure would never be truly possible.

At first, he wanted to tell Lotti everything. She must have wondered how he was affording all the expenses of medical school, knowing his humble beginnings as a Prairie boy. The sponsor who had assisted both the boys to get an education while in the care of Corrections, continued to assist them both through the Chaplain's office long after they had returned to Canada.

Many times he and Matt had tried unsuccessfully to discover who the person was, but the confidentiality around the identity was protected. They were assured that as long as they continued with their education, the funds would continue. So they had.

Matt had eventually completed his Masters in Social Work and worked with street kids in Vancouver. Due to Vaun's research in stem cell rejuvenation there had been a recent major breakthrough in patients who had been living with injuries that had left them with soft tissue damage and mobility disabilities. He had been asked to speak to the faculty here in Amsterdam on his success. That is what had brought Lotti and Vaun to the Netherlands.

The first days after Tony left had been the hardest for Hannah.

They all agreed that Hannah needed to learn all she could from Kat before she started school. Oma also admitted she was '*not getting any younger.*' She expected nothing less than to help Hannah as much as she could, while she could.

The time moved swiftly by. Massy, slowly but surely, convinced Hannah to let him treat her. She had to admit, *he did have a way with his hands that eased her aching muscles.* They had converted one of the rooms down the hall from Hannah's suite into a gym and treatment room, just for her. Her strength and conditioning program with Dr Nic Gill continued via the internet.

Getting accustomed to all the luxuries of her new life was taking some getting used to. Above all, she liked it when she could cook for all of them, and they gathered around the table each night and shared their highlights of the day.

Hannah often thought that Kat missed Tony more than she did. Whenever she mentioned any news from Lions Vineyard, Kat never failed to ask about Tony. His regular updates on team stats, progress on the farm or just about anything, Kat often brought the topic around to Tony again and again. There came a time when Hannah's highlight to share was the generous nature of Uncle Jonty. She and Tony had spoken about this matter on the phone that day, as it was time to decide which charities to continue giving to.

That day Tony had spread out all the files on the table and started the process of organising his new life. *How was he going to do this on his own?* He could not help but think that Kat would be a great help with all this. *I will start at the top. Uncle Jonty's file marked DONATIONS is as good a place as any.* "He gave in total $335,796.11 marked 'education fund' to persons with the initials V.R. and M.L. over the course of nine years through the local Chaplaincy Office. Do you know who that would be?" Tony held the open file in front of him in one hand, the phone receiver to his ear in the other.

"Oh my, he was generous, whoever it was. Sorry Bro, no idea who V.R or M.L would be. Up until a few months ago I would not even have thought Uncle Jonty had that kind of money to give away. Did you check with Charlotte? She might know something." Hannah liked these times with Tony. That he still looked to her for help felt good.

"I sure did. She kept her integrity and would not break a confidence. All she would give me was that I should be glad that the world had one more good Doctor because of our Uncle.

Yah know what, I never really understood why She and Uncle Jonty did not get together. She is a really sweet lady. Today she offered to help in any way she could. All I needed to do was ask. She told me how much she missed him. It is nice to know she can be totally trustworthy, but I did feel sad, too. I have so much rubbish to go through Sis, I might just ask her to come by and help." Tony paused. "I feel overwhelmed and have not had a chance to do any more work on the new place yet. Between managing here and practices, I had to put that project on hold." Tony felt the tension in his shoulders loosen. Talking to Hannah always helped.

"You know, Kat has not started school yet. Why not ask her to come and help before the semester starts? She would be amazing at getting you all sorted; this place practically runs itself. She has done a cracker job with Bergen Op Meer. I am certain she would be happy to help." *Was Hannah matchmaking? Nay, it did make sense.*

"Really?" Tony was genuinely surprised by Hannah's suggestion, but he did like the idea.

"Sure. Hang on, I'll go and find her. You can ask her yourself. She was in the library the last time I saw her." Placing the phone on the desktop, Hannah listened for the sound of activity. In the distance she could hear Tony's voice calling out some kind of response, but chose to ignore it on purpose.

"NOOOOO, Hannah are you there?" In one sense, Tony loved the idea, but in another, he was terrified.

"Hi, Tony, it's Kat. How are you?" Sounding a little breathless, Kat hoped that Hannah had not seen her rush to the phone.

"Good. All good. And you?" Tony kept it cool on his end, hoping he did not sound too anxious.

"Good, too. Hannah said you wanted to ask me a question. What is it?" Kat already knew what it was, but she wanted to hear the words from Tony. Twisting the phone cord around her finger, she leaned on the desk she had spent countless hours at and waited. Her grin was illuminating.

"Well......I have a huge load of files and papers of my Uncle's I need to go through and I thought you might be able to help me get through some of it." Was it just Tony's imagination or was he sounding like a complete dolt.

"I would be happy to help. Are you inviting me to your home, Tony? I want to be sure I understand. That is a long way to travel for a misunderstanding." Kat wanted nothing more than to see Tony. To hear it from him mattered.

Silence.

Oh my, have I been mistaken? The moments that they had spent together in the short time he had been at Bergen Op Meer had been so special. Kat was sure Tony had some feelings for her.

Tony now felt a little breathless. "Yes. I would like that. That would be, if it works for you." Tony was blushing and was so glad she could not see him.

"Sure. I will make the arrangements tomorrow with the agent and get back to you. If all goes well, I should be there within ten days or so and can stay at least three weeks. This fits perfectly into my schedule. Would this time frame suit you?" Kat made a mental note to also book a hair appointment and get some shopping in. Hannah was pretty much running things around here now, so there should be no issues. The start of the first semester was still two months away.

Little did she know today that these were the start of her last days at Bergen Op Meer as Katerina Wolf.

"All good with me. Thanks for doing this, Kat, I really am feeling lost." *Maybe he had said too much.*

"I am happy to help. Here is Hannah, I will call you tomorrow. Bye." Kat handed the phone back to Hannah who had eventually returned, and looked her straight in the eye. Both girls knew and understood this was a big moment. With a nod of consent from Hannah, Kat skipped out of the room.

"Well, that worked out great. Maybe you can ask Charlotte to come and help you get one of the spare rooms ready? You may be a great rugby player, but housekeeper you are not. Hahahaha." Hannah was happy. If these two could figure things out, it would ease her conscience a little that Tony was alone now. *Maybe, just maybe, everything will work out.*

"Right you are, Hannah Banana. Now I need to figure out how to keep the Bros away until I can work out what's going on inside me. I feel like I have been hit by the entire front row of the opposing team whenever I talk to Kat. Why do you think that is?" Tony had no idea what was truly going on inside himself, but he liked the feeling.

"Ton's, she may be the one." Hannah whispered this into the receiver just in case Kat had not been fully out of earshot.

"What!!!! You mean THE one?" Tony was in shock. "Like the one that Uncle Jonty said I would always find and would know it when it happened?"

"I think this is possible." Hannah's smile was so big, her cheeks began to ache.

"Well then, I had better contact Charlotte now, time's a' wastin. Night, Hannah, love you." *He felt happy.*

"Love you too, Ton's, have a great day." Hannah placed the phone back on the cradle. "You just never know."

Chapter TWENTY SEVEN

I will do this for you.

"Never know what?" Massy had gone looking for her, as it was the time of day that he reserved for her treatments.

"Oh, nothing really. Let's get my treatment done and dusted. I am working on a new recipe and want to try it out tonight." Hannah had hoped that Massy would be just as easily distracted by food as Tony was. This was not to be.

"Why do you look like the cat that has just swallowed the kiwi?" Massy looked into the eyes of the object of his growing affection, though yet to be returned in any way, and waited as he placed a hand on either side of her to block the way.

"Why, Massy, are you accusing me of lying?" Batting her eyes at him, she glided forward and rolled over his big toe. This gave her the opening she needed. "See you in the treatment room. First one there gets to choose the next movie on Friday." Hannah never knew if he let her win these contests, but it did seem strange that he never won.

Later in the treatment room, Massy thought, as he had her undivided attention, and her leg in his hand so she was not going anywhere, that he would bring up the topic most on his mind today. These quiet moments with her gave him a chance to talk about his day and other ideas he may have.

"I have been attending lectures this week. One of the speakers is a specialist from Vancouver who I would like you to meet." If Hannah could have pulled her leg out of his grasp, he knew she would have. By the look on her face, he thought he had better talk fast.

"Now, before you get all stormy, hear me out, okay? As a result of his research and work in Canada, there have been major breakthroughs that have been helping his patients, and patients here, to fully recover from injuries like yours. Hannah, they are walking again. Internal soft tissue is mending. Organs are healing." Massy gently ran the tips of his fingers down her leg in his usual show that one was done and started on the other.

Hannah was silent.

So many thoughts went rocketing through her mind. She knew that he meant well. What he did not know, it was not so much that she did not have the use of her legs, but that she would never have children. This tugged at her heart most days. *If there was any hope that this could be changed, then she would try anything.* "Let me think about it."

The sadness in her voice left Massy feeling a little sorry that he had interfered. He was coming to love this woman more and more everyday and wanted her to be happy. "It is not that I don't think you are perfect just the way you are....it's just that medicine has been advancing since the last time you were examined and I just thought...." Massy looked sad and gently placed her leg down as though it was the most precious object on earth.

"I know you mean well. How do we get an appointment?" He had been so helpful and kind all these months with the many changes in her life. If this small gesture made him happy, she would do it.

"You'll do it?" Hannah could easily come to love the man who smiled at her like he was right now.

"Yes, what harm could it do?" With a gentle smile of her own, she gave in.

"Vaun, the young man on the line is very persistent. He assures me that his patient would be happy to fit into your schedule." Lotti was feeling a little impatient herself. She was sure that Vaun had been going to ask her the other night to marry him, but something happened and she could not get it out of him. *Was it another woman?* Now that was crazy thinking. He would never do such a thing. *Then why did she get the distinct feeling that he was keeping something from her?*

"Okay, okay." Waving his hands in surrender. "If they can be here before the afternoon lecture tomorrow, I can fit them in. Tell him 2 o'clock, and then leave our evening free, please. I would like to have that time alone with just you."

Vaun had been so close the other night to telling Lotti everything. All about the lives he had destroyed and why he had gone into this medical field.

He and Matt had both needed therapy while in prison and afterward. His therapist recommended he do his own investigation and see where it took him. It was not hard to find information on the family. The local papers had covered the story extensively. When he found the obituaries and the photo of Jonty Heath, a young Tony King holding a rugby ball, and his older sister Hannah King in a wheelchair, he shared his finding with Matt and their purpose for living became clear. He and Matt both recommitted their lives to helping others.

Tomorrow he was going to tell Lotti everything and, if she still wanted him, he was going to place that ring that he had been carrying around for far too long on her finger. *His Mom was right. This may bring him closer to some closure.*

Lotti felt a jolt go through her at the words '*just you*'. Their evenings were often just the two of them. *Carlotta Margorie Dixon,* she firmly told herself, *you put your big girl pants on and face whatever is to come. Vaun is a fine man. You should trust him.* "Okay, Doctor, will do."

Though her smile was there in her reply, it did not quite reach her eyes, Vaun noticed. *It was time. He was hurting them both by not telling her everything and finally trusting fully that he could be loved, even though he had made mistakes that were impossible to live with. Was his Mom right? He hoped telling the truth would be an answer to prayer.*

God had heard often from Vaun through the years. Faith had helped him when things got really tough at medical school, the times when the dreams of the accident haunted him, when he least expected it. Lotti had introduced him to a great group of people from her church at Uni and they had all stayed in touch. If Lotti would have him, he would ask Matt to be his best man. He hoped, maybe, Matt too would find someone to build a solid future with.

155

The next day arrived quickly. "Ready? Let's get an early start, as we just don't know how crazy the traffic will be." Massy held the door open for her, noting she looked gorgeous.

"I sure am. Both ready and not ready." Giggling, Hannah made her way out into the sunshine.

Lotti had been offered a suite of offices and exam rooms for their use while in Amsterdam. From where she was sitting, it looked like the couple, *at least I think they were a couple,* who had secured time at 2.00pm with Vaun had arrived a little early. The young man, Massy Wolf was his name, had couriered Lotti the medical files on Hannah King, and she had read over them immediately.

As many stories are, this patient had a tragic one. So young, just a child when the accident happened, changing her life forever. *I wonder what caused the accident?* Lotti's detective mind started to fire up. *What a beautiful woman she was, so exotic and regal.*

The age of her injuries would be a factor, but if she was willing, there was always hope. Lotti had seen more than one miracle in the years she had been working next to Vaun. He was gifted, as though through a will greater than his own, the conditions of his patients improved through treatment along with his dedication to their recovery.

Massy was nervous. *Was it fair that he had pushed Hannah into once again being poked and prodded?* She had entrusted him with her extensive medical files when she allowed her Doctor to release them to him. As he read them, his heart went out to the young girl who had grown into the beautiful woman he knew today. When he had read that she could not conceive, this seemed insignificant to him, but as he came to know her, the magnitude of this fact struck him square in the centre of his own heart. *There would be no heirs to inherit Bergen Op Meer.* He also now believed she would not enter into a relationship with him because, as he had once confided in her, he did want a family. *What an idiot.* If he could have a life with her, that would be enough.

"This way." Hannah was now eager to get started and approached the Doctor who had stepped into the hall.

"Good day. We are looking for Doctor Vaun Rainbird's office." Hannah was all business.

"You have found it. Hi, I am Doctor Lotti Dixon, his associate. You must be Hannah King, it's a pleasure to meet you." Lotti could not help but smile. She felt a happiness just being in Hannah's presence. "and you must be Doctor Wolf."

"Yes, the pleasure is all mine. Please call me Massy." He liked her on the spot and held out his hand to shake hers.

Greetings concluded they proceeded. "Please follow me." Lotti knew that Vaun would be making his way into the inner offices soon. As time was short she wanted to have everyone ready.

Hannah had seen the inside of more than her share of doctor's examining rooms, but she had to admit this one was different. There was an element of comfort and class without losing the clinical need of efficiency and precision. The team of Rainbird and Dixon must be something special.

The excitement that she did not want to turn into hope began to grow in spite of her best effort.

Massy was now glad he had suggested they come. Everything felt right. As though there was a destiny about this appointment.

Vaun breezed through the hallway in hopes of making it to the examining room before their patient. He usually took the time to look over their files before meeting them and hoped to have a minute or two to discuss their case with Lotti. Lotti met him at the door, handed him the file with her notes, and ushered him in. "Hi, I'm Doctor Vaun Rainbird, you must be," flipping open the file, he caught the name at the top of the page and froze.

The uncomfortable silence stretched out. No one knew what to do, least of all Vaun.

It was her.

Vaun was coming face to face with his past.

Come on, man, pull yourself together. Okay, I can do this. Am I getting my chance here to right some of the wrong I had done? Look at her, stupid. Vaun raised his eyes to look at her and his knees gave out. The room momentarily broke into chaos. Lotti was immediately at his side and Massy on the other. Hannah began to experience a feeling in her stomach that something was really wrong and it had to do with her.

Eventually she glided over to the Doctor on his knees, looked calmly at Massy and the woman at his side, and spoke to the man in tears between them. "Do you know me?"

He began nodding his head, yes. Hannah gasped. The realisation of all that this meeting meant set in. "You're V.R.. Why you? Why did my Uncle do all this for you?" and then, as though lightning struck her heart, she knew.

Long ago Hannah had discussed the accident with Uncle Jonty. She knew about the two young men and how their lives had been forever changed, just like hers was. She paused. *What could this moment mean to him?*

"Haere mai, all is forgiven. Come to me." Hannah opened both palms of her hands on her lap, indicating for him to come closer.

Massy and Lotti moved back. They watched in utter amazement as Hannah ran her hand over the head of the man now weeping uncontrollably into her lap. "Shhhhhh, all is well."

Massy eventually moved to her side and rested his hand on her shoulder. If he was unsure of his love for her before today, he was certain of it now. There was nothing he would not do for her. He would never leave her side again. Her inner beauty was beyond measure.

Lotti's world was in a spin. Who was this woman? Why was she so important to Vaun? Was she the reason Vaun had never proposed? *Oh God, is my world falling apart?* Lotti had not remained close to God these past few years. She felt a pang of guilt now that she hadn't, because she desperately needed his help, and she knew it.

Vaun let himself heal in the loving touch of the girl. With each caress she pushed out the pain he had held within for so long. Lighter and lighter he became as the strength returned to his legs.

She had spoken the words he had longed to hear," *All is forgiven.*"

With all the power he had, before he lifted his head from the comforting nest of her lap, he committed himself to helping this beautiful woman to be whole, able to lead a life outside of this wheelchair.

Raising his dishevelled head, their eyes met. "I'm sorry." Vaun had no other words. They were simple and real. Lotti had a thousand questions. The spell that was over the room held them all, her tongue with it.

Hannah smiled. The kind that is released from the heart. *One very similar to Tony's.* "May I have a hug, I could use one." Hannah held out her arms and allowed herself to fall into the embrace of the man who offered her the best chance of ever having children. *Thank God for Uncle Jonty and what he had obviously done for this man.* Now she was certain there would be nothing that would prevent him from helping her to have her prayers answered. *There was hope.* It was her time to cry tears of joy.

Lotti and Massy were both at a complete loss. Looking at one another, it was obvious. Massy raised his shoulders and Lotti looked crestfallen.

Vaun and Hannah had eventually between the two of them told the whole story to Lotti and Massy, all before the start of the afternoon lecture. This became a day to remember.

The coming evening was very special. After making arrangements to treat Hannah at their Vancouver clinic where they could spend quality time going through her records and start her treatments, they said their farewells, completed the remainder of the day's busy schedule, and ordered room service when they returned to their suite.

"You are a remarkable man, Vaun Rainbird. I am sorry you never told me. That you have suffered this long and I did not know, makes me sad." Lotti gently placed her empty wine glass on the table between them.

"I just did not know where to start." Vaun refilled her glass and reached into his pocket. "I do know where to start now though. I am through wasting time. Miss Carlotta Margorie Dixon, would you do me the great pleasure of finally becoming my wife, officially?" Presenting her with the ring and seeing her joy added to this day, the most perfect ending.

"Oh yes, with great pleasure, what are you doing tomorrow?" Her laughter bubbled up and spilled out like a fountain. Her happiness knew no bounds. She liked the new sensation.

Chapter TWENTY EIGHT

1815 *Bergen Op Meer Netherlands*
Anna had been gone for more than a year when the second letter from her arrived, *carried by that sweet boy Kenyon Lewis who had spent time with them when he had delivered the first letter.* Batina knew Jude would want to know of its arrival immediately. Even more so, she wanted to know its content.

Jude saw the affection of his heart make her way faster over the hills of the vineyard than he had seen her move before, and knew whatever she had to tell him was bad news. *Good news can always wait.*

Without a word, she handed the unopened letter to Jude and braced herself. *Anna had relinquished her soul claim to Bergen Op Meer and was staying in the new land where she was running Ashton's estate.* Jude read it aloud again.

"What did you say? What has she done? What is she thinking?" Batina's mind spun. Even the gentle hand that now rested on her shoulder to calm her had no effect.

"She is a grown and fiercely independent woman, my love. Anna and Ashton would have discussed this matter in depth." Jude and Batina stood in silence, each deep within the turmoil of their own thoughts. *I want them to come home,* thought Batina.

The estate had been kept in pristine condition. The harvest would be a celebration of all that had eventually risen from the ashes. Jude's hands had healed under the tender ministrations of Batina's care. *The inside was a different matter.* Jude kept his innermost feelings behind well guarded walls. This thought, and a few others, unsettled his mind at night. *Yet even he was not able to protect them from themselves.*

To give the newlyweds their space, Damian had taken up residence in the Gate House. He walked the halls as a lonely man for years. Eventually, his only company was Captain's Jock Smit's daughter, Gata, who came to cook and clean. She was a dear girl with a warm heart. Batina had witnessed them in companionable conversation on the grounds through the years and this pleased both Jude and Batina. *No man should be alone,* thought Batina.

Damian and Gata with great joy were soon raising a child who Batina was certain should be carrying the Malefyt name. Batina and Anna had no doubt the babe was Damian's and therefore deserving of the family protection. *Oh, how complicated we can make our lives,* Batina often thought.

In her letter Anna wanted the Gate House, and all its contents, signed over to the child. *This was so typical of Anna. "I have also contacted the solicitor, and have been assured that adequate stewardship of the art collection, in which I have no real interest, will be handled professionally through the auction house. This way many can enjoy their beauty,"* Anna added in her letter.

A sizable figure would be awarded to Jude and Batina, the balance to be kept in trust to manage the estate until she could talk some sense into her twin brother. As per her letter, she had indicated she would not return without Ashton at her side. Even this seemed like a radical decision to Batina. Her intuition told her there was much more to Anna's decision than just Ashton's choices.

Jude Wolf felt the loss so deep within him. Roots wound through his soul and tied him to the children he had considered his very own.

The estate's finest treasures had been placed up for auction and his services may no longer be needed. A few weeks later, with his Sunday suit neatly pressed, as Batina had seen to it, he made his way into what he referred to as *gentleman's land* and entered the queue outside the auction house. With a fist full of his savings safely tucked into an inner pocket.

Though all the priceless paintings would be auctioned eventually, he had his heart set on only one. The painting Anna had done with her own hand of Ashton was being auctioned in the first round that day. The rest mattered little to him.

In the beginning Batina was devastated by the loss of her charges. Jude had done his best to console her and from his kindness their relationship had budded into an unexpected joy for them both. They had each other now. For him, it was enough. He planned on surprising her with the painting on her next birthday. By then they may no longer be living on the estate and she could hang it in the cottage that he planned to build for her on his family's land. It seemed it was time to return to his beginnings.

Making his way into a seat at the back that could barely hold his large frame, Jude held in his scarred and calloused hands the detailed list of priceless artefacts of the Malefyt Family that would soon be in the hands of the many collectors who had come from the four corners like hungry wolves to the prey. He was relieved to see that he would have very little time to wait as the first item was the painting he was here to purchase. Priceless to him but worthless to these collectors.

This auction house had been the establishment generations of Malefyts had used for their purchases and the experts on hand knew the artefacts well. Even to Jude the starting bids seemed generous. However he failed to see why the starting bid for the simple painting Anna had done of Ashton was valued so high. *Had he even enough in his pocket to cover a quarter of the estimated value?* Jude began to sweat.

The house came to silence as the auctioneer removed the cover of the first item and bidding started at "$5,000." No takers. Sweat trickled down Jude's back. "$4000." Still no takers. Sweat began to bead on his forehead. "$3000," and the room remained silent except for the impatient rustling of the booklet pages. *These jackals were here for the masterpieces.*

Jude hoped the auctioneer would see the painting for what it was and lower the bidding just far enough that fortune would smile on him and end this painful experience. He did not have long to wait.

The auctioneer turned to the director. With a nod from him, the starting bid was dropped. "$1000." Jude shot from his seat and yelled "sold". The place erupted in gales of laughter, but the auctioneer was having none of it. Over and over he banged the gavel until the room settled down into order once again. The sweat was now openly pouring down Jude's face in neat rows showing his obvious embarrassment.

"Are there any more bids? Are there any more bids?", bang down went the gavel "indeed SOLD to the gentleman of a discerning eye. Would you be so kind as to meet with our Director immediately? This entire auction has now been concluded."

Jude did not have to be told twice. Hastily he made his way along the row of seated auction goers to the indicated destination with great relief, hoping that Batina would truly enjoy the gift. It had come at a cost he would not want to ever have to pay again.

Jude sat in the opulent office waiting for the painting to be brought to him. But what the elegantly dressed Director said passed simply over his head. His words seemed out of order, the meaning too strange. Jude's pulse began to rise. The beating of his heart drowned out any true meaning of the words.

"The entire collection is now in your care, my dear fellow," he said. "I know this is difficult to grasp. Jacobus Malefyt felt this was the only way to ensure his children and future generations would have access and ownership of the priceless artefacts that other collectors had wanted to acquire from the family for generations. And so, he knew the buyer of his greatest possession, the painting his only daughter had lovingly crafted with her own hand of his beloved son, could become the only worthy steward."

This man had no idea how crazy this all sounded, thought Jude. *Yes, it is true, Master Jacobus had shown love for his daughter, but there was never a time, not once, that he had seen him show loving care towards his son. And what was this man saying? Were not the other items now being auctioned off?*

It was at this moment that Jude realised there was a high level of shouting coming from the main auction room just outside the office's heavy double doors. The sounds were those more resembling a brawl. *What madness was this?* "STOP!!!" Bang went the two large, scarred hands on the priceless, antique desk.

The Director was certain the massive man before him would do him no harm. He was relieved that the huge, solid oak desk stood between them, however.

"My good Fellow, let us calm ourselves." Percival Waters III was from a long line of auctioneers. He was not going to be the one that permitted their impeccable reputation to carry any stain. "Allow me to explain. There have been attempts through the millennia to acquire through various means, some dubious, the priceless items that have been in the Malefyt family for hundreds of years. These art collectors outside my door have no idea of the true item of value that you now must continue to shelter. The collection listed on the auction card today is a ruse. A deflection from a treasure that the family has owned for over one thousand years."

Percival knew this was a lot to take in; his patience would know no bounds for this gentle giant. He simply waited, relaxed and calm, hands folded neatly over the front of his waist coat.

Oh, how Jude wished this man would speak to him in ways he could understand. Nothing was making any sense to him. All he truly wanted now was to give Batina a simple home of her own.

"Mr Wolf, are you familiar with a tea set that the family possesses? At first glance it appears white, but it has a subtle blue tinge. When one holds the almost transparent, delicate cup up to the light, at the base one can see a star." Percival's father had only seen the set once. It was a day he told his namesake he would never forget. His Father, and his father before him, had kept the existence of the set a well guarded secret to be passed on only when the information was needed to be known to a new bearer. Today was such a day, and he could hardly contain his joy. If he could bring this man around to placing the set up for auction, Percival Waters III would be heralded a champion, never to be forgotten as the one that finally brought the priceless ancient set back into the public eye for the art world to anxiously bid on.

Jude knew of only one way to deal with matters that seemed out of his control. *Wait.* The truth would reveal itself. So, with patience born of a lifetime accepting the Lord's guidance, he waited. As his mind began to clear, he realised he had in fact seen one of the teacups on the day the young master Damien had tried to drink his sorrows away.

Percival could see dawning on the silent face of the man in front of him that he knew of the set. "Yes," was the only word he could get out. All Jude wanted was for his world to go back to normal.

"Miss Anna Malefyt's solicitor has informed us of the ancient protection placed on the set. Through the bizarre circumstances you and I find ourselves in today, the owner of the painting you purchased now has the responsibility for it. What I mean by this is that the secrecy must continue, and in turn protect the Malefyt descendants. When the set is brought to auction, it is then that this auction house may be rewarded, and not a day before." Percival was honoured to be entrusted with this delicate matter. He hoped that he would see the day the true auction could take place, but today it sounded more like a crime scene in the making was unfolding outside his office door.

When the painting was finally brought in, Jude stood as if in a daze. Leaving the entire amount of notes in his pocket on the desk, he picked up the painting and proceeded to walk to the nearest door.

"Mr Wolf, excuse me, Mr Wolf?" Jude reluctantly turned and saw the wall open to reveal a passageway to a quiet adjoining room.

"Thank you. I will be with my wife later today. I think it would be more suitable for you to visit us with the solicitor so we can sort this whole matter out. For now I have what I came for." With a dignity Jude did not know he exuded, he left through the exit offered.

Chapter TWENTY NINE

T *ea anyone?*

The story broke in the following morning's papers. "Collectors Robbed by Auction House". The European art world could speak of nothing else for months. The auction house took it all in good conscience, standing firm that "due to legal matters tying the collection to the Malefyt Family, the auction house was acting honourably." That was all they would say.

Batina sat in stunned silence later that afternoon as she took in the tale Jude was sharing with her. She believed him only when he presented her with an early birthday gift. The portrait was immediately placed back on the wall that it had only been recently removed from.

"Incredible, simply incredible. What is going to be our fate tomorrow, lievelling?" She said.

Jude could always count on his sweet one to bring the moment into a space of some kind of normality. She was right. They would let today be enough and face tomorrow's outcomes head on.

Batina and Jude took the liberty of meeting the solicitors from Hammer and Hammer, along with the auction house representative Jude had met the day before, in the library of Bergen Op Meer. Batina had outdone herself, having adequately prepared to serve high tea.

First Jude wanted answers.

"You will see my good fellow, from the documents that we have brought with us today, that Mistress Malefyt simply cannot sell the collection. It is not hers to sell. Though the estate was in fact hers, as her brother was believed to be dead and Damien Malefyt had no legal descendants, there is a protection clause created by Jacobus Malefyt just before he died which is legal and binding. We saw no need to bring this delicate matter to Miss Anna's attention until she had adequate time to mourn her esteemed parent.

The time simply never presented itself before she hastily departed in search of Master Ashton. Matters are even more complex now that we are aware he is very much alive according to the correspondence we have received recently. As we have no reason to doubt her, we are here today to clear up this matter with you in the hopes you can talk some sense into the Malefyt heirs." The Senior Mr Hammer tugged on his waistcoat unnecessarily to remove any folds to emphasise his point.

"She has indicated in her letter to us that protection for your futures is to be immediately implemented. That we have now done as she does have complete authority over this matter.

Miss Anna has also indicated there is a true descendant of Damien Malefyt currently residing in the Gate House. Provisions have been made for the child and her mother in the event Master Damien Malefyt does not do so himself. She has generously given the land and home to the child. But once again this cannot include any priceless artefacts currently tied to the residence. These are bound to the clause that Jacobus Malefyt added to his will only days before his death.

The Junior Mr Hammer could see that this was becoming far too much to take in for the caretaker. He thought it prudent to let the written words speak for themselves, handing over the thick, leather-bound package to his father, to be then handed on to Mr Wolf.

The Senior Mr Hammer presented Jude with a sizeable booklet of legal pages, all precisely ordered, starting with the explanation of how yesterday's events had now rendered Jude and his descendants honorary stewards over the entire collection until such a time that a direct descendant of Ashton or Anna Malefyt's family claimed ownership. As Miss Anna had herself legally indicated what was to become of the grounds and estate, Hammer and Hammer rendered this matter also completely in order, as this, too, was within her legal rights, and completed with Master Ashton's knowledge.

In awe Percival Waters III watched in fascination as the humble tea was poured into what he believed could be a priceless cup. With trepidation he slowly drained the contents between discussion and decadent cakes. When the contents had been consumed, he lifted the delicate cup to the light and gasped, gaining him the attention of everyone in the room.

Batina had held the firm belief that if you were going to keep a valuable treasure safe, keep it in plain view at all times. This is precisely what she had done with these tea cups all these years.

The legend of the tea cups was made known to her quite by accident. The two brothers had been arguing over the set. Mistress Johanna had overheard them and was so troubled by the argument, she had fainted. Heavy with pregnancy Johanna was seen to by Batina. As soon as she had recovered, her ward made an odd request to have her journal retrieved. Batina sent a maid off to retrieve it and return it to her. She remained at Johanna's bedside. Later that evening, as Johanna had slept, the journal was left open and Batina read the words she often wished she had never seen. *I do not want my children to be torn apart by those six cups. Those ancient pieces need to be destroyed. I will find a way as soon as I am able, and Batina will help me. She denies me nothing.* The words had remained as though branded into her mind. Johanna never got the chance to have the set destroyed. In time Batina was to discover why the last words to be written by her mistress spoke of this matter. The identical brothers had masterminded the unthinkable. It all had to do with this priceless and protected heirloom of six cups and saucers.

The rightful owner of the legendary set was to be Damien Malefyt, although this was now in question. Adequate proof was in the solicitors' possession that showed the set could very well belong to either Damien or Jacobus Malefyt.

Percival, with reluctance, placed the object of his fascination on the offered tray. "Mrs Wolf, I see five cups in the service. Tell me, are all six cups in your possession?"

Perplexity creased the brow of his dear wife who remained silent leaving the response for Jude to complete. "Why yes, Sir, but how would you come to know that six cups exist?"

The Senior Mr Hammer cleared his throat and all eyes turned to the document he held up. A letter addressed to Hammer and Hammer stated that: *I Damien Malefyt relinquished all entitlement of the entire set of six cups and saucers to the descendants of Johanna Heath Malefyt,* signed and sealed by Damien himself.

"Why would he do such a thing when the set was rightfully his?" Percival had spoken the words aloud, revealing he knew far more about the set than the others in the room. "You see, dear Lady and fine gentlemen, there is a record of this set being passed on to the eldest of the Malefyt family for over 1000 years. Before this, the recorded documentation has been lost. The set is believed to be in the vicinity of 1,500 years old. These delicate and priceless cups and saucers were masterfully crafted as a commemorative gift in celebration of the good news the Magi brought to the nations of the birth of Christ. Their worth is beyond measure."

Chapter THIRTY

M*illicent confesses at The Gate House.*
It was years ago that she had buried the old sea chest with all the journals safely inside. For a time she had completely forgotten about the whole matter and had simply got on with life.

When she had seen the name *Mr Tony King & Mrs Hannah King, New Zealand Guests* in the registry that morning, she had briefly wondered if there was a chance and finally decided to tell her parents what she had done. "Mumma, Puppa, I have to explain something to you and it may come as a shock. Please come sit down," indicating the two comfy chairs by the fire. Anita and Wim looked at each other and braced themselves. Their daughter had never given them any worry to date and they often wondered at their good fortune. Maybe this moment was going to explain why things had always gone so well. *Had their daughter been hiding something?*

"Whatever it is, daughter of my heart, we will work through the matter together." Wim hoped that his words reassured her. He did start to feel his heart work a little fast and did sit down right away. Indicating Anita should sit also, they both watched as their daughter formulated the words.

"Do you remember when I went WWOOFing in New Zealand?" Millicent stood before them uncharacteristically blushing.

"Yes. Go on." Wim could not believe that this beautiful woman standing before him wringing her hands could do anything that would be all that serious.

"Darling, we are here for you, no matter what." Anita was beginning to think her daughter may have gone away to have a baby.

"Do you remember when Oma fell suddenly ill?"

Both of them affirmed they did, nodding their heads. They kept their eyes focused on their daughter.

"Well, you see, I was taking care of Oma, and one night when I was putting her Bible back on the shelf," she stopped to take a breath, "I found something very interesting." She looked at her parents intently to see if they too may know anything about the things hidden in Oma's private sanctuary.

"Yes, go on." Anita was truly relieved.

"I discovered Johanna Malefyt's journals and I read them all." Once she started, the words poured out.

"There are six of them. I never told Oma I had them, as I thought they simply would not be missed. This was the reason I went to New Zealand though. The journals led me to a family by the name of Heath. This was the family I remained with for the year, as they needed help with the children who hold the surname King." She looked at the joint disappointed expressions of her parents and waited.

"My Dear, yes, I am disappointed in you. Those journals are for Oma alone to oversee, and no else until her passing. I do not know what you were thinking. But the question remains, why do you tell us this now?" Anita asked. Wim was not surprised at his daughter's actions. She had always had a protective nature and he could understand her thinking.

"Well, you see... the children I cared for are in fact direct descendants of the Malefyt family. Their names are Tony and Hannah King." The room emptied of all air.

"And you knew this all these years?" Anita was very hurt. "Are you sure?"

"Oh, yes. I am sorry, Mumma and Puppa. You know why I said nothing. Surely you can understand, please?" Millicent looked into the eyes of her parents and hoped.

"Millicent, this is too much to take in all at once. We need to keep clear heads and explain all of this to Oma as soon as possible. Goodness knows what this will do to her, but she is a very wise woman and will handle the matter with her usual grace. Undoubtedly she will want the journals back." Wim was always the practical parent and he did not fail her now.

Anita was now seething. "And you tell us this now because of the couple that is due to arrive tomorrow?"

"Well, there is a little more." Looking frightened, she continued. "I buried the journals."

"You did what? Why?" Anita looked shocked. Wim sat in confusion.

"I did not want the truth to come out. I have always felt guilty that our home is secure, and Kat and Massy have had to live under this cloud of what ifs. Oma has had too much tragedy in her life and I wanted to protect them. When I found all the documents in an old sea chest pointing directly to the truth and the heir to Bergen Op Meer, I buried them on their property. They are loved, Mumma, and want for nothing." Her shoulders dropped and she plopped down on the kitchen stool and waited.

"Oh, my girl, what have you done? These are people's lives you are controlling. This is wrong. I have always trusted, and so has Oma, that one day the balance will be completely reestablished. How I do not know, but love always finds a way." Anita had never once doubted this. "I can understand your motive, but I do not condone your actions. How will we ever get those journals back to Oma?" Her dark mood showed on her face.

"Let's not be too harsh, lieveling." Wim placed his hand gently on Anita's shoulder. "As you say, these things have their own way of working out. If you are sure there is an heir, my dear Girl, then I know Oma would be ready to hear all you have to say. We can trust her."

"Yes, I agree," Anita consulted her ever-present watch and counted down a few seconds to allow her temper to calm. "It is late. Leaving this for another day will make no difference. Tomorrow is a very busy day for us all. Let's get some sleep; this always helps." Standing, Anita opened her arms for her daughter, and with great relief, Millicent stepped into her tiny mother's big embrace.

Though the guilt over what she had done was now at the surface, Millicent knew, having the choice again, she would have done nothing different.

The next morning, from her hidden viewpoint in the kitchen, she could see that Hannah had grown into the beautiful woman she always knew she would. Her grace was ever present and little Tony was not so little anymore. *Hehehehe.* She had seen his breakfast order and made it herself. Was she ready to be seen by them? *Not a chance.*

Later that week, her mother found her hiding away. "What do you mean? Everything has now come out in the open? Hannah will inherit. They are all working out the details now. Oma looks relieved. You need to show yourself and apologise. Get on with it." Millicent listened to her logical Mumma, but knew that she could not face anyone just yet.

"I have no intention of making myself known. I expect you and Puppa to keep this also to yourself. You said Oma did not question how the journals got to New Zealand and the rightful heir is now here. All is as it should be. I am so ashamed. I simply cannot face anyone yet." Millicent looked panic stricken. "I need to get away for a while."

"And so she packed up and left." Anita finished telling a very sad husband that his daughter needed time away.

"Oh." Wim was devastated.

"When she is ready, her head will be held high and she will apologise. She has a courageous heart." Anita was sure of it.

Hannah looked forward to her weekly call with Tony. The news was explosive and she was excited to reveal what had happened. "Tony, are you sitting down? I know who V.R. and M.L. are."

Silence.

"Tony, are you there? Did you hear what I said? I met V.R. today. He will be treating me at his clinic in Vancouver later this month. He specialises in treatment for injuries like mine." Hannah's joy was beginning to sink a little.

More silence. "Charlotte and I found newspaper clippings in Uncle Jonty's things. Did you meet Dr. Vaun Rainbird?" Tony felt so sad. All he truly wanted was for the past to remain where it belonged.

"Why yes. Tony, why are you so sad?" Hannah could hear by his tone he was.

"Well, I would prefer all of that to remain way back there. Those were really hard times, Sis." Tony could not expect her to understand.

"He is going to help me, Tons. I have a fighting chance now, all because of Uncle Jonty. Be happy for me." Now Hannah sounded sad.

"I am, Banana, I am. I wish our lives had been different. This hurts all over again." Charlotte had been a great help and listened to all he had to say, but he still felt beaten up inside.

"Kat is all packed and will have a stopover in Vancouver. Why not meet her there? It will take your mind off things." She hoped talking about Kat's arrival would cheer him up.

"Man, I am looking forward to seeing her. The place looks great. I could not have done it without Charlotte. If Kat and I get going on the rest of the files and business matters right away, there will be time to show her around. That will keep her away from the Bros, too." Tony laughed and his heart felt lighter.

"Nice, good idea. Give it some thought Tons. I am told Vancouver is a great city and you could use a break. Did you want me to find Kat and you could have a word?" Hannah thought she needed to keep the momentum going.

"No, all good. I am off to practise. I have a copy of her itinerary here and plan to be in Auckland to pick her up. That is great that Dr Rainbird and you hit it off. I am hoping everything works out, but Hannah, are you okay if there is no change? I just don't want you to be let down again." Tony felt very protective of his sister.

"Sure, I feel hopeful. I would not be human if I wasn't, but I need to try. Massy and I have read some of the case studies and there have been some remarkable breakthroughs with their patients. He has been a trooper. Tons, if I could have children and Massy would have me, he would be the one I choose." Revealing this to Tony was the right thing to do.

"Oh, Sis, he adores you. Have you told him how you feel?" Tony liked having the focus off him.

"No way!" Hannah was not going to budge on this point.

"Okay, okay, I hear you. Off I go, Hannah Banana, love you. Let's talk again soon." Tony saw his teammates driving up and had to go.

"Bye, Tons, love you too." Hannah placed the receiver back in the cradle and went in search of Kat.

Tony did like the idea of changing his plans and meeting Kat in Vancouver. Timing wise it was perfect. He would stop at the travel agent after practice and check out his options.

Chapter THIRTY ONE

My meeting with M.L.

Muck, Casey, G.Dub, Owen and Bucky had survived life on the street to this point as a pack. Matt was determined to help these boys and the many more who came to the club each day to recover from their circumstances and have a chance for a better life. Year after year he saw their hardened faces and weighed down shoulders when they arrived. Most of them felt they were to blame for the abuse and troubles they faced daily; some even thought they deserved it. Guilt was a heavy load to bear for most of them.

Over time, with firm but fair encouragement each boy that chose to stay on the city rugby team, and most did, gained a sense of belonging. Some of the boys had gone on to play on scholarships; some had made pro. Others took different paths, and that was okay, too. What mattered to Matt was that they made their own good choices, and left their old way of life and thinking behind.

Matt's passion for rugby spread as the boys in his care came to know the game as well as he did. Little did they know that playing rugby became his lifeline all those years ago, when he needed a reason to live.

The boys had been given a big-screen TV for the club room. When the World Cup was on, everyone would come back to watch. The place would fill up. GasTown Pizza would be brought in, and a sense of family bonded them all as brothers. This was a time for those that had moved on with their lives to return, and were happy to tell their stories too.

G.Dub knew everything about the players on the big screen. His mind was sharp. Stats, caps, tests, he knew it all. He had a special interest in the New Zealand teams and followed players he thought would make the All Black squad.

Kat's flight was on schedule. She was glad to be on her way. When Tony had contacted her about meeting her in Vancouver and extending her stopover, she was pleasantly surprised. "Sure, I would love to explore the area. Who knows when I will have a chance to get there again. I have always wanted to see Vancouver Island, too. Do you think we can fit that in?"

"Sure, no problem. I will rent a car and we will be our own tour guides. There is a ferry that we can catch. My buddy Nicky Fitzpatrick has a cabin on the beach in a place called Salt Air. He has been telling me for years to come and stay there. I will contact him now. If you are willing to rough it a little, it should be fun."

"That sounds perfect." Kat paused. "Tony, I have missed you."

Tony took a moment to respond. "I am not that great at saying what's inside me, Kat, but I can tell you this. Your coming here matters to me, a lot." There, Tony had said it.

"That is really nice to hear." The glow from within Kat caused her to blush. "I had best let you get on with your day. I am sure you have lots to do. The rest we can take care of when I get there."

Phew, Tony was glad she knew. "Right, right you are. See you soon."

Kat was walking on air. *Is this how it felt to fall?* She wanted to make sure she was not infatuated with the idea of how much Tony looked like Ashton Malefyt but instead liked Tony for who he is. This was the main reason she had agreed to go.

Tony's flight got in at 6.00am. Kat's was not scheduled to arrive until 7.00 o'clock in the evening. He would get the rental car and make it to the rugby club and back before she arrived. He had personal matters to deal with and he didn't want anything to get in the way of his time with Kat. After Hannah had told him about meeting Vaun, sounding so happy and peaceful, Tony knew he also had to find peace. *It was time.*

He had taken all the information Hannah had given him, read all that he and Charlotte had found. It did not take him long to find out all he could about Matt Lacelle. *The man was a saint.*

He had received all kinds of awards for his social and humanitarian work. *Uncle Jonty would have been proud of him.*

Tony had called the Inner City Rugby Club Matt was associated with and was told he was on the field with the boys for the day. *Perfect,* thought Tony, *they probably won't even know I am there.*

The boys were all shapes, sizes, ages and cultures and they played with passion. The man coaching them knew what he was doing. As Tony watched from the sidelines, something in him began to break free. That age-old anger that he thought was under control reared its ugly head. *What is wrong with me?*

G.Dub saw him first. "What the hell."

"Gabriel Dubeaux, 10 minutes in the sin bin for that." Matt was strict. He knew that if he let language slide, there would be no stopping what could be the next words out of his mouth, or worse.

"Coach, look. That's Tony King, what the hell is he doing here?" G.Dub pointed at the large man standing at the other end of the field. The other boys started to take notice.

"Enough, that's 20 minutes, and your last warning." Matt was beginning to feel like he was losing control of the practice. G.Dub did not move. "Okay, tell me who Tony King is. I am listening. You have sixty seconds."

"What!!! You don't know who he is?" G.Dub hung his head, shaking it side to side in disbelief.

Matt looked down the field. "Tony King, you say, no I..." The words trailed away and his gut hit the field. "Holy crap."

Bucky, standing always at his mate's side, had never heard his Coach use language like that before. "What just happened? Does that mean Coach gets 10 minutes in the sin bin too?" he asked G.Dub.

"Go ask him if he is here to play." Matt had no idea why he said that to the young boy watching him.

"Sure, the boys and I would love to have a go at him." Bucky sprinted down the field.

Tony stood there in the silent heat that was rising from within as one of the youths who had been talking with Matt Lacelle ran down the field towards him. The rage inside him was now larger than he had ever felt. Tony turned to walk away.

"Hey, Mister. Want to step into the game with us boys? You're Tony King, aren't you? G.Dub told the coach it was you." Bucky was a complete extrovert and had no fear. He just stood there and waited. "Coach looks like he has seen a ghost. Haha, kinda funny really. My name is Bucky." He held out his hand.

The lad did not know it but his innocent words broke the dam inside Tony. "Sure, as long as <u>he</u> plays." Tony took his hand and shook.

Bucky did not like the way this big brute of a guy said '*he*'. There was a threat there. Calling over the other players who were watching the exchange, Bucky told them who Tony was. They stood there and looked at him as though he was a superhero. It's true, Tony King was impressive, but Matt Lacelle mattered more to them. Bucky felt a loyalty for their coach that spread up his back like a ridge of protection.

"He'll play if Coach steps on the field too. What do you boys think?" As always they made their decisions together. Excitement went through the group and they all agreed. "Muck, go take the news to Coach."

Nothing would stop Tony now from stepping onto the field. He removed his suit jacket and took off his tie, leaving them neatly folded on the edge of the field with his socks and shoes. *Game on.*

Matt knew this day would come. If he had any say, it would not be such a public event, but fate had not been on his side for a while. Who was he kidding? *God had left him long ago in that prison.*

He watched as the mountain of a man removed his shoes. Hundreds of times before, Matt had seen in the boys he mentored the same energy he could feel coming off Tony King even at this distance. The kind that came from being tormented.

"Coach, he wants you to step into the game." Muck looked up at Matt expectantly.

Pausing just briefly. "Sure. Let him kick." Matt knew that giving Tony a sense of control would help him right now.

Tony was on fire from the inside out. From all the years of trying to keep it in check on the field, only a seasoned player would know he was without fear and had one mission, to take out Matt Lacelle. Placing all his integrity on the shelf and risking his reputation, he stepped onto the field. Words Uncle

Jonty had said came clearly to mind. *'Fear only the Lord Tony, and be prepared to live with the consequences of fearless choices.'* After all the excitement died down, the teams lined up and Tony released the ball right into the hands of his target. He started his charge.

Matt's first instinct was to run with the ball. *So why am I just standing here?*

Casey knew right away Coach was in trouble. His instincts kicked into overdrive. With the speed of lightning he caught up to and jumped on the back of the fast-moving train that was headed right for the man he loved most in life. Muck, G.Dub, Bucky and Little Dougy soon followed as the pack tried to slow Tony down. *There was no way.* Tony was unstoppable.

As Tony ran down the field with four of the boys dangling off him, Owen, too, tried to stop the collision but he just bounced off the huge moving mass, Matt waited.

The impact was going to hurt and he was glad. He had every intention of absorbing it. Tony King needed him. It was the least he could do. The mass of body parts on impact could for a time not be untangled.

Casey was suffocating under the weight of the players on top of him. But he did not want to release the iron hold he had on Tony's neck. From somewhere in the depths of the pile he heard Coach say, "I am okay boys, you can get off him."

Little by little Tony was uncovered. "Is he dead? Did we kill him?" Owen always had a way with words.

Tony was embarrassed and was reluctant to show his face. He rolled to the side and gave Matt some breathing space. "You okay, Mate?" He said.

Matt began to laugh. Not sure if he should move yet, he lay there flat on his back looking up at all the faces staring down at him. "All good boys, give us a minute."

Muck was the sensitive one of the bunch. When the penny dropped, he motioned for all the boys to back away and give the two men room. They had something to work out.

"Hi, Tony." Matt did not turn to him.

Tony lay still at Matt's side. He had no idea what to say. Matt waited. One good thing, though, Tony's anger was gone. That place was empty. The shock of sadness that filled him now was so great, he wanted to run away as far and as fast as he could, but he couldn't move. The sky above pinned him to the ground. Matt finally turned his head to the side and witnessed the pain of a boy. "Want to tell me what happened?"

Out poured the words. "I wanted to go to the game. It was dangerous and my parents knew it. But I just would not give up." Tony was living that day all over again. *The noise of the crowd, his Mum's voice reassuring him, his sister unafraid and Dad, oh Dad....*

Matt was stunned. *Oh God, he has thought all these years he was to blame.* For the first time in a very long time the guard over Matt's heart began to release some of its tension. "Tony?" Matt waited for Tony to turn his face to him.

Slowly Tony turned his head from the blue sky above and looked into the compassionate eyes of a kind-hearted man. A light shone from them into his own soul.

"The accident was not your fault." Matt said. In that moment he released them both from all the guilt that had crippled them since the day Johanna and Alvan King had died.

Tony sat up and placed his face on his knees hidden from view. His shoulders began to shake. He did not want anyone to see him cry. Matt understood but felt no need to hide his tears. They flowed freely down his face for all to see. He no longer had anything to hide. He was finally free. Tony's release was his too. The boys watched in absolute silence as the scene before them continued to unfold.

What now? thought Tony.

Wiping his eyes on his sleeve, he looked over and saw Matt for the first time, through the eyes of a new inner calm.

Getting to his feet was not an issue, as Tony was used to being banged about. Matt was not so capable. "Need a hand up, Mate?" Tony offered his hand and placed his other under the shoulder of the man still lying flat on his back.

Matt practically flew up into standing position without using a single muscle of his own devices, while Tony still had the ability to pick up the ball as well. After steadying himself, Matt filled the awkward moment. "I owe you a long overdue apology."

"My Uncle would want you to be forgiven and so do I." Tony held out his hand and Matt took it and pulled him in for a bear hug. Though Tony was big, Matt was not a small man either. Matt held the boy safe in his arms for as long as needed.

"Thanks, Tony, that matters more than you know." As they pulled away, Matt was curious "Your Uncle, why is that?"

"He was your sponsor." Tony was proud of Uncle Jonty and this could be heard in his statement.

"My sponsor?" Matt's brows wrinkled in thought.

"Yup. You, Vaun, me and Hannah, we all had a guardian Uncle." Tony had an impish grin that spread across his face and shot from his eyes.

"You mean to say that your Uncle, the guy who raised you two, is the same guy that paid for all those expenses and years of schooling for me and Vaun?" Matt could not believe it.

"He is the one." Nodding his head in affirmation, a smile that started from Tony's heart spread on his face and he shone.

"Excuse me, mister, can we have the ball please? There is not much daylight left and we need to practise." Dougy, the smallest guy on the team with the biggest heart and never short on courage, handed Tony his jacket, tie, shoes and socks, offering a trade.

"Sure, Lad." Tony had not even realised he was holding it.

"All good?" Tony looked at Matt after tying his laces and waited, knowing that he needed to be making his way to the airport to pick up Kat.

"Oh, yah, we're all good Mate." The smile on Matt's face was genuine. Tony was glad.

Chapter THIRTY TWO

1819 *Lions Vineyard in the new villa.*

Anna loved her son to distraction at times. Tony had finished the villa in the spring of 1819 and they lived happily as a family, often seeing Rawiri at their table. These were enjoyable times. Koraka was getting into everything and had the most extraordinary protective nature, as though he was born to it. Anna appreciated any help she could get from Rawiri. "Kory, come see the new sheep." Anna watched as Koraka made his way on steady feet to the fence rail. With glee he laughed at the sight. Mother and son relished the joys of new life and a warm, sunny spring day before heading back to the ever-constant chores to be completed.

"Uppee" Raising his hands to his mother when it was time to go, Kory tried one more time to charm her into carrying him back.

"No, my little warrior, God gave you two strong legs to carry you, come." Anna turned from the object of her deep affection. Kory tried several times a day to be taken here and there in her arms and promptly fell asleep. *What a clever lad,* Anna thought.

"Noooooo, com, Kee com." Kory tore after Anna with determination, even though she was merely a few steps ahead of him. Tony was just returning from assisting with the work on the new wooden Church and stone buildings at the Mission and was sitting at his joyful leisure watching his sister and nephew make their way back through the vineyard from the paddocks. He was certain Anna was attempting to tire Kory. Their little man had enough energy to go strong for an entire day non-stop. When he did stop, he slept like a bear in hibernation.

"Kia ora, and hello, you two. What has occupied your day?" Tony was glad Anna had decided to stay on and it always showed.

"Kia ora, brother." Sweeping up her little charge, Anna ran the last few steps and placed a kiss on Tony's upturned cheek. "We have seen the new sheep and inspected the work on the stone outbuilding. Paulo will be under his own roof in no time," Anna informed Tony with a grin.

Paulo Santos had moved back in before Tony had arrived, after the sinking of their Uncle's ship. Talbot Heath had included a space for his long-time shipmate on his land. Over time a type of peace one could call a truce with boundaries was called between Tony and Paulo.

Though Tony's one time shipmate had been kind to Anna, Tony could not find it in his heart to trust him, so he decided keeping him close was best. Anna had tried to convince Tony to forgive him and make a more permanent home for him. So far the sailor had not shown any sign of his old self. Tony had this gut feeling though. He had no intention of letting his guard fully down. Kory had not warmed to him either and Tony trusted his nephew implicitly.

Anna was endlessly kind to Paulo, including him in meals and sharing happy memories of their life as children at Bergen Op Meer. He in turn filled their evenings with harrowing tales of adventure at sea, tall tales of him and Captain Tally sailing through rough seas and enjoying many seafaring years together. Tony was always glad that he kept his adventures from being too dark or not proper for Anna to be hearing. *That did give Paulo one plus mark in his favour,* thought Tony.

"Captain Tally never truly embraced the killing we did, but money does strange things to a man. Trading with the locals got him a foothold here on this land," Paulo said, pointing to the ground at their feet at the outdoor fire pit. "He always wanted to have his sister join him. Family was everything to him. He was making this into a legacy to pass on to you." Paulo shared this news with a head nod towards Tony. "And now look, here you are enjoying a life with a path ahead that has no end. You have all a man would ever want." Paulo looked out at all the land around them and marvelled.

Paulo was content with his life but Anna was sure Tony wanted a family of his own. "But what about faith and all the other things we all need?" Anna was always thinking of everyone's social and wellbeing needs. "We need the Lord, each other, enough food for everyone and to all be equal citizens, Paulo. There is so much more. Do you know that I have less rights than you three?"

The four sets of eyes looking at her stared in fascination. Rawiri, Tony, Paulo and Kory, were all good listeners. "Being a woman is, in many ways, a gift that I thank God for, but I do not see man's wisdom in not allowing me to vote. We are all equal to the Creator, aren't we?"

Tony could see that Anna was passionate about equality and passing on the Lord's message. He had to admit that it was unbalanced that she could be a property owner but have no say over the governance of the land. "I hear you, Anna Banana. The question is, what can be done about it?" Popping the last heated biscuit in his mouth, Tony chewed and waited for the response he knew would come.

Anna could always rely on Tony to come around to the matter at hand. She needed to think this through. "Hmmm, you're right. I will take this little warrior of mine and get him all settled in and consult with my journal." Anna reached out to take Kory from the comfy lap of his Uncle.

"Nooooooo, Kee stay wit Unc Toee." Kory held on tight to his Uncle's neck. Tony tried to dislodge his nephew, to no avail. Anna knew how to deal with this. Artfully placing her tickling fingers in just the right spots soon left the tot in gales of laughter and unable to hold on any longer. Off mother and son went inside leaving the sweet sound echoing in Tony's ear.

Paulo had slipped away unnoticed before the warm tender moment had come to a full end. He tolerated them most days because he needed them, but some moments just became too much for him. The young Miss was taking a slow and steady hold of his heart and Paulo was not at all sure if he wanted this. She had been the first woman he had ever known who wanted nothing from him but for him to receive her kindness. Paulo knew that, had he been closer to God, he was sure this is how a loving father would want his children to be. Kind, generous and strong. Willing to give without thought of measure. The sea had been his nurturing mother. To have a flesh and blood female take any space in his heart was foreign to him.

The stone dwelling that was being built on the land would be perfect for Paulo's plans. Life with Captain Tally had been lucrative for him. Until he could find safe passage to move all his gold, *the next best thing was having them think I belonged.* Paulo had even considered helping with the work on the building from time to time. He could see Tally's nephew didn't trust him. *That one was sharp. He shouldn't trust me. And that little orphan is just as bad,* thought Paulo.

Paulo had been watching for his chance to pop Malefyt off. He would then convince the locals the Health land was now his. *It shouldn't be too difficult,* he thought. Things got complicated when Miss Anna arrived.

Maybe it was time to buy my own ship and captain it across the Seven Seas. Paulo liked the thought so much, he began to plan how he could start mustering sailors. Buying a ship and paying for a crew was not going to be an issue.

Later that evening, when all was quiet, Anna found Tony enjoying the glow of a full moon so bright he could read a book by its light. The stars filled all the other spaces in the sky and the night was a true show of creation's glory. "Anna, I have been informed of a sickness spreading that has already killed hundreds on the South Island. I insist you and Kory keep a safe distance from the village until whatever this is passes." Tony expected complete compliance from his sibling and this showed in his firm stand on the matter.

"Sickness, Tony, you know I will be called on to help at the Mission Hospital if needed and I will not refuse. How could I when many hands may be needed if this is as bad as you say it is." Anna was going to hold firm on this.

"And what of Kory? If something happens to you, what then?" *Tony had a point.* Thought Anna.

Little did they know that Jude and Batina were holding a very similar conversation also, at Bergen Op Meer. "What of the child, Jude? She is now alone." *And resting peacefully in one of the guest rooms upstairs.* Batina had finally returned to the estate after caring for the residents of the Gate House. The child had not succumbed to the plague, yet both her parents had died within hours of each other. Batina looked exhausted. Jude was concerned she would fall victim also.

"The little one is getting stronger by the day, my Tina, and she is now ours to nurture and love. Other than Captain Jock, we are all she has now." Jude was happy to have a child who they could love as their own. He knew Batina was not young anymore. She often felt the weight of responsibility of Bergen Op Meer. Having a child to raise herself would bring her joy, he was sure of it. "It is time for you to rest. She will need you to get her through this difficult time. Off with you. I will finish up here and will join you soon." Jude turned to the ever-present washing up and rolled up his sleeves.

Batina was happy to surrender. Truth be told she was ready to fall over on her feet. "You have the eyes of a hawk. I will check on the little one. So much loss for someone so small is hard to imagine. I have asked Reginald and Josie to set up a spare bed for me in the child's room. I will be there if she needs me. When you see them tonight, ensure they are reminded to not venture anywhere near the village. We can manage quite nicely with all the stores we have for now. Now that the death toll is decreasing, I am confident the Mission will no longer be needing so much of our supplies also. Good night, man of my heart." After placing a kiss on his weathered cheek, Batina shuffled off.

Reginald van der Land and Josie Doek had been hired at Bergen Op Meer when they were both new to the work. Jude needed more hands to deal with the many tasks that had to be completed each day on such a big estate and was happy to train an apprentice himself.

Batina could manage with day staff but felt a more permanent member on hand was needed also. As she told Josie, "I am not getting any younger," though she had only recently reached the age of forty. Jude and Batina liked having the young staff around. They were lively, hard working and kind. Reginald learnt quickly, could do his sums and found the work rewarding. Josie's many capabilities and firm ways made Batina's burdens lighter. Recently her menses had ceased to flow and change was coming over her that made her feel tired more often. The effects of ageing were happening to Batina whether she had planned for it or not. It did not help that her weight was increasing. She made a mental note to let out some of her sturdier dresses she used for day work as soon as she could. Josie may even be of help on that matter.

When it was obvious to Jude and Batina the young couple were well suited for each other, they simply let nature take its own path. When they fell in love and married, they took over the caretaker's cottage. It was then that Jude and Batina had finally moved permanently into the west wing. At first this move seemed presumptuous but practical thinking won out. They both soon surrendered to the many comforts of their new home. Anna, being of practical mind herself, *would understand the reasoning.* When she returned, it was then the decision would be revisited.

Batina looked down at the tiny child sleeping peacefully beneath the luxurious duvet and knew she belonged here. Little Miss Sophia Debra Smit was now fully under their protection and everything seemed right again. *Now to get her Mistress and Master home to take over the many needs that such a large establishment had on a daily basis.* But for the moment Batina was pleased that both Ashton and Anna had been saved from the outbreak of disease that had taken thousands of lives this year. *Tomorrow I will send a long and convincing letter explaining everything.*

Chapter THIRTY THREE

Who will survive?

Anna was called on within a few days to assist with the many casualties needing care. The Mission Hospital overflowed with sick bodies everywhere. Extra tents had to be erected from the old sails that had been frugally saved. Anna sent a message home to Tony explaining the need for her to stay on and that he would have to take responsibility for Kory, as she would not risk bringing the disease to them. Whatever this was, it attacked the native population with a vengeance and not many of the missionaries seemed to fall ill.

"Well, sport, it looks like it is just you and me now." Tony threw the happy child up into the air and artfully snagged him from his downward fall, repeating the game much to both of their delight.

Ataahau had been surviving on berries and water for the past few weeks. When her people in the south began to fall to the ground at her feet, she had to make the choice of protecting her sister's son or stay and fight the demon that no one could see. Koraka was never far from Ataahau's heart and she could sense a need to be with the boy.

As she stood hidden from view at the edge of the dense forest, she watched the joyful exchange of manhood playing out on the land of Koraka's whānau. *Would she be welcomed?*

Tony suddenly had the strong sense of being watched. "Let's get you settled in, little man." He made his way into the villa and placed Kory securely in his chair along with a healthy helping of raisins, then exited out the back door.

Years of practice came in handy. Tony came up behind the intruder without her knowing. There was obviously no threat. Tony was far more cautious than ever, because he did not want to be dealing with Anna if he put Kory's life in jeopardy. So far the illness that was spreading through the village had yet to touch anyone on his land.

He was pretty sure he had not seen her before. He would have remembered her if he had. She was tall with a regal bearing. "Kia ora!" said Tony. *A simple 'Hello' will do for now.*

She turned in an instant and faced him almost eye to eye. Obviously unafraid but wary.

"Tēnā koe. Hello" Ataahau responded without fear. "The child is my sister's son. He needs me. I know his whaea whāngai is in the village and will not bring the illness to him. She is a strong warrior woman. I am here to help. I carry no illness with me." Ataahau waited in silence.

Tony believed her. This would be the way of her family. Now he would make it the way of his. "You are welcome, Sister. I am Tony Heath. This is our home," sweeping his hand out, indicating the expanse of the property.

"I am Ataahau, this is the land of Atua. All belong to our God." She left no doubt who she was and what she meant. She carried very little with her but what she did have Tony put in the spare room and introduced Kory to his Aunty Ata. He, of course, was delighted.

Tony wondered for a moment how he was going to explain this to his sister. The first chance he had, he sat down and began to write to her. It was the only way they could communicate while she was in contact with the villagers who had been infected.

When Anna received the daily communication, along with the supplies Tony sent regularly, at first she felt a pang of jealousy but it soon passed. Kory needed his family. *What mattered is that he was safe.* So many of the villagers had already succumbed. *Ashton knew what he was doing.* So with her blessing Kory gained an Aunty. Anna hoped when this was all over she would also have gained a friend.

The routine was the same each day at the Mission Hospital. The men and women who cared for the sick took long shifts, easing the pain as best they could, using every method known to them to bring the fever down. Yet one after another, the families in the village became smaller and smaller. Anna often felt powerless. Only two of the missionaries had become ill. They had recovered but each time one of the local iwi came in contact with the illness their chance of recovery was proving minimal.

The villagers who had not been affected continued to supply food to those at the hospital. Rawiri often checked in on Anna, as he refused to leave her. She entrusted him with the daily notes and letters she wrote to Kory and Tony, at the ardent request to keep his distance from them. Tony and Rawiri had devised a way for communication from Anna to the villa to stay open. Kory enjoyed hearing from his Mother but could not understand why he could not see her. Anna had even sent a note for Paulo. This he received with great surprise.

Dearest Friend Paulo

Have you been making progress on the stone cottage? Your own permanent place to call home is a joy we all need and when I return, we can say a blessing together and I will bake your favourite cake. The one you like, with the raisins.

As you know, I remain at a distance from you all, because there is always the risk of me bringing disease into our home. It is true that the villagers are far more affected than we have been, so I feel safe. My purpose is clear, I need to help.

I hope you are making the most of this time of isolation and studying the Bible I gave you. You may enjoy the book of Jonah, as in it you will find a whale. This one gets away. Not the ending you are accustomed to but a wonderful message all the same. Jonah was in the belly of a whale three days as our Lord was in the tomb for three days. Both have happy endings.

Keep watch over the boys for me; they can get into mischief.

Until we are together at the hearth,

Your Miss Anna

Rawiri wanted the pain of so much loss to leave his chest. *How many of his iwi was he going to no longer have in his life?* He had just come back to the Mission Hospital after partaking in his tenth tangi in less than three weeks. He was not sure he could face another funeral. *So much loss. When will it end?*

In truth, he wanted to leave his own body, so great was his sorrow. He now sat outside the quarantine tent waiting for a glimpse of Anna. She had become his strength giver. He had only to look at her and he felt stronger. Her ceaseless energy brought life to everyone around her. She gently touched the brow of the sick, read quietly from her bible to the healing patient, spoke tenderly to those dying and was always peaceful. He loved her and knew that if he was ever to have an eternal partner he wanted her. Anna was not this kind of woman, he knew that, so having her as a sister was all he would ever need, *so he told his heart sternly*.

Anna had thought that Rawiri had moved just a little slower today, and no wonder. With so much loss his heart must be crushed. Nonetheless she kept a watchful eye on him. When she brought her daily message to him for those at home, she placed her hand on his brow and was not surprised to discover he was burning up. "Rawiri, my brother, you are unwell and need to come inside." Anna knew she was going to have a fight on her hands. "I do not have the spare energy to fight you, as I can see one coming into your eyes. Please, just take my hand and come, let me take care of you?"

Holding out her hand, palm up, Anna waited for the mighty man who was failing before her very eyes.

Rawiri looked into the eyes of the woman he loved. He did not want to bring her any more hardship. With dread, he placed his hand on hers and took hold. He could see the relief in her eyes. For this he gave thanks. "I will be at your side through whatever is to come. Let's face this together, my brother. Come." Hand in hand the unlikely pair walk into the quarantine tent.

Rawiri fell into the cot like an old growth tree finally releasing roots from the earth and keeling over. He was done.

Anna tenderly washed his feet, and removed any extra outer garments. She knew he was about to go through an ordeal. Soon the evening breeze blew in. It helped to cool his temperature. Anna remained true. She stayed at his side until he fell into a deep sleep that could either take him from her or restore him. Anna would have no way of knowing which one. Rawiri was strong in heart, body and soul and had come to love the Lord. Anna slipped away for a private moment later that evening and found a quiet place to pray.

Loving Father, in all earthly matters you feel our suffering and somehow bring forward a perfect outcome. I ask that you take special interest in your child, Rawiri. Give me the strength to care for him and all your children who suffer today who you have given me to nurse back to health and those souls whose time on earth has come. Hold them, loving Father, in your protective dwelling place until we all meet again at the coming of your beloved Son. Father, may Tony, Kory, Rawiri, Paulo, Kenyon, Ataahau, little Sophia, Captain Jock, Batina and Jude come through this tragic time on earth so that we may all embrace again and glorify you as one loving family. I ask this all in the name of our loving saviour Christ Jesus, Amen. It was all Anna had time for, yet she had no doubt that God had heard her prayer.

Each night everyone at the Mission Hospital gathered to pray, those not too sick to join in and those not too exhausted from long hours administering care. God was listening. Anna left these times of gathering and belonging with a heart full of hope lifted and restored.

When no letter was forthcoming from Anna that day, Tony knew that his companion had fallen ill. It would have been the only thing that would keep him from holding open the line of connection everyone needed. He began to wonder for the first time if he should break the safety barrier and venture into the village. *But what of the boy and Ataahau? Had he not promised Anna that he would guard her son?*

Rawiri lay in a state of delusion for five days. Anna's prayers deepened, the plea for his life never leaving her heart. They became a chant sung in the silence of her inner being. Desperation clung to the outer edges of her mind, refusing to leave her in peace. So she prayed, night and day, for the life of this man who she had come to know, as the love she never thought she would want. When her heart began to change towards him, she could not say, as day and night seemed as one. The fight for his life became her only focus.

Chapter THIRTY FOUR

True love finds a way.

The Mission Hospital began to see fewer cases each day. It seemed as though the worst had passed. Anna began to relax. She had been told that all was well at home.

They all prayed each day for Rawiri. Someone had taken news to them. *She hoped the messenger kept their distance.*

On the sixth day of Rawiri falling ill, Anna fell to her knees at his feet and gave her heart over to the Lord in absolute surrender. "Almighty Father, your will be done on earth as it is in Heaven. If you have made this strong, brave and loving man for me to walk this life with, I accept. " Anna spoke her prayer aloud from her knees.

"Then you are mine and will be for eternity." Rawiri's voice was soft, as though spoken from a place far away. Anna thought she might be the delusional one now, slowly raising her eyes in the hope she would see him on the path to full recovery. His smile was so bright she would come to believe that light had been shining from him at her first sight of him, the man she would now spend the rest of her days with. Kory could now have an earthly father of his own.

Though her patient was still weak, he was showing remarkable signs of recovery by the end of the day. Anna knew he would not remain still much longer. "Here, drink this, it will help you become strong." She was glad he had recovered, yet the newness of their eternal bond had set them both at ease in heart and awkward physically towards each other. Rawiri wrapped his hands around the slender hands that held a cup to his lips. He was sure he could do this for himself but was enjoying the tender care he was now awake to enjoy.

"Taupuhi, loved one, your hands are ice cold, yet you are warm to the touch." Rawiri became instantly alarmed as he reached to cup her cheek.

Anna leaned into his touch in full surrender "It is nothing a little rest and some nourishment won't cure. Wipe the fear from your eyes, lieveling, my loved one," Anna gently smoothed back the rogue, night-black curl from his temple.

Tony had been told earlier that day the good news. The last patient was coming right and his dear friend and brother would be fishing with him again in a day or two. Well, *maybe a week,* but Tony had to go see for himself.

He stood in the opening of the medical tent and was witness to the tender exchange between the two people his heart held as a value equal to his own. *Am I intruding?* not likely, but he was glad at heart to see them both after all this time. He had to admit Anna did look far too slim and a little flushed. Tony waited for the lovers' moment to pass before announcing his presence. "Anna Banana?"

"Tony, this is too soon." Though Anna was happy to see her brother, she did not want him to take an unnecessary risk now.

Tony stepped into the tent. Anna was torn between wanting to run to him and hug him and admonish him for taking the risk to enter the village. Tony could see the concern on his sister's face, so he waited for her to come to him.

Anna stood and reluctantly released the hand that held hers now. Her world began to spin. If not for the warrior reflexes of Rawiri, she would have ended up in an unladylike heap on the floor.

As he held the limp and feverish body in his arms, Rawiri commanded his friend to leave the tent. "Out." Tony moved forward. "She is mine and I will let no harm come to her. You risk your life and that of the child she loves. OUT!" Rawiri was fierce in his stand. Tony was not helping anyone by arguing.

"Brother, she needs us both." Yet Tony knew Rawiri would be as good as his word.

"Yes. So be there when she is well. Bring the child she loves when no harm can come to those she has fought to keep safe." Rawiri could feel her body temperature rising.

He looked into the eyes of the only man alive who he knew loved Anna as much as he did, feeling his pain. He then turned away carrying Anna to the Doctor who Anna had told him was to be trusted. Tony stepped out of the tent leaving behind a part of himself, the agony from his heart reaching his mind and causing explosions in his brain.

Ataahau had come to the place of wanting this life as her own, the life of another woman. Koraka and Tony had become more to her than her own existence. They had both claimed her centre and changed the course of her life for all time. *She knew the moment Tony entered into her heart.*

The two males of her attention had been harvesting on the vast property, older teaching younger with such patience. Tony was showing Kory the need for gentleness when picking the tender crop that grew in abundance on the land. She had made them a noon day meal and was bringing the basket to them.

Hidden she watched the tender vision. Kory had crushed the cluster of grapes in his child-sized hands releasing the delicious juices and began stuffing them into his mouth. Tony's laughter took flight and filled the skies. *A moment that sang to my heart and the music was witnessed by Angels with pleasure, surely. I will hurt by the loss I will have when Tony's sister and Koraka's earth mother return to a life in which I will no longer have a place. My sister's son will always have me as guardian but that did not mean I could stay with him always.* This was a bittersweet moment for her.

Tony was heartbroken. He knew his sister was a strong woman but she had obviously been caring for the sick with all her soul. She was tired. Bone tired. Anna had poured herself out in the care of others. He was rendered powerless.

Faithful and kind Ataahau met him at the base of the hill leading up to the villa. He could no longer hold back the tears. She opened her arms and he allowed himself to be held in her tender embrace. She did not ask anything of him, simply gave him a space to grieve and so he did. Fear poured from his soul. "She is unwell. Anna has been taken ill." Like a child Tony wiped his wet face with the front of his shirt.

Ataahau could see the adorable child he must have been.

"Where is Kory, Aroha, Love?" The endearment was from his lips before he had realised what he had said. Ataahau had suspected his feelings for her had taken flight. Now, when he was most vulnerable, whether he meant to or not, Tony had revealed his heart to her.

"He has fallen asleep on the mat in the lounge, waiting for you. I did not want to wake him. He is so peaceful, and you know how rare the times are that he sleeps in the day. I think he waits all day for his mother to return." Ataahau could see the mention of Tony's sister brought him pain. She opened up her arms to him again and he gratefully stepped into her embrace.

They were becoming one. Ataahau wanted this life of family. "She is a strong wāhine, a blessed woman. God will protect her." Tony had been teaching her more about the man Christ, she was sure if there was any way to help, this would be done for Anna.

Rawiri gently wiped Anna's forehead with a cool cloth as he had seen her do hundreds of times. She was delirious and had become much worse in the night. She was struggling for breath. The doctor's face showed no sign of what he was thinking, but Rawiri knew. *It was bad.* Anna had no reserves. She was exhausted and her body was being taken over by fever.

That God had dominion over all that is seen and unseen, the missionaries had told him to pray. "I do not know how to speak the words in my heart to God." The anguish on Rawiri's face gave the doctor all the insight he needed, to know that the young warrior would not want to hear what the doctor now knew. *This brave woman was very ill. She was succumbing to the illness that she had brought many through. Anna Malefyt was dying.*

The doctor placed his hand on the shoulder of the man who obviously loved her and shook his head. "She is not long for this world. We need to send for her brother."

"I will not leave her." Rawiri was determined to fight for her life.

"We must get Tony now." The Doctor gave a last look at Anna and left the tent.

Rawiri watched in horror as Anna's breathing became slower. He called out to the God who Tony had told him so much about and believed in with all of his soul. "Save her! She is your child."

He heard the words: *Take her to the ocean.* Yet no one had spoken.

Rawiri gently lifted her into his arms and carried her out of the tent towards the sea. Her body was warm, she was becoming peaceful as though entering into a deep sleep. Her breath was leaving her.

Tony knew. His sister was dying. He could feel her life leaving this world as though it was his own. Nothing would keep him from her now. He took off in a run leaving Ataahau and Kory staring after him. Ataahau grabbed Kory and took him to his Mother.

The water gently lapped over the still form in Rawiri's arms. She was beautiful. He turned to the man he loved who now slowly walked into the sea with tears streaming down his face.

Tony knew she was gone.

Ataahau saw the scene for what it was. *Was this the closing of one life and the opening of her future?* The ocean called her and Ataahau understood. "Take the child." Tony caught Kory midair. Ataahau snatched Anna from the arms that held her and dived beneath the waves.

Had the moment not been so serious they would have laughed at the look they saw now on each other's faces. The two men and bewildered child watched the surface of the water and waited, wide-eyed, anxious and expectant.

Into the deep Ataahau took the still form of the woman who was the other half of the man she loved and the mother of her own sweet sister's child. The voice that spoke encouraged her to take the still form deeper and deeper until her own lungs began to ache in great pain. Ataahau did not want to give her life for this woman. *Even though she knew Anna was not just any woman.* For Tony, she would do anything.

Anna felt the shock of ice-cold water. She wondered if she had been pushed into the lake at Bergen Op Meer and she was not happy about it. The thought foremost in her mind as she surfaced was to give the fool who had such an audacity a firm piece of her mind. Sputtering and coughing, Anna surfaced with a power of determination to keep herself afloat. Three shocked faces greeted her.

"Mummaaaa!!!!!" Kory leapt from Tony's arms, creating a new level of madness in his wake for he had yet to learn to swim. Ataahau was prepared. She rose up out of the water next to him, protectively guiding him over the surface of the water to his mother.

Chapter THIRTY FIVE

E ster *Wolf Blass and Markus Wolf.*
Yes, at times not remaining home more often was in question. *Mumma needed more help at Bergen Op Meer and Thomas and Katerina did need stability.* But when Ester thought of the adventures they had had, her concerns melted away like snowflakes falling on the sand of a sun-baked beach.

Markus loved the sea and Ester loved him. The research they had done on the life of seabirds in the South Pacific was extensive. Markus had agreed this would be their last adventure, *an odyssey into the deep.* The opportunity to deep sea dive in the new, two-person submersible was too much to turn away from. They would then return as a family of adventurers to settle down at Bergen Op Meer and enjoy lecturing on their combined research. Ester was relieved.

Stepping into the vessel gave them both the thrill of doing something new. *What would they see?* They had been known for years as the Aqua Duo. Ester had to admit, the opportunities that had come their way often caused her to wonder what made them so lucky. It was as if a force of nature on the tide saw them as a destination for opportunity.

It was true, the discoveries they had made both thrilled and often surprised the science world. They hoped that today would be no different.

So, with undersea cameras ready and their family photo placed front and centre, they headed into the deep. Thomas and Katerina watched as the bobbing of the machine that would take their parents to places they could not go, *because they had asked,* motored from sight.

"Lieveling, man of my heart, whatever we discover today, we agree to head home tomorrow, okay?" Ester looked deep into Markus's eyes and searched for any reluctance.

"It is time. I can see that the children need a little more from us. Just think how happy Oma is that we will all be with her. She gets lonely. I know she never complains, but I see it." Markus was sincere. These years had been wonderful, but even he wanted to be on land a little bit more.

"In that case, I have something I want to tell you." Taking his hand she placed it on her extended belly.

"What!!! We are turning back right now." Even though the space was confined, he was thrilled and swept her into his arms. They had been trying for years to have more children and had resigned themselves to the fact that two wonderful children may be all they could have.

"No, you are not. This is our last trip. This is all the more reason for you and I to enjoy it." Giggling with the sheer joy of his reaction, Ester placed herself back in the seat and clipped her harness on for emphasis.

"Are you sure? You know you are not as young as you used to be. Hahahaha." Markus always teased her about her age, mainly because he was so much older than her.

"Oh, Trit, you're such a funny bear." With a friendly punch to his shoulder, Ester settled in for the journey. "We are staying right here." Affectionately she patted her belly.

Markus felt the waters of his soul ripple when she used his pet name Trit, short for Triton. Giving the gears a push, off they went into the deep blue.

Johanna had kept regular contact via carefully scheduled phone calls and seasonal cards and letters to Batina. Both had continued to keep in confidence the secrets that only they knew.

Their mutual respect through the years grew, as did the understanding that the truth would need to eventually come out.

When Hannah and then Tony were born, Batina had stated she wanted them to call her Oma when they met. Once again she explained to Johanna that the inheritance of Bergen Op Meer was Hannah's now, too. "When will you pass on the legacy, dierbaar, my much loved? You know I will not push, but I also have to think of Thomas and Katerina. Their parents are now settling down with them here this spring."

"But Hannah is so young, Batina. I see no need to say anything. Leaving things as they are until she is an adult is what I want. All this will come as a shock to her. And what about Tony? What will this mean to him?"

She also knew Alvan wanted to provide for his own family, much to Jonty's protests, and Johanna had followed her husband's lead. Jonty lived in the Villa and the children were often with him on the land. This was a comprimise.

"I have always been honest with my daughter. She knows we are beneficiaries of the land and the conditions that can change circumstances. I don't think she is concerned. She and Markus have done very well for themselves. Yes, I want them to live here, but they have the means to live anywhere they choose." Batina sighed in relief that they would soon be home for good. The children needed stability and a regular schedule.

A few days later their phone rang very early in the morning. Alvan quickly sprang up, ran down the hall and picked up the receiver. These random calls came in from time to time for him. Johanna settled under the covers and waited for his return. "Ma'am, can you slow down please. I can't understand you. Did you say your name was Batina Wolf Blass?" Alvan did not hear Johanna run down the hall, so intent was he in attempting to get pertinent information from the anxious female caller.

"This is my call, love, you go back to bed." Johanna held out her hand for Alvan to place the receiver in hers. Looking calm and collected, though hardly feeling either of these, Johanna waited for her husband to hand over the phone.

Well, this is odd. "Excuse me, Mrs Wolf Blass, here is my wife," handing over the phone and mouthing the words to his wife, *"Who is it?"*

Johanna made a shoo, shoo motion with her hands and closed the hallway door.

"It is me, what has happened?" Johanna knew that Batina would only call at an unscheduled time if matters were dire.

"My daughter, it is my daughter." Batina paused to catch her breath. "Markus and Ester were on their last and final assignment and the submersible they are in has gone missing in the sea off the coast of New Zealand." Her heart was racing.

"Oh, my friend, you must be terrified. How can I help?" *How am I going to explain this to Alvan? Johanna, stop it, be here for Batina.*

"The children are with them." Batina was having trouble getting her thoughts in order.

Johanna gasped.

"No, no. Not missing, they are on the ship with the crew waiting for news. Lieveling, they are alone." When speaking to Johanna, a small amount of relief began to aid in slowing her heart rate to a normal pace.

Johanna would understand, she had children around the same age. "Where are they? How do I reach them?" She found a pen and paper and took down all the information. "That is less than an hour from here. I will call you when I get to them."

"Thank you, dierbaar, my precious one. I will be waiting for your call." Relief flooded in.

"Oh, and Batina, I don't know what this all means just yet, but we will face it together. Okay?" In these times Johanna was a rock.

"I am grateful. Bless you and God's protection upon you." Batina slowly put the receiver down and took the first real breath since she had received the news.

"Alvan, I can't explain everything right now but I need to get to the coast. There has been an accident and I need to go there." Racing around, she quickly changed and grabbed the items she thought she may need.

"I hope they have good insurance. Just slow down, my girl, let me help you." Alvan held out her slicker. First placing a kiss on her forehead, he slipped her into it.

Her wellies were there at the door and on to her feet they went too. She was off. "Oh my gosh, the children." *Where is my head?* turning back to Alvan standing in the door .

"I got the kids. You drive safe, you want to get where you are going in one piece. Call me when you get there." He was worried as it was raining heavily.

"I will, you're my hero. Love you." With a final wave over her shoulder, she walked towards the car.

Thomas and Katerina waited in the kitchen with the cook for any news. The plate of cookies between them sat untouched. Cook could see they were scared. He had never been around kids and had no idea what to do. What a relief when Johanna King showed up. She knew exactly what to do.

"Hi, you must be Thomas. And you must be Katerina." Two little faces looked up at her as though she was a lifeline. "I am a friend of your Oma." The little girl let go of her brother's hand that she had been holding and stepped into the waiting open arms. She began to cry. Thomas sat in frozen silence. "Come here, little man, let's figure out what to do next." Johanna gestured for Thomas to step into the circle of protection his sister was in. That he did eventually approach was a good sign.

After thinking about it, he jumped down from the stool and took the nice lady's hand. Although he was glad to be getting away from the cook, he did want some of the cookies because he was getting hungry. "Can we go now? I want to go home. We both want to go home."

"Hey, boy, would you like to take some of these with you?" Cook gestured to the untouched plate on the table.

"Yes, please." Thomas held out his free hand for the bag now being filled. With his other hand, he kept a death grip on Johanna's.

"Where can I make an overseas phone call?" Johanna asked. Speaking to their Oma would help these two frightened children.

"Up those stairs and to the left. The Professor will want to have a word. I will see if I can locate him now." Off the young man went, who looked more like Popeye's twin than a cook of any kind.

"Thank you. Come on, kids, let's call Oma." Batina picked up on the first ring.

"I have them, they are right here. Hang on. Who wants to go first?" Still holding Thomas's hand and with Katerina on her lap, they were both instantly ready.

"Let Kat go first." Thomas pointed at his sister with his free hand holding the bag of cookies.

"Thank you, Thomas." Taking the phone in both her little hands, Katerina placed the receiver to her ear. "Hi, Oma." The children spoke perfect english.

"Yes, I understand what is happening."

"Yes, there is a nice lady here to help us."

"Yes, I want to come home right now, but I want Mommy and Daddy to come too." The child's dam of tears burst.

Batina suddenly realised she was firing questions at the frightened child. *Slow down old woman, they need you more than you need them.* She took a deep breath and started again.

Thomas reached in and patted her head and then took the receiver. "Hi Oma, it's me."

"Hello, my Thomas. You understand what has happened, don't you?" Always the more serious one, Batina thought. Until they were home, Batina would speak to their strengths. They still had a long journey ahead of them. In the time that Johanna had been in transit to the children, Batina had heard the unthinkable news. *They would be out of oxygen by now. All hope of finding them alive was lost.* "I am going to ask Mrs King to bring you both home." Batina was finding it hard to breathe again.

"Is she the nice lady here right now?" Thomas pointed to her as if Batina could see him. "She will be bringing us home?"

"Yes, lieveling. Please put her back on the line. I will see you both soon." Oh how Batina hoped this would all go smoothly for the two frightened children.

"Okay, Oma, bye for now." His voice was hollow. Thomas handed the phone back to Johanna.

"You have more news." This had to be bad if Johanna was going to be needed to travel to Bergen Op Meer.

"Yes." The pause was deafening. "They would be out of oxygen now. There is no hope of finding them alive." Batina found it hard to focus.

"Oh, Batina." Johanna drew in both children and held them as the news continued its destructive path, leaving pain in its wake. "The children are safe with me. You want me to bring them home, don't you?"

"I know this is asking too much." Batina was in tears and exhausted.

"It is the least I can do. Do you know where your daughter would keep their passports? I know this is difficult for you too, but the sooner they are with you the better." Johanna was going to move fast.

"Yes, yes, you are so right. Ester travelled with a large, black folder in her briefcase. All their documents should be inside. Do you need funds for expenses? I can wire those to you."

Johanna could hear Batina's voice steady.

"No, we can work that all out later. I am going to pack up their things now and take them with me. Neither one of them is going to let go at this rate, anyway. Being in our home may even help a little."

"How are you going to explain all this to your family?" Batina's voice was fading again.

"No worries. They will take it all as it comes. I will call you later today. And Batina..."

In a very small voice she answered. "Yes?"

"I love you." There were no other words.

"Thank you," and the call dropped.

The King family rallied around the two orphans as Johanna made plans to travel. Alvan had seen the news that morning. He knew before Johanna got home what had happened. What he wanted to know was, why was she involved? "I have been asked to take them home. You see, when I was in the Netherlands before you and I married, I came to know their Grandmother. She was kind to me and I want to return the kindness." Johanna hoped this simple explanation would be enough for now.

"Strange that you have never mentioned anyone by the name of Wolf Blass to me. I would have remembered it." Alvan knew something was amiss.

Johanna did feel the sting of guilt for not telling Alvan and for that matter Jonty more. And now, here is his niece and nephew right under his nose. Jonty had offered to advance all the funds needed for the trip as the revenue from Lions Vineyard was rightfully Johanna's as well. She had never pushed Alvan to include this in their budget and trusted Jonty to invest it wisely for future generations.

"Sure. If you can have the bank transfer the funds into my personal account today, that would be great. The agent is looking into our tickets right now. I will get back to you with the amount soon." News travels fast. Everyone in the area had now heard what had happened and who the children at the King house were. Johanna wanted to move fast. The less she had to explain the better.

Alvan felt hurt. He would have gladly paid for the tickets. Johanna had enough to deal with at the moment. The matter of his feelings could be left to a time when things settled down again. "How long will you be gone?"

"Just under two weeks. We leave within the next ten days or so." Johanna kept the conversation short.

As children do, the four that had been thrown together just a few days before had made the best of it. Tony and Hannah did not ask them any hard questions and Katerina and Thomas forgot their pain from time to time as they became completely lost in the adventure that Jonty took them all on at Lions Vineyard.

Had they been any older, this would have made matters impossible for Johanna. As it stands today, she thought they would all be too young to remember each other well, certainly way too young to start and have regular correspondence. However, Tony had loudly stated one evening, much to everyone's amusement, that *if he could have anyone for a wife like his Daddy had, he wanted it to be Kat.* She blushed sweetly.

When the day came, the whole family travelled to the airport. All four children enjoyed the adventure, seeing the planes, checking in luggage, and eating in the coffee shop. Johanna, for a split second thought of telling Jonty who these children were, but the moment passed just as quickly.

Alvan noticed Johanna was not being herself. *Sure the recent events had been unexpected, if not highly unusual,* Johanna had a big heart though. Her wanting to give back started to make some sense.

Taking her in his arms, "Love, whatever this truly is, all that matters is you come back home." He placed a kiss on her lips.

Johanna leaned in and sighed. "Oh, I will, that you can count on. You are the love of my life, where else could I possibly want to be." Her smile was deep and penetrated his own soul.

Hannah looked up at her parents. She knew when she grew up, she also wanted to be loved like Mummy was by Daddy.

"Come here, kids, come give me a hug." Tony and Hannah dived in and were held in the safety of their Mother's arms. Kissing each cheek, and telling them to behave for Uncle Jonty and Daddy, Johanna stepped back and offered her open hands to the two little ones standing by, looking a little sad.

Thomas, now known as Massy - Tony and his mates gave him the name in a show of friendship - stepped forward first, then Kat. She really liked it here. She was not sure if she wanted to leave her new friends, especially Tony.

Massy on the other hand wanted to go home. "Let's go." Turning, he waved. Kat blew an adorable kiss at the group left behind. The three travellers walked out of sight.

Chapter THIRTY SIX

J *ohanna returns to Bergen Op Meer.*

"They are wonderful travellers." Johanna remembered the photos she had in the hope of bringing Batina a little good cheer. "Oh, and I did bring you some photos of Jonty. Here they are."

The children were both once again safely tucked into their own beds. Batina was relieved.

Johanna handed Batina the stack of photos she had been saving and was glad she could hand-deliver them. *Batina had aged.* The death of her daughter and son-in-law had come as a hard blow. Again Johanna ever so briefly thought, *Should I claim my birthright and tell Jonty everything?*

The time passed quickly. Batina and Johanna together made all the arrangements for the memorial service. Markus Wolf and Ester Wolf Blass had both been well known and very involved in their chosen scholastic fields and charity organisations. Hundreds turned out for the service and enjoyed the hospitality of Bergen Op Meer with the help of Anita and Wim van Dam and their enchanting daughter Millicent. Had this not been such a sad occasion, Johanna could have fully basked in the majesty of the moment and place.

"My dear, do you want to see the solicitor before you leave?" Batina was certain Johanna was having second thoughts about the arrangement they had made. "As you say, your daughter is now next in line. One day she will need to know."

"Oh Batina, have you not been through enough these past few weeks. Do you want to leave all this? Is that why you mention this now?" indicating with a sweep of her hands the vast holdings around them. "Massy and Kat do not need any more disruption either. This is the only home they have ever known."

Batina's heart was broken. With a need for healing she felt at peace in her home and told Johanna so.

"And as long as I live, so shall it remain. And that is that. As long as you are happy being the one that is responsible for all this, who am I to complain? Mind you, you now have two young grandchildren to also raise. If they are anything like mine, this will be no small task." Compassion radiated from her heart and enveloped Batina as Johanna spoke.

"Oh, I am not without the right help for all of these matters and the estate is a profitable one. Would you like to see the accounts before you leave?" With transparency, Batina Wolf Blass had mastered the successful running of Bergen Op Meer.

"No. I see no need. If you do not mind, though, I would like to explore the estate for the rest of the day. I have no idea when I will be back and I want a solid blueprint of the place etched into my memory. Can we meet again for dinner at 6.00 o'clock tonight?"

"Of course, my dear. In truth, I need some solitude." With a gentle smile radiating out, Batina softly touched Johanna's cheek. "I love you, my dear."

"Did anything seem strange to you with Oma and Johanna?" Wim found the foreigner who so kindly returned the children to have a relationship that seemed more, much more than just two people who had met briefly years before.

"Now that you mention it, yes." Anita paused in wiping the last of the crumbs off the counter top of The Gate House that had seen hundreds of years of use. How sad today that once again the food was prepared for a funeral.

In truth, Anita was not close to Markus. Largely because he and Ester had always been on one adventure or another. *Oh how she was going to miss Ester.*

They had shared many happy life moments. When Millicent was born, Ester was a great help, as Anita and Wim were often busy with the running of their popular establishment. Ester was good with children from the start. It was no surprise that she and Markus had made it known they would have a large family, even though he was much older than the woman he adored.

"Johanna may be one of those people who it is easy to trust, but it is true, I have never seen Oma so relaxed with someone she hardly even knows. The children are mad about her too." Anita began once again to vigorously complete her final task of the day and leave the countertop glowing.

"Her handshake is firm and confident. I liked her from the first moment. Millicent is quite taken with her as well. She obviously has nothing to hide." Wim had seen how hard she worked when the many preparations had to be made for the huge gathering that had only today been a part of the historic fabric of the estate. *Saying farewell was never easy.* Wim was going to miss Ester dearly. Tears formed in the corners of his eyes.

Anita felt the stillness of the only man she had ever loved and dropped the cloth. "Come here, lieveling." Opening her arms, she gathered him into his safe place and held him as the sadness of loss washed through him. "You have been going for days and need to slow down now. All the work here is done and the rest can wait for another day. We need time to grieve."

The two weeks had seemed much more like two minutes to Johanna. "Kids." It was her last moments at Bergen Op Meer and she wanted to be sure they knew that their pain would change over time and get easier to handle.

Massy and Kat heard the call from the library. "Coming," Massy yelled from the bowels of the house. Johanna heard the many beats of footsteps charging through the house on the wooden floorboards and wondered just how many 'kids' would be answering her call.

Millicent skidded into the room a full pace ahead of Massy with Kat quick on his heels. They looked happy. This lifted Johanna's heart, giving her even more conviction that she had made the right choice to keep all matters as they were.

"I have called the taxi and will be on my way within the hour. Oma and I have already said our goodbyes. Now, it is our turn." Johanna watched the three faces in front of her fall to various degrees.

"Can you stay just a little longer?" Kat had a depth to her eyes that getting lost in was not in the least difficult. With her left hand she showed a small gap between her thumb and finger as she peeked her eye through the space.

"No, little one. Tony and Hannah need me and you know how much Uncle Jonty depends on me." Johanna had to giggle at this for he truly was their Uncle. "Lions Vineyard is far too much for him to manage on his own."

"I love it at Lions Vineyard. It is very pretty." Kat was being sincere and she had a dreamy look in her eyes.

"Will you come see us again and maybe bring Tony and Hannah? I really liked being with them." Massy knew exactly how to zero in on the hard questions.

Millicent could tell that her new friend was struggling. "Come on, you two, let's show Mrs King the present we have for her. We hope you still have room in your case for what we made you?"

"I am sure I will." Johanna was relieved she would not have to lie to Massy. She took the little hands offered to her and walked into the well-used art room with Massy on her left, Kat on her right, and Millicent leading the way.

Chapter THIRTY SEVEN

1823 *Lions Vineyard Aotearoa New Zealand*
Life fell into a gentle routine as the days moved by. Anna had kept in contact with Batina and Jude, with the regular communication kindly delivered by Kenyon Lewis. Jude and Batina now knew that the chances of them returning was increasingly becoming a greater issue.

Anna and Tony spoke at length as to the best options. When making the final decision, they both felt a weight lift. Home had become right where they were and neither of them wanted anything else for the time being. On September 16th, Rawiri and Anna, and Tony and Ataahau, celebrated together becoming husband and wife.

Theirs was the first wedding, rather weddings, to be recorded in the new church that still had the smell of fresh whitewash about it. The first baptism had already been recorded and Kory had been an angel, much to everyone's relief.

It did not take long for the family to expand by one. To Tony's joy he became a father almost nine months to the day after the nuptials, June 17th, 1824. Rory Arlo Heath was a welcome addition to the family and Kory enjoyed having someone to teach new things to. From day one, the two were never apart. Rolo, as Kory called him, became his self proclaimed brother. The stone mission buildings had eventually been completed, as had Paulo's home. He was less and less at the Heath table and this did worry Tony some. *Paulo was up to something.* He could feel it. It was as though the more happiness grew in the hearts of the family in the villa, the less Paulo liked it.

Paulo had come to truly care for the sweet girl, Anna. He often wondered if this is what it would feel like to have his own daughter. The jealousy that overtook him at times was blinding. Anna had been the first woman that had ever got in and he did not like it at all that he had to share her attention. He had kept all her letters. When she had blessed his home, all he truly could fathom was to sail away with her. *That was saying something big, because she was both a woman and a Malefyt.*

The little Bible she had given him was in constant use now, although he had to confess the words on the pages seemed like a story that was hardly relevant to anything that mattered to him. *Gold coins mattered to him, so why would he go about giving it all away? This thinking was crazy madness.* Paulo loved coins. He protected his golden stash with great determination.

No one would ever know where he had long ago safely hidden all the gold that he had earned while sailing with Captain Tally.

From time to time, in the late hours of the night, he would take it from its hiding place and stack the coins neatly in rows on the table.

The sound they made as Paulo dropped one on top of the other played out a sweet melody of *mine, mine, mine.* Even the thought of spending any on his own crew and ship was not an option as he no longer desired parting with any of it.

One evening, he was finding it particularly hard to deal with the mess that had become of his heart.

As he was looking at all his wealth, an amount that nearly covered the entire space of his table ten coins deep, he drank to his good fortune and misfortune, lifting his glass over and over to the glow of gold filling his entire view with the hope some ease would come to his heartache. It was not to be.

For the first time ever, Paulo, deep into his cups mind you, cried. Tears streamed down his cheeks. *You are becoming soft in the head, Sailor, pull yourself together. Was his heart softening? Were the words from the book Anna had given him making a difference like she said they could? Who could truly love him? This Jesus was kind, like Anna. Maybe there was something to it. Should he give it all away? Would that ease the pain in his heart? I would like to live forever in a place that had no pain. That would be nice. Just like the one promised in his little book.* Paulo wiped the back of his sleeve over his dripping nose and filled his glass with the other hand.

There had been many times when he could have used a friend like Christ. Captain Tally had been that friend and look how Paulo had behaved the last time he had seen the man.

More tears began to fall. Guilt poured into the empty space where his heart should be and pushed out even more tears. Years of the wrongs he had done flashed before his drunken eyes.

Forgiveness was a word foreign to Paulo before he had met Anna. When she had been ill and near death, for the very first time Paulo spoke to God. He just could not imagine a world without her, nor a Father that would let his child die. That God had let his own Son die was still a mystery to Paulo. Anna had told him once, *'the Son of God does live'* and he believed her. He had yet to realise that the turning point of his heart rested upon the answer to his prayer when Anna had recovered.

She had been as good as her word. Soon after she returned to Lions Vineyard, Anna brought him the promised raisin cake and blessed his new home, the first one on land he had ever truly known.

The silence that filled the room now held Paulo in its embrace, yet he knew he was not alone. There was a presence. Something calm and whole. He knew without a doubt that the One with him now had been there all his life. Watching over him, keeping him safe. *It had not been the mistress of the ocean who nurtured me but the Creator of it keeping me safe.* The words passed through his mind as a complete and whole truth.

Paulo put the full glass down and waited. For what or who, he had no idea. "Lord God, I want to give this gold to you." The words came from deep within and cleansed him as they passed by his lips. Joy overtook him and laughter filled the room. He was instantly sober.

Kory enjoyed daily adventures. Today was going to be no different. After he finished his chores he was going to complete the work on the small fishing poles he had been making. One for him and one for Rolo.

"Kory." Anna had one last errand for Kory today that would be more a test than anything else. Though she would not let him know it.

"Yes, Mumma." Kory gently put the last of the eggs in the pantry and turned to smile at his mother.

"I have a raisin cake for Paulo here that I need you to take to him this morning." Anna indicated the package neatly wrapped in a cloth on the benchtop. "If you do this, then I can start on the biscuits that are next on the list."

"Sure. Will those be ready when I get back?" Kory was a big fan of biscuits.

"I will have some sitting right here" indicating the now empty space with a tap of her hand on the benchtop "for you on a plate when you get back." Anna smiled at her only child, tousled his adorable curls, and marvelled once again at her blessings.

Kory reached for the raisin cake, kissed the cheek his mother was indicating he should leave a kiss on with the tapping of her finger, and hurried out the door. *Wait a minute. I have never done this before. What was going on here?* Kory was never permitted to venture into the area of the land that everyone considered to be Paulo's. *Why today, why now?*

Paulo woke to a symphony of birdsong just as the sun's light filled the room and bounced off his treasure still stacked in neat rows on the table.

Something felt different inside him. The place where his heart was seemed alive, as though a light had pushed out all the darkness.

He picked up the bottle on the table and dumped the balance of the contents out. *He would not be needing this anymore. Now, about this gold.*

He decided the place for it was the same place he had been hiding it all these years, for now. Later today he would talk to Miss Anna about the best way to deal with it all. Maybe she could use it at the Mission House. The Hospital always needed supplies. If he could somehow make amends for all the suffering he had caused the beautiful creatures of the sea, that would be nice too.

The tears dared to come to the surface again. *I now understand you, my friend.* Captain Tally had once confessed to Paulo that he felt it was wrong what they were doing. *"Profiting from the death of these wondrous creatures is wrong."* Paulo now understood.

Kory squared his shoulders, determined to complete his task with pride. In truth, he was more than a little afraid of Paulo. He had never thought Paulo liked him. He could see that made his Mumma sad. Doing that was not okay. Mumma had said that we need to meet our neighbours as though they were Jesus. Kory loved Jesus and he loved his Mumma, so he would try.

Paulo placed the last coins in the chest that fitted to perfection into the flue of the chimney, and pushed it into place. From his knees in front of the fireplace, with eyes closed and head bowed, he prayed. "Heavenly Father and your Son Jesus Christ, I am sorry for all I have done. Please help me to be a better person. Thank you for my friend Tally and his sweet niece Anna. Help Tony to forgive me too. I would like us to be friends." Paulo had the sense he was being watched.

Kory looked in utter shock at the scene in front of him. Quietly he placed the cake on the window sill. As he turned to go, his eyes locked with those of the man he had truly never known. He froze, and then ran for his life.

Oh no, what have I done? thought Paulo. The boy looked terrified. How could he know that the change that had come in the night meant they could also be friends. Paulo's heart was full of joy. He quickly got up and ran into the woods after the boy. He wanted to tell him and the whole world that he saw life differently now, *he was a new creation.*

Kory's heart was beating out of his chest. Could he outrun the grown man that was now chasing him. *Probably not. But I can climb and he can't.*

Up the tallest tree he flew, hoping that he could hide behind the huge widowmaker resting in the branches.

Holding his breath, Kory heard his own heartbeat. He willed it to be still, so that Paulo would not hear it also.

Oh no, I have scared the boy. Slowing his step Paulo listened for any sounds that would point him in the direction the child had just bolted.

How much longer can I hold my breath? thought Kory. Paulo was directly beneath him. The pain in Kory's chest began to swell. *Just a little longer.* With a gasp, Kory took the much needed breath and knocked the massive plant from its life-long resting place.

Paulo did not suffer. His neck was instantly broken.

Chapter THIRTY EIGHT

B*onds forged from light.*
Anna placed the last batch of biscuits on the benchtop to cool. She looked at the small plate with cold biscuits and frowned. "What's that look for, Anna Banana?" Tony could smell the baking a mile away. Popping one of the warm ones into his mouth and grabbing a second, he waited.

"I gave Kory a new responsibility today because I thought he was ready, but I am wondering if I was mistaken." Anna trusted her intuition implicitly. On second thought, knew she could trust Kory too. "You know the raisin cakes Paulo likes so much?"

Tony nodded as his mouth was still full.

"Well, I made one this morning and gave Kory the task of delivering it with the promise a batch of his favourite biscuits would be waiting for him. These are his favourites and they are now cold." Anna lifted up the plate and looked at Tony with such concern, he got the message.

"Here, give them to me. I will go over now and see what is keeping him. I am sure it is nothing." Tony took one of the cloth bags Anna put all her baking in and filled it, being sure to add some of the warm biscuits too.

"Thank you, Ashton. He is a good boy. I am sure all went well." Anna was slightly relieved.

She very seldom ever called him '*Ashton*' anymore. He preferred it that way and she knew it. *She must be very worried.* Tony thought.

When he arrived the stone cottage was quiet. An eerie quiet. The kind that happens just before an earthquake, or in death. The hair on the back of Tony's neck stood up. Leaving the biscuits next to the cake sitting on the window sill, Tony looked for any signs of where Paulo and Kory could be. The fresh prints leading into the dense forest were all he needed. Tony took off in a run.

Not far from the cottage he found the body. Paulo was dead, very dead. Was Tony sorry, no. But this would hurt Anna and for that he felt a pang of regret. "Kory," Tony called out for his nephew. "Koryyyyyy." Nothing. *Where could he be?* Thinking through the whole situation, Tony thought it best to go get help. Rawiri was often at this time of day at their favourite fishing hole. He would start there.

Rawiri had done all he could think of to win Kory over as a son. He understood at times that the boy wanted his mother all to himself, Rawiri wanted that too, sometimes, but that was not their reality. They had come together as a family in a way that none of them had planned. *God knows the plan, all is well.* Now that it had been over a year, with Anna not carrying his own flesh and blood within her, he wanted Kory to warm to him even more. *This may be our only child. What can I do, Lord? Show me.*

The fish had been jumping onto the line today, *at least I can bring home enough for the table tonight. This is good.* Rawiri let the gratitude he felt fill his heart.

Kory had heard the sickening sound of Paulo's neck breaking and knew, just knew, what he had done. He started to run. Blinded by his fear, he did not see Rawiri until he ran right into him.

"Ooph." The fish flew through the air.

Had Rawiri been a weaker man, he would have been knocked off his feet. "Boy, what is it?" Holding Kory's shoulders, he bent down and met the frightened child eye to eye.

"I killed a man." Kory blurted out the truth, not fully believing it himself.

Rawiri saw the look of terror in his eyes. He opened his arms to hold Anna's son, and Kory gladly stepped in. He gave thanks for the teaching of his Anna. She had shown him through the years that holding those you love close can sometimes be all we can offer them.

"Let's go hang these fish back in the water and you can tell me everything." With his hand firmly resting on the back of the frightened child, they walked back to the fishing hole in silence.

Tony came into the clearing and saw the man and boy bonding. *This is beauty.*

Rawiri had his arm around the lad, intently listening to every word he was saying as their feet dangled in the cool water of the pond... *Phew, finally.* Tony had witnessed Rawiri's attempt to draw Kory in as his own with little success to date. *It looked like today things had changed.* Leaving them to their moment, Tony returned home to tell Anna the news.

Anna stood in silence allowing the truth to settle into her heart. She loved Paulo. She always hoped he would be awarded his portion of faith to guide him into a life eternal. Now it was too late. "Are you sure?"

"Oh yes he is very dead." Tony tried to sound compassionate. In truth he felt relief.

Anna walked out onto the veranda and wondered when Rawiri would bring Kory home. And so she waited.

With ease Rawiri lifted Kory, *his son*, onto his shoulders and headed home to Anna.

Today his prayers had been answered. The boy told him everything Paulo had said, why he had run and the fear he had felt when he knew Paulo was dead. The two bonded over trust. Kory poured out his heart, also confessing he wanted to call Rawiri Papa. "From this day on you call me Papa," Rawiri confirmed. Kory gave a weak smile and nodded his head in affirmation. The two touched forehead to forehead and shared a breath.

Anna watched with pure joy the two of her heart's desires appear at the edge of the forest. The smile on Rawiri's face as he carried the child on his shoulders would be a sight Anna would never forget.

Not many attended the funeral. Anna was glad to have her loved ones around her as she listened to the readings. Tears finally came when the Lord's prayer was spoken by all in the native language. The beauty of sound and word was a song from her heart to the heavens.

Kory had eventually told his mother the words that he had heard Paulo speak from his knees that day. The happiness on her face made the healing of his own heart take a giant leap. "We will see Paulo again." Taking her child into her arms, Anna rocked him back and forth and lifted words of praise to the Almighty for the blessing her son had given her.

Rolo was a great distraction in the weeks after the funeral. Tony acquired for both boys their own black merino sheep and it was decided to use the stone cottage as the sheep shed.

Anna cleared out all Paulo's belongings, of which there was not much. The whalebone stool she brought to the villa and the small Bible she returned to the shelf. Paulo had never spoken of next of kin, so passing on the items that could be used seemed prudent. Once the rest of the furniture was delivered to the Mission House and the floor swept, Anna took a moment to pray.

Returning to the last spot anyone had seen Paulo alive, Anna knelt before the hearth and gave thanks to God. Their lives had been enriched knowing Paulo and she was always glad that Uncle Tally had known a good friend. He was often away and she wondered if he had been lonely. *How could he be, with a friend like Paulo always at his side?*

"Thank you, Father, for creating a place for you alone to take root and grow within us as Love. Your child Paulo, in the end, found faith in your son Jesus and I am now comforted to know that a day will come when we will all be united once again for you have given us the promise that this is so through your Grace and I believe. I now ask that my prayers are brought to you in the hope that Christ Jesus finds great joy in passing them on to you too, as I pray these words in his name." Anna sat quietly for a moment and let the stillness of the warm day and cool interior of the stone cottage comfort her. It was then that she noticed what had been always overlooked. The fireplace had never been used. *How strange.*

Later that evening, when the villa settled down and the adults gathered on the veranda, Anna brought up the subject. "Did any of you ever notice that the fireplace in the stone cottage has never been used?"

"Well, no I hadn't. How odd. There must have been winter days that the interior would have been like an ice house. Even on warm days, it is always cooler than the villa." To be fair though Tony had not spent much time through the years inside.

Rawiri reached over and took her hand, and proceeded to hold it close to his heart. Anna blushed. "The man and his life was a mystery to me. The one thing I did know about him was how much he enjoyed your raisin cake."

"Maybe I am just being silly. Now that the stone cottage has a new purpose, I doubt that the black sheep will be needing the warmth of a fire anytime soon." Laughter broke out and filled the night sky.

Chapter THIRTY NINE

1823 *Bergen Op Meer Netherlands*
Batina sat in her spot before the fire and wondered just how many times she could let out her dresses before she would need to replace them with a complete set of new ones.

Months ago she had noticed that her diet changed when her monthlies had stopped. She could not get enough of the bread and butter that Josie made each day. She simply had no willpower to stop herself from enjoying each delicious bite, then going back for more each time the aroma of fresh baking filled the air. It was as if she could smell the baking from any room.

Having little Miss Sophia living with them had been a great joy and Batina often felt full of vigour and restorative energy, as though a source of life was flowing from within her.

Josie began to wonder at Batina's odd behaviour these past weeks. She was glowing and gaining an enormous amount of weight. It was true that she often indulged in the bounty of her baking efforts, but Batina was full of energy and worked tirelessly all day, always with a sweet smile on her face.

It was when she was assisting Batina with the alterations on yet one more of her work dresses and the ladies sat in companionable friendship that the most extraordinary event occurred.

Without warning water gushed out from between Batina's legs. The older woman was completely taken off guard, humiliated. It was when the intense pains shot through her back in regular intervals that Josie began to understand what moments before would have been the unthinkable. Batina was going to be a mother.

"Batina, you are going to have a child, now, today. We need to get you to your room." Josie was calm and firm. She took complete control of the moment. Batina looked both to be in shock and overjoyed at this precise moment.

"I cannot move as my bowels are emptying out as I rise to stand, child. This simply cannot be happening."

"Oh, but it is. Here and now." Josie quickly grabbed as many of the empty sacks that were neatly stacked in the corner and laid them on the floor, gently lowering Batina onto them.

This was not the first time Josie had delivered a baby and she knew one was coming into the world today, possibly right now.

With one mighty push the child entered without a single complication. "You have a son." Josie had to laugh at the miracle of birth and the look on Batina's face. "Lets get him swaddled, then you can hold him as I deal with the matters yet to come." *Thank goodness thread was on hand to tie off the cord.*

Batina held her son in complete awe as tears spilled from her eyes onto the most enchanting face she had ever seen. It mattered very little that she was lying on the floor in a heap of what would now be unusable cloth.

"Okay, my friend, let's get you up, to your rooms and into some clean night clothes." Josie held out her hands for the child.

Reluctantly the baby was passed to waiting capable hands and placed in a basket lined with dried corn husks. Once in her room Batina was exhausted. She soon fell into a deep and peaceful sleep, with the child resting next to her in his basket. Josie watched over them in complete wonder and then thought of Jude for the first time.

When Jude entered the kitchen carrying the afternoon's supply of wood he simply could not understand what he was seeing. The area that normally was the meeting place of his beloved wife and Josie was in a state of disaster.

"My friend, place the wood down and come with me." Josie entered the kitchen with the strangest look on her face.

"What has happened? Where is my Tina?" Jude was beginning to sweat even though the room was cold.

Josie extended her hand. "Come, I have a great joy to bestow on you this day, my dear man. All is well. Very well indeed."

Jude first placed the wood in the box next to the stove, and uncharacteristically took the hand offered to him.

When they got to the door of the rooms that he and his wife shared, they stopped. Josie held her ear to the door and the most radiant smile presented itself on her face. Jude had never seen her look more beautiful. "Open the door," she said.

With a gentle hand Jude moved the handle ever so slowly. With heart-stopping anticipation he opened the door and gingerly stepped into the room. *Why is my precious Tina in bed at this hour?* was his first thought.

He turned back to look at Josie. As she was still smiling, he knew not to fear. She motioned him forward towards the bed.

"Go," she whispered. Josie was ready at hand, preparing to place a chair under him when he saw the babe peacefully sleeping in the basket next to his mother.

Jude moved one step at a time towards the bed. His sweet one was dishevelled and completely beautiful as she slept with an angelic turn to her lips.

The babe in the basket chose this moment to make himself known to his father by letting out the sounds of what was most likely hunger. He started off softly. By the time Jude made his way around the bed, baby Wolf had also woken up his mother who was smiling up at the bewildered look of her husband. Sweet laughter from Batina filled the room. "Here is your son."

Just as Jude was about to collapse, Josie slipped the sturdy chair underneath him. "My son. How can this be?"

Batina blushed. "Well my dearest, we are husband and wife."

The child was now making sounds of real hunger and Batina knew just what to do. Josie helped her sit up, discreetly covered the top half of the soon-to-be nursing mother, and placed the child in her arms. Silence soon filled the room.

"Batina, I think your husband needs you also. I will be back with fresh linen shortly." It was time to give this new family a moment together.

"How can this be?" Jude was in shock. Leaning in, he lifted the covering and saw a suckling child nestled into Batina with the smallest of hands resting on her bosom.

"He is our miracle, a gift from above. I am as surprised as you are. I simply thought my menses had ceased to flow due to old age and I was gaining a wider girth as a result." Batina looked down at her son and smoothed the dome of soft hair. "Simply put, he is perfect and is ours."

"Are you well, my Tina?" Jude looked on with concern.

"Yes. He gave me very little trouble and his entry into the world was, as you can see, quick." Batina beamed up at her husband. "He has no name, my husband."

"Name? Oh, yes, of course. Let's just call him Baby Wolf for now." Jude sat back into the chair just as Josie reentered with fresh linen and a glowing smile.

"Anna and Ashton will simply never believe me. That sweet lad Kenyon will be leaving soon. I will be sure to send a letter to them explaining the miracle of life that has today become part of the family." Batina once again looked very tired.

Josie gently removed the sleeping babe with a sweet pop. "We won't be long. I have made the fire and this little one needs a bath. Jude, I will leave you in charge of his mother."

The news eventually arrived on the tide at Lions Vineyard. Hand delivered by Kenyon Lewis. "A baby!!!!" Anna simply could not take in the news.

"Yes, truly and just. They have a son. He is healthy and strong, the apple of his father's eye." Kenyon smiled with delight to bring such news. Samuel Judah Wolf. Well, better known as little Sam. But I am sure Batina has included this all in her letter. She is besotted with him." Kenyon had to smile over the true depth of little Sam's parents' devotion to him.

"Hahaha. Oh yes, Jude would be a great father. He was the only father Tony ever knew. By a strange twist of fate, our Puppa believed himself to be our Uncle, knowing no different until a few days before his death."

"Extraordinary! You must tell me the story one day."

"One day I will." Anna said.

"Miss Sophia is great with him too. She is a lovely child." The love he had for her showed in his eyes.

Anna had never seen Kenyon look the way he did when he mentioned Sophia. "You love her, don't you? Sophia that is."

"Yes. She is the image of you, just younger, and her gentle spirit is endearing." Kenyon smiled.

He sat at the large table in the villa enjoying one more helping of sugar biscuits.

He and Anna had long ago become friends and for this he was glad. To be the messenger of this family gave him a family of his own to belong to and he could see now that that had been his desperate longing. With each trip across the vast ocean with Captain Jock, he would faithfully deliver letters back and forth and tell Anna, then Batina, all that he could that was not in the letters. With each trip he would also find a special gift to take home for Miss Sophia. She was a delight, always happy to see him. Jude and Batina also loved her as their own. They now had a son to love too. *Life is filled with blessings, he thought.*

Chapter FORTY

The truth is revealed by Damien.

Jock Smit could see that his daughter and Master Damien had fallen in love. When the birth of his grand-daughter was announced, he was certain they had become a family, although not in name. *Why had Damien not asked for my daughter's hand?*

Anna also had her questions.

One day when seeking out information about her inheritance and the distribution of assets, Anna ventured to the Gate House to speak to her Uncle. She made her way along the tulip-lined pathway that meandered from the estate gardens to the Gate House humming a happy tune.

She was enjoying being a woman of means, and her many freedoms as much as her many responsibilities. Her Uncle Damien and his family were now her concern. Today she was determined to speak with him about his future before finalising her plans to join the Mission group.

"Thank you, Miss Gata, would you like to join us?" Damien looked into the eyes of the woman he had come to love and gave an encouraging smile.

"No, Master Damien. My little Sophia will be needing me soon and I will take my tea in the nursery." Gata loved this man with all her heart and cared very little if anyone else knew it.

"Of course." Turning back to his niece who waited patiently. "What brings you here today, my dear?"

Gata quietly closed the library door, also wondering at the reason for Mistress Anna's visit. It was rare that anyone ever bothered them here at the Gate House.

"Well, Uncle, I shall come right to the point." *Finally someone to talk to.* She took a deep breath. "I have been beating a steady path to the solicitor over the last fortnight and have come to the conclusion that both Junior and Senior Hammer see me as a woman of deep mourning, incapable of dealing with my own affairs. This is quite frustrating and has led me to seek you out. You see, I wish to be assured that we both are well represented in all our affairs as I will be taking a long journey soon with Captain Jock and the missionaries to the land that Ashton was destined for. I do not believe his life has ended and I have every intention of bringing him back here to Bergen Op Meer for him to assist with the many responsibilities as my equal. To be completely forthright, I had always thought that you and my Puppa should have shared equally in the estate." Anna lifted the tea cup to her lips and took a delicate sip.

Damien watched in fascination as his dear sweet niece lifted to her lips the priceless piece. She truly had no idea what she was holding. Damien had instructed Gata to use this set for their meeting today. In truth, he wanted to see if Anna noticed. "My provisions are adequate, my dear. I have for many years been very content in the Gate House. As you do not seem to mind having me stay on here, I hope this arrangement is now even more suitable to you, because I can assist with matters arising while you are on your quest." Damien's hand shook slightly as he paused to lift his cup from the equally delicate plate.

"Oh my, yes! Thank you, Uncle, I accept your generous offer. You do not think I am delusional, as some have said?" Anna sat in happy readiness to hear his reply.

"Not in the slightest. A twin knows these things. Jacobus and I delighted in this gift." For a moment a shadow passed over his face.

With compassion Anna asked, "What happened?"

The room suddenly felt very heavy, as though a shadow blanket had been laid on them both. The feeling of oppression filled the room.

"My dear ...... your Puppa and I had a close bond but we both loved your mother. We all grew so close. We both knew that one of us would ask for her hand. He asked first. As you know, she said yes."

"But why did you not ask?" Anna spoke the words before even really thinking about them first.

Shall I tell her? There is so much to lose if she knows. But if I don't ,I will never be set free. "You see your tea cup?" Damien pointed to the delicate cup and saucer she now cradled in her hand.

"Why yes, Uncle. It is unique and quite lovely, but why does it matter?" Anna began to think of all of the other matters she needed to get on with and did not want to sit here for a history lesson on the serving of tea.

"It is the most valuable artefact you now own. This set has passed through the family for over a thousand years. The six cups and saucers were commissioned to commemorate the birth of Christ. When your cup is drained, you can lift it to the light and see the star that led the magi to the birthplace of the Messiah." Damien began to sense the lifting of a long-held burden.

"Uncle, this family has had some very fancy ideas through the years. This is just too much to believe." Anna did hold the now empty cup to the light and enjoyed the sight. The cup was enchanting.

"The first one to marry would relinquish the set to the other brother who married second. It was why it took us so long to ask her. Neither of us wanted to give it up. Please forgive us, we were very young. We both loved your mother and she wanted a family. It was Jacobus that saw the true treasure and married for love and family." More oppressive weight left his shoulders and the room.

"How very odd that my mother would want it destroyed. This was her final journal entry the day before we were born. Why, Uncle?" Anna was beginning to feel the tea hit her stomach like a stone hitting the bottom of a lake.

"You could say I was more than just a little bitter on their wedding day and made my twin the unthinkable offer." Demain had the good grace to look sheepish. "I am ashamed of myself to this day." He paused. "The tea set came to mean nothing to me and I wanted somehow to hold onto a piece of your mother. So I offered it back to Jacobus if he would allow me to enter the bridal chamber before him, as him. I thought this would give me some peace."

The colour drained from his niece's face.

"Now before you jump too far ahead, let me explain. Nothing happened. I loved her too much and could not go through with it. I thought Jacobus must have known."

"I simply do not understand. How could she not have known?" Anna sat dumbstruck.

"The only way she could tell us apart is the mark on the palm of my hand. The one that is identical to Ashton's. The candlelight was dim in the chamber and I used the hidden doorway. Jacobus simply slipped in after I slipped out. What I did not know was the fact Jacobus thought you and your brother were mine, not his. This is simply impossible." He paused. Looking sad and lighter.

"For years I tried to speak to him and make amends. He was utterly lost after the death of your mother, we both were. In the hope of saving your brother more heartache, I stayed away, thinking Jacobus would come to love his son as he obviously did you." Damien thought back to the day he knew his brother was dying.

"I could feel his life slowly slipping away. Captain Jock has been a good friend to us both through the years. Without knowing the full sad tale, he suggested I place my heart on parchment and give it to my twin brother in the hope he would read it and also to release me from my prison. And so I did.

Miss Gata delivered it a few days before Jacobus died but not before he read it. I know this because Jock was with him when he died. His last words were 'Ashton and Anna are mine.'"

Anna sat in utter silence. Was she even breathing? *This explained so much.* The room began to take on the light filtering in through the tall windows again. "Uncle, there has been suffering, too much suffering. This needs to end today." Anna wiped a tear from her eye as she thought of all the pain Ashton had endured.

"Can you forgive me, child?" Looking at her with longing, Damien hoped with all his heart she could.

"There is nothing for me to forgive, Uncle. Ashton has suffered a far greater loss than any of us and I am even more determined to find him. Let us hope this extraordinary turn of events brings him peace for I know he has suffered the loss of it on many occasions. It would now seem that Gata and Sophia need you well of heart also. Will this be so?"

Anna's bearing showed her focused determination. She placed the cup and saucer aside as though it meant very little. Leaning forward she took his hand.

"Yes, my dear. You are wise beyond your years and I give thanks to the Lord that I may find peace once again. I love Gata and little Sophia deserves to have all the protection that I can give her." Damien's shoulders began to lift from the burden of the past.

Dusting the crumbs from her day skirt, she became all business. "Now, let's get matters sorted as I leave within a fortnight."

Kenyon could not believe his ears. "Extraordinary!"

"Indeed. Now just give me a moment or two to put my thoughts to parchment. I have a few things to say to Jude and Batina and would like to send gifts to the children. Ataahau has been teaching me to weave." Anna sprang from the table but not before slipping the half empty plate in front of Kenyon to finish just as Tony and Rawiri walked in. "Tony, could you get your own, please. There are more in the pantry." She blew a kiss to her heart's desire and off she went.

Kenyon enjoyed the time he had at Lions Vineyard. Tony was a fine man and Rawiri an even better storyteller. He sat back and claimed his biscuits. What was to come would be a tale to take home with him.

Rawiri did not disappoint.

Chapter FORTY ONE

Vancouver British Columbia Canada

Kat saw him in the waiting crowd immediately. This was not hard to do. He would stand out anywhere. "Hi." She stepped into his welcoming arms as though she had belonged there all her life. He smelled of fresh air, musk and grass. *Is that a grass stain on his sleeve?* "What have you been doing?" Kat smiled up into his eyes as she stood in his arms.

"Oh, it's been quite a day. I will tell you all about it over dinner. We can eat on the ferry." Tony was happy, so much so he kissed the top of her head without giving it a second thought.

His mate Fitzy was out of the country playing for a team in France. He had messaged Tony early that day the location of the key, explaining that Tony would need to bring food as *'the place is not big enough to hold enough for him'* for the three days they planned to stay on, although *'the fridge was well stocked with cold beers as well as a connoisseur's selection of local wines and artisan waters.'*

After picking up a sizable take-away at Tim Hortons in the novelty of a 24 hour drive-through on the way to the cabin, Tony and Kat found the key hidden under a massive wooden carving of a bear at the entrance to the property. Tony wrapped the bear in a big hug and lifted it off the ground.

Without fear Kat reached underneath the obviously heavy, solid timber and grabbed the keys. "It is a very good thing you are made the way you are." Kat laughed at herself. She was feeling light-hearted and very happy. Besides, she loved it when Tony smiled at her and this he did again and again.

"This is enchanting, Tony. Thank you for making this happen. I can hear the surf. And look, a faint outline of what must be the coastal mountain range. How beautiful! Do you know the meaning of the name ERCAMALO?" Kat stood leaning on the driftwood railing that separated the cabin from the drop to the beach below and pointed to the name over the door.

She was so beautiful in the glow coming through the French doors. Tony found it difficult to respond, so he took a second to just smile at her. "Yes. It is the first two letters of each of his children's names in order of their birth."

"That is very thoughtful. Family is everything." Kat at times missed having her parents to confide in and she wondered if Tony felt the same.

Tony was not sure where to take this conversation. "I will grab our things." Off he went, leaving her to put away the food they had brought. It was then she noticed just how much space they had. Kat was not at all ready for any new level of intimacy.

"Here." Passing Kat her bags, "You take the bedroom, I will take the couch. I am sure it is a pull-out and there will be plenty of blankets somewhere. There is a nip in the air tonight and I think we are in for a cold day or two."

"Oh my, Tony, could you just imagine if it snowed." Though Kat already had all she could ever hope for, she did think a little snow would be enchanting.

"Well, it has been known to happen at this time of year here, or so Fitzy tells me. He said the place is well stocked with extra coats, and boots too. I'm ready for a snack, then we can both settle in for the night. What do you say?"

"I will freshen up first, then the bathroom is all yours." Kat wheeled her bags into the bedroom and quickly selected the things she needed. She did not want to miss a moment with Tony.

He was right and Kat got her wish. A white blanket of snow lay over the landscape in the morning.

Tony found the coffee pot and had already drunk his first cup when Kat made her way into the living room that overlooked the most spectacular view of God's snow-covered creation.

Kat was enchanted.

Tony placed a cup of hot brew just the way she liked it into her hand and led her over to the freshly made couch. And there they sat in companionable silence as the last snowflakes fell onto a landscape of white trees, misty seas, all framed majestically by the coastal mountain range.

At Bergen Op Meer, Hannah was excited. Vaun had started working on her case as soon as he returned to Vancouver. He began assembling a team of trusted specialists who could meet with her and Massy much earlier than expected. So it was not long after Kat left that more travel arrangements were being hastily made.

Vancouver was truly a beautiful harbour city. Vaun's offices overlooked Stanley Park from the North Shore. The view was breathtaking. "Thank you for coming with me, Massy. I know it was complicated for you to juggle all your clients. I promise somehow I will make it up to you."

"I will never let you travel alone. I promised Tony I would always take care of you and so I shall. Let's get you into your gown." Massy was glad that they could share every detail of this journey and would see it through to the end.

Hannah would be staying in the private clinic in the best of care with Massy close by at the Coastal Renaissance Inn.

Lotti had explained the first procedure would be exploratory, the second much longer with more recovery time needed. They could expect to be with them for at least two weeks.

"Are you okay, Banana?" Tony had called her room that evening from the cabin. The snow affected international departures for twenty-four hours which meant Tony and Kat would be leaving Canada five days later than expected.

"I'm good, Tons. Kat told me what happened. I bet you feel like a total dolt now?" Kat had found out why Tony had a grass stain on his dress shirt and was given the okay to tell Hannah everything the next time the girls talked. Which they did, often.

"Hahaha, I am over that bit now. I feel free. Matt is a good man. I can see those kids love him. He knew exactly what I needed. I think he is free now too. Hannah?"

"Yes." Hannah twisted the phone cord through her fingers as she enjoyed the view of the city lights from her bed.

"Uncle Jonty was really special. He asked for nothing from any of us and look at what all of us have now. I wonder if we ever really knew him." Tony pulled Kat a little closer to him.

"I know, Tons. I am feeling that way too as I look out at the city and think of the possibilities tonight. But even more so, I feel loved. The kind of love that cannot always be explained, but is known, a love deeply alive. God is truly good. When Mom and Dad died, I felt cut off from the feeling of belonging at first. Over the years that changed. I've changed. He sure loved God and look at all he lost and suffered. Did you ever hear him complain? Not once." She paused in thought. " I miss him."

"Me too. Well, Sis, tomorrow is a big day and you need your rest" Tony's arm remained firmly around the woman he was holding close. Kat silently mouthed the words to Tony, *Say goodnight from me!* And she blew a kiss.

"Kat says goodnight too. You are in our prayers. We will be in Vancouver in a few days, that's if the ferries are running from the Island as they have had their share of issues too. We will stop by the clinic on the way to the airport. I am excited to show Kat Lions Vineyard." Tony hoped she would never leave.

"Nite, and Tons,"

"Yah?"

"Love you." In fact she was a little scared.

Tony could hear it. "You are the bravest woman I know, and I love you too." Tony ended the call there and turned to Kat at his side and surrendered to her open arms. He needed a hug.

Looks like more than one big bear needed to be hugged, thought Kat.

Chapter FORTY TWO

T*reatment continues at the clinic.*

"Now that we have seen what we are dealing with, I am confident that rejuvenation repair can be made to some of the areas affected by the trauma of the accident." Vaun had left Hannah with Lotti and gone in search of Massy to tell him the news also.

"Vaun, I do not need to tell you how important the outcome is to her. Please be brutally honest with me. Is there real hope?" The weight on Massy's shoulders pushed down on him and it showed.

"We have had success in the past but it really depends on her body's response to the next treatment. Let's leave hope in who it belongs to and stay positive. She is determined. This is good," slapping Massy on the back. The two men understood just how powerless they truly were.

"You know, I love her just as she is but she won't have me. I am certain it is because she can't have a baby." Massy looked beaten.

"She is awake and asking for you both." Lotti could see she had interrupted, but the patient's needs are always first and these two men could work out the rest later.

Hannah looked so delicate in the bed. "Hello, lieveling, how are you?" Massy simply could not hide his feelings.

Hannah opened both her hands and indicated the chairs. Vaun on one side of the bed took one. Massy on the other side took the other.

"Let's move forward tomorrow. Lotti has explained your findings and I have waited long enough. For now I would like to sleep as I am very tired. Okay?" She trusted them and knew they would not let her down.

"Okay." Vaun did not think she heard him as she was already peacefully resting. This is good.

The weather was bright and beautiful for the ferry crossing and Tony was ready to be going home. "Massy will be waiting for us at the clinic. Hannah is resting comfortably and can see us today. This is a relief. I need to see her." Kat held a little tighter to the hand she was holding and Tony blessed her with one of his smiles.

The memories flooded in of the days after the accident. Hannah had told Massy Tony would be affected this way and to watch out for it. They got to the entrance, Tony could not take another step. For a moment he stood in the entry to the elegant clinic with beautiful surroundings and waited for the wave of the past to flow through him.

Massy soon stepped into his line of vision with a tall and confident man in a clinical jacket. The moment ended, *thank God.*

Kat moved from Tony's side and leaned in to receive a kiss from her brother on each cheek. "Tony, did you hear what the doctor said?"

"What? Oh no, sorry Mate, could you repeat that?" Tony shook his head to clear the debris.

"We have never met. I am Vaun Rainbird." He extended his hand to the mountain of a man in front of him and held his breath.

"We know each other well, don't we? I am pleased to meet you, Doc." Taking his hand gently, Tony held on for a moment and let the last remnant of the past leave his life, he hoped for good.

Vaun began to breathe again. "So true. I am giving all I am and have to Hannah now. She is asking for you both. Tony?"

"Yes"

"There is nothing I wouldn't do for either one of you." Love shone through Vaun's eyes.

Tony gave one of his smiles. Turning to Kat, polite introductions were then made. Everyone now knew the whole story and Vaun was relieved, yet again, that everything was out in the open.

"Hello, Tony and Kat. I am Lottii and in charge of things here." Lotti gave a giggle. She had yet again interrupted the conversation and really *couldn't care less.* She was just too happy to care. "She is waiting for you and no one wants to keep Hannah waiting." Kat was sure it was this woman who was never kept waiting. She was tall, beautiful and had a regal bearing.

"Lead the way." Kat took Tony's hand and followed *Miss Lotti long-legs* down the glass-walled walkway, lined with native wood carvings, that overlooked the most stunning view of the city.

In the Netherlands, Millicent hid in Amsterdam. It was a city one could easily get lost in. Which is exactly what she did. She lost herself in the many sights and sounds hoping that the guilt she felt would lift and she could go home and face everyone again. That she disappointed her parents is what bothered her most.

To take her mind completely off painful matters, she knew that enjoying the art to be seen in the Rembrandt House would be a soothing balm.

No one really paid her too much attention as she walked from room to room, enjoying a sense of being home again. The paintings of this artist were the reason so many came to Bergen Op Meer. The family collection of art and artefacts was among the very few private collections in the Netherlands open to the public.

It was this and the home of those she loved that had led her to make such a crazy choice all those years ago. For she could now see what she had done was *a bit foolish, these beautiful works were for everyone to see and enjoy.* She should not have stopped the rightful owners from enjoying them all these years. It was time to go back home, face Oma and apologise to Hannah and Tony. She sure hoped they would come to understand and trust her again.

"Oma, I am sorry. It was in those nights you were recovering and I would read to you. When you were sleeping one night, I found the journals and took them. I know I had no right but I felt so protective of you all. After reading them I could not come to terms with you, or Kat and Massy, not having all that I have. Tony and Hannah also deserve so much more. I see this now. As soon as Hannah returns I will give her my apologies in the hope she can forgive me."

Millicent sat with her back ramrod straight, hands folded neatly in her lap in the library at Bergen Op Meer and waited for Oma to respond.

"Better than most, I understand decisions made out of love. I do not condone your actions, but do understand why you made them. We are all blessed to have everything work out exactly as things should. I have a confession of my own. Do you know that you have met their mother, right here at Bergen Op Meer?"

Millicent's brows shot together in thought. "What? How can this be?" This seemed so impossible and certainly not the conversation she thought to be having with Oma today.

"I knew her for many years. Long before the children were even born. What you discovered was not news to me. Johanna King herself worked it out and came to see me before she married. You see, I kept the secret far longer than you. We are both guilty. Yet I feel no guilt." Oma patted Millicent's hand in comfort.

"Johanna and I agreed to keep two secrets. She did not want her life to be anything more than what she already had. She was happy." Suddenly Oma looked sad. "When Ester and Markus died, I needed to turn to her, as the children needed someone to be with them and bring them home. I contacted Johanna and she did just that, without question. All the children were small, so they do not recall meeting each other. You were older. I am sure if you think for a moment, you will recall a gentle, sweet foreigner who was so helpful during the first few weeks after they were killed and helped with the many plans and preparations for the funeral here on the grounds."

"Why yes, I do. Her name was Johanna Heath. Holy Flipping Sea Monkeys!!!!" Millicent sat in complete shock.

Oma giggled. "There is more. Do you know, my dear, who their Uncle Jonty is?"

Catching her twirling thoughts, Millicent took a moment to consider what in heaven's name could possibly be revealed next. "I can tell you he is a very dear man who deeply loved the Lord and the two children in his care. Other than this though, I do not understand your question, Oma." Millicent's shoulders began to relax ever so slightly as the weight of her guilt began to lift.

"Long ago, I believe I mentioned to you, I had been very much in love and was separated from the father of one of my children before we could marry. Jonty is that child. He is my son." The smile on Oma's face was radiant.

Millicent knew she was hearing the most impossible truth, but the truth it was. Flashbacks of the time she had spent at the villa came flooding in and there was the truth for her to see, over and over, as plain as the nose on their faces. Uncle Jonty was very much like his Mother. How did she never see it? *Well, she knew how. It was too fantastic for even her active imagination to fathom such a possibility.*

"Tell me everything you can about my Joshua, lieveling. Leave not a single detail out. And I shall tell you how all of this is possible"

Millicent did not disappoint. "Oma, I even have some pictures somewhere that I can dig up for you."

"That would be wonderful. I find myself now quite fatigued and wondered if you could help me to my rooms, please?"

"Of course. And Oma" Millicent was standing at her elbow.

"Yes." Rising was getting difficult for her unassisted.

"Do you think Tony and Hannah will ever forgive me?" Looking now right into the eyes of the woman who always loved her, she waited.

"They already have." Oma knew from her core this to be true. These two children had been raised by her son to love, and love they did.

Chapter FORTY THREE

Tony and Kat arrive at Lions Vineyard.

Kat could not believe what she was seeing. "Stop, Tony, stop the car." Tony had never heard her use that tone before and he sure was not going to argue with her. They were just coming over the rise and the villa had come into view. He looked sideways at her and saw the strangest look on her face. She sat frozen as though she had seen a ghost. "I have been here before," said in barely a whisper. Kat was finding it hard to breathe.

"Sorry, love, I did not hear what you said?" Tony leaned forward to get in a little closer.

Kat slowly turned her head and looked at Tony as if seeing him for the first time.

"Tony............" She was white and was staring at him in the strangest way.

"How about we continue and you can tell me all about it over a cuppa. What do you say? Mum would always say everything could be worked out that way." He brushed the back of his hand over her cheek and hoped for the best.

"Tony," Kat raised her hand and cupped his cheek "I have been here before. It was your Mum who picked us up after our parents were killed and brought us home. We stayed with you and spent a few very happy days here with your Uncle Jonty. I remember now, I never wanted to leave here."

"What are you saying, Kat?" Tony looked for any evidence of the truth of what she was saying in her eyes.

"Tony, don't you remember. It was you who first called Thomas, Massy. Tony, it was you." Kat looked deep into his eyes and waited. And she knew the moment he remembered. She could see it in their depths.

Tony slowly raised his hand and covered hers that still rested on his cheek. "Welcome home, Kat, you belong here and always have."

"Let's go home, Tony." She radiated and knew they would never be apart again.

"First this." Tony drew her in and kissed the woman he had always wanted.

Charlotte wondered why they had stopped at the top of the hill. The fridge was full, the house was ready and she was happy that Tony was home again. She had missed him. *Maybe Tony was explaining the lay of the land to Miss Wolf.*

It took every ounce of his self control to stop the kiss he had waited a lifetime to plant. "Wait till we tell Charlotte. She is waiting for us now." Tony slowly and reluctantly released Kat but kept his hand firmly in hers.

"Can you just imagine what Hannah and Massy will say? They will surely remember also, don't you think?" Kat sounded elated and breathless. A beautiful glow had returned to her cheeks.

"Yes. I am surprised Hannah never figured it all out. This is nuts, my Kitty Kat, but it is now time to get you home. Are you ready?" Tony was very serious. Never more serious in all his life. He would never let her go again. Tony gave her one of his gorgeous smiles and, with no hesitation, she nodded her head and off they went.

At the clinic, Massy enjoyed these quiet times with just the two of them. They had decided to continue with her massage treatments as Vaun and Lotti both thought this would be helpful for recovery. Hannah was feeling different. Her body was responding to new sensations now which she had never experienced before. Massy's hands were strong and soft. He knew exactly how to ease her body and keep her muscles supple. Lotti had asked her to keep a journal of any change and if there was a significant one, to notify her right away. Hannah reached over to grab her notebook and pen.

"What is that for?" Massy had never seen Hannah break into their time with journaling. "Are you okay?"

"Yes. I want to capture this new feeling and need to write it down now." Hannah slipped on her glasses and attempted to write as he continued to work on one leg and then the other. *What is happening? I am feeling tingly and my skin from head to toe is starting to heat up.* "Lotti..... I need to speak to Lotti right now. Can you please see if she is still here? I need to see her, alone."

Massy felt alarmed but did immediately as requested.

"Here I am." Lotti looked as though she had been napping. She had not left since Hannah had arrived, so this made sense.

"Please, close the door. I do not want anyone to hear this. I think this might be good news but I want to be sure." Hannah was glowing.

"Do tell, you have my complete attention." After ensuring the door was firmly closed, Lotti pulled up a chair and waited. If she was not mistaken, she could swear her patient was blushing.

"I am not sure how to start as I do not know what I am talking about, but here goes. Massy was massaging my legs and for the first time ever I liked it. I mean, really liked it." She was fully blushing now. "It felt wonderful and I did not want him to stop."

"And this has never happened before?" Lotti's clinical mind was going into overdrive.

"Maybe it is nothing and I should not have bothered you. I simply have never felt his way before," Hannah felt silly.

"Oh my dear, this is why I do what I do. Thank you for calling me now. I would like to perform a test right away. May I examine you?" It could be possible that Hannah was stimulated and Lotti wanted to know if she was ovulating. If this was the case, that would mean a huge breakthrough for them and Hannah.

Massy waited outside the room. Standing right next to him was a very dishevelled Vaun Rainbird. "Is she okay?" Vaun asked Lotti when she emerged from the room.

"Oh yes. Give me a minute or two and I will get right back to you." Off Lotti went down the hall as both men turned to watch her speedy exit from Hannah's room. Vaun and Massy looked at each other and both made the decision to follow right behind her. Lotti closed the door at the end of the hall firmly on them both.

The test did not take long.

Lotti looked very pleased with herself when she opened the door. She promptly congratulated her husband with a kiss and headed right back to Hannah's room.

One after another her room filled with her wellness team. Hannah was feeling alive. In fact she had never felt better. Vaun had warned her. Though her energy would return quickly, she would still need to physically take life slow for a time.

"What is it?" Hannah knew the news was good. The look on Lotti's face said triumph.

"You are ovulating." Her smile radiated as the excitement of what this meant took hold.

Silence.

"Did you hear what I said, Miss Hannah King. Your reproductive capabilities are waking up." Lotti was glowing with happiness. Massy plopped down on the floor.

"Hannah, do you know what this means?" Vaun stepped over Massy and stood at her bedside taking her hand.

"I hope I do." Looking into his eyes, Hannah searched for the truth. To her absolute joy it was there.

Nodding his head. "You sure do, my girl. The blockages are repairing, at least in this part of the body."

"Tell me now in words, can I have children?" Hannah was squeezing the life out of his hand.

"Yes." Vaun knew his business well and was completely confident. "The question is, can Massy?" Turning to him, "Come with me, Chap, let's find out for sure." Vaun gently extracted his hand from hers and kissed the cheek of Lotti as he passed by. Lifting Massy by his collar, the two men left the room, leaving behind gales of laughter.

"Well, I guess we all know where this is going. Do you have any questions for me, Hannah? I suspect you have not had much guidance in this department." Lotti was serious.

"Well, now that you mention it, I do know about the birds and the bees from growing up on a farm. If you could just hear me out as I tell you about my fears, I would appreciate it." Hannah was so glad to have someone like Lotti in her life. There are things only a woman in love would understand and this was clearly where Lotti was at in life.

Back at Lions Vineyard other matters were unfolding. "Should we call and tell our siblings?" Suggested Kat. They had so much they wanted to share with Hannah and Massy but were sensitive to Hannah's needs as she recovered.

"What would be great is if they both came here before heading back to Bergen Op Meer. They are already half way." This made the most sense to Tony.

"That would be wonderful. I will be calling Hannah tonight and can mention it to her then." Kat and Hannah kept a regular schedule for calls and this one was perfectly timed.

"Sure. Let's keep our news until they get here. I am certain Hannah will want to make the trip if she is up to it. No pressure on her, though, she has been through enough." He had made a lot of progress on the business end of things and there were a few legal matters that he and Hannah had to deal with. This would give them the chance.

"They are coming. Do you think they suspect?" Kat hung up the phone in the hall that evening, then headed for the kitchen where Tony was helping himself to some of the fresh Anzac biscuits that Charlotte had dropped off earlier that day.

"How could they? They are probably way too busy anyway. Hannah is so focused on recovery, I am sure she has not given us much thought." Though Tony did suspect things had changed somehow between Massy and his sister, it would be good to see just what was going on with his own eyes. And see he did.

Chapter FORTY FOUR

M assy and Hannah arrive at Lions Vineyard.
"Give me but a shake." Massy was delirious with happiness. He immediately stepped out of the car and practically ran to Hannah's side and opened her door when they arrived at Lions Vineyard.

When they had both received the news they desperately wanted, he knew Hannah would confess her feelings without delay. This had happened on the flight from Vancouver over the Pacific. He was ready.

Having had time for shopping when she had been resting, he had found a Michael Hills Jewellers in the city that had exactly the ring he wanted. With discretion the Air New Zealand steward brought them two glasses and a bottle of the finest champagne and let them be alone. Massy had had a slight moment of guilt as he wondered if he should have asked Tony for Hannah's hand in marriage first, but it did not last. *Tony will understand.*

Hannah liked this side of Massy. He was adorable. There was not much that he did not know about her now. That he loved her so openly and with so much affection filled her soul with gladness. She was enjoying a slice of heaven and was glad to share the joy with Tony. *He would be happy for her.*

"I feel a little nervous now that they are here." Kat stood in the circle of his arms as they both looked out the picture window and saw the scene unfolding in front of them.

"By the looks of things, I don't think all of the attention is going to be on us. Just look at how he is holding her." Tony nodded at the two in the yard, as Massy had yet to put Hannah down. He had lifted her from the car and simply had no intention of releasing her.

"Massy Wolf, put me down this instant." Hannah was serious but did not sound at all firm about the request.

"Make me." Massy knew he had her where he wanted and there was not a thing she could do about it.

Tony, with Kat at his side, stepped out onto the veranda. After waiting long enough for them to notice they were there, he cleared his throat.

Oh my, that will do it. Massy gently relinquished his prize and they both headed for their two stern looking siblings waiting none too patiently. Hannah saw it first. Her mother's rings were on Kat's wedding finger.

Raising her arms she greeted her brother, and Massy took his sister into an uncharacteristically exuberant bear hug. As soon as the excitement of being together had washed over the four of them, "Is there something you two want to tell us?" Hannah looked right through both of them. They knew she knew.

"Charlotte married us on Saturday." Tony felt awkward and hoped it did not show. "I knew you would not mind if I gave Kat Mom's rings. I hope I am still right." *Would Hannah want them for herself?*

"Married." Massy was taken completely off guard. *And here he was worried he had not asked Tony.*

"Yes." Kat stepped forward and showed her hand to her brother while firmly holding onto Tony's other hand for support.

"Oh, Tons, I am thrilled and am truly happy for you both. Come here you two." The veranda that had sheltered generations of Heath descendants became once again a place of celebration for the next generation of Kings and Wolfs.

"How about Massy and I get your luggage and you two ladies head inside." Tony did not wait for an answer and put his arm around his brother-in-law's shoulder and off they went to the rental car.

"Are you truly okay I did not ask you, Bro? I have a legit reason and want to share it with you." Tony was feeling the weight of his choice. He did not want anything to come between him and his new brother-in-law.

"It is fast but I know how you feel and Kat is happy. I am wondering why though." Massy popped the boot and started to take out the bags, so he did not notice Tony was blushing.

"Well, this is a bit strange for me to admit but before meeting your sister I had never been with another woman. I wanted my first time to be as husband and wife." To the roots of his curly, blond locks he was almost bright red now. "If the Bros find out it will be the end of me. I let them think otherwise, because I wanted them to leave me alone. You see, I had found Kat when I was just a kid and have been looking for her ever since."

"What do you mean kid? And by the way I will never tell a soul. Thanks for trusting me. It really matters." Massy gave Tony his complete and undivided attention, a quick hug and then lifted their bags from the rental car he had insisted they rent. He always wanted to be the one to care for Hannah, even though Tony had offered to drop off Hannah's vehicle at the airport or be there to pick them up.

"The place looks wonderful, Kat, I can see your touches everywhere." Hannah meant it. This was a home.

"Thank you, Hannah. I am very happy here. The amazing thing is I had always thought that I belonged here. Now I know why." They made their way over to the window and watched their men deep in conversation.

The two sisters analysed the scene outside with great interest. "Don't you want to know what they are talking about?" Hannah sure did. "Wait a minute. What do you mean 'your whole life?' You have never been here."

"Oh, but I have and so has Massy." Hannah turned her full attention to Kat. "Give me a minute."

Kat went down the hall and took a drawing off the wall that had been done by a child. Their mother had had it professionally framed. Uncle Jonty had thought that if she had gone to so much trouble, he had better keep it. It had hung in the hall here at the villa as long as Hannah could remember.

"This is me, this is you, this is Tony and this, this is Massy." Kat pointed to four of the five figures in the drawing. "Massy, Millicent and I drew this for your Mom before she came back to New Zealand. You see, our parents died in an accident not far from here. Oma had nowhere else to turn, so she contacted Johanna King and she came and got us from the research ship, brought us to her home and then we spent time here with your Uncle Jonty. Come to think of it, he is our Uncle Jonty too."

"You're serious!" Hannah stared at the drawing, perplexed.

"Yes, I have never been more serious. Don't you remember? Hannah, it was Tony and his friends who gave Thomas the name Massy and it stuck. I did not want to leave here. I felt as though I belonged even then. Tony does remember me. It took him a moment too."

Hannah dug deep into her childhood memories and sifted through years of images of times here at the villa as she played with the ring on her engagement finger. She would like to remember meeting Massy as a boy.

Kat let out a gasp, "Hannah, you're engaged?" Taking Hannah's hand, more to quiet it than any other reason. Kat was beginning to feel guilty for putting so much news on her as she was recovering. Even though Kat knew the news was positive and Hannah was strong, she made a mental note to go a little slower.

Massy and Tony stepped into the kitchen with all the luggage just as Kat looked up from Hannah's hand.

Tony stepped forward. "What is this?"

It was now Massy's turn to look sheepish. "Tony, she is the one and I could not wait. Hannah said yes. Are you happy?" Massy to this point truly had no idea how important Tony's approval was. He waited in the space of Tony's stunned silence.

Tony really did not mind at all, but he had a moment of not wanting anyone else to take his place. "That was fast." *Who was he to talk?*

Hannah reached up and took his hand. "You will always be my Tons and as soon as possible an Uncle Tons."

"I know, Banana, I need a minute to let all this change settle in. Do you know it is less than a year since Uncle Jonty died. I sure could use his steady-on ways right about now." Turning, Tony held out his hand and shook Massy's hand in sincere congratulation.

Phew. "That's a relief." Massy truly looked relieved. He started to breathe again.

"Come here, Tons." Hannah raised her arms. Without hesitation Tony leaned in and lifted her into his arms. She rested her head on his heart and listened to the strong beat. Wrapping her arms around his neck, they held each other.

Kat and Massy exchanged looks of complete understanding. With the arrival of these two dear souls into their lives a short time ago, they also felt the effect of the speed of change. Everyone needed a moment. Kat held out her hand for her brother and he took it. She did not want to disturb the moment and silently mouthed the words, *Congratulations my Brother!* to the happy, grown man she loved dearly standing next to her. Placing a kiss on each of his cheeks, on either side of his big smile.

"I am good now, Banana. You picked a good man. I approve." First kissing her forehead, Tony gave his sister one of his smiles saved for special moments only. Hannah basked in his light.

"I need a cuppa." Hannah was all in.

Tony gently released his sister as Massy stepped right in.

Kat took the drawing she was still holding over to the benchtop and put the kettle on.

They soon all settled in around the table. "I honestly do not recall being here before. May I see that drawing again?" Massy just could not wrap his brain around the fact all of them had been together as children. Tony reached over, grabbed the drawing, and handed it to him. "Everything in that time is a blur. Even today it still seems surreal and I expect our parents to still be somewhere. They were always going here and there, this was nothing new. You say we drew this for Tony and Hannah's Mum?" Shaking his head, he hoped it would help him remember, but it didn't.

"Yes. You particularly liked being at the airport and were very ready to go home." Kat could remember every detail of this time as it was a painful one for her, and hard to forget.

Some memories began to form in his mind. "I can recall a stone house. This I remember because the kitchen was like ours at Bergen Op Meer. We ate cookies there one day when we were exploring, didn't we?" Massy looked for confirmation from his sister.

"Now I know why the kitchen at Bergen Op Meer and The Gate House seemed so familiar to me. They are an identical layout to the Stone Mission Building here in the North that was built with the help of Tony Heath, our ancestor." Hannah was wondering if the light that finally went on in her head was shining on everyone at the table because it was so bright.

"One and the same." Kat was pleased.

"I wish I could remember being all together." Hannah looked a little sad.

"Do you remember that time when Dad did the cooking and Uncle Jonty picked us up from school and took us for ice cream every day for two weeks?" This was a solid memory for Tony because Dad was not a great cook, so they did takeaways every day. Having ice cream daily was a dream come true.

"Why yes, I do. Mum had left all those meals in the freezer. We never touched one of them. She was not at all happy with us when she got home. This was when she really got going on my cooking lessons. My first cookbook had some of the recipes in memory of her. I think she taught the wrong child to cook though." Laughter broke out.

"Well, Mum was with them at Bergen Op Meer." Tony waited as he could see it all coming back to Hannah now.

Everyone waited. The fog of lost memories was clearing and it was written all over her face. Turning and pointing to her fiancé, "Massy, you're Massy. I remember. You wanted to go home the whole time you were here and" pausing, Hannah remembered, "Kat, you never wanted to leave. I remember. Welcome home, my sister." The two girls touched hands in complete understanding of knowing a true homecoming. The villa was full of peace and understanding as the two happy couples spoke of the future.

"When will you two marry?" Tony was thinking about the upcoming season and he wanted everything to work out. Kat had already decided to change her education plans. She would do distance learning and take on more of the running of Lions Vineyard. At first Tony was concerned she was giving up too much. After she had reasonably explained to him this was not the case, he gave in completely. As long as she came to as many of his games as possible, he was in complete agreement.

Massy spoke first. "Well, my little Kiwi, how about we get married here too. Whoever this Charlotte is, she must be very capable. What do you say, my Bro." Looking expectantly at his brother-in-law, he waited.

Tony had to laugh. *My Bro.* "Sounds about right to me, what do you think *my wife*?" Tony turned to Kat and gave her his best shine.

Kat giggled. "Of course, but no one has asked Hannah?" She could not help but think all of this was moving very fast.

"Oma." Hannah let the name hang there in suspension.

"I know! Millicent can travel with her. I am sure Oma would come if she would not have to travel alone." The light was now over Massy's head.

With a nod of her head affirming her choice, Hannah let the woman who was now in charge of this household know she approved.

Kat rose once again to hug her new sister-in-law. "Let's call Oma in the morning."

Chapter FORTY FIVE

1824 *Bergen Op Meer Netherlands*
Sophia held little Sam's hand as they skipped their way through the vines with their basket. Today they would have a picnic lunch with Puppa Jude, and Master Simon.

"Hello, dearest Simon, have you brought your appetite to the task today?" Sophia was always happy to help on the estate. She knew that the Gate House would be her inheritance and she was glad that she and Sam would always be together.

"Why yes, I have, my dear. What have you got in your basket today?" The first time Simon had laid eyes on her she was a very small child, doing all she could to try and move the dead horse he had found himself crushed under.

"Mooder Tina has filled it to the top for us all. I will lay out the blanket in the shade and set them out now." Sophia liked having Simon van Dam around. Opa thought that his grand-daughters' holdings needed a no-nonsense manager, and he had taken a liking to him. It had not taken much convincing for Simon to leave his military career. Captain Jock's offer was a lucrative and secure one. It was an easy choice for Simon.

After spending a pleasant meal in close communion with her loved ones, Sophia could see little Sam was in much need of a nap. "Off we go, little one."

Reaching for his hand, once the remains of the meal had been packed, and waving farewell, off they skipped, back into the perfect home that offered up constant calm and security. Sophia would spend the rest of this pleasant day baking with the others and enjoying much laughter. Her life was idyllic and her confidence that this would always be so rested firmly within her heart.

In no way was she prepared for the day that was actually unfolding.

No one was in the kitchen to greet her. This was highly unusual at this time of day. *Where could they all be?* "Come here, little Sam." Placing the basket on the table and lifting up the now very sleepy child into her arms, the two made their way through the hallways to the nursery. Before Sophia could even reach his little cot, he was fast asleep in her arms.

Gently laying him down, she placed a kiss on his forehead, and said a blessing: "*As I lay you down to sleep, heavenly angels guard your keep, standing watch until you wake, to join in all the Lord does make.*" Sophia then quietly closed the door. *Now to find the others.*

She was presently a little unsettled. Her routine had never been upset before and she hoped all was well. *Surely I would know if lightning had struck and there was an issue that had harmed someone keeping Mooder Tina busy elsewhere. Oh my, what if SHE has been harmed?*

This thought prompted her to take off in a very unladylike run.

She would start her search in the library. If she trusted her well tuned ears, that was the direction the sound of voices was coming from, many voices. Sophia could hear Master Kenyon's voice and knew all was well. Tonight the table would be a place of storytelling. Her speed picked up.

Kenyon was enjoying the moment to the fullest, this loving family had a very sweet way of displaying all the inner joy they felt. There was always much excitement when he arrived. *What will my dear Miss Sophia think when she sees what I brought her?* He did not have long to wait, for into the room she burst shortly thereafter.

"Oh, I am pleased to see you, Mistress Anna. I simply am not prepared for your arrival." Batina was glowing as she held the hands of her mistress.

"We will all help." Anna was so happy, she simply had to laugh at the small matter that Batina was fussing over.

This is how Sophia found the woman at the centre of her world behaving when she burst into the room.

"Mooder Tina, I was looking for you and was worried." Sophia was trying to catch her breath. She had no idea what to say next as she took in the whole scene. This was highly unusual for her.

Standing in the library was a huge savage, a very elegant woman, and a boy who looked more as though he belonged in a jungle book, rather than alive, right here in the library.

"Well hello, my pet, have you got a greeting for me?" Kenyon was happy to see her, noting how much she had grown since he had seen her last. She had in fact not looked his way, so distracted she was by the others in the room.

With glee she refocused her attention, threw herself into his arms and allowed herself to be spun around.

Anna would never have believed it without seeing it with her own eyes how much she and Sophia resembled one another. The child was undoubtedly a younger version of Anna in appearance.

Rawiri had seen this style of greeting before, on the beach, the first day he had met his wife. He was glad he knew it was not expected of him. In truth he found it disturbing to see an exact likeness of his beloved Anna in miniature form. *What kind of world am I stepping into?* Anna had come from a place that to him looked like a royal seat to a humble life with him. He was not at all sure what he thought of himself and where he now belonged.

Kory looked on, standing between his parents. He did not think he belonged at all. *What is Rolo doing right now?* He wondered.

"My dear one, let me introduce you to the Mistress of this great house, Anna Malefyt Kavinga, her husband Rawiri Kavinga, and their son Master Kory." Taking her hand and presenting her to the family of this home was a true joy for Kenyon, for he loved them all.

Sophia was never one to be shy, but even for her this was a big moment. She gave the most delicate curtsey and spoke these simple words, "Welcome home."

Master Kenyon's stories and letters had made this family real to her. Now here they stood before her. *Would they like me? Do they know who I am? Will I still be welcome here?* Tears began to form in the corner of her eyes.

Anna could see her distress. Curtsying in response, she offered her open palms to the child into which Sophia quickly placed her hands, but not before looking up to Mooder Tina and seeing her reassuring smile.

Anna smiled sweetly. "I see you have been taking great care of my home and I must thank you. I hope the task has not been too great and that you have had much help from others?"

"Oh yes, My Lady, everyone is wonderful. You see, we all work together." Although Sophia was beginning to breathe normally again, she thought how odd it was that the woman she was speaking to looked so much like her. As though they were sisters.

"I would like for you to meet our son Kory, it is customary to say hello little man." Bringing her son forward to present him was no easy task. His feet were firmly rooted to the floor.

Rawiri was just about to lift him from his spot, when Sophia stepped forward, without any fear or reservation, right into his safe space between his parents.

"Do you want to see the horses?" Sophia held out her hand in full expectation of being obeyed and was not disappointed.

Kory looked into her eyes first and immediately thought he was looking at his own mother in small size. "I have a horse too. What is your horse's name?"

His accent was enchanting. Sophia knew not to laugh, yet inwardly she was delighted. "Madam Silver. She is very pretty. What's the name of yours?" Kenyon had long ago told her stories of the beautiful beasts that roamed the hills of Kory's home.

And as only children can do, Kory trusted her and placed his hand in hers. "Whatitiri. Mumma says it means Thunder."

Off the two children went, chatting away about horses. Not before Sophia turned back and explained to the adults in the room that they would not be late for their meal, and that Little Sam was currently napping upstairs. Sophia did not think Mooder Tina would mind if she did not help with the baking until later in the day, as it looked like the lady of the house was finally home. She looked very capable too.

Chapter FORTY SIX

Have they truly returned?

The conversation was indeed to become very lively that night around the big table. Jude and Simon had been introduced to Kory by Sophia herself earlier in the day. She felt very important doing so. "But, child, are you saying this is Mistress Anna's son?" Jude was not sure he understood her at first. They had spotted her at the paddock late in the day. This being unusual, Simon and Jude went to investigate.

"Yes, Puppa Jude, and she is currently in the library with another traveller who is the likes you have never seen before." Sophia really liked Kory. He was gentle with her horse and she could tell he was going to grow up to be a good horseman. *He had this in him.* Simon did not look at all pleased. *Would this mean his position here would be overtaken? Surely not! Sophia mused.*

"Well, my dear, let's all return to the big house and see for ourselves all that has transpired today." Simon turned to make way as any good soldier would. With immediate haste.

"Will you not first properly greet my new friend and show the hospitality we are accustomed to sharing here? May I introduce Master Kory." Sophia showed her upbringing and for this Jude was pleased.

"As always, you are right." Getting down on one knee, Simon finally greeted the fierce looking child at Sophia's side. "Hello, young Master, I am Simon van Dam, how do you do," extending his hand. Kory looked at it and took Sophia's hand.

"I would like to return to my Mumma and Puppa now, please." Kory was not at all sure about these two men who now seemed to stand over him. It was time to return to safety, even though he did think Sophia had everything under control just like at home with Mumma.

"Yes, little Master, let's go." Sophia once again skipped away from the two men for the second time that day, fully in charge of her surroundings, with not a care in the world.

"Jude!!!" Anna had been watching for him. After Kory had returned, Anna was certain the man he described who would be soon following them, was Jude. She was very unsure as to who the other man was.

"Mistress Anna, you bring great joy to an old man." Jude's heart was soaring. She looked the picture of good health and very happy. "I have met your charming son and see you have brought who I presume to be your husband?"

Rawiri liked the look of this man. He loved Anna and he knew she adored him. "Rawiri Kavinga, sir. Are you the kind Jude Wolf then?" The size of Rawiri was impressive. Even Jude had to tilt his head slightly to meet him face to face.

"At your service. Welcome home, Master Kavinga." Jude was happy. *Did this mean that there would be more capable hands to assist with the ever demanding needs of Bergen Op Meer? And one his size would be very helpful indeed.*

"I answer to Rawiri, sir. I had not thought of this place as my home." Rawiri had enjoyed the trip on Captain Jock's ship. This matter of greeting all Anna's relations was not the pleasure Tony said it would be, nor was entering into the world of Anna and Tony.

Kory slipped his small hand into his Puppa's large one, as he too was feeling homesick.

Anna looked at her two men and her heart fell. She had wondered if they could embrace the life she had known here and had hoped to introduce Kory to it. This was her legacy and now his also. *This is not the best start.*

Jude saw for himself a need for discretion. He wanted the smile on his Mistress's face to remain firmly planted, so he took no offence and found other topics that would be much lighter.

All the introductions and happy chatter took up the better space of the next hour.

Reginald and Josie had also heard all the excitement and wisely put together a hasty but delicious tea for everyone. It was when a very sleepy child entered the room dragging a tattered blanket that the new orders of the day took hold.

"My little Sam." Sweeping the small child into her embrace, Batina drew her son to her bosom. He rested his sleepy head on her shoulder and stuck his thumb in his mouth. From the safety of his mother's arms, he looked out at the gathering with drowsy-eyed interest. Anna had no intention of overwhelming the boy. She simply smiled at the tender sight of mother and child.

"Batina, shall we first have our men do the heavy lifting and get all these cases to our rooms? I am sure there will be plenty of fresh bedding and you and I can start on the evening meal." Anna was now gaining her bearings and once again took charge.

"Splendid idea, Mistress Anna. Follow me, Master Kavinga, Kenyon, Simon and Jude. If you all put a shoulder to it, we shall be done in no time." Batina was walking on air. The Mistress was home and all was right again.

"Rawiri will be my name," said in a tone he hoped would be understood but not taken as disrespect.

"Of course it is." With her free hand Batina patted his big shoulder, as one would a child. She could sense this man needed some understanding. How to deal with him was going to be a new adventure for everyone. He did not look threatening. Kenyon had long ago explained how Rawiri's people were fierce and honourable. "Come, Rawiri, and show these men how hard work is done." With a giggle Batina led them from the room.

"And I shall personally settle Kory into the nursery. That is his trunk there." Anna pointed to the smallest case with the markings KMK. Kory was ready to do his part with the men and was first to the cases.

"And I shall assist with the baking." Off Sophia went with Josie, carrying her share of the remains of the afternoon tea.

"My goodness, Miss Sophia, how wonderful to have Mistress Anna home once again. I do hope this means she is here to stay. We need more children around here. You would then have suitable guidance, as you too will be mistress of your own great home one day and need the correct tutoring." Josie was already busy kneading the dough for the many loaves she was now planning to bake.

"Well, truth be told, I am very content and have had excellent help from you." Sophia had also rolled up her sleeves and was elbow deep in a bowl. Spoken as though from a much older person yet, the kind words filled Josie's heart. She had in fact done her very best. A gentle blush filled her cheeks, one not from the warmth of the hearth in the room but the one from within. Happy chatter from the hallway could be heard. Josie and Sophia turned to each other with the look of female confidence, nodded an affirmation of knowing to each other, and continued with the tasks of the day.

Anna and Batina had settled the children and most of Kory's things, leaving them both eventually in the care of their capable husbands.

"Yes, let's carve the remainder of the meat from the roasted lamb and make shepherd's pies." Anna was pleased to see that some bread was already rising and scads of fresh vegetables were laid out to be chopped. The kitchen had remained well run in her lengthy absence. *This is God's gift of abundance.* "Mrs Doek and Miss Sophia, what do you think of making a feast from all of this and calling it Meer Pie?" Anna was happy and wanted everyone here to share in her joy.

"That will be wonderful, Mistress Anna. We have a - I mean - you have a wonderful herb garden that Josie takes great care of. Would you like to see it?" Sophia felt a little silly. *Always one to speak without thinking first.*

"I would love to. First I need an apron as I can see we are going to be very busy in the kitchen today and for many days to come. There will be loads of things you will need to show me. Can I depend on you and Mrs Doek to help me?" Anna could only imagine how unsettling showing up unannounced must be for those already very busy and hard at work in the kitchen today.

Josie placed her arm around the sweet child who was obviously finding the sudden changes in her life a little too much to bear. "Mistress Anna, with hand on heart, we are here to serve," using a tone of voice like that of a soldier-at-arms. Anna could see the happiness in this kind woman. After a brief pause the gathering of women burst into gales of laughter.

Wiping the happy tears from her eyes, Anna eventually composed herself. "I insist you call me Anna. May I call you Josie, and you sweet girl, Sophia?"

"Yes, I would like that very much." Josie did look very pleased.

"Me too." Displaying complete conviction, with the firmness of pumping her fists towards the floor to show it, sending clouds of flour through the air, Sophia felt solid in her place again. All would be well.

"Good. Now tell me, what do you think of my beautiful Rawiri? I am sure you have never seen the likes of him before." And so the afternoon passed in pleasant conversation. Batina had truly missed the young Mistress. *It is good to have you home, child.* Wiping a happy tear from her eyes with her apron, she got to work.

Chapter FORTY SEVEN

What do we do now?

The weeks flew by. In the daytime Anna hardly ever saw Rawiri or Kory, so busy were they all with the work needing to be done leading up to the harvest. The evening meal was when everyone gathered, including the children.

Kenyon and Captain Jock had taken up residence at the Gate House until they would depart on the seasonal tide, Rawiri was glad to fill in the details that had been missed in the many tales Kenyon had already told. Weekly, after the church service, was a time for play.

Jock was pleased to see his granddaughter's interests were well looked after. Simon had in fact proved to be the best choice as Manager. "Mistress Anna, may I have a word with you at your earliest convenience?"

"Now is quite suitable, I shall ask Batina to bring us some tea in the library." Anna placed aside the ledger she had been writing in and rose from her desk.

"Have I ever properly thanked you for all you have done for Sophia?" They had both settled in their respective leather chairs facing a pleasant fire in the hearth.

This was not what Anna was expecting. "Yes, my dear man, you have. Simon has also taken great care in shrewdly managing her interests also. I am very pleased. Have you any concerns?"

"No, my dear, not a single one. The matter I must speak to you about is you." Captain Jock looked into her eyes.

"Me?" Now very intrigued. "Why?" Anna had no concerns and raised to her lips the delicate tea cup that had been in her family for as long as she could remember. She noted how Batina used the priceless set at every opportunity and thought this was wise.

"As you know, I will be sailing to the new land soon and have made the decision to make this my last trip. This has been a prosperous venture for me but I am no longer a young man. I want to be closer to my granddaughter. As you and I can both see, she is a beauty, and I want to see her happy and well wed in her future. This will give me peace." Jock was not certain if she knew what this meant.

"I understand your thoughts, but why does this concern me?" Anna was not at all sure she wanted to understand. Her constant connection to Bergen Op Meer was a direct result of Captain Jock's enterprising trade venture and it had not crossed her mind that this would end anytime soon.

Anna could see Rawiri had not taken to life at Bergen Op Meer, and Kory was only truly content when he was with the horses or fishing on the lake. On numerous occasions he had asked Captain Jock if he could go on the ship as he wanted to see Rolo.

Anna's heart began to fall. *She was going to have to choose.*

"My dear child, I have seen this before with the men who have taken wives from lands that are not their own and placed them far away from all they know and those they love. This rarely works. I think you know, as I do, that you did find happiness in the new land because of Tony, but Rawiri and certainly Kory have not done so here. The voyage is yours as a life journey, yet it is your happiness that concerns me."

Tony and Rolo also spoke often of their predicament. "I miss them too, kleijnman, my little man." This had been the fourth time in as many days that his son had asked where Kory was.

Life simply was not the same without the Kavinga clan.

The villa was more than big enough for them all and seemed too empty without them. Tony and Anna had spoken at length about what to do with Bergen Op Meer. The bizarre circumstances of Jude and his descendants being stewards over the estate had become acceptable to both of them. Now that Sam had been born, there was a possibility that nothing would need to change until Kory, Rolo, or any future descendants of Tony and Anna took full ownership of the estate.

Anna had informed him, "I have no interest in being apart from you, Tony, so unless you are planning to join me at Bergen Op Meer, we will all be staying right here at Lions Vineyard. That's if you will have us of course." Anna had no doubt Tony wanted them all to stay as one bonded family.

"You know being together is all I want. What is knocking at my conscience is the fact that we owe it to Jude to know what he wants." Tony had already made plans to add onto the villa, as he was certain Ataahau would be telling him any day now that their family will be growing by one in the autumn.

"Kenyon is returning in a fortnight. I shall send a lengthy letter to Jude explaining our thoughts." Anna was certain this would suffice.

"Don't you think it is time you went and saw for yourself how things are truly going at Bergen Op Meer with your own eyes? It has been more than ten years. Rawiri is a capable sailor and would be fully up for the trip. Take him to see how you have lived and where you are from. The timing could not be better." What he meant was , she was not expecting.

"Why Tony, are you trying to get rid of us?" said in the voice of teasing to hide her hurt for she knew his meaning.

Tony felt sad. There was no win in this matter for him and the possibility of a great loss.

"I will speak to Rawiri tonight." She said, Anna could not see an easy answer to this dilemma. *Tony is right, I need to go home.*

As it turned out, Rawiri would not leave his son for that length of time and would also not let her go alone. Captain Jock made room onboard for the family of three as Kenyon had offered to relinquish his quarters and sleep with the crew. Their sea voyage began on a very peaceful and calm sea.

Back in the library, Anna responded to Captain Jock. "I have no desire to hurt anyone nor put anyone in a lasting position that is not to their liking. I am now at a loss." Anna rarely felt this way. "I will speak to my husband tonight." *But first I will seek out Jude.*

He was to be found later that day repairing one of the horse's saddles that had been recently damaged in a race that Simon, Rawiri and Kenyon had partaken in, much to Sophia's horror. She had since banished them all from the stables. Because Anna fully agreed, the three of them had stayed regrettably away.

"Hello, my friend, may I bend your ear as you mend?" Anna scratched the sweet spot of the newest colt yet to be named.

Jude moved over on the bench and patted the space next to him. "I am your servant."

Anna got right to the heart of the matter. "It is about the bizarre circumstances that came about as a result of the purchase of the painting. I am going to come right out and ask. Do you mind the position this places you and your family in?" *There, she said it.*

"I had wondered when you would come around to this conversation. And this is my answer. Had it not happened, I would not have all that my life is today. My son will have a loving family as his very own all the days of his life, as I am certain you and Master Ashton will always see to it. Our world is filled with threats and troubles. We experience far less than many others because of that painting. No, my dear, I do not mind." Jude had put down the leather in his busy hands and patiently waited.

"I want to go home, Jude. I want to go back to Ashton and stay in the new land. Rawiri and Kory belong there and I belong with them." Anna hung her head. "Is it too much to ask that this arrangement continue until the next generation works out what is best for their lives?"

Jude placed his calloused and scarred hand over hers. "I would be honoured."

Had she heard him say yes? "Jude, truly. This is not too much?" With hope from deep within , Anna dared to look into his eyes and saw conviction.

"All is well child. Batina and I are very happy here. With Simon managing Miss Sophia's estate, all other matters can be dealt with. We have seasonal workers and Josie and Reginald ensure nothing becomes too much for us. We do truly miss you and Master Ashton, but what matters more is that you are both happy." His gentle smile said it best.

"Oh we are happy Jude, thank you." Anna entered into the open arms of a man she had loved with all her heart her entire life.

The unnamed colt chose this tender moment to chew on her hat. "Oh you rogue."

Batting his nose gently away from the brim of her hat, Anna had to laugh, both with joy and relief.

"Well, I think the colt now has a name. Rogue it is." Jude's eyes twinkled.

"Rogue it is." Anna practically floated back to the kitchen.

"Opa, is it true you are coming back and will never leave me again?" Sophia had heard the news that much of the life at Bergen Op Meer would be going back to its old ways. Anna, Master Kavinga, *she could never bring herself to address him as anything less*, and Kory would be returning to the new land and would have no regular means of communication, as her Opa would be taking his final voyage.

"Yes, my child. I am returning and will stay right here to see you happily married and with a family of your own." He knew it would not be long before this took place. She was blooming before his very eyes.

"Oh Opa, I am so happy," wrapping her arms around his neck and placing a kiss on his weather-beaten cheek.

Jock delighted in the child and briefly felt a deep sadness for his friends Damien and Jacobus. They had never known such a sweet joy. In his heart he gave a thanksgiving prayer to the two men as a result of whose lives he had been greatly blessed.

Ataahau had eventually been accepted into the local iwi and was exchanging feathers in the village when she saw the sails in the distance. Tony had not been the same since his sister and her family sailed away last spring.

She had hoped the news of having another little one join their family would bring him joy. For a time he was restored and soon became preoccupied with the building project at the villa.

Though heavy with pregnancy again, she did not find it difficult to ride back to the villa in search of him. "There is a ship on the horizon." Ataahau called out to Tony before she reached him.

As autumn began to shorten the days, Tony had hoped for the return of his family. *Life simply was not the same without them. Could this mean their return?* "Whoa, my dearest. I know you are strong but we do not need you taking any unnecessary risks." Tony helped her down from the lightning quick, prancing beast Diddy.

She remained briefly in the circle of his secure embrace.

"All is well, the baby is strong. Let's not keep the captain waiting. Where is our Arlo?" Ataahau had left their son and daughter earlier this day in the care of a sweet village girl who enjoyed spending time with them at the villa.

"Today he has joined the other children in the village who are learning to fish with nets." Tony led the horse towards the paddock. "This beast needs a cooling down and you and I can enjoy a pleasant walk to the shore."

And there they stood as the majestic ship entered the harbour, the family of four hoping to find that Captain Jock Smit had returned with those they loved.

Anna saw them first. "Kory look, Rolo is waiting for you." Had Rawairi not been as quick as a flash, Kory would have dived over the side, so happy he was to be reunited with his cousin.

The number of the landing party soon began to swell. The Captain had made many friends through the years; this trip would be bittersweet.

Anna could feel the struggle that Kenyon was also faced with. He had to accept his time with the Malefyts was coming to a close or find another ship to sail on.

"And there they are, Arlo. The Kavinga Family has returned." Tony was elated. "Let's hope it is for good."

Kory was the first to place his feet again on land and within his first steps came a jubilant cousin. Their excitement was all Anna needed to confirm her choice to leave Bergen Op Meer in safe keeping for the next generation to manage. Tony was next in line to lift his sister from her feet and give the customary spin. "I am home, my brother, we are home indeed." That was all he needed to hear.

Chapter FORTY EIGHT

A dam Heath buys a horse.

A Everything was out of place and yet Joshua felt secure in his future. *He knew his loving Father would never leave him.* The message of how his chosen children had been saved from slavery in Egypt and safely guided to a new land was written into his own heart. Joshua could hear the Creator's still quiet voice.

Will I ever see Oakley again? Of all of the things Joshua missed most it was his pony Oakley, a descendant of Madam Silver and the mighty Rogue. This new land had horses too. Here he sat looking at the beasts that he hoped would soon find new homes just like he needed.

The Missionaries had explained to him that he would become part of a family here in the strange land they had sailed to and never again be afraid and have to hide from danger. His family was gone. He was the soul survivor. *God, if you find me a new Mumma and Puppa, I will be their son. You now hold my Mumma and she is safe from scary people. Please help me until I see her again with you.*

At the tender age of five, Joshua Samuel Wolf knew lots about life. He had had to be very clever to keep himself safe from the mean soldiers who wanted to snatch him from his home at Bergen Op Meer and take him to a place that no one ever came back from.

Adam Heath was prospering. He and Stephanie had had years of happiness together except for one major setback. They had no children.

Today he needed more muscle for the many tasks at Lions Vineyard. As labour was in short supply due to the war, Adam went in search of a horse.

Weston Wobble was known for his ability to tame the wild beasts that roamed the hills freely here in the North. Today one of these majestic creatures would be added to the Heath stables.

"Wobbly, what have you got in the line of working muscle for me to look at today?" Adam was never one to waste time and got right down to business. He knew the amount he was willing to hand over. Getting there was going to take most of the morning.

"Well, mate, there is one with your name on it and you can take the lad into the bargain." Wobbly had been dealing with these farmers for years and knew how much to get out of them.

The Missionaries often came in to preach to him about his high prices. Today was one of those days. Those pesky do-gooders were always after him for one reason or another and today had been a doozy. Jewish children were being shipped around the world and new homes were needed for them. The local Mission left one of them to adapt and enjoy being with the horses today, as they were looking for a family to take him in and had yet to find one. In a rare act of compassion Wobbly let the lad sit on the fence. Sternly warning him to stay put.

"Lad? What are you on about, old man?" Adam found it hard to be charitable. Wobbly was cantankerous, probably why he had it in himself to work with the wild horses. *Rein it in, man, you need him.*

"Yup, one more of those Jewish kids has made it to our shores and needs a home. You and the Missus want him? He is sitting on the fence, or had better be, in the west paddock." He leaned back in his chair and placed his booted feet up on his desk, showing he was in no rush at all.

Adam's heart began to speed up. Walking over to the window, he wiped the dust from the pane. Sure enough, there sat a small boy obviously enjoying the view. He was happy and Adam loved him on sight. "You're serious! How did you end up in charge of him?" Thinking better of it. "Never mind. I will be right back. Get the dappled grey ready and name your price." Without delay Adam made his way to the nearby Mission house, found the Head of Missions and signed all the paperwork before the sun had reached the Western hills.

Stephy was getting a little nervous. Adam was running late and this was highly unusual for him. He was her everything. From the time she was a small girl, she knew her life was entwined with his. Of course, she thought they would have at least a dozen children by now but so was not her fate. The cruelty of having so much and no one to pass it on to often played on her heart.

Adam never complained. If anything, his reassurance of the Creator's hand being within their lives gave her often the comfort she was seeking when her longings for a family became too much to bear. Adam swore to her that matters would somehow come right one day and she loved him all the more for it.

"I will finish this last batch of sugar biscuits and saddle up Old Smokey." Speaking to the open spaces in the kitchen, and Poppy the cat, was a common occurrence for her. She expected no answer.

Stephy Heath was simply happy. She knew those who had guarded generations of family in the villa could sympathise with her. *I just want to add more to their numbers.*

She was in the process of removing her apron as the last batch was now cooling on the bench top, when she heard the wheels of the wagon coming over the rise. *Thank the Lord. Old Smokey was not easy for her to saddle up.*

Stepping onto the veranda with a much lighter heart, she expected to see Adam with the new horse. *Were her eyes playing tricks on her?* Was that a small child holding the reins? The light that began to fill her heart soon revealed in its glow the reality. *This was her child.*

As they approached, she could see the overwhelming joy on Adam's face.

Stephy knew with certainty he was bringing her promised son home. Without hesitation she approached the wagon, opened her arms, and in fell their son, *finally.* "Welcome home, my jonty boy." *God is good.*

Adam wiped the tear from his eye. He enjoyed seeing his wife so happy and gave thanks for all that is and is to come. The miracle of their faith was overwhelmingly beautiful, he knew with complete certainty, *there is great joy in knowing you are a parent.* Raising his face to the sky, he spoke "All glory and honour are yours, almighty Father, forever and ever, Amen."

"How is my Jonty boy, come see all the biscuits I have made for you." Putting the feather-light child down, Stephy placed her arm around her small son and steered them both into the warm, welcoming kitchen with all the sweet smells. Turning back to her husband without breaking stride, she mouthed the words, *"Thank you, my dearest one, he is beautiful."*

Chapter FORTY NINE

1981 *Jonty Heath at Lions Vineyard.*
"I need to give blood. It is the least I can do." Jonty had arrived at the hospital and was now waiting on news from the Doctor. Tony was in recovery and Hannah was in the operating theatre.

Bet could see Mr Heath was desperate to be of assistance in some way. This happens when trauma rips into a family. This one had been hit hard today. "Of course, do you know your blood type?"

"Both of my parents were O. I hope this information helps." Jonty knew this, because his parents had left meticulous records of the family medical history.

"Yes, it sure does. This would mean you will also be O. Please relax. I will get you some juice and a biscuit." Without hesitation and with precision Bet had started the extraction.

Later that day as Jonty sat in prayer and waited for Tony to wake up, he received the strangest news.

Bet entered the room and signalled for him to step into the hallway. "Mr Heath, I have checked and double-checked. If your parents are in fact O, yes, you should also be O. However your blood type is AB. I thought you would want to know." Bet Willson was efficient at her work and never left a stone unturned.

"Oh. Yes, I may be mistaken." Jonty inwardly was shaken.

All he wanted was to have this day come to an end. It went on and on, doing his head in. "Thank you."

Turning back into the room that held his sleeping nephew, he returned to the chair he had recently vacated and cried.

Jonty had wondered through the years why he had memories that made no sense to him, why Johanna looked like their parents but he showed no likeness to either of them. In truth this news was not a shock, just a lot to take in today of all days.

You need Charlotte. The words came into his mind, as though spoken by an all knowing voice.

They had been friends for years. Johanna had encouraged him to make more of the obvious connection they had. Jonty had been afraid to. Not that he thought Charlotte did not return the affection, but for fear of losing what he did share with her. He feared losing her.

There was much to do in preparation for the funerals. Charlotte stepped into the planning role and never pushed too hard. She had a knack for bringing everything that was needed to its rightful outcome. "Jonty, have you any pictures of Johanna as a baby?" Charlotte was looking over her list as they sat at the kitchen table later that week. Jonty looked tired. She did not want to push but a picture would be nice to have. *She was so glad he had finally called.*

Looking up from his tea mug, Jonty let thoughts go through his mind of where to look. "Those would be in the attic. It would be best if I got those for you now, before I visit Hannah today. Tony and I are going to stop at the nursery and get her some potted red roses. Tony thought of that, isn't that nice?" A gentle smile briefly crossed his face.

Charlotte leaned forward and patted his forearm resting on the table with the empty cup. "He is a very sweet boy. Need any help?"

"I might lose you in all those boxes up there." Again a weak smile. "Best to let me have a look." Off he slowly went.

"Where to start?" Jonty could see where Johanna had previously been sorting, as there was a stack of boxes in one area that was neatly organised. "This is as good a place as any." All the boxes had been clearly labelled.

Through his pain, he gave a little thanks for his sister's organisational talents. The wooden sea chest marked AM he eventually found in a place behind all the other boxes, as if hidden away. "Why would she have done this?" Jonty really needed to stop talking to himself out loud. *Tony and Hannah were going to think he was crazy.* "As long as I don't answer myself, it should be okay." With a little chuckle he lifted the lid and found what he was looking for. The album was directly on top of a stack of documents. "Charlotte," Jonty called out, hoping she could hear him and come and see what he had discovered.

She soon joined him. "Well done. I am sure I will find what I need in this album."

"What do you suppose all this is? And why would Johanna put the album in a place that seems hidden? I found the old sea chest behind stacked boxes, as though she did not want me to see it. Why?" He was hurting.

Jonty was certain his sister had never kept anything from him. Even when she travelled, she had meticulously written letters from each of the locations where she had stayed. That was why he found it odd that he had never heard of the Wolf family when Johanna assisted the two children from the Netherlands a few years ago. *Something was not adding up.*

"That is very odd indeed." Charlotte could see Jonty had opened Pandora's box and she was beginning to feel guilty for asking him for the photo. *Can I do anything right for this man?*

"How about we take the photo book down and deal with this mystery after the funeral, what do you say?" Placing her hand once again on his forearm, she hoped to restore calm.

"Right, right you are." As though he had been in a trance, Jonty began to have flashes of pieces which on their own made no sense, but grouped together the unthinkable was coming into focus.

Tony was at the funeral of his parents. Jonty found no harm in letting him take his new rugby ball which Tony held onto the entire day.

When the day was done, with Tony exhausted and sound asleep, Jonty could wait no longer.

He went into the attic, opened the sea chest and pieced together what he came to believe his sister had known. This was the reason she had suddenly gone to the Netherlands before settling down. "What do I do now? I need to talk to Charlotte. She will know what to do. Did I just answer my own question out loud? Maybe I am losing it." *What a day it has been.*

The next day Charlotte and Jonty went through the contents of the sea chest. They poured over Johanna's letters which he had kept, and looked into the news reports of the accident off the coast linking everything together. Within a few days they had pieced it all together. "I need to go there, but how can I leave Tony and Hannah?"

"I don't understand. What could possibly be gained by you going there now." Charlotte wished with all her heart that this man would not have to deal with so much.

"Johanna obviously wanted to keep everything as it was. You said so yourself, she loved her life and would not change a thing. Yes, you, Tony and Hannah need to know the truth at some point in time, but now?"

"You are right. There is enough to deal with today." Leaning forward, Jonty in truth wanted to have a hug but had no idea how to step into one. So he awkwardly patted her forearm as she had done to him in comfort recently.

Chapter FIFTY

Tony and Hannah settle in at Lions Vineyard.

The days began to take new shape as Hannah and Tony settled into life at the villa. In the back of Jonty's mind was the truth yet again hidden in the old, wooden sea chest upstairs.

Did he feel sad that he was not a true blood relation to these children? *Yes,* but in his heart it didn't matter. God knew the truth. What he wanted to know was, *who was he?*

Jonty loved having the house full most of the time and Millzy was a great help. It was on the day that he had arrived home when obviously not expected that he saw something so odd, he knew it was time to dig a little deeper into the truth.

"Anybody home?" *Guess not.* Jonty needed the new shovel, as the old one had finally been rendered of no use by years of digging.

He had thought to find Millzy busy in the kitchen but on second thoughts, maybe she had gone for a walk. *Now to get that shovel.* He knew exactly where it was. So when he got to the shed and found it missing along with his wheelbarrow, this seemed strange. The farm hands had their own tools, seldom needing anything from Jonty. "Who could have taken it?" Certainly not Tony, and definitely not Hannah. He did not have long to wait for his answer.

Millicent hummed a tune as she placed the items in their rightful place and returned to the kitchen without seeing another soul. Jonty felt a little guilty for not revealing himself.

There seemed something odd about the reason she needed these items. *Maybe he could bring up the subject later.* Curiosity got the better of him. He followed the tracks to the place the fresh ground had been turned over. "What could she have wanted to bury?"

Later that evening Jonty hoped to bring up the subject without giving anything away. "How was your day today, girls?"

"I am working on a new recipe with Millzy." Hannah was first to answer.

"Nothing unusual. I continued the work in the attic and enjoyed girl time. How was your day?" Millicent revealed nothing about her need to bury anything.

"The work is almost complete on replacing some of the fence posts in the north paddock. My Dad and I had originally dug those when I was just a boy. I even had to use the new shovel." He hung the word out there and waited.

"That's nice." Millicent's response was natural, though she did give an inward sigh of relief that she had put the shovel back where she had found it.

He trusted Millzy. Deciding to let the matter drop, at least until later that evening when the house was quiet and it struck him what she had said. "*The attic.*"

Jonty had forgotten that he had given the okay to clear away the dust and cobwebs. He knew before he got into the attic what he would find.

The space was indeed spotless. Everything was packed away neatly. The old wooden sea chest was nowhere to be found. He felt both sad and confused. Discussing the matter with Charlotte later that week did help with a decision he knew he needed to make.

"I need to find out what is really going on. How can I travel and be gone without the kids or Millzy knowing? Especially so close to Christmas. I don't think she meant any harm. Johanna obviously kept it all a secret for good reason, too."

"You can take the opportunity to finally accept the offer of the Master vintner Montague Blass who has been coveting some of the vines here at Lions Vineyard. No one will think anything of it. On your way home you can look into who this person is who Johanna spent time with in the Netherlands. If you are lucky, all this will tie together neatly and you will be back before you know it." *Always the practical and trusting advisor. Her faith knew no bounds.* Jonty thought.

"You're right. The children are in good hands. If you keep an eye on things, I will feel confident all will be well while I am away. The timing could not be better, come to think of it. Thank you, my dear, what would I do without you," again reaching forward and patting her arm.

"What an extraordinary coincidence this is. My late cousin's wife, Batina Wolf Blass of Bergen Op Meer, has the identical noble grape vines. These are exceptionally rare and I am deeply grateful. Name your price." Jonty recognised the name 'Bergen Op Meer' immediately.

Montague could simply not believe his good fortune. "I am curious though, what finally brings you to my humble vineyard, good man?" Jonty had no intention of explaining the full nature of his trip, but he saw no harm in speaking of the loss of his sister and how he was now the guardian of her two young children.

"Condolences, my friend." Montague had also known tragedy in his life and could understand Jonty's pain and need to move forward in life. He thought it best to find other matters that could take Jonty's mind off these sad thoughts and maybe infuse some joy into his life at this festive time.

"Your cousin's wife, you say. Yes, this is quite something. Let us discuss the price later. First I would like to hear more about your cousin's wife." Was it possible that he would not need to go any further?

Montague was overjoyed to share the happy story of how the family came to be overseers of a vast estate that could at any point be handed over to a legitimate heir if one were ever found. "And yet there has been great tragedy also. My cousin died of cancer far too early in life, you see. Also their daughter Ester Wolf Blass and her husband Markus Wolf, no family relation of course, were lost at sea in a freak accident several years ago. Their two children were left orphaned." Jonty felt as though he had been struck by lightning. "Oh, I see you are saddened. Yes, Batina Wolf Blass has had to deal with many hardships and survived them all. She is an extraordinary woman. She was thought to have been killed in the camps during the war. Her only son was saved by missionaries and was adopted by a family somewhere in your country. She has no idea where and hopes to be reunited with him still." Montague refilled their glasses. "I have kept in touch with her and we remain friends." And struck by lightning again.

Jonty immediately knew he was Batina's child. The memories flooded in. *Whatever happened to his horse Oakley. This man speaking to him now was speaking of his mother.*

Johanna had faithfully sent Christmas cards each year to Batina. She herself could not write back as there was no way for Johanna to explain the letters to her husband. From time to time a call was arranged and they could speak privately. Batina cherished these letters and eagerly awaited their arrival. Photos accompanied the many pages and they were all safely stored, in order, under lock and key in her private sanctuary. Johanna was punctual each year. So when the days passed and no card arrived, Batina began to worry. *Who can I reach out to?* She decided to call Monty. He knew everyone in the industry. He may know something about Lions Vineyard that may help in solving this mystery.

"Hello, my dear, how extraordinary. Just last week I was speaking of you to a fellow vintner and here you call. How are you?" Monty was in a joyful festive mood, glad he had interrupted his dinner party to take the call.

"All is well here. We enjoyed an extended season, as the weather remained unseasonably warm well into October. I can hear music in the background and hope I have not interrupted you?" Batina always enjoyed her chats with her late husband's cousin.

"No. No, all is well. The children have all come home. They will still be there when you and I have had our time together." Always charming and ready to be available for anyone who may need him.

"I am calling in hopes you may have some information." Not wanting to give too much away, Batina gave thought to her next words.

"Always, my dear, I am an abundant well of this commodity. Ask away." As this request was highly unusual for Batina, he was now hopeful he could be of service.

"It is customary for me to receive a Christmas card from a young woman who years ago I had met by chance, and this year, you see, none has arrived. She travelled here from New Zealand and is from Northland. She did mention that her extended family owned an interest in a large vineyard and I thought you may have heard something. The estate is known by the name Lions Vineyard."

"Why yes. As a matter of fact I recently acquired the noble grapes that are identical to the ones you have at Bergen Op Meer. This is extraordinary. Jonty Heath finally accepted my offer and visited me a mere fortnight ago. He is now the sole owner of Lions Vineyard as his sister was tragically killed in a fatal car accident this year along with her husband. He is now the guardian of her two children. Would you care to have his number? I am certain he would be open to receiving your call, he is a very likeable fellow." Monty sincerely hoped he had not added yet more tragedy to this dear woman's life.

"How sad for him. I would not want to trouble him. I will look for an opening in my diary and write the young woman a letter, I do not know why I did not think of this before. I am sure all is well." Batina was devastated and wanted to get off the call.

"There you have it, my dear, I am sure she will enjoy the gift of your words." Monty could hear the joyful sounds from the dining room escalate and he was now ready to return to his loved ones. "May this season bring you rejoicing and peace, my dear Batina."

"Thank you, Monty, please extend my love and greetings to the children."

"I did not need to go any further." Jonty and Charlotte sat once again in the comfort of his kitchen.

"Did you not want to meet your Mother?" Charlotte had not been surprised to get the call that he was coming home early, asking if she could pick him up at the airport. However, she had no idea why until just moments ago.

"Johanna only wanted a simple life and thought she was protecting Hannah, this I understand. As I now think, Millzy is protecting Massy and Kat. Johanna must have known I was adopted and not the heir to Bergen Op Meer, because she would have never kept the truth from me otherwise. What I am not sure about, is if Millzy knows who I am and what I want to do about it. That's why I came home. I need time to think."

"Oh, Jonty, this is all too much. What can I do to help?" Charlotte so desperately wanted to give him a hug.

"Just listening helps. Millzy is with us for only a few more months. Let's keep this between us. I do not think she meant any harm and Tony and Hannah have been through enough." Jonty was exhausted.

The farewells did come with a few tears. "Millzy, will you remember me?" Tony liked having her around and thought it was nice for Hannah and Uncle Jonty too. Though recently Uncle Jonty had been a bit off. Tony wondered if he was sad or something.

"Oh yes, my boy, but it is now time to return to my parents and help them with their thriving and very busy Bed and Breakfast establishment. They have missed me." The words had slipped out without her thinking about what she may have just revealed.

Jonty heard it though. "I am sure they need you too. You have been a great help to us all. Has the establishment got a name?"

Best to stick to the truth as much as possible. "Yes, The Gate House."

"Lovely, I am sure." Jonty had decided to let this sleeping dog lie, for now.

"Yes, my parents were both born at this address. The place has an aura of destiny about it. Well, I had best be on my way. Thank you for a year I will always treasure." First one quick last hug to Tony and Hannah.

Walking through security, she did not look back. The guilt was showing on her face.

"The Gate House is very well known. I was able to get information from the travel agent. Here it is," sliding the glossy brochure across the kitchen table towards Jonty. Charlotte simply could not let this go. *She could not fathom how Jonty could.*

Jonty slid it back to her. "I am not interested. Johanna had a reason to keep this all quiet and I trust her."

"She is no longer here, Jonty. You need to finish what she started." Charlotte wondered, *if all this was resolved, would he be free to share a life with her? Was this keeping him from her?* On more than one occasion, she had thought he wanted to get close. She wanted him to make the first move.

Jonty was torn. He loved Charlotte. He had even gone so far as to have a custom ring made for her, but he loved his sister also and the pain in his heart was just too big for him. He missed her everyday and did not want to do anything that would hurt the bond he had with the mother of the children he was now responsible for.

"I can't, Charlotte." He could not look her in the eye and did not see the tear slip down her cheek.

Their relationship changed after this. It was as if an invisible wall was separating them. Charlotte came by less and less. It was just too painful. Jonty focused on managing the new investment portfolio he was now responsible for, as well as the needs of two growing children, a huge plot of land, stock and revenues.

Chapter FIFTY ONE

1836 *tragedy strikes at Lions Vineyard.*
The last rays of sunshine filtered into the room as Anna finished the final stitches on the shroud that would cover her son's casket at his funeral. The gauzy fabric had once been a gift from Batina. Anna had saved it, hopefully to make a christening gown for her grandchildren.

The bold, black cross stood out on the white cloak that would cover him during the church service. *Koraka was born under a crescent moon with the last star of the evening sky fading with the dawn.* Anna thought as she stitched.

The images began to take shape on the cloth. Completing the markings were the red and black pātiki patterns Anna had first seen long ago on Anahera's kahu huruhuru, the feather cloak she often wore with pride. It was adorned with diamond shapes representing the flounder fish in black running along the top edge, with soft, downy feathers falling like a waterfall to the cape's hem. Anna had stored it safely away in the attic. This was Anna's reason for choosing these colours today.

She would have found it comforting to share the task with the women of her family who lived across the circle of the earth. As Anna stitched she reflected on the last letter she had received from Batina and wondered how all were doing today at Bergen Op Meer.

Sophia had finally chosen the love of her life and had children of her own. When her heart was ready Anna would write of her devastating news. Sophia and Kenyon will be saddened to hear of the death of her only son. *These were the letters that were hardest to write.* How Batina had managed to get all the words out in her final letter was a mystery to Anna. So ill had she been, that it would have taken every ounce of her energy. *If she can do it from her deathbed, I can write one from a broken heart.* Anna thought.

The years had been good ones. As a large family, they had survived the many changes that had overtaken the land and the people. The suffragette movement was seen as a non-threatening pastime of the gentler members of society, though Anna and a few other ladies knew differently. Their determination to be equal citizens in every way would simply not be curtailed. The Church Mission was flourishing, with Māori clergy leading entire regions of the ever-expanding parish. As a result of the Word of God being spoken, there was new birth everywhere. To Anna all these historic patterns being woven into the history of Aotearoa New Zealand gave her confidence in the choice she made so many years ago. In her moment of solitude, Anna's thoughts also turned to Arlo.

Kory and Arlo both knew the forest as well as the back of their own eyelids! The night could be in total darkness and neither of them would have any trouble getting from place to place. They moved as one creature, with the speed of a lion on the hunt. "I belong right here with all of you, and right here is where I will stay." Kory was determined to put the message that had come just this night from the South out of his mind, but no matter how far he had run, escape was impossible. He was the descendant of a chief, expected to return and take his rightful place.

Arlo no longer answered to the name Rolo. He had refused to do so, ever since his cousin had sailed off when they were both still *no bigger than a loaf of bread*, as his Aunty Anna would say. During the time that his soul brother was gone, hearing the name from anyone was simply too painful. "No one calls me Rolo again," he had firmly stated to the family at large.

His wise and understanding father had said, "How about Arlo, then?"

After a little thought, the confident and firm reply that came from someone so small was fully respected. "Arlo, yes. I am Arlo." Of all people, Tony understood the need for change when great pain had been experienced.

The cousins had both grown into men, with men's responsibilities and issues. They had always known where Kory had come from. The story of how both Kory and Ataahau came to be *a* golden thread in the tapestry of the land at Lions Vineyard' was told often under the stars around the open fire.

So much was changing. In her heart Anna knew the day would come when Kory would be called. He was from a royal line. Rawiri had been approached just this morning by the iwi from the South. They would not acknowledge Anna as a member of the family to be considered an authority. This jolted her nerves, moving her to consult her journal to clear her mind.

Anna later closed her journal and looked out over the landscape.

With the new land developing, Anna wanted to ensure women had access to education, employment, equal rights, the right to own property, custody of minor children, full control over their own bodies and the right to vote. This was no small task, yet with the guidance she had often experienced, her confidence inevitably received the lift needed when all hope seemed exhausted.

The family was growing. Tony and Ataahau had been fruitful and the gathering at meals was always lively and entertaining. *After six children this will happen.*

Tony had once said, after the birth of his third daughter, "I tell you, every woman who brings children into the world should get a chair with a soft pillow in heaven."

All the children were her godchildren and the love of the Lord had taken hold of each heart. Arlo had taken vows to serve in the church, having no intention of ever settling into a life of working the land as his father had done. His five sisters all had their hearts set on having families, with two of them well on their way after both marrying fine young men.

Jock had made the right choice when he made his final voyage. Sophia had grown into a stunning beauty and was like nectar to the bees. Three suitors rose to the occasion. Even Jock could not fault a single one. Day after day she remained oblivious to their intentions, as her sole focus was her ageing and ailing Mooder Tina.

"I have brought you a delicious broth that has been made with great care. Here, let me help you." So much attention had in fact gone into the brew. Both Jude and Sam had partaken in the seasoning of the rabbit broth and they would not let anyone else have a say. No one wanted to argue. It was plain for all to see they were both deeply distressed. *How would they handle it, when the end finally came?* Sophia wondered.

Kenyon and Simon found themselves at a loss. They had been unable to get close to Sophia for weeks now and neither wanted to lose their advantage. They both wanted her, and Sam was getting all of her attention. Simon was mildly jealous but Kenyon was beyond containing the obvious issue he was having with the whole matter. Sam, on the other hand, was revelling in all her attention.

"It will give this old woman a pearl of peace if you settle on one of them, my dear." Batina had been restored and was enjoying her time with such a sweet woman. They sat companionably by the fire in the rooms that she and Jude had so long ago moved into and, by the looks of it, she would be leaving them feet first.

Batina was not afraid to die. She was weary, ready to depart this life for a peaceful rest. She had come to know with certainty that the Lord loved her, and that all would be well when this life ended.

"They can all wait. Opa included." Sophia leaned in and gave one silky, paper-thin cheek a kiss and then the other. "I have other matters to attend to at the moment."

"If you are referring to me, I can still take care of myself." Though Batina knew this not to be true, she enjoyed the idea.

"Well, in that case, shall I return to the kitchen then?" with an impish grin. The teasing brought a smile to both their faces.

Batina held out her hand and the two companions took time to pray before once again transferring the once robust Batina, now very small and frail, back to the refreshed bed.

"I would like to write a letter. These will be my final words to the children of my heart across the sea. Please get my lap desk and all my things, and then I must be alone." Doing so, Sophia then placed a gentle kiss on Batina's head and quietly closed the door.

Dear Master Ashton and Mistress Anna ,

LIONS VINEYARD

The Almighty has blessed me throughout my life in ways that I could not have foreseen for myself. When my dearest Johanna came into my life, I was but a child also and knew very little of the world. My life was one of being settled in tradition and family. But times were hard for my parents and having one less mouth to feed, I knew, would bring them some relief.

I secured the position through a fellow Jew, who, I later discovered, knew the entire history of the Malefyt legacy and had his own agenda that, through sheer good fortune, my beloved Jude derailed when he purchased the painting. Of course I speak of the tea set.

There has been another family who has attempted to take possession of the set through their generations to no avail. They will certainly be on hand when, and if, the set goes to the auction house. If this in fact occurs in Percival Waters the Third's time at the auction house the Malefyt family has entrusted the task to, you will be bestowing on him a great honour.

I have for my part kept the set in plain sight all these years, and will be entreating our sweet Sophia to oversee the guardianship of the set in your absence. I believe this will be agreeable to you both. She is wise and will discern for herself the best means to also become a guardian of this delicate star of your legacy.

In truth, my loved ones, I have found the task to be a sad one. The things of this world taking on such value can be a trap, for it is wisdom that is of greater price than anything else, hand-crafted or otherwise.

Your entry into my life gave me the security of a life I often felt I had done nothing to deserve. You both needed me and I needed you more. You are my children and I have always loved you as my own.

LOYOLA VAN ROOYEN BUCK

It is the ardent hope of my heart that Jude and I have placed within your souls the knowledge that you are loved deeply through us, and guarded by the One who sees and knows all. The One who has done it, defeated death and has promised to return for all who believe.

I now turn to you in what I am certain is my final day among the living. You see, my dearest ones, I am tired and must ensure that those I have been entrusted with share in the last breaths I will take. This is my dying wish.

As I write to you now, the love that has been alive through us surrounds me. There is a light so pure and perfect, my hand is guided by the uplifting presence filling the room I am resting in now. I give thanks and feel at complete peace. Jude will not be long behind me, I fear, for he too has joyfully given himself in devotion through the years. He also needs to have a rest before the return of our Lord and Saviour. Our little Sam has kept him young at heart, but his body has aged and, as all must, will soon return to the earth.

I am at peace in knowing Sam has the Malefyt family protection and love. His understanding of duty is fully agreeable to him. As Sophia will be here also, Jude and I have peace.

My loved ones, I now entrust you with one last concern that surfaces, Sophia. Captain Jock has the best of intentions, but has caused the greatest of issues for his only grandchild. She now has three suitors and is often distressed. Her desire to please him clouds her clear thinking on this matter and the wisdom I spoke of earlier seems to wrestle with her heart at times. If I could but know she was happily settled, I could truly die in absolute peace.

I know you will pray for her.

I must end what I am sure looks like scraping now on the parchment, as my vision is beginning to blur. I have complete faith I will see you in eternity through God's gift of grace, in the fullness of time. You have my love, we have our memories, and may God have mercy on us all.

Place a gentle kiss on the faces of the children. Give Master Rawiri and Mistress Ataahau my blessing also. I entrust you to find a perfect use for the bolt of fabric that this letter will accompany.

Your devoted, Batina

Chapter FIFTY TWO

You are forgiven.

Rawiri found his son deep in the forest at the same fishing hole where their lives had changed forever years before.

Today would not be as joyful. Kory would need to make his choice and Rawiri would need to stand his ground with Anna. "Son, the shadows are lengthening and all still remains the same. We must travel to the land of your iwi and discuss matters there."

"Do you not know the pain I feel? Does it not show that I suffer the consequences of another's choosing? Puppa, how can I leave Mumma?" Kory hung his head so that the tears would not be seen.

A piece from Rawiri's heart tore as he sat next to the only child he would ever call his own.

Anna felt a renewed strength through her core and was ready when they both returned later that night in the dark. Arlo had returned hours before to the waiting family. She could do nothing to comfort him. That had to be done by one much greater than she, *the one who wrote this day from the beginning.*

She sat alone on the veranda and waited, while the house and all its occupants silently waited in their beds. Even the newest addition, a granddaughter, to the family seemed to know silence was needed in the waiting stillness.

Anna stood as they both walked into the glow. All she could do was open her arms and hold the man Kory had become, the child he would always be. Rawiri embraced them both and wept.

Kory had not slept. The closer they came to the village the next day, the stronger the beat pulsed within him. He could feel the life of the land entering in through his bones. There was a signature of remembrance surfacing in his heart that he had never known existed until now.

Many were gathering for trade, as this was an area easily reached by waka and ship. The port was bubbling with activity.

Recently a naval ship had arrived and the soldiers had been welcomed onto the land. They were not a new sight to the small travelling party, Rawiri, Kory and their guide. The three of them passed through the hub of activity in solemn stature.

"Baxter's Lung Preserver, get your Baxter's Lung Preserver here!" John Baxter believed in his product and was determined to make it a complete success. "Is your breathing embarrassed? Use Baxter Lung Preserver. Do you spit up blood? Use Baxter Lung Preserver. Are you suffering from sore throat? Use Baxter Lung Preserver."

Travelling the country was hard work. He longed to be with his wife and the little ones but there was truly no other way. He knew going where the people are was essential and the North Island was far more populated than the budding South.

This day he could sense something of significance was about to happen. Larger than normal crowds were gathering and this was good for business.

John loved to watch people, and paused to take a moment to watch the three men walking through the centre of the busy village. He noted something was different about the two walking in tandem behind the one who was obviously a guide. They were in truth no bigger than the other massive warriors he had seen, but they were by far the largest in presence. Their appearance was beginning to draw attention. A stillness was spreading through the village like a shadow flooding the ground on a sunny day.

Angus Macdonald was proud to be a soldier. His mother, Ruth, had stitched into the seams of his uniform jacket the words of God so that he took them with him, always. *Isaiah 66:13 "As a mother comforts her child, so will I comfort you; and you will be comforted over Jerusalem."* This verse shows that a mother's love is a reflection of God's love and care for His children.

Angus had every intention of returning to her with news of how the word of God was spread by him in his travels as a soldier. He had yet to be compelled to use in battle the musket which he was now showing to the natives, who had in curiosity come to enquire of its use. Angus found them to be enchanting, fierce, and he wanted to please them.

For effect he thought he would load the weapon and shoot the paua shells the children had lined up on the stones along the shore line. One by one he picked off the shells, with precision shooting, to the delight of the onlookers.

The musket ball entered clean. At first Rawiri thought Kory had stumbled. When he saw the life blood of his child draining into the soil at his feet, the anguish he felt was so great, it tore from his heart and passed his lips without him even knowing that the animal sound made came from him. Kory was leaving him. Tenderly, he laid him on the ground and looked into his eyes.

Kory knew. Peace washed over him. There would be no meeting of his other people and iwi today.

In the crowd stood a woman who he knew but had never met. "Mumma."

Kory's eyes closed and he was gone.

John pushed his way through the crowd. He tried to stop the flow of blood pumping from the chest wound of the young man he had just seen, but even he knew there was no elixir that could help him now.

Angus at first did not understand what was happening. He heard the wounded cry of an animal and jumped from his skin. Joining the flow of the crowd, he pushed his way to the front of the circle. When he saw the musket hole in the boy's chest, he froze. The unthinkable had happened. He had killed a man.

The tangi was held over three days. At the funeral, sitting in the stillness of peace that opened to her just before the Lord's prayer was spoken in the language of her child by the many who filled the church to overflowing, Anna knew without any doubt that Kory was now resting with Anahera.

With strength to mirror the power felt within the church today, the entire congregation spoke the words Christ taught his children to pray:

Te Karakia O Te Atua

The Lord's Prayer

E tō mātou Matua i te rangi
Our Father in heaven,
Kia tapu tōu Ingoa
hallowed be thy name.
Kia tae mai tōu rangatira-tanga.
Thy kingdom come,
Kia meatia tāu e pai ai
Thy will be done
ki runga ki te whenua,
on earth,
kia rite anō ki tō te rangi.
as it is in heaven.
Hōmai ki a mātou āianei
Give us today
he taro mā mātou mō tēnei rā.
our daily bread.
Murua ō mātou hara
Forgive us our sins,
Me mātou hoki e muru nei
as we forgive those who sin against us.
Aua hoki mātou e kawea kia whakawaia;
Lead us not into temptation,
Engari whakaorangia mātou, i te kino:
but deliver us from evil:
Nou hoki te rangatiratanga,
for thine is the kingdom,
te kaha,
the power,
me te korōria,
the glory,
Āke, āke, āke.
forever and ever.
Amene.
Amen.

Arlo looked out to his Aunty from the altar and held her with his gaze. Their understanding of mutual pain was understood. He marvelled at the flow of strength he felt as he led the gathered congregation.

The memories would always bring into his heart the love known by him for Kory. This love would now become his new companion. He could rejoice through his pain and find solace in knowing eternity is, by sacrifice and of the grace of God, for them all.

The funeral would soon be over and Anna would follow the casket out. No force on earth, or chief from any tribe, could stop her from walking these last steps at Kory's side. Anna stood as Tony, Rawiri, and the young women of the Heath family lovingly lifted the casket onto their shoulders, with Arlo giving the final blessing. As he sprinkled them all with water, Anna felt the cool drops land on her face and remembered Kory's baptism.

Angus could not stay away. What he had done was unforgivable. *How would he tell his mother?*

Anna saw the lone soldier sitting in the back pew.

Rawiri had eventually spoken to Angus Macdonald as he required consoling. The accident was causing him deep pain also.

Anna had also tried to speak to him, but he simply could not look her in the eye. As Kory was being carried out, she reached up, took the cloak from the casket, folded it neatly, stopped at his pew and handed it to him. "All is forgiven," and walked on.

Chapter FIFTY THREE

1995 *Bergen Op Meer Netherlands*
"Of course you are going." Millicent would not let Oma miss being with Massy and Hannah on their special day.

"My dear, I know this is not easy for you. You have yet to see Tony and Hannah and will also have to explain yourself to Katerina and Thomas." Batina did desperately want to make the trip and knew she could not do so alone. What Millicent did not know, she also wanted to place flowers at the place her daughter and son-in-law had been lost to her, not far from Tony and Katerina's home and Joshua's final resting place.

"I have given this much thought and find this the perfect opportunity to make things right again. I trust you and I also believe they will all understand. Especially now. They are all so happy. I should have trusted that all would work out as it should. Besides, I really miss Kat and would like to see her settled in at the villa." Millicent paused to reflect. "Oma, you will love it there. You also get to see where your son grew up. How do you feel about this?" Millicent leaned in and took the cold hand that was resting on the arm of the well-worn leather loveseat in the library at Bergen Op Meer.

"I do hope somehow I will come to know more of the man he grew into. And thank you, my dear, for helping this old woman travel across the world to be with the newlyweds. I am pleased to be joining them." Batina could not help but reflect on the beach wedding her daughter and Marcus had celebrated, feeling a little melancholy.

Matt, Vaun and Lotti could also make it to the wedding.

After confirming with Charlotte, the date was set. Wim and Anita could not leave their busy B&B as they were fully booked for the next few months. Their attending was simply not possible with Millicent travelling with Oma, which they were both very happy about.

The nuptials would be a simple affair, with a few family members and close friends in attendance. Anita would be sure to send plenty of fresh stroopwafels. The soft syrup waffle biscuits they all enjoyed.

Kat and Hannah used the time to strengthen their bond. They spent a pleasant weekend in Auckland searching for the perfect dress. The flowers for her bouquet would come from the red roses that grew at the entrance to the villa, since these were the ones Tony had given her in hospital all those years ago. Kat would be her matron of honour and Tony, Massy's best man.

It was when Charlotte and Hannah were making the final arrangements at the church that Hannah felt she needed to confess.

"Charlotte." She did have one burden that she needed to share with her.

The afternoon had been so pleasant and Charlotte was happy to help in any way possible, but there was one obvious question that kept coming to her mind and she did not know how to bring it up. *Who would be giving this bride away?* To her relief, Hannah did get around to it herself.

"Yes my dear, you sound serious. What is it?" Charlotte was so glad she had not pushed. She had learnt her lesson the hard way, when she had tried to convince Jonty he had to act on a matter. She never wanted to push any of her loved ones away again, ever.

"I cannot walk down the aisle." The two of them sat in complete silence in the old wooden church that had seen generations of Hannah's family celebrate the sacraments through the passing of almost two hundred years.

Inwardly Charlotte prayed for the guidance needed. It did not take long to come. "I know exactly what to do."

By the time they had worked out all the details, Hannah was once again all smiles, glowing with the knowledge she was loved, loved others and knew all would be perfect on the day.

The airlines had accommodated all the travel needs Oma had for the long journey. Millicent was enjoying the trip but had to admit, now that they were boarding their last flight, she did feel a little nervous to be facing them all.

The attendant indicated it was time to settle his passenger into her seat, because the other passengers would be boarding soon. "I will push the wheelchair." Millicent stepped behind the chair and indicated he could lead the way, her regal gesture ensuring no one would argue with her. *She would be boarding with Oma.*

Matt was glad to have been invited. Surprised, and happy. He had not been in New Zealand since leaving all those years ago, and thought he would never return again. He had to admit meeting Hannah was a bit nerve-wracking too, but both Tony and Vaun assured him he truly had nothing to fear. He was now hoping to bring a cool souvenir home for the club house, though he would not know how to explain it to the boys. He had not told them about how he knew Tony King. Amazingly enough, they did not push for details after Tony had left the field that day. *Leaving the past where it belonged seemed right. He would work out the finer details when he got home. Maybe he would ask Tony to sign a jersey and it could go up on the wall at the club.*

What he really wanted was to have someone in his life, like Vaun had. *Lotti was great.* They were so happy and perfect for each other.

Matt looked over at the two of them, heads leaned into each other, both looking at the same magazine. He loved them. *Surely it will be time to board soon.* He thought.

Matt looked up. He watched a tall, blonde drink of water in designer clothing, and with proud bearing, walk toward the entrance to their gate, obviously travelling with her elder companion. *Man, it would be nice to have a woman like that at my side.*

Kat, Tony, Hannah and Massy found themselves once again at the small regional airport together. So much had happened in their lives since the last time they had all been here as children.

"Tomorrow is going to be full on. I hope Oma has it in her to get through yet another busy day." Tony knew she was tough, but travelling can take it out of you.

"So true, Tons, I was thinking the same thing." Hannah kept her gaze on the plane that had just landed and was taxiing towards the terminal building. Massy and Kat looked at each other realising these two did not know Oma as well as they did.

"Trust me, you have no need to worry. Oma draws energy from a place inside her that has never been exhausted." Massy gave Tony that look that said, *believe me she is a tough old bird.*

"Oma will be last off the plane, as Millicent insisted on a wheelchair." Kat was certain Millicent would get her way on this one.

"I am anxious to finally be meeting her. Tony and I never got the chance when in the Netherlands. And I have yet to meet Matt, but Tony assures me this will go smoothly." Hannah only wanted those closest to her tomorrow. She could already feel her emotions lining up to take their own flight, making her nervous.

Especially when she thought of those who would not be in attendance. It was one of the reasons this wedding day would be a simple and small affair.

She spotted Lotti first. *She is very hard to miss.* "There are Lotti and Vaun. Let's make our way over to arrivals."

Arrivals at the airport are a place of happiness. A basket that overflows with joy streaming from people of all ages, stages and graces. Today was no different. Matt stepped into Tony's embrace as though they had known each other all their lives.

In some respects they had.

Then Tony introduced Matt to Hannah.

Lotti had so much to tell and ask the girls. They all, within a few months of each other, had become or were becoming wives to the men they loved.

Massy and Vaun simply stood back after their handshake greeting and watched the loving exchange unfold.

"Hello." Millicent decided to pull the plaster off the wound quickly. She left the capable Air New Zealand staff to their job and reached the group entangled in greetings before Oma had set foot on the ground.

Matt turned from Tony to the gorgeous woman he had seen earlier, thinking he had heard her say something. "May I help you."

"Millzy????" Tony could not believe what - or who - he was seeing.

"Hi Tony, it's me." Tears began to form in her eyes.

The other conversations came to an abrupt halt. Massy and Kat saw her for the first time.

"Millicent!" Massy gently leaned in and gave each of her cheeks a kiss.

As did Kat. "Let me introduce you."

"Millzy!!!!" Hannah and Tony stared at her perplexed and had no idea what to do.

"Yes, it is me." She froze.

Lotti slipped her hand into the hand of the man she loved, giving thanks for this enchanting family of human beings. *It seems everyone has a story.*

"Hi, I am Matt." He extended his hand in the hopes she would take it and the awkwardness of the moment may pass.

"Hi, Millicent van Dam, pleased to meet you. Excuse me, I think I am going to be sick." And off she ran to the nearest toilet right past Oma, who had also now arrived.

Chapter FIFTY FOUR

All is revealed.

A"Hello, my loved ones. I see you have all seen Millicent." Not only did Oma not look tired, she looked radiant.

Into the moment once again poured the joy of being together.

Introductions were made. After the new rounds of greetings had been completed, Oma gave a little insight into why Millicent might be having some difficulties. Kat thought it best to go in search of her. *God knows, we all have our moments.*

"I am coming with you." Hannah needed some kind of explanation from the horse's mouth. Kat let her go first.

Millicent brushed her teeth and wiped the tears from her eyes. Looking at herself in the mirror she said, "keep it together, van Dam".

"Hi, Millzy." Hannah saw the beautiful woman who had been such a big part of her recovery and knew there was nothing she would not forgive her for. Opening her arms, she waited for the loving hug she hoped for. After only a brief pause, in stepped her friend.

"I'm sorry, so sorry. I should not have interfered." Through fresh tears, out poured the whole story. "I just could not face you, when you both showed up at Bergen Op Meer. Can you ever forgive me?"

"There is nothing to forgive. Everything has worked out so perfectly. I love you Millzy, and am thankful you are here. If you really think about it, all your actions led us to all find each other again." Hannah's smile shone from her eyes. "Let's go tell Tons. He is probably having a fit out there."

The luggage had all been collected and loaded into the cars. Oma was sitting in the front seat of Hannah's vehicle with the sweetest smile on her face. "Millzy, you go with Tony and tell him everything on the way home." Massy had already left with their rental car and the other guests.

"Okay. Kat, do you mind if I spend this time alone with him? By the looks of things, it may be the only chance I get." Millicent indicated the obvious, as Tony was sitting in his ute with his back to them. *A truck she was sure she had seen Uncle Jonty drive.*

"Of course. I will ride with Oma and Hannah. See you at the villa. It is about a twenty-minute drive from here. Oh, but I guess you know that." Kat leaned in and gave her an encouraging kiss on each cheek, leaving her standing there.

Tony was watching everything in his rear view mirror. He could not believe it when he saw his wife leave with Hannah.

There stood Millzy, alone. He felt betrayed. *I can't just leave her there.*

Millicent waited for him to come to her. She was not going to budge. It never occurred to her that he would not step from his truck and approach her. She was right.

"Hi, Tony. I guess this is all pretty crazy for you. Do you want to ask me anything?" She stood as still as a statue, though she longed to draw him in.

"You hid the truth from Uncle Jonty. He trusted you, we all did. I don't know what to think. Here you are and so is everyone else we love. All I want to feel is happy, but I feel confused. I keep hoping that life will no longer be so complicated, but things just keep happening that hurt like flat stones skipping over the surface of a still lake and then sinking to the bottom with a thud. I don't like it. I want to feel safe and have all those I love around me always." People were starting to stare.

"Come on, let's get in my ute." Tony gestured for her to walk in front of him to his truck. This gentle suggestion mattered to her. If she had to look at his retreating back, she would have gone back home on the next flight and never returned.

The landscape had not changed.

Kat was right. All she had was about twenty minutes. "I had no right to keep the truth to myself. I am one of a long line of others who knew. Each one of us had what we thought were good intentions. Your Mother and Oma included. I am not condoning my actions, but I want you to know, I thought I was protecting Massy and Kat. They had been through enough."

"And Hannah and I hadn't?" Tony was hurting. She began to cry. Tony pulled over on the side of the road and waited. "I'm sorry. None of that was your fault. You actually made it even easier on how tough it was. What would Uncle Jonty have done without you? What would any of us have done?" The sadness he felt showed on his face.

"It is me who is sorry. You are right. All of you have been through far too much in your young lives." She went looking in her bag for something to blow her nose into. "My life has been charmed, Tony. At times I feel so guilty."

Tony reached over and opened the glove box. "Here is a tissue for your issue." He gave a weak smile and waited.

"Millzy, does it ever get any easier? Loving, I mean. Will there always be so much hurt included?" Tony loved her and it showed again. He was glad to be feeling it too. *Have I ever said thank you to her?* he wondered.

She was so glad to hear him call her by the name that touches the heart when she hears it and instantly fills her. "We are not saved from these trials but saved through them dearest Tony." Years ago she had taken Oma's advice and had deepened her relationship with a loving Lord. She was now ready to share the truth to the best of her ability.

"What do you mean?" Tony gave her his full attention. He could feel a life lesson coming on. One that would change him today. Of the many things that Uncle Jonty had taught him, this knowledge of *when to pause all and pay attention* stayed with him as a lasting reminder.

"Christ gave his life out of a perfect love in obedience to his Father's will, so that you and I could live for eternity through faith in Him alone. Those of us who love do the same thing in our own small and big ways. Oma raised two small children, as did Uncle Jonty. Your parents loved you enough that you can feel it today. All around us are people who love us. Oma explained to me that even Vaun and Matt have dedicated their lives to helping others. Each moment we are given, tough or easy, is precious." *Was she saying this right?*

"We need to surrender, day in and day out through our own free will. All that is asked of us is to obey a few simple and very clear rules" She hoped she was doing a good job explaining. "If you look back over your life you will see God at work. Helping, guiding, saving."

Tony sat in stunned silence. *Is it really this simple?* "I have faith, Millzy, I think I always have. At times it has kept me sane and prevented me from giving into the anger that I thought protected me from the sadness I felt. Matt has been helping me to see through the hurt. Seeing you reminded me of that little boy with the broken arm."

Reaching forward, she put her hand on the arm that had so long ago healed. "You are a man now. By the looks of things, you will be a father yourself one day. All the goodness that has been passed to you through the generations you will pass on to your children, and so on. God's character is of this nature and we are made in his image. Love always finds a way through anything. Just look at us now. No one could have ever thought of the crazy way we have all become one family. His hand is in this, Tony. What's important is what we are going to do with the gift given to us, as his beloved children. I for one am going to treasure each moment as it comes and seek to do his will in new ways. Come to think of it, Matt must be a special man to have found his way into your circle of bros."

"He is a saint." Tony paused as he looked out at the landscape.

"I love you, Millzy. I don't know if I have ever said thank you to you, though." Tony gave her one of his rare smiles, saved for only those whom he truly loved with all his heart.

She raised her hand to his cheek and he leaned in. "I love you too, lieveling, and yes, you have. Each time I served you star-shaped potatoes for breakfast. Let's go home and I will make you some, and you can reintroduce me to Matt. I might like to have a saint in my life too."

Charlotte had prayed for these boys many times with Jonty, as they came up from the depths of despair while in the care of Corrections, and as they continued their commitment to leave the pain of the past behind through education streams.

Both boys had tried to discover their benefactor through the Chaplaincy office she had been associated with for over thirty years, to no avail.

In her devotions, there they had remained all these years.

Now she would be seeing them again, face to face. *Will they remember me I wonder? Will they be okay seeing me? Will they want me around?* Charlotte left all to God and waited.

Matt and Vaun sat in silence in the back seat with Lotti happily chatting away as the scenery of Northland flowed by. *Was this the final step in the line of many since that fatal day?* Each time Matt thought about his time in prison, it hung in his heart as a heavy cloak, hanging on a nail in a sealed cupboard. Today he opened the door and there it was. *I wonder what Vaun is thinking right now?* If he could forget those years, he would. *Yet, even I know they formed him into the man he was today.*

As Charlotte put the final touches on the banquet she and Kitty had prepared, her mind wandered through the many faces that she had come in contact with through prison ministry. Some of the men were easy to enter into engagement with, others not so much. It was these men that God often had to gently remind her, *they are my children also, and are deserving of My love. Remember the thief on the cross.* And she always would.

Vaun and Matt were deeply troubled when she had first met them, but as they found their way through those first years after the accident, it was clear to everyone that they were two very sweet kids from a small town and life had dealt them a cruel blow.

A team of onsite and offsite prayer-warriors fought for them day and night. The results were obvious. They had both taken the time to deepen their relationship with the Lord and in doing so had discovered their callings.

Charlotte often thought the mysterious ways of the almighty playing out could not be done by human thinking. In the case of all the people gathering now, *God's got it right, as always.*

The first car had arrived.

Charlotte stepped onto the veranda in anticipation of finally greeting the two young men she had loved and not seen in a very long time. *What will be, will be. I will be still in you Lord.*

The land was impressive. As far as the eye could see it stretched out like a blanket of lush versions of green in all directions. Matt was glad he had made the decision to come. He looked over at Vaun also taking in the beauty. Their eyes met and they understood each other. "Let's get out of the car." Matt said.

"Kia Ora, and welcome to Lions Vineyard." They had simply not changed. Charlotte hoped once again they would know her, as she wanted to hold them for the very first time. *Touching the men while in the care of Corrections was forbidden.* Two stunned faces looked at her as though seeing a ghost.

"Boys, don't be shy, I am sure she is friendly." Lotti stepped forward and introduced herself. "Vaun, stop being so silly. Matt, what is wrong with you two?" Lotti was beginning to get annoyed as they both remained as if rooted to the ground.

"Let me explain. Matt and Vaun may be experiencing minor turmoil. They may not want to have the relationship with me renewed." Charlotte's gentle smile remained in place and she waited. Kat had told her that everyone knew the whole story. She felt no fear in revealing she did know them.

"Oh, but I do." Matt stepped forward and held the woman who had saved his life all those years ago. Her arms slowly came around him as though he was delicate. She enfolded him in her love, *finally.*

"I love you, Matt." Spirit through the soul can whisper at times on the breath and give life. This is exactly what happened, for Matt alone to hear. He was completely renewed.

"I need my hug too, man. Step aside." Vaun had waited as long as he could.

Matt slowly detached himself from her but not before saying, "Thank you, thank you, for everything."

Charlotte shone like the sun as Vaun stepped into her welcoming warmth. "Hello, my boy, I have missed you." Lotti was seldom ever brought to silence. She was learning the folly of her ways right at this moment. The glory of the moment came from on high. In silence was the only way to allow the beauty to wash over her. *This is Love.*

Other vehicles began to arrive.

Oma was happy. Massy could see it. *What an incredible life she has had.* And now here she was, in the home of her own son.

Tomorrow was his own wedding day.

As he looked around at all the happy faces at the breakfast table overflowing with food, he realised he had not thought of his own parents and wondered if Hannah had thought of hers. Life had not always been easy but it was rich. Vaun and Lotti had assured them there was no reason they could not become parents themselves. The years ahead looked bright.

Hannah felt his stillness next to her. Reaching her hand into his, their fingers locked into a perfect love knot that they both knew nothing could undo.

Tomorrow, everything will change. Their vows would be spoken in front of their loved ones and they would be joined in a holy contract. To be honest, she was nervous. *What would it feel like to wake up with this man every day for the rest of my life?*

Charlotte was in her element. She knew these couples loved each other. She took in the joy and let it fill that place in her that had never been filled before.

That space she thought would have been shared with Jonty.

Love was everywhere, in so many different forms, too. Oma adored her grandchildren, Matt was sharing his life story with Millzy, and Hannah and Tony did not feel alone. *God is so good.*

"Well, my dears, I have a few matters to attend to at the church and will see you tomorrow. My sincere thank-you to you, Kitty, for the delicious meal, you have outdone yourself." Charlotte winked at Hannah and blew a kiss to Kat, now known to all as Kitty.

"I will see you out." Tony had a matter of his own to discuss with her.

"Bye everyone, have a lovely day, and may I say it again, Aotearoa New Zealand welcomes you, blessings." With a final wave to them all around the huge table, she made her way to the door.

"What is it, Tony, you look serious." Charlotte knew all would be well, but this was unusual behaviour for Tony. "Out with it, lad."

"Well, I found this with your name on it in Uncle Jonty's things." Tony handed her a small box. Charlotte's world froze as he gently took her hand and placed the box in her palm. "We always wondered why you two had never made it official. It was no secret how you both felt for each other. Open it." Tony watched her gently pull on the ribbon, her hand trembling.

"Oh Tony, look, it is beautiful." There in the velvet box was the most exquisite band of gold, woven together by delicate feathers encrusted with pearls. They were her birthstone. "Jonty had never forgotten a single one of my birthdays. Tony, today is my birthday." Their laughter filled the air. Tony took Charlotte into his arms and gave her a big hug.

The day dawned bright with the morning chorus reaching new heights. It seemed as though all the birds wanted to join in the celebration. Everyone got busy, even Oma. She wanted to make Hannah's bouquet and had picked the roses the night before, scanning the property for equally beautiful blooms to accompany the perfect red roses.

Kat made sure everything ran smoothly.

Hannah was sent off to Charlotte's home to prepare, with the promise that she would join her long before the church bells rang.

Tony took charge of Massy. He was a bag of nerves.

Matt and Millzy teamed up to oversee the outdoor set up.

It was obvious to all that there was every chance of their relationship budding into something more.

Vaun and Lotti busied themselves in the kitchen as they had both proved to be able bodies with a knife. *Who knew?*

Kat surveyed her surroundings, satisfied. She could now collect her dress, give a last word of encouragement to her brother, transport the exquisite bouquet, and leave for Charlotte's home. It was time to spend these last moments with her new sister-in-law.

Hannah was a vision in white. Charlotte had ensured nothing would be forgotten. She had a team of the best standing ready to assist the bride with any need she may have, though she did not truly need it. For the rest of her life Kat would never forget this moment. It was for her the coming together of all that began hundreds of years before. They were all one and everyone knew it. "You are the most beautiful bride." Kat leaned in and gave each cheek a kiss.

"Thank you. I do feel it too. Charlotte has seen to everything." Hannah held out her hand for Charlotte to take, and the other for Kat to hold, and they did.

Charlotte knew what to do now. "Shall we pray?" Both girls gave affirmation.

Bowing their heads, Charlotte began." Heavenly Father, you have brought us, your daughters, to this day of celebration. Receive our thanks for all of the prayers you have answered. Bless the union of all those who come together through your divine will. For it is your will alone that we desire to accomplish. Your Son gave his life for our everlasting freedom and made the ultimate sacrifice. How can we ever thank you enough? And yet, Father, we are brave and have the courage to ask for more, for you have spoken the word that you would be with us always and would give your children good things. Father, make this union a fruitful one. Bless both your daughters here today with children of their own. As the years pass and the fullness of their lives are revealed, protect them, Father. And may they all continue to always see your work in their lives and seek to serve you forever. I ask this in the name of your holy and perfect Son, Christ Jesus, who sits now safe with you in Heaven above. Amen." Giving both girls' hands a final squeeze, and anointing them by placing a kiss on their foreheads, Charlotte knew her life had come full circle somehow. "Let's finish up here and get you over to the church." She said.

Oma was first to arrive with Matt and Millzy. Charlotte ushered them in towards the stunning bride waiting at the altar. As the other quests arrived, each one understood and remained standing. Tony and Massy were the last ones through the doors. There was no need for music; the sound of birdsong was enough. Side by side they entered, as Hannah watched them walk towards her.

She would be leaving one of them today and joining the other. Tony leaned in and kissed her upturned cheek. He placed her hand in Massy's sweaty palm and joined his wife at his sister's side. Massy had no words. She was a vision of perfection.

Hannah could see her reflection in his eyes and knew a new kind of joy. She was his. They were becoming one.

The words of a vow spoken before witnesses, sealing them through a holy bond, took very little time to say. When it was time to kiss his bride, Massy lifted her into his arms for the kiss and proceeded to carry her down the aisle. "I have a little surprise of my own, Mrs Wolf." Prancing in readiness was her horse, Hero, harnessed to a carriage.

Charlotte ensured later that day that all documents were signed and filed as required. The celebration went well into the small hours of the night.

Dawn found the newlyweds waiting for the first light of a new day to spread over the hills of Lions Vineyard, while the discarded remains all rested silently forgotten on the white linen tablecloths.

"I am the happiest woman on earth." Hannah snuggled in just a little closer to her husband. He had long ago placed his suit jacket, warm from his body, over her shoulders. There it stayed through the night.

Kissing the top of her head he also thought the same of himself. They truly were one. "Will you dearly miss this, lieveling. It is beautiful." As though dawn wanted to place a kiss also, the sun chose this moment to alight on their faces.

With a sleepy reply, Hannah did not have to give the answer much thought. "I will miss Tony. Where you are is enough for me. Bergen Op Meer is ours to share. I could not ask for more."

Massy drew her in even closer and held on with all his might. The fabric of her wedding gown rustled under her weight and she giggled. He loved this woman and gave thanks that she was his and God's alone. For a while he did not want to share her with anyone, but the day was coming into full life. The birds had long ago begun their daily symphony and the peacocks were looking for leftovers under the tables.

"Massy, Charlotte spoke so beautifully yesterday, a prayer that rings in my heart. She prayed for our children to be born." A tear began to form in the corner of her eye.

"How beautiful." Massy felt peaceful. A stillness overcame the moment, so much so that the male peacock came to investigate the quiet alcove on the veranda where they were hidden away. Their eyes met.

This big feathery male was the master of his domain. Thought Massy.

"For a little while I want you all to myself." Massy spoke the words softly so as not to frighten the majestic bird. The movement was just enough, and the bird's tail fanned open in full view for all the females to see.

Tony did not want to disturb them and stood at a discreet distance. A clear voice came into his head that said, *have the camera ready,* and so he did. They never knew he was there until the framed photo arrived a few months later as a belated wedding gift. To this day it remains the Wolf family's most valued artefact at Bergen Op Meer.

THE END *for now.*